A COMPROMISING POSITION

A COMPROMISING POSITION

Carole Matthews

headline

First published in 2002
by HEADLINE BOOK PUBLISHING

10 9 8 7 6 5 4 3 2

Cataloguing in Publication Data is
available from the British Library

ISBN 0 7472 6974 2 (hardback)
ISBN 0 7553 0334 2 (trade paperback)

Typeset in Times by
Letterpart Limited, Reigate, Surrey

Printed and bound in Great Britain by
Mackays of Chatham plc, Chatham, Kent

HEADLINE BOOK PUBLISHING
A division of Hodder Headline
338 Euston Road
LONDON NW1 3BH

www.headline.co.uk
www.hodderheadline.com

To Andy Keech, Carl Thomson and the team at the *Milton Keynes Citizen* for all your kind help.

Chapter One

Have you ever seen one of those weepy films where the distraught and usually love-lorn heroine cries silently and beautifully, tears coursing down her perfect Estée Lauder foundation leaving not a blemish? Yes? Makes you want to weep, doesn't it?

I don't cry like that – I howl. Like a banshee. A banshee who's been hit about the head with a baseball bat. And I go bright red and blotchy round my neck and my eyes swell up as if they've been punched by Lennox Lewis. My nose generally contributes too, producing, on average, two buckets of dribble per second. *Nice*.

This is what I'm doing now. Howling. Why? Because I, Emily Miller, have left my boyfriend of five years, one Mr Declan Patrick O'Donnell, fully paid-up member of the Bastard species. And, in doing so, have rendered myself homeless.

At the tender age of thirty-two, you'd have thought I'd have the wherewithal to get it together by now, wouldn't you? But no. At this point, my tissue disintegrates, having clearly reached its Critical Snot Limit. The receptionist looks at me with a mixture of pity and terror. Oh, I forgot to mention, I'm not indulging in this bout of hysteria alone. Oh no. I am doing it in the reception area of the *Hampstead Observer*, a nineties conglomeration of uncomfortable tan leather sofas, stainless steel and beech coffee-tables and undernourished Yucca plants in terracotta pots.

I sniff and make a little gulpy sound. The receptionist clutches her phone nearer to her, and tries to give me an encouraging smile which basically says, 'Pull yourself together, woman!' The trouble is, my lip wobbles alarmingly every time I fight to stifle a sob, so in the end I give up and blub some more.

'Is Cara there?' the receptionist whispers in a pantomime style. The look in her eyes reminds me of that bit in *Watership Down* where the nice bunny gets caught in the headlights of a not very nice car. I take it that Cara isn't at her desk. The receptionist lowers her voice a bit more, but I can still hear her. 'I have a slight emergency.' Ha! *She* does? If only she knew. 'Her friend's here. In reception.

1

Now. She's a bit upset.' She smiles at me like I'm completely insane. And I have to admit that I probably do look a tiny bit unhinged at the moment. 'Tell her to get down here,' she hisses. 'Quick!' She hangs up and looks reassuringly at me. 'She won't be long.'

I nod speechlessly.

'Are you all right?' the receptionist asks kindly, if a little point-lessly, since it must be obvious to anyone with half a brain that here is a woman more devastated than she has ever been in her entire life.

I heave out, 'I'm fine. Thank you.' But I'm not fine. I doubt I'll ever be fine again. And with that thought, I dissolve into tears once more. There's nothing quite so bad as someone being kind to you when you most need them to be, is there? Except for someone being cruel and unkind on an unprecedented scale when you least expect it, of course.

I don't know quite where to start really. Should I explain about Cara, my closest and most irritating friend and confidante? Or should I just cut straight to the chase and talk about Declan, ex-boyfriend as of half an hour ago, and his stupendous, mind-blowing betrayal? Oh, I don't know. How on earth can I be expected to think straight when I'm creating my very own papier-mâché sculpture with a Kleenex?

Just let me make one thing perfectly clear. This is totally and utterly Declan's fault. One hundred per cent. You know when you hear people discussing their friends' relationship break-ups and they say stuff like, 'Well, it was six of one and half a dozen of the other . . .', or, 'No one's really to blame . . .' or the equally vacuous, 'They just drifted apart . . .'? Well, it's all bollocks as far as I'm concerned. Ducks drift apart. Humans get pushed away. No one will ever say that about this particular situation. I did not drift, I was shoved. Heartily. If I were a soap star instead of a boring old English teacher, this would fill the pages of the tabloids. You mark my words. The demise of our lovey-dovey coupledom is entirely due to my bastard boyfriend. *Ex*-boyfriend. And, very soon, when you know the whole story, I think you'll agree.

Chapter Two

Adam stood up and had a quick glance round the office again before he spoke. 'Cara's not here,' he said. 'I'll pass the message on as soon as she comes back.'

He replaced the telephone receiver on its cradle. The news desk was empty – apart from the Himalayan mounds of paper in this supposed age of the paper-free office and Cara's usual barricade of bells, Buddhas and Oriental what-nots – but then it was late in the day and, apart from those on the newspaper's aptly named graveyard shift, they should all be heading home or, more probably, to that home-from-home the British call 'the pub'.

'Where's Cara?' he shouted to no one in particular.

'Our esteemed News Editor is in the toilet,' Chris supplied.

Adam sat down again. 'She's been ages.'

'She's probably Feng Shui-ing her arse.' Chris leant nearer to his computer screen. 'Bloody hell. Look at this.'

Adam raked his fingers through his hair and clasped them behind his neck. 'It'll make you go blind.'

Chris closed his eyes and fumbled around his desk with his hands, knocking over his pen-holder. 'What?'

They both laughed tired laughter. It had been a long day. Not long as in interesting, long as in the most boring day imaginable. To say that it was a slow news day was an understatement of mega proportions. As Chief Photographer, Adam had been sent out to take snazzy pictures of a car that had been vandalised by the owner's batty sixty-two-year-old female neighbour (who refused to be photographed), a child who had won a place to the local theatre school and a man whose lost dog had returned home of its own accord after two weeks missing in the wilds of Belsize Park. Not much to get the old adrenaline whizzing round the veins, although it was a very cute dog – some indeterminate ball of frantic fuzz that had adored Adam on sight and liked to lick a lot. Adam sighed inwardly. If only women were the same.

Adam shuffled his chair over to Chris's desk where his friend was

3

doing what he did for the majority, if not all, of his working day – surfing the Internet. His favoured sites were those that contained the headings NUDE, NAUGHTY, NAKED and NIPPLES – among other things.

'Now *that* is a sight for sore eyes,' Chris said, breathless with admiration as he pointed at the image on the screen.

Adam peered over Chris's shoulder and pursed his lips. 'Not bad.'

'Not bad?' His friend scowled at him. 'Are you gay? That is the most luscious pair of legs you're ever likely to see. I would give up all of my worldly goods to walk arm-in-arm with a young lady of such delicate beauty.'

'I don't think a fiver would get you very far.'

Chris looked crushed. 'No?'

Just then, Cara came out of the ladies' loo and walked across the office. She cuffed Chris across the head as she passed behind him. 'You'll go blind.'

'It's been done,' Chris and Adam replied in unison.

'It's also very politically incorrect. I could report you for sexual harassment in the workplace,' she warned. 'You do know that it's now a sackable offence to surf porn sites?'

'It's research,' Chris countered. 'For an exposé piece on the dark side of technology.'

'Yes. Right. And Davina McCall's going to be the next Prime Minister.' Cara went to ease Adam out of the way. 'Let me see.'

'You haven't got time.' Adam shielded the screen. It wasn't nearly as bad as some of the stuff Chris liked to surf, but he didn't feel happy about one of the bosses seeing it. 'There's an upset woman in reception asking for you.'

'Who?'

'Bethany didn't say. Sounded urgent though.'

Cara scooped up her coat. 'I was about to head for home, anyway. Will you tie up any loose ends for me please, Chris?'

'*Ja, mein Führer,*' he said, throwing a Gestapo salute at her.

'I'll see you boys tomorrow.'

'Not if we see you first,' Chris muttered under his breath.

'I heard that,' Cara said.

Adam smiled at her. 'Hope it's not bad news.'

'If it's who I think it is, it probably will be.'

'We're going to the pub if you want to join us,' he offered. 'If she's nursing a broken heart, strong drink works wonders.'

Cara shook her head. 'I think this is going to be a tea and sympathy job.'

'Have fun,' Adam said.

'You too.' Cara eyeballed Chris and then the corner of her spotlessly neat desk and the Burger King polystyrene box poised conspicuously at its outer reaches. 'Chris. Burger. Out of my wealth corner. Now.' Then she turned and marched crisply out of the office.

Chris looked up hazily, still intent on drooling at the screen. 'Adam, do you think Cara's a lesbian?'

'No.'

'She eats a lot of vegetarian food.'

'I don't think the two things are necessarily connected, mate.'

'Oh,' Chris said. 'You sure?'

Chapter Three

'Oh, heavens-to-Betsy!' Cara is standing at the steel swing doors that open out into the reception area, coat slung over her arm, hands on her hips in a nonchalant-aggressive pose. Cara doesn't do swearing. She says it sends out little poisoned arrows into the universe which come back to fall on your head when you're least expecting it. I dread to think how many 'bastard' and 'bugger' arrows are up there waiting for me. It'll be like the Battle of Hastings if they ever decide to let fly.

As a consequence of her non-swearing policy, all of Cara's expletives come straight from the Beatrix Potter and Enid Blyton book of bad language. This is just one of her deeply irritating habits. Sometimes I really wish that she'd let go and have a really good 'fuck' every now and then – metaphorically speaking. That's the other thing that Cara doesn't do at the moment – she's been celibate for over a year now. She says by choice, I say by default. Cara thinks she's being saintly and going through a period of spiritual cleansing, whereas I think she's desperately unlucky and hugely frustrated. Whichever way, it makes her very bad-tempered.

Cara tuts and bustles across to me, sending a 'thank you' glance at the relieved receptionist. She dumps her coat and throws her arms around me. 'What have you been doing?' she sighs.

And despite all her idiosyncrasies, quirks, foibles and fetishes, she really is a dear, dear friend who would abandon everything to help you out of a crisis. Even though you have to indulge her belief in the healing power of hugs. Cara tries to squeeze the last breath out of me, and although I'd finally managed to get the weeping under control, it starts again. 'I've left Declan,' I say in between sniffs.

Cara eyes for the first time the two very large suitcases which stand stoically beside me on the floor. 'Oh flip. This looks permanent.'

'It is.'

'You can't leave him, Emily.' Cara holds me away from her and fixes me with her most earnest stare. 'Where will you go?'

6

'Er . . .' I can't help but look at my suitcases.

'Oh no,' she says before I have the chance to get even one syllable out of my poor trembling mouth. 'Oh no.'

'Oh no, what?'

'Don't even think about it,' my friend says in a threatening tone.

'It won't be for long.'

'You're right. It won't!'

'Cara!' I am gobsmacked. 'You're supposed to be my friend.'

'I don't want you living with me,' she says. 'You're untidy.'

'I'm not,' I protest.

'You never put the lid back on the toothpaste,' Cara says.

'That was one incident, Cara. About ten years ago.'

'You leave the loo seat up,' she says as if it's a hanging offence.

'You're just anally retentive,' I point out. 'Howard Hughes was probably more relaxed in his bathroom than you are.'

By now, my tears have been shocked into an arrested state. Look at me – I have come to my friend in my hour of need and she is about to close the door of her three-bedroom, Victorian terraced cottage in my face. 'You've got a perfectly nice spare room,' I choke out.

'I stack my ironing in there.'

'Well, thank you, friend.' I can't believe this. Cara's spirituality is about as substantial as a pair of seven-denier tights and you can poke holes in it just as quickly. 'I am trying not to be hurt that your ironing pile takes precedence over your closest friend. If you knew what had happened, you wouldn't deny me.' My chin gives an involuntary shudder. 'This is not your common or garden everyday break-up. This is serious stuff.'

'Is there someone else?'

'No.' My lip wobbles. 'It's worse than that.'

'What can be worse?'

I eye my cases hopefully.

Cara lets out the long, weary breath of defeat. 'Let's go home,' she says, 'and you can tell me all about it.'

7

Chapter Four

Cara is in the kitchen. I'm getting camomile tea when I'd rather be having a Tetley's hairy-arsed brew and gin. My cases are ensconced in the spare room and I am lying prostrate on the sofa, having been given a hefty dose of Bach Flower Rescue Remedy, a lavender pillow for my neck and a rose quartz crystal to put inside my bra, for reasons I didn't enquire into. There is a thick cloud of nostril-twitching incense hanging in the middle of the lounge.

I don't think Cara and I could be more different as people. I am normal. Cara is not. I look ordinary. Cara does not. I am tall, naturally blonde, apart from my intellect, curvaceous and have a chest that could have inspired Jordan. Cara is tiny, waif-like with crimped hair that veers between curls and dreadlocks in a variety of shades of Burgundy and pink. I like business suits, button-up blouses and stilettos. Cara's style is more Madonna meets Mother's dressing-up box. This makes her sound like an ugly bag lady, but she isn't. She's stunningly beautiful but not in the traditional sense – a bit like Morticia Addams, who is, in her own way, utterly gorgeous.

I believe in hard work, never going overdrawn at the bank and filling in Income Tax Returns on time. Cara favours the New Age approach to life, opening herself up to the divine benevolence of the universe and the healing power of Angels. Personally, I believe in the healing power of strong drink. I think the tooth fairy may well live at the bottom of Cara's garden. If not, I'm sure she'd be made very welcome.

Our taste in furnishings differs wildly too. I like pastels, stainless steel and natural wood, no fuss, no frills. Cara is more artistic by nature, which means every wall is a different colour and is festooned with ethnic artefacts – tat – from around the world. And she thinks *I'm* the untidy one! She mixes red with green, which was always a no-no in my book, yellow with purple, hot pink with deep blue. Sometimes I wonder if Cara has decorated with the sole intention of destroying the optic nerves of any visitors. Some may say it has a certain charm, but at the moment, it feels like I'm lying in a migraine.

Cara lives in the heart of Hampstead village, just down the road from Keats – or where Keats used to live when he was writing *Ode To A Nightingale*. I know that because there's a little brass plaque nailed to a tree that tells me so. It's very posh and bijou. She has original, ornate wrought-iron railings, a blush of Virginia Creeper curling round the door and an original Victorian lamp-post on guard just outside the gate. It's right in the middle of a conservation area – or if it isn't it should be – and Cara can't sneeze without someone complaining to the council. I'm amazed she's allowed to get away with the colour of her front door. It's painted a lurid mauve shade – the colour of people's armpits who are suffering from Bubonic Plague. Cara says it symbolises the rich fullness of life. I say it symbolises someone with pretty awful taste in front-door paint.

This isn't strictly Cara's house. It's owned by her parents, who are currently away running a charity school to save young girls from prostitution in Thailand. Cara's parents, Jade and Yang – not their real names, I suspect – have always been keen to support noble causes. I don't think they've ever done a day of paid work in their entire lives. How on earth they came to own this house is a mystery. Even if you won a million quid on the lottery tomorrow, you'd be hard pushed to afford a place here. I think it was inherited by Cara's father, Yang, from his grandfather, or so the story goes. The truth is he's probably the secret love-child of a member of royalty, but don't quote me on that.

Anyway, property millionaires or not, Jade and Yang are sort of sixties throwbacks – which is *so* Hampstead. Despite their rather privileged upbringings, they wear kaftans and embroidered slippers and say 'cool' and 'fab', but in a very spaced-out and non-now sort of way. They dragged Cara round most of the hell-holes of the world when she was growing up, claiming that it was better than being educated in a bourgeois private school in bourgeois southern England (as they were, of course). That may be, but it left Cara totally without roots and a feeling that she never does enough for people, because she has sufficient money to eat and drive a capitalist bastard's car – or a Citroën 2CV which, personally, I don't think is anything to brag about.

Wherever there are people in need, that's where you'll find Jade and Yang – Tibet, Nepal, Glasgow – pretty much anywhere but in their house in Hampstead. Cara is fiercely proud of them, desperate to live up to their bohemian ideals, and she fails on almost every level. They turn up once every two years, sleep on the floor of their

9

own lounge because, presumably, beds are also a sign of being a capitalist bastard, empty their daughter's bank account of her hard-earned savings and then swan off on another mission to save the world. The only needy person Cara's parents don't have time for is her. Sometimes, I wonder why Cara and I are friends. I think this is one of the main reasons. Without me, she'd have no one.

If I were a product of *my* parents' making, I'd be wearing a sensible cardigan, having lunch in the Wisteria café of the garden centre once a week, driving a Volvo 240 Estate with a fur cover on the driver's seat to save it from excess wear, and I'd have no idea how to work my answerphone. Sometimes I get the distinct feeling that I'm heading that way.

Cara comes in carrying a tray of tea and sets it down beside me. She has her sympathetic look on. 'When did you last have your chakras cleansed, Emily?'

'Er . . .' I won't admit it, but I'm not entirely sure where my chakras are. Or, indeed, if I have them. 'I don't think I've ever had that pleasure.'

'That's probably why you have so much negativity,' she says. 'We must do them.'

A lot of what Cara does involves wailing and candles and it isn't usually pleasant. Perhaps her theory is: how can it be good for you if it's not horrid?

'Well, despite my negativity, I'll be a great housemate,' I say hopefully. 'I'll pay you rent on time. I won't drink all your milk.' Mainly because soya milk makes me want to throw up and Cara wouldn't dream of drinking anything else. Am I the only one who thinks it smells like syrup and vomit mixed together? Cara is a strict lacto-vegan and I'm sure she wouldn't even injure vegetables by eating them if there were a suitable alternative. If you could buy tofu carrots, Cara would be at the head of the queue. 'I will also try very hard not to re-enact the ten-year-old leaving-the-lid-off-the-toothpaste scandal,' I promise. 'I won't deposit hair in the plughole and I'll always put the loo seat down.'

'I'm not being fussy, Emily,' Cara says sincerely. 'That's simply good Feng Shui. If you leave the seat up, all your money dematerialises down the toilet.'

'See?' I try a weak smile. 'I'm learning already.' I don't bother to point out that my money dematerialises without any help from my u-bend, mainly on my mortgage and the contents of Sainsburys.

Cara pours us both a cup of camomile tea and hands one to me. I feel as if someone should be soothing my fevered brow.

'You still haven't told me what's happened,' she says.

I feel my jaw tighten. 'We need to log onto your computer.'

'Why?'

I give her a knowing look. 'You'll see.'

I dispense with the lavender pillow and hitch the crystal into a more comfortable place in my bra and, taking our tea, Cara follows me as I trudge quietly upstairs into her box room which serves as an office.

Cara is writing a novel in her spare time. As she has no spare time, she's been doing it for about ten years. I don't ask about it any more because she gets very stroppy about its lack of progress. It's a worthy novel, full of meaningful things, apparently. It's also destined to be an unfinished novel, I think. My friend sits at her computer and taps away until it springs into life with a series of beeps and whirls and happy tunes.

Cara thinks her computer sends out bad vibes, radiation fields or something. Computers that aren't turned off use up twenty-five per cent of the world's energy resources, she once told me. I think she read it in *Rainbow Warrior Monthly*, so it must be true. Hippies don't lie. She has it boxed in by bowls of little crystals and pretty stones, plants and other indeterminate objects that are supposed to protect her from it. I hate computers too. I don't get road rage, I get computer rage. Five minutes on one of the damn things and I'm ready to throw it out of the window. I have barricaded mine in with pen-holders and computer manuals to protect *it* from *me*. What's more, I've invented a whole new vocabulary while working on the computer – all of it obscene.

These days, teachers are expected to be computer literate and we're sent on expensive courses to learn about the delights they can offer by people who work with them everyday at a lofty level and cannot understand why they strike terror into a real person's heart. 'Real people' being those who can't programme video recorders, get toasters to work and even have to resort to giving the channel changer a hefty whack on the arm of the chair before it will change channels. I'm so *not* in the computer age that I don't even have my own email address – Declan has to do it all for me. He persuaded me, once, to do my supermarket shopping on-line. What a disaster! It took me about two hours to fill my virtual basket, by which time I could have whipped round Sainsburys with my eyes closed. And when, several light years later, my shopping finally arrived, I got twenty-seven packets of Penguins, ten iceberg lettuces (I hate iceberg lettuce!), an industrial-sized tomato ketchup that would take even the most dedicated of chip lovers about five years to use up and a Tweenies video. None of which I had ordered. I didn't, however, get the cheese, butter, tea bags and loo rolls that I *had* ordered. Grrr. Give me a manky wire basket and a tatty list to stomp round with any day. Though preferably not Saturday.

I wish we didn't have computers. I could live without one. We all managed well enough without washing machines and faxes and microwaves and mobile phones. Didn't we? Although I wouldn't be quite so willing to dispense with those now. Computers, however, are nothing but trouble. Like men.

Declan works with computers. He is what's commonly known as an expert. Declan is going to be a dot.com millionaire. Or so he keeps telling me. He has his own string of Internet companies, strung out, presumably, in cyberspace just waiting for the pounds to roll in. Except they aren't. And that's pretty much where I come in.

Grabagadget.com, a site advertising loads of useless gadgets you never knew you needed and probably never did, sadgits.com, a sad site for sad gits everywhere, and datewithastar.com, where you can have a virtual relationship with a celebrity of your choice, are not quite the cash cows that my other half had dreamed they would be.

I run my fingers over Cara's bookshelf. She has titles such as *A Woman Empowered Is A Woman Set Free* and *The Complete Guide To Becoming A Serenely Magical Being*. She's obviously not read that one yet. It's heartening to see that the majority of her books are covered in dust, as are my bookshelves. Mine contain mainly English set texts and the odd well-thumbed Jackie Collins novel left over from when I was fifteen. I would like to read some of Cara's life-changing books when I have time and, in the light of what has happened, maybe I should have done it sooner.

Cara twizzles round on her chair. 'OK,' she says, flinging her crinkles of hair out of the way. 'It's all yours. We're on-line.'

I take over her seat. 'You're going to be shocked,' I say.

'Nonsense. I'm a rufty-tufty News Editor,' she scoffs. 'Nothing shocks me.'

'As you like it,' I sigh and reluctantly tap a web address into the appropriate box. The search engine does its bit, creeping and crawling across space until it finds the right site. I have a vague feeling of distorted reality as I wait for the images to appear. This is a shock to me too. I only found out a couple of hours ago and, even now, part of me hopes that it is all a big mistake and that Declan couldn't really have done this.

The computer grinds away. Site located. Transferring document. 10%. 30%. 50%. Chunter. Chunter. Chunter.

'Sorry it's so slow.' Cara is chewing her fingernails.

It's that time of night when children are closeted into their bedrooms jamming up the airways surfing things they shouldn't be, when instead they should be downstairs watching *EastEnders*.

60%. 80%. Done. Bingo! The page opens. The banner heading reads: SAUCY SANTA SHARES HER FESTIVE JOY! and a little box with a cross in it appears where soon a picture will be.

'Christmas was ages ago.' Cara looks puzzled.

'Four weeks,' I say, monotone. I'm not likely to forget in a hurry.

A hazy, pixelated image appears and quickly clears into a start-lingly clear, full-colour photo. And there I am on the page. I have a bare bottom, directed at the screen, and bare breasts, although I am not totally in the nip. Oh no. I am wearing a red, fur-trimmed, flimsy Santa costume fashioned in chiffon, a red hat with a flashing light on the end, dominatrix stilettos and a very stupid grin. I also have *HO-HO-HO* written cheekily in marker pen on one buttock.

Next to me Cara has turned white-faced. 'Oh my giddy aunt,' she gasps.

Again, I feel stronger language might have been appropriate in the circumstances.

'It's you!'

'Yes.' I know that.

'You look ridiculous.'

'Yes.' I know that too.

'This is the sort of stuff the guys at the office look at all the time.' Cara points in disbelief at my bottom on the screen. 'Why did you put it there?'

'I didn't, you wombat! Why on earth would I want my arse on the Internet?'

Cara stares wide-eyed at me. I can feel the tears welling again. 'Declan?' she asks in hushed tones.

'Of course, Declan. Who else would have access to pictures of my bloody backside?'

'I didn't know that Declan did.' There seems to be a grudging sort of admiration in her voice and she nudges me out of the way to get a better look.

There is one main photo and four small ones, artistically arranged, underneath.

'Oh golly,' Cara breathes.

From whatever angle you look at them, they are still undeniably me and my bottom.

'I gave Declan a digital camera for Christmas.'

Cara zooms in for a close-up. 'Looks like he's been using it.'

'That's enough,' I snarl and grab the mouse, clicking it over the Exit button.

'How did you find out?'

'I was going through the desk drawers looking for my cheque book and I came across a print-out.'

Cara snorts, heavily. 'What are you going to do?'

'Do?' I snort a bit too. 'I'm going to put the house on the market and sod off with my share. If we were married, I'd divorce him.'

'Not about that,' Cara tuts. 'About *this*.' She flicks her thumb at the now blank computer screen.

'Declan said he'd take it off. Immediately.' It occurs to me that it is still very much there.

'Why did he do it in the first place?'

'For a laugh.'

'For a laugh?' Cara looks deeply sceptical. 'I take it you didn't find it very funny?'

'About as funny as Declan would have found being hit round the head with the frying pan.'

'Which is what you were trying to do to him moments before you left.'

I nod.

'Emily?' Cara sips at her camomile tea, which must be stone cold by now. 'What on earth possessed you to let him take photographs of you tarted up like that?'

I might have the exterior of a cool, in-control professional, but beneath this breast (these breasts), I throb with unrestrained passion. I haven't been blessed, or cursed, with a glamour-girl chest for nothing. 'It was a bit of adult horseplay.' I can feel myself glowing with shame.

'You look like a two-bit whore.' Cara likes to be comforting. 'Making love should be a spiritual experience. Prancing round like that smacks of desperation. It's the sort of thing that couples do when they've been married for twenty years and are bored to death with each other. I thought you were a feminist?'

'I am.' My red cheeks burn.

'And you let your boyfriend take pictures of you in a see-through Santa suit with no knickers?'

I can hear my guilty gulp. 'I was expressing my sexuality.'

'You can do that without taking your knickers off.'

'Declan has always appreciated my adventurous side.'

Cara narrows her eyes. 'And now hundreds of others can too.'

Hundreds? I hadn't actually considered that. My redness gives way to blanching. 'What if someone I know sees it?'

Cara shakes her head, a look of extreme frustration on her face. 'Get Declan to take it off. Now. Before it does any more damage.'

This could actually be a lot worse than I thought. And I thought it was pretty bad before.

Cara heads for the door. Clearly being in the same room as me is bringing on a need to meditate. She turns to face me and she has her schoolteacher's expression on. I know because it was me who taught her it. 'And next time you feel like being adventurous, Emily, try white-water rafting. With your clothes on.'

Chapter Five

The local pub, the Jiggery-Pokery, could only be categorised as a dump. But, in its favour, the Jig was a hop, skip and a jump from the office, it churned out good bacon rolls all day until they finally remembered to turf the clientèle out, and the beer wasn't bad. There was very little else that the average journalist required in a watering hole. Stencilled flowers, sponged walls and designer distressed furniture – rather than distressed by aeons of abuse – largely went unnoticed by members of the press.

Tonight, however, wasn't a bacon-roll night, it was a two-bags-of-Scampi-Fries and two-pints-of-Guinness night. Adam put the packets of chemically manufactured snacks between his teeth and carried the brimming drinks over to the table.

Chris sat staring into space. Adam clinked his pint down in front of him, jolting Chris out of his reverie. 'If you keep drooling like that, someone might come along and try to revoke your day pass.'

'Just daydreaming, mate.'

'Well, don't do it in front of Cara or she'll think you've got the hots for her and then where would we be?' Adam said.

Chris tried an exploratory taste of his Guinness. 'Would you . . .?'

'What?'

Chris shrugged. 'You know . . . with Cara. If it was on offer.'

'No. No. *No*. No way!' Adam was affronted. 'She's a great News Editor, but she's totally emotionally unstable. And she's the boss. And she's into all that "alternative" business. It would be like going to bed with the Dalai Lama. Do I need any more excuses?'

'So you've asked and she turned you down?'

'No.' Adam sighed into his drink. 'I wouldn't dream of it. She's a friend, a work colleague. She's the last person I'd want to go to bed with. Besides,' he pointed out, 'you know I have a deep vein of bitterness running through my body when it comes to women. These things start out all right, but they invariably turn horrid.'

Chris tried to look smooth. 'I wouldn't mind giving it a go.'

'Now tell me something that doesn't surprise me.'

'No. Seriously,' Chris said. 'I could teach Cara a lot.'

'Oh, I'd like to be a fly on the wall to watch that.' Adam folded his arms across his chest and smiled.

Chris wouldn't be swayed. 'We all have our perversions, mate.'

'Yes,' Adam said. 'You just have a lot more than others.'

'It's taken years of practice,' Chris said proudly. 'Anyway, how are things with Laura, the woman to whom all your bitterness is owed?'

'Oh fine,' Adam nodded. 'She's just had my maintenance payments increased to the sort of level that any skilled extortionist would be proud of.'

'She's still giving you grief?'

'She gave me grief from the moment I said "I do".'

Chris's attention wandered to the two girls wiggling over to the juke box, bare-midriffed and bottoms bound into tight Capri pants. Adam followed his gaze. The girls turned round and grinned at them.

'BOBFOCs,' Chris said in a voice that it was best not to argue with.

Body off *Baywatch*. Face off *Crimewatch*. Chris's standard description for anyone who didn't come up to his exacting standards i.e. Julia Roberts.

'Do me a favour, Chris. When you find your soulmate, don't propose to her.'

'Propose what?'

'I was thinking of marriage.'

Chris dragged his attention back from the two giggling women, whose taste in music appeared to be confined to Westlife, and stared at Adam wide-eyed. It was a good job he wasn't swigging his Guinness, as he would have spat it out. 'Are you mad?'

'I was once.' Adam sighed. 'But that's enough. The only good thing to come out of my three years with Laura was Josh.'

'He's a great kid.'

'Yeah.' The one downside of it was that Josh's presence tied him and his pay packet to his ex-wife for the foreseeable future. Even the thought of it dragged his heart a little bit nearer to the floor. How could you say that another person's life was the result of a stupid accident? Particularly a freckle-faced twelve year old who was so irrepressibly cheeky and gave meaning to an otherwise mundane existence.

The fact was, though, that Josh was the product of a split condom, in a time when the focus had been taken off unwanted pregnancy and put on unwanted life-threatening disease. It was months before Laura realised she was pregnant and it was shortly afterwards, when they were grinning inanely at each other in Wimbledon Register Office, that Adam realised he was marrying someone who was, in every way, wrong for him.

Still the dirty deed was done. They struggled on gamely for three unhappy years before he left her to live in a box-sized bedsit in the bleakest part of Bermondsey and retain what was left of his sanity. Within weeks Laura had latched onto another man – Barry, the manager of the building society where she worked part-time when they had been together – and whom she had since married. She'd left her job immediately after the nuptials and now sat on her backside all day watching house makeover programmes – *Changing Rooms*, *Rooms for Change*, *House Doctors*, *Garden Doctors*, *Gardening Neighbours*, *Neighbours' Gardens* – she knew them all. The rest of her spare time she devoted to turning into the ex-wife from hell. Adam wondered if she was taking night-school classes in it. He heaved a lengthy sigh. This was too depressing a subject to consider with only a bag of Scampi Fries for solace. Licking the orange chemical coating off one, Adam then popped it into his mouth in the hope that all the E Numbers would stave off his depression. 'Is Toff coming tonight?'

'Expect so,' Chris replied, his interest in the girls having waned momentarily.

Toff, otherwise known as Sebastian Atherton, had formerly occupied the position of Chief Photographer before Adam, but he had left the *Hampstead Observer* the previous year to form his own photographic company specialising mostly in glamour shoots. The top end of glamour – no pun intended.

Toff was one step away from the Pirelli Calendar type of material rather than *Hustler* or anything featuring Readers' Wives. This was primarily down to Daddy's contacts. It wasn't that Toff's talent was in question. He was a completely competent and even talented photographer; it was just rather a mystery to everyone who met him why he bothered to work at all.

His father owned a country pile the size of Buck House somewhere down near Brighton and several other homes organised alphabetically around the world – Antigua, Bali, Cannes, the Dordogne, Evian, and a little ten-bedroomed ski-lodge in Gstaad. His parents were Lord and Lady someone or other, or Earl and whatever an Earl's missus is called. Toff lived in one wing of a sprawling mansion with spectacular views over the Heath, the rest of which was occupied by a pop star Adam had never heard of and a celebrity chef whom he had. Toff's lifestyle clearly hadn't been funded by his salary from the *Hampstead Observer* – and quite how he came to be chief snapper on a local rag is anyone's guess. He was infinitely

18

more suited to doing portraits of Iman with tyre-marks over her bottom. Toff wasn't so much struggling to get to the top, rather the top was sitting there waiting to welcome him with open arms when he deigned to arrive.

Still, he was a great bloke despite driving a Morgan and sounding like he'd been in *Gosford Park*. A valued member of the drinking brethren, he usually turned up at the local a couple of evenings a week. The other nights he spent with a harem of different women only linked by a common tendency to names like Felicity and Charlotte and Samantha and the need to start every sentence with 'Yah'. The only other trait that ran through his choice of women was their ability to cope with his total lack of commitment to anything and their unadulterated non-accusatory delight when he saw fit to spend time with them. It was a highly commendable one in Adam's view and he wondered why, after even a few paltry dates, he always got the feeling that women were waving their engagement fingers in his direction. It wasn't that he was a great catch, being on the far side of thirty, permanently penniless and an embittered divorcé with a nearly teenage ankle-biter in tow. Not your typical qualifications for a dreamboat.

Toff arrived and pushed his way through the crowd of hardened late-evening drinkers to join them at their table.

'Hi, Toff,' Adam said. 'How's it going?'

'Pretty damn fab, old boy.' Toff pulled up a chair and lowered himself into it, brushing his ever-flopping fringe from his eyes. Toff had typically aristocratic hair – strawberry blond and with a mass of curls on top that mothers and women with maternal tendencies just adored. He always wore linen suits with absolutely the right number of crumples. His father's tailor probably put them in especially.

Chris stood up. 'It's my round. What do you want, mate?'

Adam jiggled his glass. 'Same again.'

'Campari and soda, sweetheart.'

Toff could also drink girls' drinks and get away with it. Just about. While Chris ambled over to the bar, Toff nicked one of his Scampi Fries.

'You're looking a bit glum for a Tuesday evening, old bean,' he remarked to Adam.

'Less of the "old".'

'Lacking the love of a good woman?'

'I'm off women,' Adam said sourly.

'I've known you for five years, maybe more, and you've always been off women.' Toff eyed Adam wryly. 'Are you sure they aren't off you?'

'I was just thinking about life, Toff.'

19

'Ooo. Scary subject.'

'I want to do something with it.' Adam rubbed his toe over some long-dried chewing gum on the floor. 'I don't want to spend the rest of my days photographing school harvest festivals, church fêtes and bouncing baby competitions.'

'Come and join me,' Toff offered. He grinned a louche aristocratic grin. 'Different sort of bouncing babies.'

Chris came back with the drinks and plonked them on the table. 'I'll do it.'

'You're not a photographer.'

'So. How hard can it be?' he said, voicing the typical antipathy that existed between reporters and photographers when it came to appreciating each other's respective talents.

Adam and Toff exchanged a glance.

'Chris is in love with a cyberbabe.'

'And what's wrong with that?' Chris looked affronted. 'I've forwarded that celestial image to several of my deserving friends and not one of them came back with the riposte "not bad".' He turned Bambi eyes on his friend. 'Gissa job, Toff.'

'No.'

'Please,' Chris begged.

'We're talking about Adam,' Toff reminded him. 'He's tired of life.'

'He's always tired of life,' Chris whined. 'Even when Manchester United win, he can barely raise a titter.'

'That is because he has a burdened soul.'

'That's because his ex-missus is emptying his wallet. Again.'

'I want to make a difference,' Adam said thoughtfully, savouring a sip of his pint. 'I want to get out into the big, wide world. Do you know, until the paper sent me to Bosnia, I'd never been further than Ibiza? I want to go back there. Or to Kosovo.'

'I would treat someone who wanted to ship me out to a war zone with the utmost suspicion,' Chris concluded.

It had been a turning point in Adam's life when he'd been sent out to Bosnia by the *Hampstead Observer* at the beginning of December. His brief was to do a feature spread of photographs showing how local boys who were in the Armed Forces spent their Christmas. Adam had seen it as a jolly. He'd entered into the festive spirit totally and taken two Santa hats, a foot-high, battery-operated, fibre-optic Christmas tree and some garish scarlet tinsel with him.

After seven hours' bouncing around in a basic Army issue plane, with no in-flight entertainment other than how to keep warm, he and the reporter, a crusty, seen-it-all-before hack called Andrew, had been dumped in a pile of rubble that used to be a town, given flak-jackets and hard tin hats, a crash course in how to avoid land mines and had been sent on their way with two heavily armed guards to take cheery pictures and report cheery thoughts.

When they'd reached their eventual destination, the village was so bombed out that there was nothing left worth exploding. Adam had taken ridiculous posed pictures of the boys who called themselves soldiers sporting Santa hats, blood-red tinsel draped poignantly round the barrels of their guns, the tiny Christmas tree twinkling in the background for all its worth. They'd left them huddled against the cold behind damp sandbags valiantly defending a few ragged houses and a few ragged people.

Two little girls, barely Josh's age, dressed in threadbare clothing and paper-thin shoes, had laughed as only carefree children can do as they bombarded Adam and the reporter with snowballs. It was the single uplifting moment of the entire trip. He and Andrew had left their thick, fleecy man-sized gloves behind to warm the children's tiny, red-raw hands, and sometimes, in the wee small hours, he wondered whether they were still alive.

When they returned home Adam had sat in the fugged-up warmth of the Starbucks coffee bar in Hampstead High Street and marvelled at the British ability to moan about every single aspect of their cosy little Christmas and their self-inflicted, obsessive commercialism. He could hardly bear to listen to the indulgent mothers laden with bursting carrier bags reeling off all the needless toys they were bestowing on their spoiled brats, complaining about all the retail excesses they still had to endure. Life is tough. I don't think so.

After twenty long years as a journalist, Andrew had resigned from the *Hampstead Observer*, waved his comfortable company pension goodbye and gone off to work for the Voluntary Services Overseas building mud huts in Namibia. Adam had lacked the same courage and commitment to walk away from it all, but an unidentified restlessness had stayed in his heart ever since.

'Bosnia. Bollocks,' Chris said succinctly, breaking Adam's train of thought. 'Why would you want to spend your days getting your arse shot at?'

Adam scowled. 'I want to experience the difficulties of living in conflict.'

'I thought you'd have had enough of that with Laura.'

'We have it so cushy, mate.' Adam tried to explain. 'You've no idea. I want to do something to help these people. I want to know what they feel like. I want to make a contribution to improving their lives.'

'Have you ever thought of entering Miss World?' Chris put on a girly voice. ' "My ambitions are to meet people and help animals, cure cancer, reverse global warming and create world peace." '

'Don't you want to be remembered for something, Chris?'

'Being a great shag.' He grinned widely.

'Be serious.'

Chris looked hurt. 'I am.'

'Has it ever occurred to you that you might be considered very shallow?'

Chris put his beer down as a barricade. 'Compared to what?'

Adam huffed wearily. 'Don't you want to make a difference?'

'No.'

'Why not?'

'It sounds too much like hard work.'

'Don't be ridiculous. It'd be great. Challenging. I'm talking about life-changing stuff.'

'So why haven't you done it?'

Adam sagged. 'It sounds too much like hard work.'

Chris grinned smugly. 'I rest my case.'

'You have also one other small matter to consider.' Toff looked at Adam sagely. 'What about Josh?'

'You don't need to remind me.' Adam shook his head. It was something that always brought his lofty ideals down to earth. He had fought long and hard to stay involved in Josh's life – and not just financially. If it meant sacrificing his own ideals he would have to do it. Josh was growing up fast and his father wanted to be around while he did so, and if that required him to spend his days snapping prize-winning vegetables, toddler groups and the tennis club trophy dinner then he would do so. There was no point going halfway across the world to help deserving causes while neglecting your own offspring. He was just going to have to knuckle down and make the most of it.

'So are you going to give me a job, Toff?' Chris interjected.

'No.' Toff swirled his Campari. 'But if you're very good, you can come and watch sometimes.'

Appeased, Chris rubbed his hands together in glee. 'Great!'

Chapter Six

Declan could charm the birds out of the trees. He had looked at investors in the same way and found he could also charm individuals out of large sums of money with nothing more to offer than a wing and a prayer – and, of course, the possibility of becoming ridiculously wealthy at some time in the future. At the moment, that time was looking further and further away. And there was another thing about investors – they were rather more demanding than birds once you had got them out of the trees.

It was a skill he had cultivated over many a year. Charm. Or perhaps it was part of his Irish inheritance. That and a good sprinkling of the old blarney. At the moment, though, words seemed to be failing him. Declan was sitting in front of a whirring computer, hands over his eyes. It was late and everyone else had gone from the offices except him and Alan, the nerdy computer programmer who'd helped him to launch his business in its fledgling stage.

He'd been in the right place at the right time. Everyone had wanted to invest in dot-coms. Was it his fault that the floaty, fragile bubble had quite spectacularly burst? No it wasn't. Every day, the newspapers were full of doom and gloom stories of yet another trendy young website gone to the wall. There was no way *his* failure was going to grace the business pages. But if that wasn't to be the case, he'd have to do something pretty nifty and pretty fast.

He risked a look at the screen again. Emily smiled back at him, cheeks full and rounded – not the ones on her face. He could hardly bring himself to do this, but unless he wanted to retain his manhood, which Emily had threatened to part him with, he had to ditch the Saucy Santa images pronto. It was a desperate situation and one that he hadn't really foreseen. Emily was the least computer literate person he knew, and she'd probably never have found out – as was the plan – until he'd foolishly printed a copy out.

Declan chewed his lip. This had been a very sound business decision, if not the best choice for improving domestic harmony. But then domestic harmony wasn't really his top priority at the moment.

Hanging on by the tips of his fingers, still hoping to cash in on the Internet explosion *was*. There was bound to be a turnaround soon and he wanted to be there at the front of the race when it happened. And in order to do so, he'd set up three surefire, money-spinning winners – except that they were turning out to be backfiring, money-munching losers. In the face of mounting bills and rising pressure from investors, he had been forced to take drastic action. And he could think of nothing more drastic than starting up a soft porn site starring his unwitting girlfriend in private bedroom shenanigans.

The legitimate sites were all great ideas. It was their execution and logistics and lack of funding that were the problem. Grabagadget.com was a fantastic site, selling all sorts of now products that no self-respecting technoed-up city boy could live without. Except they could. In droves.

The relatively few orders they'd had for bargain-basement glow-in-the-dark palm-top computers, radio-controlled flying saucers and James Bond-style wrist cameras had all disintegrated into a disaster of demand, lack of supply and an unwillingness in the office for anyone to take responsibility or control of the mounting pile of brown cardboard boxes whose ownership had been downloaded into cyberspace somewhere, never to be found again. As they had no sale or return arrangements, Declan's company was now the proud owner of two hundred and seventy personal GPS systems, five hundred adult-sized space hoppers and an unknown quantity of Office Voodoo Kits. Who would not die to own one of those?

Sadgits.com was a great idea too. Funny, original and a potential cult site. Except that it was failing to find favour with advertisers, who didn't particularly want their product linked with *Anorak of the Day* or *Eighteen Ways to Be Extremely Boring*. It was doing OK, with around two million hits per week, so there were enough people out there who wanted to nominate their friends or colleagues for the *Wanker of the Week* page, but that wasn't good enough if he couldn't get Tesco to cough up a few bob for banner advertising to plug their fruit and veg on it.

Datewithastar.com should also have been a corker. For a few quid each month, any lonely housewives or particularly desperate men could sign up to receive virtual emails from virtual celebrities and indulge in a virtual relationship. Virtually a certain winner! Or so he had thought. The trouble with Datewithastar.com was that it required a full-time writer to sit and compose the daily emails required by the clients, who probably should all have featured on Sadgits.com.

All three businesses were gobbling up money at an alarming rate. The office overheads were staggering, as he'd wanted a prestigious

24

address befitting a young, thrusting, techno-savvy company. They had the upper floor of a converted chapel in Camden with huge arched windows overlooking the Grand Union Canal, which was great, very funky, very inspiring – and a shitload of rent-money every week.

The size of the staff was growing at an alarming rate, too. He'd started off with a young secretary, one nerdy computer programmer, (the aforementioned Alan), and a cleaner called Madge. Now he had an office crammed full of dot.snots – young know-it-alls of the techno age. There was an Office Manager, several young secretaries, an equally large number of expensive Webmasters alongside the nerdy computer programmer, and two young and hungry Sales Executives who, Declan was convinced, were creaming off half of the business they gained for themselves. It gave him very bad headaches.

The decision to go porny had been born out of genuine desperation. While all his business endeavours were slowly sinking without trace, all he'd done with Emily's photo was circulate it to a group of contacts as a bit of festive fun and frolics – not wise, not exactly moral, but done without malice aforethought. And it had snowballed – to use a suitably festive analogy. He knew Emily was a stunning-looking woman, but he hadn't quite realised how many others would appreciate that too. The whole thing had gathered momentum, rolling down the hill of cyberspace out of control and soon he was being emailed copies of his own creation. At the time, it seemed a sin not to capitalise on it.

Now, a paltry few weeks later, Emily's bottom was attracting four million hits per week, all by itself. Every search engine happily chucked it up with very little prompting. Nearly half of the people who accessed the Internet did so looking for material of a dubious nature. Forty-two per cent, to be exact. That was a scary statistic. Not too many years ago you had to go out of your way to find sites like that. Now you had to take steps to avoid them. And there was no shortage of people who wanted to peddle their wares on porn sites. It had the potential to be huge. The site, not the bottom.

It was a pity Emily had launched herself into orbit when she'd found out. But then he always knew that she would. It was, primarily, the reason he hadn't told her.

Alan shuffled towards him. He was the only person who looked out of place in the trendy offices and he was the only person Declan felt he could really trust. Alan was as gaunt as a heroin addict, due to the fact he rarely went out in daylight because he rarely ventured far from his beloved computer screen. He wore his hair down to his

25

waist and parted in the middle, flares from the first time round, basketball boots and the look of the permanently stoned.

'Hey, man. Late night,' Alan said and sat down next to him.

The light from Declan's desk lamp bounced off the stark white walls. Madge had pulled down the black Venetian blinds as she left, shutting out the cold night. Declan felt trapped in what used to be his sanctuary, his baby, his dream and his life.

Declan sighed before he said, 'Yeah.' He sat back and nodded at the screen. 'Emily found out.'

Alan grimaced. 'Heavy.'

'Very.'

'Emily's page has to go?'

'Yeah.' Declan rubbed his fingers round his lips. If only there was a way. 'I didn't really want to go into porn, Al. It's not my style.'

'It's big money.' Alan pulled a tobacco pouch out of his jeans and rolled a tiny joint. There was a strict no-smoking policy in the office which saw everyone else who indulged huddled outside in the chapel porch, exposed to the elements. Alan was the only exception. Without a roll-up in his mouth, everyone was terrified he would implode, desiccating into a pile of dust on the non-static flooring before their eyes. He looked as insubstantial as the liquorice papers he used to encase his suspicious-smelling tobacco. 'A friend of mine was a lap-dancer who got tired of doing the clubs. I set up a basic site for her. She makes seven million a year from guys ogling her in a g-string.' Alan shrugged as if mystified by the ways of the world.

Declan inhaled sharply and not because Alan looked like *the* most unlikely person in the world to have a friend who was a lap-dancer. *Seven million*. It was a considerable amount of money in anyone's book.

'What did Emily say?' Alan enquired, lighting his spliff.

'Nothing that was fit to broadcast on children's television.'

'I guess it's to be expected.'

'Yeah,' Declan agreed. 'Except I didn't expect her to find out.'

'These things have a way of escaping into the universe.'

'Yeah?' Declan wound his fingers together, leaning back in his black leather chair and trying to look as if he hadn't a care in the world, when it actually felt like he had too many to count. 'She's left me, Alan. I didn't expect that either.'

'Hea-*vy*.'

Declan looked up. There was no one else he could talk to. He certainly hadn't been able to tell Emily how much he was in for with the business. The numbers were racking up daily and they were now starting to scare him. 'I don't know what to do.'

'We need this site, Declan.'

'I've told Emily I'd ditch it.' He pressed his lips hard together. 'Tonight.'

'It's the only thing that's bringing us any cash in.'

'I know.'

'Declan. The damage is done,' Alan wisely pointed out. 'Go out. Fast. Get some models. Get some pictures. It can't be that difficult. We'll replace Emily.'

Replace Emily. Just like that. It might be easy to do that on the website. Quite how it would work in real life was a different matter. 'Phone the lap-dancer for me.'

'I can't, man. Competition.'

Declan tutted. 'It's money, Al. Money that I haven't got.'

'It's your only hope, Declan,' his friend said. 'Buy yourself some time. Leave Emily's butt on there for a few more days. It can't do any more harm. Maybe she'll even see the funny side of it. Women can be like that.'

'Yeah.' Declan wished he felt as hopeful as he sounded. 'And maybe she won't.'

'Then you've lost her anyway.' Alan eased his gangly frame from the chair. 'I have to go, man.'

'Yeah. Yeah. Thanks for your help, mate.'

'No worries.'

'And Alan – not a word of this, OK?'

'Declan. You're the man. You'll fix it.'

'Yeah.'

Alan shambled off, making the office look untidy as he progressed.

Declan heard the front door bang as Emily looked out at him from the screen. He hadn't imagined making his money from sleaze when he'd entered this business. He'd had aspirations of being a bright young thing, a dot.com whizz, a star. He'd wanted to follow in the footsteps of Martha Lane Fox and her online ticket agency Lastminute.com, and others such as Zoom and Boo.com which burnt brightly but were blown out far too fast. Declan wanted his dream to be bigger, bolder, better and without the inevitable crash that seemed to be afflicting all dot.coms and turning them into dot.bombs. What had happened? They were the new gold rush, everyone vying to stake their claim in cyberspace. And now they were all in one big shoot-out, with only the wiliest not ending up full of holes and dying in the dust.

Instead of trailblazing, he'd now joined the lowest of the low in the lowest of the low way, selling out the only person who cared about him. And yet it had to be done. There was no way he could let all this

27

crash around his ears. 'I'm the man,' he said flatly to her trusting, grinning face.

Standing up, he stretched his aching shoulders and turned off his desk lamp. Leaving his girlfriend staring inanely out into the gloom, he walked wearily out of his office without looking back.

Chapter Seven

I hardly slept a wink last night. When I did drop off, I had all these terrible nightmares about computer bugs with millions of legs and viruses that looked like Anna Kournikova chasing me with tennis rackets. When I was awake the reality was even worse.

It's strange not being in my own house. Normally, if I can't sleep, I get up, make a cuppa, read for a bit, something slushy and mind-numbing if possible – and I don't mean students' essays – then I go back to bed when my brain's calmed down and I nod off straight away. Sorted. In someone else's house you can't do that. Not even in your best mate's. You can't prowl round in the dead of night without arousing alarm. Instead I lay awake counting the array of lucky, fat-bellied Buddhas with cheesy grins that Cara has lined up on the bookshelves. Thirty-one, to be precise. One of them that actually worked would do me.

Cara had to go to work first thing this morning and I was already awake when she kindly stuck her head round the door bearing a cup of nettle tea – mmm, *yum* – before she shot off to do important news-type things.

I had the urge to spend the night looking at my near-naked image on the screen, willing it to go off, yet now that I'm up and about, I haven't got the courage to face myself in my full glory. Instead I'm rooting around in Cara's cupboards looking for something to eat that hasn't got the word 'organic' in the title. Even the loo cleaner is 'organic'. How can you have organic loo cleaner? What am I saying? I'm just trying to avoid the fact that I have more pressing problems.

I phoned the School Secretary first thing and told her that I was sick. Which I am – to my stomach. Thankfully, most of my colleagues are as computer illiterate as I am and probably haven't seen me doing my bit to spread goodwill to all men. The School Secretary, who is a harridan, tutted loudly down the telephone at me, because my absence means she'll have to draft in a supply teacher for Form 5S of Year 10 who were due a double lesson of Shakespeare. Personally, given what I'm going through, I reckon it's lucky I

29

haven't taken to my bed and am refusing to come out ever again.

I also have to go to one of the rash of estate agents on the High Street and arrange for someone to come and do a valuation on the house. I wonder idly what Declan and I will get for it and my stomach rolls again. It is still a struggle to fit this into my structured shape of reality. I can't believe that he has really done this. Oh, don't get me wrong. Declan is no angel. Not by a long chalk. Over our five years of fairly turbulent relationship there have been more than a few sticky patches. He's been very stupid at times. And stubborn. And reckless. But I don't think he's ever been deliberately cruel. I'm talking more about missed anniversaries, crap birthday presents and an inability to share cooking duties. Which, given the global scale of this particular misdemeanour, was mere fumbling foreplay.

I look out of Cara's window into the garden. January is a good time to be betrayed. The greyness I feel inside matches perfectly the bleakness of the day outside. Imagine being dumped in July when the sun is cracking the flags. That truly would be awful.

It's drizzling – that miserable type of rain that Britain does so well and so frequently. Even in the relative sparseness of winter, Cara's garden looks a bit overgrown and the ivy, which seems to be overtaking everything else, is being batted about by the wind.

It's a shock being betrayed like this. I trusted Declan. Trusted him enough to risk playing 'adult games' involving photographic equipment. Lesson number one learned. You can never truly know someone, I guess. You can love them, lie in their arms, iron their shirts, make their favourite meals for them, allow them access to your bank details, lose yourself in their life, you can think you know them. But you never really see what's in someone's heart.

Declan bought me the wretched Santa outfit as a joke – so I thought, although I now suspect deeply ulterior motives. We had a few drinks, I put it on, pranced around being silly and posing as Declan snapped away for half an hour, then we made love and the outfit and the camera have remained in the cupboard ever since. The Santa hat played a tinny, mechanical version of 'Rudolph the Red-Nosed Reindeer' and had a little red light that flickered on and off at the end. This is not a serious sexual deviation. I am not the whore of Babylon. It's fun. Right? Not what you might call your classic turn-on. We had a laugh. When I let Declan write HO-HO-HO in black marker pen on my bottom that's what I assumed we both thought it was. Funny.

I am an open-minded, millennium sort of woman. I have needs, a sex drive and hormones that clank together occasionally. I am still in sex bomb rather than biological clock mode. And I don't think that's a bad thing. Or didn't. Declan and I were not like most of our coupley friends, whose sex-lives appeared to be flatter than a two-week-old bottle of Coke. Ours had fizz, sparkle, adventure. We made love outside in secluded places, when the weather warranted it. I have an array of feather boas and velvet gloves purely for entertainment purposes only. I have been known, on occasions when I didn't feel fat and bloated, to wear stockings and suspenders instead of Marks & Spencers' 10 denier tights – and very little else. I was liberated and felt free to indulge my sexual fantasies. Now that I have my arse on the Internet, however, I'm taking a different view. If we'd had a quick straightforward shag under the duvet on a Saturday night like everyone else, then I wouldn't be in this trouble now. And trouble it is.

With luck, Declan has been true to his word this time and has taken it off – pronto. If not, there is something I'd like to remove for him – pronto.

Still, I can't stand here staring at the rain all day, bemoaning my lot. I have my life to get on with. A life that no longer involves Declan Dead Meat O'Donnell. I am going to force myself to carry on. Force myself to live life to the full (so long as no one's pointing a digital camera at me). Force myself to love again – in the fullness of time. And, first and foremost, I am going to force myself to eat.

I ferret round the kitchen a bit more. My batty friend even practises her Feng Shui in the fridge. I adore Cara even though she is slowly driving me insane too. We probably have the most prosperous, well-aligned cheese in North London. My search for calorie-laden comfort food is in vain. Cara has a loaf of *organic*, wholemeal, wholewheat, wholesome, wholly disgusting-looking, shrivelled brown bread covered in sunflower seeds lurking in her bread bin. Frankly, the packet looks more appetising. I shut the lid and decide that it would be better to face the day on an empty stomach.

Chapter Eight

Adam had got to work early, before the others. He was already at his desk when Cara arrived and scurried his bacon sandwich into his drawer when he saw her approach.

'Hi,' she said brightly.

'Hi,' he mumbled. 'Sorry.' He flicked an apologetic glance at his drawer.

'It's OK,' she said. 'I don't like to inflict my principles on everyone.'

Adam choked on a crumb and Cara felt the urge to pat him on his back.

She liked Adam. He was still a gorilla, like most of the other blokes in the office, but he was a nice sort of gorilla. Lovable in an undernourished way. He was tall, dark and sruffily handsome. His mad black hair curled round his pale face in a gloriously unkempt way, and a vaguely worried look stretched permanently between his eyebrows. Adam had a natural designer stubble due to an apparent aversion to shaving and he always wore black, which made him resemble a cross between a depressed New Romantic and a cheerful Goth. His green eyes were flecked with brown and he generally looked like he needed more sleep. He had a low, gravelly voice that made him sound like he smoked, but he didn't.

'How was your friend?' he asked when he'd recovered from his coughing fit.

'Bad,' Cara said, dumping her bag down. 'Very bad. The twit she lives with has seriously blown it this time.'

Adam's look was genuinely sympathetic.

'I've got a new lodger,' Cara informed him. 'Not out of choice, I might add.'

'I'm sorry.'

Cara flicked her hair. 'You can't let a friend down and Emily is my best friend. No, *the* best friend a girl could have.'

'I've got a spare room. It's not much bigger than a shoebox, but if it gets too much, she could shack up at my place for a while.' Adam shrugged. 'I could do with the company.'

Cara shuddered inwardly. If a man could leave his hair so untidy, just imagine what his kitchen sink must be like. 'It'll be fine. We just need to establish some ground rules.' At this, she thought she saw Adam flinch.

Reaching over to Chris's desk, Cara picked up the day's news list. As she did so, her hand brushed the mouse lying next to his computer and it activated his screen, whisking aside the screensaver.

'Oh flip!' Cara sank into Chris's chair, biting the end of the news list.

Adam leaned over. 'Oh shit,' he said. 'Sorry about that.'

Cara looked up at him, stunned. 'It's Emily.'

'Who?'

'My friend, Emily. The one I was just talking about.' Cara glanced at the screen again. 'What on earth is Chris doing with this?'

Adam blanched slightly. 'What do men usually do with porn-site pictures?' He wetted his lip nervously. 'Chris is totally in love with her. Besotted.'

Cara closed her eyes. 'This is terrible. A nightmare. Her ex put it on the net. She didn't know about it until yesterday. That's why she's left him.' Cara lowered her voice. 'Emily's a schoolteacher.'

Adam sucked in his breath. 'Not good.'

'He was supposed to take it off last night. Clearly, he hasn't. I bet tons of people have looked at it by now.' Cara pulled at her lip. 'I'd better ring her.'

'I'll tell Chris to get rid of it,' Adam offered.

'Yeah,' Cara said distractedly and headed back to her desk to phone Emily straightaway.

Chris wandered in ten minutes later. Adam gave him a look that said, 'Hurry up.'

'What?' Chris glanced at his watch. 'I'm not late.'

'No. But we have a little crisis.'

'Ooo,' Chris said, rubbing his hands together appreciatively. 'I like the sound of this.'

'You won't,' Adam said, lowering his voice. 'It's to do with Miss Noel Knickers here.' He nodded towards Chris's computer screen.

'My lovely Saucy Santa?' Chris sat down and wiggled his mouse so that the image appeared again.

'Don't do that!' Adam hissed, glancing across the office. 'Cara'll do her pieces.'

'Not that sexual harassment stuff again!'

'No.' Adam checked that Cara was still out of earshot. 'It's her mate.'

33

Chris's eyes widened and he flicked a thumb at the screen. 'That is?'

'*She* is.'

'Bugger me.' Chris twisted his lips. 'Cara's not going to be the Easter Bunny Girl, is she?'

'Don't be stupid.' Adam sighed. 'Look, it would be a really good idea if you could tear your eyes away from her and ditch it before too many people see it.'

Chris looked puzzled. 'Isn't the point of it being there precisely so that lots of people can see it?'

'No. Not in this case.'

'I've already forwarded it to all of my address-book chums.'

'What?'

'It's a bloke thing. You know, Adam,' Chris said with a wink. 'Share and share alike.'

'That wasn't a good idea.' Adam shook his head. 'Cara will go ballistic.'

Chris spread his hands. 'She'll never know.'

'Make sure she doesn't,' Adam advised. He nodded at Chris's screen and Emily's fur-trimmed but otherwise bare breasts. 'She's a schoolteacher.'

Chris roared with laughter. 'You what?' He tilted his head to get a better view. 'We never had teachers who looked like that at my school.'

'Neither did we,' Adam admitted. 'Apparently, she's distraught. That was her crying in reception last night.'

Chris's eyes widened. 'She was *here*?'

'Yup. With her clothes on,' Adam added drily. 'You wouldn't have recognised her.'

His friend looked gutted. 'She was here and I didn't even know.' After a moment of sulking, he brightened considerably. He glanced up at Adam. 'If she was here, that means she's local.'

'Yeah,' Adam agreed. 'I suppose so.'

'She's a local schoolteacher and porny pics of her have been on the net?'

Chris had a mind like an abacus. You could hear the beads clicking into place. 'Looks that way,' Adam agreed.

'Why was she upset?'

'Wouldn't you be?'

Chris nodded indifferently.

'Apparently, she didn't know anything about it,' Adam explained. 'Her boyfriend slapped it up there without her knowing.'

Chris snorted. 'I bet that's what they all say.'

'Well. Who knows.' Adam shrugged. His bacon sandwich was long past its best and he'd lost interest in Miss Saucy Santa, not that he'd ever had much in the first place.

Chris jumped up. 'I have died and gone to heaven!' He could hardly contain himself. 'What a brilliant news story!'

'What?'

'And on my patch.' Chris gazed at the ceiling. 'Thank You. Thank You, God!'

'Wait. This is not a news story. Repeat – *not* a news story.'

'Not a news story?' Chris was standing now. The only time Adam had previously seen him so animated was when Manchester United were about to score. 'This goes to show why you're a mere snapper and I'm a hot-to-trot news hound.'

Adam shook his head. 'You won't be allowed to run with this one, mate.'

'Are you mad? This is *the* news story of my career. We are the newspaper that makes a front-page splash of a library book being stolen from the Heath branch library.'

'It was a rare edition library book,' Adam protested.

'Oh, excuse me,' Chris countered. 'That makes all the difference. Adam, sweetheart, we ran an in-depth exposé about a leaking pipe in a toddlers' group toy cupboard.'

Adam opened his mouth.

'And before you say it,' Chris held his finger up to shush him, 'I know that the ickle-pickle toys all went mouldy and all the teenie-weenie toddlers cried.'

Adam closed his mouth again.

'If that is a fucking *news* story, mate, how can we possibly ignore this? We have a teacher, possibly a *primary* schoolteacher, romping about in obscene poses on the Internet for any pervert's delectation.'

'You were one of them half an hour ago.'

Chris looked hurt. 'That's before I knew the full story.'

'You would have married her, given half the chance.'

'I didn't know then that she was a scarlet woman purporting to be an upstanding pillar of our society. Instead she's a scourge among us. Secretly corrupting our young.'

'She didn't know anything about it,' Adam said flatly.

'Pah!' Chris tucked his thumbs behind his lapels and paced about a bit, like a barrister summing up a trial.

Adam twisted one of his curls round on itself in frustration. 'This is exactly the sort of trumped-up scandal that I hate in the tabloids, let alone the *Hampstead Observer*.'

35

'It's news, mate,' Chris declared loftily. 'This is a *news*paper. And we are *news*breakers.'

'She's Cara's friend, Chris. Be very careful how you go about this. You are going to stamp on a lot of toes in your size tens if you don't tread gently.'

'She cannot stop me from running a story just because it's about her mate. *Particularly* if it's about her mate. Haven't you heard of the freedom of the press, Adam? It's one of the few joys of living in Britain – apart from the beer. And Manchester United. It's not a police state. Yet.'

Adam tried to be reasonable. 'All I'm saying is, go easy.' He wished to hell he'd never let the cat out of the bag now. Although if the pictures were already halfway round the Internet, it probably wouldn't stay quiet for long. These things took on a life of their own once they were out there. Friends copied them to friends and the damage spread like wildfire. Poor Emily. This was going to take some living down, whether it was her fault or not.

'This story will run, Adam.' Chris narrowed his eyes. 'I will make sure of it.'

Adam wanted to curl up in a ball and go back to bed. He'd always wanted to work in a danger zone – but then he'd assumed he'd have to change jobs to do it. He just hoped that he could stay out of the firing line on this one.

'It'd be great if she's a primary schoolteacher,' Chris breathed hopefully. 'Just imagine the headlines.'

Adam hung his head. He was afraid he could. Very afraid.

Chapter Nine

I'm standing outside my own house, my key in my hand, feeling like an intruder. I'm acting so furtively I might as well be wearing a striped jumper and carrying a bag marked SWAG. Yet all I am doing is stealing in to get a valuation of my own home. The estate agent is going to meet me here to give it the once-over and this feels very much like the first nail in the coffin that is my relationship. I get the urge to phone Declan at work and ask him to try to find a better excuse for his behaviour so that I can stop this excruciatingly painful process. But I don't.

I live – *did* live – in a slightly less salubrious area of Hampstead than Cara. It's still extortionately expensive, but people's eyes normally just bulge disbelievingly when we tell them the house prices; they don't die of shock on the spot. When people think of Hampstead, they picture a green, leafy oasis in the smog of London. Well, it isn't – not all of it. The bit we inhabit is in Scaffolding City, NW1. Every road is Skip Alley. There is so much building rubble around that bits of it look like Beirut on a bad day. Every house is being renovated, restored and refurbished to within an inch of its life. And ours is no exception.

We paid way over the top for this place. When we bought it, it was a two-bed terraced hovel in a nice-ish street – that says it all, doesn't it? They never come with bargain price tags, despite the fact that this one was all but falling down round our ears when we moved in. This is what used to be called a house with room for improvement, suitable for a DIY enthusiast. Now, several property booms later, it would be classed as 'a period cottage retaining original features, with unlimited potential'.

For years a dear old lady had owned our particular haven full of original features before shuffling off to God's waiting room – the nearby Retirement Home for the Terminally Bewildered – and dear old ladies are not generally renowned for their DIY skills. We had a mottled, cracked Victorian bath, turn-of-the-century rising damp and ancient plumbing that required hours of coaxing before it would perform even the most basic of plumbing-type duties. We were probably the only couple in Hampstead who cheered every time our loo deigned to flush. It was pure luck that the old dear hadn't been electrocuted by the pre-war wiring or felled by one of the many ropey ceilings falling in on her over the last few years. I'm sure the whole structure was only held up by ten ageing layers of wallpaper. But, of course, our survey didn't reveal that.

Since then the house has consumed every available penny that hasn't already been consumed by Declan's business. Everything – and I mean *everything* – had to be ripped out and replaced. I'm on such good terms with the Homebase staff, they invited me to their Christmas party this year. The amount of paint I've bought over the year would easily have paid for all their mince pieces and bottles of Lambrusco.

Now Declan and I are broke. Utterly. There are phenomenally rich people in Hampstead and there are ordinary people – but not many of them. Declan and I are impoverished paper millionaires. We now have a very shiny, non-lethal house worth, I would guess, a King's ransom, probably more, but we do not have one brass razoo left to our names. Our bank account is full of moths and our mortgage is big enough to give any sane person sleepless nights.

Taking a deep breath, I open the door. It's funny how your own home smells quite different from any other. Cara's home reeks of exotic scents, is heady with lavender and vanilla and spices. Mine is filled with newness – paint, carpet, furniture all still bearing a faintly chemical odour that I hope will fade with time. I also catch a whiff of Declan's aftershave, fresh green grass on a summer's day, which takes me by surprise.

When I open the lounge door, he is sitting at the far end, surrounded by a litter of papers spread all over the dining table. He has his hair held back from his forehead and is barking into the telephone. 'I know. Look – I've said I'll pay, and I will. I need two more weeks. Just two weeks. That's all.'

I stand inside the doorway and watch him, and already I feel like he is a stranger to me. The pull I normally experience when I see him has gone. Instead there's a gap inside me where Declan used to be that's been replaced by a creeping nausea. And it feels very weird, because only yesterday I adored him. Really, I did. No one has been more pampered and cosseted than Declan. He demands it. Every fibre of him needs constant attention. He only has to turn on his little-boy smile and I'm gone. I have supported him all through his business difficulties and believe me, there have been a few. I have cooked and cleaned for him, laughed with him and loved him. And, call me foolish, but I sort of expected his undying devotion in return. Not for him to slap pictures of my comely figure on the Internet.

'Ooo,' he says with a certain amount of nervousness as he looks up and notices me. 'I'll call you back,' he says briskly into the phone and hangs up. Declan smiles tightly and stands up. 'Emily. You've come back.'

Declan is a bit of a stunner in anyone's book. He's a trendy old soul, as befitting the owner of a blossoming dot.com corporation, and favours Paul Smith suits over jeans and T-shirts. He has hair the colour of bitter chocolate, worn long, curling over his collar onto his shoulders. His skin is smooth, olive and unblemished, and even in the middle of a prolonged, grey British winter, Declan manages to look tanned. I think his mother must have had it off with a gypsy because his father is fat, red-haired and typically Irish whereas Declan is a brooding, high-cheek-boned movie-star type. He pouts just like Johnny Depp, which could never be classed as a bad thing.

As he comes closer, some of the gap inside me starts to fill, but I can't give in to this. I can't. 'I've arranged for an estate agent to come round,' I say in as steady a voice as I can muster. 'Why are you at home during the day? Why aren't you at work?'

Declan does his Johnny Depp pout. 'I'm sorry, Emily. I am so, so sorry.'

I can't look at him when he's like this. He looks so depressed I think he might throw himself on the carpet at my feet. His shirt collar is skew-whiff and my fingers itch to straighten it.

'I never meant to cause any harm,' he goes on sorrowfully.

'You should have thought of that before, Declan.'

'I know.'

'How on earth could you even contemplate that I'd be happy about it? You've made me look an idiot. *Hundreds* of people could have looked at that.'

'But they won't know who you are.'

'That's not the point. How would you have liked it if I'd circulated pictures of you tied to the bed with silk scarves to all and sundry?' We have done this too, so it is a possibility, not just an idle threat.

Declan chuckles. 'I'd have thought it was a great crack.'

'Oh, yes?' I fold my arms. 'Then that's where you and I differ.'

'Don't leave, Emily,' he begs. 'I promise you, I'll take it off.'

'You mean, you haven't already?'

Declan hesitates and I can see a gulp travel down his throat. 'Not exactly.' He scratches his neck and pulls his ear and does all the sort of things that body language books tell you to watch out for when you're being lied to.

39

'You promised me!'

'It's just . . .' Declan sighs. 'It's just proving a bit tricky.'

'How tricky can it be? You managed to get it up there. You have no idea how upset I am about this.' And getting more so by the minute, I can tell you. 'There's no going back from this. I want the house sold. I want my share and I want out.'

'It's not going to be quite as easy as that,' he says.

'Why?' I am rapidly losing patience with Declan, which is a good thing. 'This place will be snapped up.'

The ex-love of my life casts a very furtive glance at the mess of paperwork on the table. 'I think you'd better sit down.'

When I do sit down, Declan sits opposite me. He crosses his hands on the table and tries to look meek – which he does very badly. Declan is by nature confident, self-assured and, on occasion, borderline arrogant. He does not do humble.

'Ha!' I say as I spy my cheque book. 'I've been hunting high and low for that for weeks.' I snatch it back and hug it to me as a sign of my independence. 'What are you doing with it?'

Declan says nothing and for the first time I notice that he's got dark shadows under his eyes, purple smudges like bruises that spoil his perfect complexion and I don't believe he got them from one sleepless night over me.

'We'd better get on with this.' I gesture at the paperwork, whatever it is. 'The agent will be here soon.'

'We can't sell the house, Emily.' Declan's voice has an underlying shake that I've never heard before.

'We have to,' I inform him coolly. 'I don't want to live with you any longer and you can't afford to buy my share.'

'We can't sell the house, Emily, because it's about to be repossessed.' Declan's eyes are unflinching. They are the same colour as his hair, bitter chocolate. And I'd never seen them look quite so bitter before.

My eyes do flinch. They blink several times, uncomprehendingly. 'What?'

'I'm in deep, Emily. Way over my head.'

All this dazed blinking has still not succeeded in kick-starting my brain. 'You'll survive. You always do.'

A slow shake of the head. 'Not this time,' he says. 'This time we're in big trouble.'

I don't like the way 'we' has crept into this conversation. 'What has this got to do with me?' I demand. 'And, more importantly, what has it got to do with the house?' I look round at my Laura Ashley

40

sofa and soft furnishings. 'I thought we agreed we'd always keep the business separate.'

'I remortgaged it,' Declan admits with an apologetic smile. He too looks at our Designer's Guild wallpaper, but I don't think he sees it in quite the same way as I do.

'How?' There's a horrible ringing sound starting in my ears. 'How could you do that? This is my home too. How did you manage to remortgage it without me knowing?'

Declan has the grace to look shamefaced. 'Remember when you signed those documents for travel insurance?'

'Yes.' Only just. I was in the middle of making dinner at the time, or something, and he just shoved them under my nose, gave me a pen and then high-tailed it the minute I'd put my scrawl to them. Oh, Lord.

'That was to remortgage the house?' My voice is barely audible although it's crashing inside my head, and if I wasn't sitting down I think I'd collapse.

Declan chews his lip. 'You should always read the small print, Emily.'

'I certainly didn't when I got into this relationship.' I put my head in my hands and try to convince myself not to weep. 'How could you do that to me?'

'I was desperate. I didn't know what else to do.'

'You could have talked to me about it.'

'What good would that have done? You never would have agreed.'

'Of course I wouldn't have agreed! You've put our home on the line.'

'I had no choice.'

'There must be something.'

'Believe me,' he says with an icy undertone. 'I've tried everything.'

I feel completely defeated. Battered around the head by my boyfriend's betrayal. Inside I'm reeling like a punch-drunk boxer. 'How much are you in for? Are *we* in for?' I correct.

'A hundred,' Declan states, avoiding my eyes.

'I take it you mean thousand, not pounds.'

He nods and twines his beautiful long fingers together. 'I never, ever meant to do this to you,' he says and, for a moment, I can almost believe him.

'When they sell the house,' the words nearly stick in my throat, 'we should have enough left to clear that, shouldn't we?'

'No,' Declan says. 'That's what we still owe after we've used up everything from the house.'

One hundred thousand pounds. Even with all my worldly goods

being sold from underneath me, we still owe one hundred thousand pounds. Whichever way I say it, it sounds like an insurmountably large sum of money. One hundred thousand pounds. I've gone cold all over, even though the central heating is kicking out for all its worth, and it's a good job I didn't have any breakfast, because otherwise I might have to throw it all up in the loo.

The doorbell rings and I look at my watch. It's the estate agent. He's late. Several months too late, by the sound of it.

Chapter Ten

Cara paced the room. 'You cannot do this,' she said, tugging at one of her wannabe dreadlocks in anguish.

Five very sheepish men sat cramped round the table in the Editor's office. The air was heavy with smoke and the table was strewn with dead polystyrene coffee cups which festered in cold dribbles of machine Nescafé. Chris was tearing bite-sized lumps out of the rim of his spent cup and throwing them on the floor, anger blazing in his eyes. Adam looked at Chris, who looked at the Chief Reporter, who in turn looked at the Deputy Editor, who looked nervously at the Editor, who looked back at Chris. All of them looked at Cara, who glowered back.

Chris thumped the table. 'We have to!'

'We do not,' Cara shouted. 'We are playing with people's lives.'

'Sit down, Cara,' the Editor instructed.

'Just because she's your friend,' Chris shouted back.

'Shut up, Chris,' the Editor instructed.

Cara sat down, heavily, rattling her chair as much as she could while she did it. She banged her notepad and pen down and glowered a bit more at them all. Chris opened his mouth.

'Shut up, Chris,' the Editor said again.

Chris shut up.

Adam did not want to be here. In fact, he decided, he'd rather be anywhere else but here. In Outer Mongolia, in outer space, in a coma. And, even more, he wondered why he actually *was* here. He crossed his feet on the table and munched the end of his pencil thoughtfully. There was no need for him to be. None at all. Other than at some point he would be dispatched to take a photograph of Cara's friend, should the *Hampstead Observer* decide that it was in the community's best interests to inform them of an Internet porn-site model masquerading as a schoolteacher in their midst. Which it no doubt would. Presumably the photograph would require her to sport more clothes than had otherwise been evident.

He was also there, he knew, because he was considered to be the

43

voice of reason. Whenever the editorial meetings descended into a riot of accusations and recriminations, Adam was invariably the one called upon to sort it out. The Editor, a mild-mannered man named Martin from Macclesfield with less spine than a plankton, sent him a case of Côtes du Rhone every Christmas to thank him for the fact.

'It's a brilliant news story,' Chris said petulantly, when it appeared no one else was about to speak.

'It isn't,' Cara countered with a barely disguised snarl. 'It's scandal-mongering. As a local newspaper we should be above it.'

'Every school round here is stuffed full of celebrities' kids. Their parents have a right to know what is going on. Would you want your toddlers taught by her?' Chris snapped.

'Yes.' Cara leaned low over the table. 'Emily is an excellent, caring teacher. And she doesn't teach toddlers, you cretin. She teaches teenagers. Which you'd know if you'd done a modicum of research.'

'Even worse!' Chris was elated. 'How would you feel, knowing that your teenagers were being taught by someone who gets their tits out on the net – and who knows where else.'

'Children, children,' the Editor said firmly. 'Let's not have all of our toys out of the pram.'

'It's a good story,' the Deputy Editor said, entering tentatively into the mêlée.

'It's not!' Cara said, shooting him down in flames.

'You don't think your judgement might be ever so slightly skewed on this, do you?' Chris enquired waspishly.

The Editor took a deep drag on his cigarette, trying to extract some relief from his Silk Cut low tar brand. On no, Adam could feel it coming. The Editor blew out a smoke ring, which drifted up towards the brown nicotine-stained patch on the ceiling to join all its friends. 'What do you think, Adam?' he asked.

'Well . . .' Adam removed his boots from the table in what he felt was a considered manner and sat up straight. Why did Martin always do this to him? Why did he always put him on the bloody spot?

'Well . . .' Adam said again, to buy some time. He'd just been having a lovely daydream about lying on the golden sand of a palm-fronded beach, skipping through the edge of the surf with a bronzed babe in an itsy-bitsy Geri Halliwell-style bikini.

'Well . . .' Adam reiterated, noting that everyone round the table was hanging on his every word, particularly Cara, which was very disconcerting. 'I think it *is* a newsworthy story.'

He didn't. He thought it was a load of old tosh. The celebrity kids might have a teacher who was a part-time porn star, but then half of the celebrity parents had probably done a lot worse in their time. And who on earth cared these days how people got their kicks? Hampstead was a hotbed of lust and who gave a toss? No one, that's who. Apart from journalists, it seemed, who were more than happy to go through the wastepaper bins of people's lives in order to fill column inches. Sometimes – like every morning when the alarm went off – he really wished that he didn't have to count himself among them. 'But I can see both points of view.' Everyone relaxed slightly, assuming Adam was going to work his magic once again. 'Cara is in a very difficult situation. This woman is her friend.'

'Best friend,' Cara interjected.

'Best friend,' Adam echoed wisely. 'On the other hand, Chris feels he has a great story.'

'It's a blinder, mate,' the reporter snapped. 'And you bloody well know it.'

Adam sighed silently.

'If we don't run it and the tabloids get a whiff of it, which they will . . .' Chris warned.

Adam knew that they would because Chris would make sure that they did.

'They'll crawl all over it,' his colleague continued. 'And then we'll look right twats. We want a scoop on them.'

Oh, dear. It was all so tiresome, Adam thought. Grown men, and women, tying themselves in knots to get news stories printed a few paces ahead of their rivals. Why? What was the point of it all? They weren't in the race to cure cancer or to put men on Mars. It was a titillating story about . . . well, about someone's tits really. Nothing more, nothing less. The saying used to be that today's news is tomorrow's fish and chip wrappings, but now that the EU had stopped British chip shops from wrapping fish and chips in newspaper, today's news merely ended up in tomorrow's bin bag.

'I've got a solution,' he said, hoping that they would all buy into it and then they could piss off down to the Jiggery-Pokery for a well-earned pint. 'Why don't we cover it from a sympathetic angle? Cara said that this woman . . .'

'Emily,' Cara supplied.

'That Emily didn't know anything about it.' Adam spread his hands. 'Surely that's the story. We do an exposé on the boyfriend and why he did it. Give *him* the hard time. Get her off the hook as a silly woman who's made a mistake in the context of a caring adult relationship.'

Cara wasn't looking convinced. Neither was Chris, come to that.

'Let's run it tomorrow. That gives Cara time to warn Emily and it

45

also gives Chris time to go large on it with the boyfriend.'

Chris gave a triumphant little smile.

Cara twisted her hair and pouted a bit. 'I don't know.'

Adam wondered, not for the first time, if Cara was cut out to do her job. She seemed more suited to running an animal sanctuary or an organic health food shop or some crap like that. She was too principled to be a hack, that was for sure. But then again, so was he and he stuck it out.

The Editor stubbed out his cigarette which was usually a sign that the meeting was to come to an end. 'It has to run, Cara,' Martin said, in a surprisingly decisive manner for him. 'Sorry, but that's the way it's got to be. Adam has come up with a good compromise. Let's go with that.'

He stood up and gave a small wink to Adam. A wink that said, Thanks for getting me out of the smelly stuff again, mate, there'll be some more French plonk on the way for you. Adam rubbed his neck to ward off the tension that was mounting in his muscles.

Cara walked past and squeezed his shoulder. 'Nice try, Adam.'

He smiled a thank you to her.

Chris followed, doing a celebratory dance and giving Adam a concealed victory punch. Adam slunk down into his chair. Would he have this much hassle if he was a postman?

'Cara!' Chris caught up with her before she reached the door. 'How about you fix me up with an interview with the lovely Emily?' he suggested. 'Over dinner tonight would work for me.'

'Bog off,' Cara said fiercely. 'Just bog off!' And she bounced out of the office.

Chris turned to Adam. 'What?' he said, looking bemused. 'What did I say now?'

Adam shook his head and grinned to himself. 'Beats me, mate.'

Chapter Eleven

The estate agent leaves, smiling as insincerely as I am and the minute he is safely back in his car, I slump down into the sofa and try to hide this all behind my hands. This is such a nice house, my home, and I've worked so hard to get it just right. Just right so that it was our little sanctuary to come home to after a hard day's work. And Declan has signed it away without a second thought.

'We won't get anything like he suggested for it if the bank sells it, will we?' I ask.

'No,' Declan says starkly and crushes any little glimmer of hope I might have been harbouring.

'This is why you put my picture on the net, isn't it?' I ask. Declan perches on the edge of the sofa, slightly out of hitting distance. 'You were trying to get some money back.'

'Yes.'

'I don't know whether that makes me feel better or worse,' I say. And I don't. All the processes for logical thought have gone sailing out of the window, along with my trust for Declan.

'It's the only site that's making us any money,' my scheming bastard ex-boyfriend admits.

'Oh good.' I fix Declan with a steely glare which is totally wasted. I want to smash things, but as I look around at my Habitat vases and carefully selected, strategically placed ornaments, I realise I care about them all too much to break them.

'You're a very beautiful woman, Emily.'

'Well, a lot more people know that now, don't they?'

Declan snakes his fingers across the sofa and takes my hand in his. He always has hot hands, warming, comforting. I used to call them healing hands. Now they're only hurtful and I pull away from his touch. 'You could do some more posing for us,' he ventures.

'Us,' I say. 'Us?' I bite back the tears. Declan will not see me cry over this. 'I did that for you. You alone. For fun. Because I loved you.' I hope he noticed the past tense, but if he does, Declan doesn't register it in his eyes. They have taken on a vaguely sparkly

47

appearance and he soldiers on regardless of my black looks.

'Nothing too awful,' he says brightly in an attempt to be reassuring. 'Arty. Erotic. Not porn.'

'Oh?' My eyes close down to slits. 'Like appearing in a Santa suit with *HO-HO-HO* written on my bum? That sort of art?'

'They're lovely, fun pictures.' Declan looks at me as if I'm mad. 'You should be proud of them.' He smiles condescendingly.

'I'll tell you what, Declan. If you're so keen, you do it.'

Declan inches away from me. 'What?'

'You've not got a bad body.' It is, in fact, totally gorgeous, but I'm not in the mood to tell him that now.

'Don't be ridiculous!' Declan really does look shocked.

'There must be sites where women go to ogle men,' I say. There must be, but I hadn't really thought about it before. Perhaps I'll start to surf the net a bit from now on. 'Or gay sites.' I'm getting into my stride now. 'You could make a fortune with your cute little bottom.' Declan has blanched. My jaw clenches. 'Or does it suddenly seem less appealing?'

'I'm a businessman, Emily. I'd lose my credibility completely.'

'I'm a schoolteacher, Declan. You didn't think about that.' My heart is pounding very slowly. 'What will happen if they ever find out?'

'Of course they won't. Don't be silly!'

'I'm not being silly,' I insist. 'Don't you see how serious this is? How damaging?'

'I think you're going a bit over the top . . .'

'Oh you do, do you?' Weariness attacks my bones. 'I suppose I should be grateful that you didn't secretly put a webcam in our bedroom.'

'I did think about it,' Declan says without batting an eyelid. 'They're very popular sites. They make a lot of money.'

'Then perhaps we should do one,' I say, hoping that he detects the sarcasm in my tone and doesn't whip out a webcam to take me up on my offer. 'I can't think how else we are ever going to pay off these wretched debts.'

'I'll work something out,' Declan assures me. 'You've no need to worry.'

I want to beat my head against the Natural Calico Dulux Emulsion but, instead, stand there impotently, worrying on a scale I've never previously experienced.

'Come back to me, Emily. We can see this through. Together. Come back.'

As I look into Declan's eyes, I can tell that he honestly thinks I will.

Chapter Twelve

Cara took the tomato juice from Adam and he sat down on the red plastic bench beside her, so close that his thigh nestled against hers. But then the Jiggery-Pokery was packed, as always, and they were all pretty squashed together so she tried not to read anything into it. Chris, however, had stayed standing up, leaning against the bank of fruit machines, talking to some blonde bimbette from the Promotions department which she took as a definite snub. 'Thanks.'

'Don't you drink?'

Cara shook her head. 'Not much. I don't like to put too many toxins into my body.'

'Right,' Adam said and eyed his Guinness. 'Me neither.'

Cara wasn't a huge fan of afterwork drinking. She hated the smoke and the noise and the forced air of joviality and the sticky, smelly carpets. At the end of a day at the *Hampstead Observer*, all she wanted to do was to go home to a nice rose-scented bath, a few smouldering ylang ylang joss-sticks and some green tea. Heaven! But if you wished to be one of the boys, part of the team, which she desperately did, then going to the pub was the thing to do. And it was nice that Adam had made a point of coming after her to ask her to join them. He could be quite a sensitive person when he wanted to and he'd clearly realised that she'd taken a mauling in the editorial meeting. She smiled at him gratefully.

'Feeling OK now?' he asked, licking his Guinness from his top lip.

Cara shrugged half-heartedly. 'I don't know how I'm going to face Emily.' She huffed out loud. 'What am I going to say to her?'

Adam's eyes softened. 'Tell her the truth. Tell her you tried to fight her corner. You can't do any more than that. At the end of the day, this is Emily's mistake. She's the one who has to live with it.'

'I do, too, now that she's my housemate,' Cara pointed out.

'She'll understand.'

'I hope you're right.'

Adam turned towards her and stretched his arm across the back of the bench, resting his cheek against his hand. His face was awfully

49

near to hers, Cara thought with a nervous gulp. She didn't think she'd ever been in such close proximity to him, although she'd worked with him for ages now. His skin looked temptingly soft to touch and, despite the best efforts of the smoky pub, she could smell a tang of citrus soap.

'How come you two are friends?' Adam asked.

Cara pursed her lips. The hidden question was, How come a wild, winsome, bottom-baring broad like Emily is hooked up with a strait-laced pillar of morality like you? And it rankled slightly, because it was one thing trying to live your life in as healthy and abstemious way as possible, but entirely another if people viewed you as a boring old fart because of it.

'We met at university,' Cara said. 'We both studied English, Emily because she's always had a burning desire to teach, and me because I wasn't good enough to get on the art course I really wanted to do. We've stuck together ever since.'

Through good times and bad, Cara thought. Even though they were entirely different characters. And it was strange that Adam had formed his opinion of Emily from a one-dimensional glimpse of her on the Internet, because that really wasn't Emily at all. In fact, the most shocking thing about this for Cara was that Emily, behind closed doors, had seen fit to be a brazen hussy in the bedroom. Emily was sensible. Emily was down-to-earth. Emily was organised. Emily was neat. Emily wore Marks & Spencers' work suits. That is not the trademark of a woman who has a penchant for kinky sex. And even though Cara was entirely grateful that it was Emily's bum on the Internet and not hers, there was also a small green pain that nipped at her, reminding her that despite her devotion to sensual massage oils, scented candles and velvet bedthrows, her sex life had not been all that she might hope for. The thought that Emily had been romping round with gay abandon for years was a tiny bit hard to swallow.

There was part of Cara that liked being independent and self-sufficient, but on the other hand, it was infinitely better to share the trials and tribulations of your life with someone. And it had been a long time since she'd had someone to look out for her. Too long. It gave her a warm glow to think that Adam had tried to be so protective of her today. She looked up to see that he was finishing his drink. He was a nice guy. A bit scruffy for a knight in shining armour, but at least you wouldn't have to fight him for the bathroom mirror in the morning.

Adam clinked his glass down onto the stained table swimming in the dregs of someone else's beer and smacked his lips in satisfaction. He had good lips. Pink and full. Strong.

'Right,' he said, rubbing his hands together in a particularly decisive way. Cara hurried down her tomato juice. When Adam said, 'Come for a quick drink,' he evidently meant it.

'Doing anything tonight?' he said as he stood up. 'I mean, as well as telling Emily she's about to become a local celebrity.'

'No,' Cara said. 'Nothing.' She'd planned to spend some time meditating to help her clear her head of today's stress, but suddenly it sounded rather pathetic to mention it. 'No,' she said again, clearing her throat. 'You . . . er . . . you don't fancy grabbing a bite to eat, do you? There's a new veggie restaurant on the High Street. It's supposed to be OK.'

'I can't,' Adam said. He looked flustered. A pink tinge came to his cheeks which may have been due to the Guinness or to embarrassment. 'I've got other arrangements. Plans. Stuff to do.'

'Oh, right. Right,' Cara said, struggling to gather her coat together in a rush. 'A date. You've probably already got a date.'

Adam shuffled a bit. 'Well, sort of.'

Cara rolled her eyes and punched his arm playfully. 'You guys! What are you like?'

Adam rubbed his arm. 'Yeah.' He forced a laugh.

Now Cara was embarrassed. 'I didn't mean anything by it. I just thought . . . well, I thought . . .'

'Yeah. Yeah, I know,' Adam said. 'Oh, is that the time? I'd better be off.' He looked down at his wrist and he wasn't wearing a watch. They exchanged a glance and Cara had no idea what it meant. Adam scratched his stubble uncomfortably. 'Maybe another time?'

'Well, yeah. Maybe,' Cara said. 'Maybe another time.'

Adam eased round her, without touching her, heading for the door. 'Hope it goes well with Emily.'

'Yeah. Me too.' Cara gave him a wave. 'Hope it goes well with . . . whoever.'

But Adam was gone, disappearing through the squash of backs and elbows and beer glasses.

Cara folded her arms and let out an unhappy snort. 'Oh flip,' she said.

Chapter Thirteen

There were wire hanging baskets containing the long-dead remnants of geraniums dangling either side of the porch and it had started to rain. Adam shrugged himself a bit more deeply into his coat. Reluctantly, he rang the doorbell.

If he cared to examine it, which he most certainly didn't, it had been a bit of a shock for him when Cara had asked him out to dinner. He supposed he shouldn't read too much in it. You only had to flick through the *Daily Mail* to discover that women did that sort of thing all the time these days – only usually not to him. And then out of the blue, Cara popped the question. Cara, from whom he would least expect it. The weird thing was, he'd sort of wanted to go to dinner with her. She was very small and cute and always looked as if no one loved her – and that was a feeling he could readily identify with.

At that moment Laura, his ex-wife, opened the door and promptly walked away from it. She looked over her shoulder and said, 'You're late.'

'Five minutes,' Adam countered.

With a cry of 'Dad!' Josh rushed down the stairs, nearly knocking his mother over, and jumped into Adam's waiting arms. Adam spun him round.

'Don't you think you're getting a bit old for this?' Adam puffed as he got his breath back.

'No.' Josh jumped back to the ground. 'But you are.'

Laura's jaw was set. 'It's a school night. I don't want him out late.'

They had gone through this little ritual every week since Josh had started school and now he was twelve. Every week it got a little harder to bite his tongue. Adam ignored Laura and spoke instead to Josh. 'Have you done your homework, champ?'

'You ask that every week, Dad,' his son chided. Perhaps Adam too liked his own little rituals.

'And you always say you have, but you haven't.'

Josh grinned and Adam cuffed him round the head. Laura looked on, unsmiling. But then, Adam thought, there probably wasn't a lot to laugh about if you were married to a short, fat, balding building society manager called Barry.

It was strange how time changed things. In the last few years, Laura had somehow managed to metamorphose from a beautiful butterfly into a hairy, scary old caterpillar. When they'd first met, she'd been an untameable, attractive woman with a mass of tumbling black curls, a penchant for leather trousers and tops that left the world in no doubt about her cleavage. Now she was a tight-lipped harpy who lived in cardigans and scraped her hair back in a knot and whose only joy in life seemed to be to make Adam miserable. It was ridiculous. They'd split up nine years ago. Nine long years. Laura was the one who remarried within the blink of an eye and he was the one who was still sitting alone at nights in a flat with only McCain's Home Fries, a six-pack and *Survivor* for solace. What had she got to complain about?

Perhaps it was significant that after several years of marriage to Mr Barry of the Alliance & Leicester, there were no brothers or sisters for Josh to play with. Or perhaps it was the fact that Adam was still very much around, determined to remain in Josh's life when Laura would really rather he'd been exterminated from the face of the planet. The term 'ex' was a bit of a misnomer really, because Laura would never truly be a complete 'ex' as long as Josh was around to bind them together. Not that he was complaining. Josh was his only reason for getting out of bed some mornings. Most mornings. Every morning.

'Luigi's?' Adam said.

'Yeah!' His son whirled round on the spot.

The thing Adam most liked about Josh was his enthusiasm. Luigi's was a small family-run Italian restaurant nestled beneath one of the towering oaks that lined the leafy part of Rosslyn Hill, just before Hampstead slid quietly into Belsize Park. It was cheerful, cosy and they were always welcomed like old friends. They went to Luigi's every week without fail and yet Josh never seemed to tire of it. That was probably down to the fact that Mrs Luigi thought Josh was the cutest thing that walked the earth and told him so, regularly. She also gave him huge helpings of ice cream to reinforce it. And they were comfortable there. Adam never felt like he was doing the Single-Father-Trying-To-Entertain-Bored-Kid syndrome at Luigi's.

The thing was, it would have been quite easy to invite Cara to come with them – as a friend – but he never talked much about Josh at work. He wasn't even sure if Cara knew he had a son. But then that would have intruded on his time with Josh and that was a very precious commodity. It just seemed easier to let her think that he'd got a date. As if.

'Come on, Dad.' Josh tugged at his sleeve, eager to get to his four-cheese pizza.

'Right.' Adam smiled wearily at Laura. He really wished that they could make peace with each other.

'Don't be late,' she said and slammed the door.

His son looked up at him and shrugged. 'Women,' Josh said.

Chapter Fourteen

The minute I walk through Cara's front door, I can hear a dreadful din. It sounds like a cat having its teeth pulled out. One by one.

The noise is coming from the lounge and, believe me, for a minute there, I feel like going straight up to my room. Instead, I decide to face it. Tonight, I do not want to be alone. Tonight, I want to find something alcoholic lurking in the fridge, in among the organic tofu and the beansprouts, and drink it. All of it. Whatever it is.

I open the door and Cara is sitting on the floor, in the Lotus Position – what else? She has her eyes closed and is clinking little bells together that are attached to her outstretched fingertips. The tortured cat noises are coming from somewhere in the back of her throat and I wonder what she'd be like at 'I'm Every Woman' in the local karaoke bar if this is the unholy row she makes when she's clearly trying to do something spiritual.

I throw my bag on the sofa, which makes her jump, and I think she's not quite as deep into her trance as she'd like me to believe. To confirm it, she opens one eye.

'What are you doing?' I ask, following my bag to the sofa.

Cara opens the other eye. 'I'm trying to attune to the universe.'

'Ah.' I cuddle one of her tie-dyed cushions. 'Bad day?'

'Dreadful,' Cara admits, de-trancing. She picks the little bells off her fingers. 'I have some bad news.'

'Ha!' I say in my most sympathetic voice. '*You* do?'

Cara unwinds her legs and comes and curls up next to me on the sofa. She pulls her floaty skirt down over her knees and leans towards me. Cara looks like a very troubled person. 'How did it go with Declan O'Cheeky Bits?'

'Bad,' I say with a vehement nod. 'Very bad.'

Cara inclines her head as a signal for me to continue.

'The dot.com businesses are all going down the pan,' I start, not needing an excuse to launch into my monologue. 'Except the one featuring my arse, but I'll come to that later. Our house is being repossessed and Declan has emptied *my* bank account of *my* money by forging *my* signature in *my* cheque book.' I look at my friend and, not for the first time today, my heart feels literally as if it is going to break – just snap quietly in two and that would be the end of it. 'He has, without my knowledge, made me a director of his company and I am now jointly responsible for his debts which are, at a conservative estimate, one hundred thousand pounds and rising.' I sigh heavily, which does not even come close to expressing how I feel. 'My life could not be any worse, Cara.'

'Mmm,' she says thoughtfully. 'I think it could.'

'No way.' I shake my head. 'I am already contemplating taking a long walk off a short cliff.'

Cara shrinks back into the cushions, holding one in front of her like a barrier. 'The paper is running a story tomorrow,' she says as she bites her lip.

I am arrested in my flow. 'Which paper?'

'My paper.'

I don't think I like the sound of this and it's clear that Cara isn't expecting me to. I purse my lips tightly. 'On what?'

'You,' she supplies flatly.

'Me?'

Cara nods, wincing slightly.

'Your paper?' My eyes are out on stalks again. '*Your* paper is running a story on me? Why? Why are they doing that? Why are you letting them?'

'I couldn't stop them, Emily.' Cara looks distraught. 'It's a good news story.'

'It's not.' My hands are sweaty with panic. 'It's a terrible story. My life is crashing around my ears and now I'm going to do it inside the *Hampstead Observer.*'

'Front page,' Cara says quietly.

'I've made the front page?'

She barely nods.

'Great,' I say. 'Oh, that's just great!' Try as I might to pretend this isn't happening, I know that it's only too real. 'I'm going to get that bloody Declan O'Donnell, rip his heart out and castrate him! Not necessarily in that order.'

Cara puts her arms round me. 'Some good could come of this, Emily.'

I sink against her, feeling wretched. 'Like what?'

Cara looks at me earnestly. 'I have absolutely no idea.'

'I need to be drunk, Cara,' I mumble. 'I need to be very drunk.'

'I have bought some Smirnoff Ice for that specific purpose.'

Cara is a truly wonderful friend.

'Then, when we are too drunk to function,' I warn her, 'we need to think of a cunning plan. A very cunning plan indeed.'

Chapter Fifteen

Luigi's restaurant was busy as always, but nicely busy, not can't-hear-yourself-think busy. Adam liked it because it was one of the few places in the area that didn't require you to take out a second mortgage in order to eat there on a regular basis. Josh liked it because it made him feel grown up, whereas McDonald's was now relegated to the realms of comfort food in times of crisis, and as Josh approached the joys of adolescence, his father suspected there might be plenty of emergency trips to the Golden Arches.

At Luigi's, they always sat at the same window seat, watching the well-heeled of Hampstead strut their stuff. The streets were quieter during the week, not thronging with tourists and window shoppers like they were on Sundays. While Adam daydreamed, Josh liked to arrange the objects on the table, making geometric designs with them that he tried to keep within the bounds of the red and white check pattern on the tablecloth. First it was the salt and pepper, then the sugar bowl piled with rock-hard crystals of sweetness in livid colours, the obligatory knackered Chianti bottle with rainbow-coloured melted candle and, finally, the simple white vase usually containing a selection of flowers which rotated between a wilted rose, a wilted carnation and a wilted daisy-thing that neither of them knew the name of. If he got really bored, he started on the cutlery and the red paper napkin. Adam wondered whether it was an indication of what profession Josh might eventually lean towards. If it was, Adam hadn't a clue what that might be.

Adam savoured his glass of wine while Josh slurped his Coke. Eventually, Adam turned his attention from people-watching back to his son, feeling a smile curl his lip as he looked at the boy, rapt in the task of unnecessary organisation of condiments. 'What have you been up to this week?'

Josh shook his head. 'Nothing.'

Their conversation always started the same way. Adam would ask what Josh had done, to which his son would duly reply, 'Nothing.' That would then be followed by a half-hour, non-stop download of all the things he had actually done that week.

Mrs Luigi delivered their pizzas and they tucked in, momentarily diverting Josh from his story about somebody-or-another's dad buying them a wrecked Mini that they were going to do up together, from which Adam was evidently supposed to conclude that they should be doing similarly expensive father-son bonding activities.

Adam looked aimlessly around the restaurant and as he did so, his perma-frown started to deepen. Everyone else in here was part of a couple. All of them. Why had he never noticed that before? The two thirty-somethings on the next table could hardly keep their hands off each other, which wasn't exactly on in the middle of a family-orientated restaurant on a table next to a twelve-year-old boy. At their age they should know better, or at least be able to wait until they got home. Adam treated them to a glare, at which they glared back and groped each other a bit more. Josh swizzled round so that he could get a better view.

The couple beyond them looked as if they were on a first date. They were talking to each other too animatedly to be comfortable, tripping over each other's sentences, laughing just that little bit too hard. It had been ages since he'd taken anyone out on a real date. He'd almost forgotten what it felt like. Well, actually he *had* forgotten. Completely.

'You need a woman,' Josh said.

Adam pointed his fork. 'Eat your pizza.'

'You do,' Josh stressed.

There were times when he was sure that his son and heir was a mindreader. 'I don't,' Adam said. 'Eat your pizza.'

Belligerently, Josh stuffed a forkful of pizza in his mouth. 'It's been ages since you had a girlfriend,' he mumbled through it.

Adam scowled at his son. 'I don't tell you everything.'

'You do.' Josh's mouth was surrounded by a circle of tomato sauce. 'You've got no one else to talk to.'

'I've got loads of friends,' Adam insisted.

'All blokes,' Josh said dismissively.

'And what's wrong with that?'

'When did you last have a girlfriend?'

'Shut up, Josh.'

'When?' he persisted.

Adam put down his fork. 'Remember Serena?'

'Of course I do. How could I forget?' His son shuddered at the memory. 'All she ever made for us to eat were things with broccoli in them.'

'Quite.' Adam took a glug of his Chianti. It was coming to

something when you were quizzed on your flagging love life by your twelve year old. 'She was a psycho.'

'If you keep saying nasty things about women, I'll grow up gay.'

'I wouldn't mind that.'

Josh looked outraged. 'I would!'

'Have *you* got a girlfriend?' Adam said, trying diversionary techniques.

'Yes,' Josh said bashfully. 'She's called Imogen and she's eleven. She's in Mrs Bleesdale's class and she's very good at sums.' He puffed up his chest proudly. 'She can sing like Britney Spears.'

Adam longed for the days when these gifts were all that you required in a woman. He smiled at his son. 'That's nice.'

'She lets me be my own person,' Josh said. 'Matthew's girlfriend is always nagging him to get a new bike.'

'I'm glad you're happy.'

'I could see if Imogen's got a mum,' Josh offered. 'Perhaps you could go out with her?'

'I do not want to double-date with my son, thank you,' Adam tutted. 'I'm perfectly OK on my own.'

Josh stopped eating and looked serious. 'I worry about you being lonely.'

'I'm not lonely. I'm fine,' Adam assured him.

'I could come and live with you,' the boy volunteered. 'If you like . . .' Then his voice tailed off.

Adam's throat closed. This was the hardest thing, seeing his child for a few snatched hours each week, but how could he explain to Josh about the complications of custody arrangements and the difficulty of him working shifts and the awkwardness of his other parent?

'I'd never get a woman if you came and lived with me,' he said simply. 'You'd scare them all away.'

'But you will try to find someone?'

'Yes,' Adam sighed. 'I will try. Eat your pizza.'

Josh gave the smug smirk of the triumphant and happily got on with devouring his pizza.

Chapter Sixteen

We are lying on the floor in a state of complete inebriation, brought on by a surfeit of Smirnoff Ice. The migraine colours of Cara's decoration are all swimming together in the manner of a particularly exuberant kaleidoscope, and it reminds me of one of those disco scenes in 1960s films where oil blobs morph across the walls and everyone dances really badly to B-side Rolling Stones tunes.

My pain has receded to the point where I'm no longer worried that we haven't come up with a wonderful solution to my current predicament. At least, I don't think we have. If we did, it can't have been that wonderful or I wouldn't have forgotten it already. Would I? I don't know. I need another drink. As if by magic, Cara rolls over and pours me one.

'I loathe men,' I say, forcing myself upright. 'All of them. They're all bastards.'

Cara props herself up on her elbows and squints at me. 'I haven't had a decent man since women wore puffball skirts with straight faces.'

'I loved Declan.' I wave my Smirnoff Ice at Cara for emphasis. 'I loved him so much. And look what he did.' I can feel my lower lip trembling. I am lucid enough to appreciate that I'm at the Maudlin/ Regretful stage on the Drink Consumption Index. 'Just look what he did.'

'Put your bum on the Internet.'

'Exactly,' I say. 'Exactly.'

I know I'm going to wish I hadn't drunk so much in the morning. I have to go back into school tomorrow. Really, I do. You're not supposed to let the state of your love life affect the education of our future actors, television presenters, politicians and brain surgeons. I will get a severe bollocking from the Head, I can tell you. I'll just have one more drink and then I'm off to bed.

'I hate men,' I repeat, helping myself to another bottle. Cara has clearly laid in supplies for us to get completely off our trolleys. The odd Pringle might have helped to stave off our worst excesses, but we are doing this completely without calorific accompaniment. Cara thinks Pringles are loaded with deadly chemicals that are going to rot our brains in years to come. But, hey, we've all got to go sometime. I can think of worse ways than death by excessive Pringle consumption. I have another drink in lieu for our foodless state. 'I'm never, ever going to go out with another man ever, ever again.'

'Me neither,' says Cara. And I hate to point out to her that her main problem seems to be getting one in the first place.

'I think this house is on a gateway into the underworld,' she decides as she takes in her vivid decoration. 'Or on an ancient leyline. I reckon that's why I can't get a decent man.'

'I don't know what a decent man is.' I am feeling ridiculously sorry for myself now. It can't be too long before Aggression or Blissful Oblivion kicks in. 'I have no idea what I want from a relationship, Cara. Since I was fifteen, I've drifted from one bastard boyfriend to another.'

'Lucky you,' Cara mutters drunkenly.

'I have spent the formative years of my life cowering on football terraces, never understanding the off-side rule and not really caring. I have had my brains knocked out on the back of speeding motorbikes, stood shivering alone on windswept beaches while the love of my life has indulged in the love of *his* life – windsurfing. I've trailed round golf courses, gone to Van Halen concerts, sat through sci-fi films when there was a perfectly good romantic comedy starring Hugh Grant being shown on the very next screen – and for what? They've all bled me dry of money and love.' Although, it has to be said that Declan has done it on a much grander scale than anyone else I have loved. 'I have no idea who I am, Cara. I am merely a man's appendage.'

'Oo er, missus.' Cara giggles raucously.

'I mean it,' I say, trying to sound serious, which is quite difficult given the level of alcohol abuse I've enjoyed. 'I don't even know what kind of music I like. For the last five years I've been into Irish music, for heaven's sake. Who, out of choice, would listen to stuff with titles like "Bernadette's On Her Back Again" or "Patrick's Lost His Wellies"? I've pretended to like all of this crap purely to keep Declan and his supposed love of tradition happy. He wouldn't give a fig for tradition if it wasn't trendy. And what's he ever done for me?'

'Put your bum on the Internet.'

'Put my bum on the Internet,' I echo with feeling. 'Are there men out there who don't like football, who want conversations and who aren't afraid of commitment?'

'Yes,' Cara tuts. 'Of course there are. And the Abominable

Snowman and poltergeists exist too.'

It is a bad state of affairs when even Cara doesn't believe it. Cara believes everything. She reckons that wind chimes are all it takes to make the world a lovelier place.

'I want a man who's in touch with his feminine side, yet who's still laddish enough to be manly.' I've gone all wistful now. 'I want someone who'll walk in the woods on a crisp, frosty day and who'll curl up beside me in front of a roaring log fire at night. I want a man who appreciates fine wines, but who can still down a pint of lager in one. I want someone who can discuss philosophy, but who still thinks Ben Elton's funny.' I sigh into my Smirnoff. 'Oh. And I want someone who's brilliant in bed and particularly skilled in the art of massage.'

Cara gives me a sideways glance. 'I think you actually want ten men, not one.'

'I need to give this some serious thought,' I say. 'Doesn't it strike you as strange that after five years Declan and I have never, ever discussed marriage?'

Cara looks vaguely surprised. 'Would you have wanted to marry him?'

'I don't know.' And I really don't, which isn't a good feeling.

'I don't think you were ever compatible,' Cara offers gently. 'You're a water sign and Declan is an earth sign. And you know what that means?'

'Mud,' I say. 'Together we were mud.'

'You know, there is a lot to astrology, Emily,' Cara says crisply. 'It's been scient . . .scient . . .scientifically proven.'

I think my friend's tongue has alcohol anae . . .anaes . . .anaesthetisation. Oh nellies, I'm doing it now. 'Oh, I know.' I try to placate her. After all, she is nearer the stash of booze. 'I'm being flippant. It's just that I don't really believe in all that stuff.'

'Typical Pisces,' Cara huffs.

'Help me, Cara,' I plead. 'Help me get out of this mess.'

'I think you need to draw up a five-year plan, Emily.' Cara goes into business mode. 'You need to decide where you're going, how you're going to get there and who's going with you.'

'And how I'm going to clear my debts.'

'That goes without saying.' Cara takes my hand in hers and puts on her deep and meaningful voice. 'I can help you.'

With all this vodka sloshing around inside me, I'm finding it very hard not to laugh. I press my lips together, banishing the smile behind them. I might take the piss out of my best friend – a lot – but sometimes I really envy her naïve optimism.

'I'm very skilled in the art of creative visualisation,' she informs me. 'I can guide you. Whatever you picture for yourself, you can bring into being.'

At the moment, I have an image of Declan swinging from a very high beam at the end of a very thick rope.

Cara composes herself into what appears to be a creative visualisation kind of pose. It's only fitting that I do the same, I feel, and I rearrange my legs accordingly. 'Let's start with something simple,' Cara says, giving me an encouraging smile. 'Imagine who you would most like to be stuck in a lift with.'

'A lift engineer.' No problem there.

Hey – this stuff is easy!

Cara narrows her eyes to mean little slits. 'I think, Emily, you're somehow missing the point,' she says tightly and downs her Smirnoff Ice.

Chapter Seventeen

'Good morning, Cara,' Chris bellowed brightly across the office and waved a copy of the *Hampstead Observer* at her.

'Get lost,' Cara hissed from behind her sunglasses as she made her way gingerly to her desk.

The office walls were white and harsh and the throbbing light from the banks of fluorescent tubes tried to creep round the edges of her shades and burn into her retina. The modern *Hampstead Observer* building had totally the wrong colours for fostering creativity – and for nursing hangovers. It had too many sharp corners and not enough curves, which never helped. Adam frowned at her as she sat down.

'I had a bonding and commiseration experience with Emily last night,' Cara croaked in explanation.

'Ah,' Adam said.

Cara held onto her desk in an effort to stop it swaying about. 'It involved lots of vodka.'

'Coffee?'

'No, I . . .'

'At this moment, caffeine is good, Cara,' he interrupted. 'Believe me.'

'Yes. Coffee. Coffee's good.' Cara slunk down into her chair and Adam wandered off to the coffee machine with a slightly superior smirk on his face.

Cara smiled to herself even though it hurt. It was nice to have Adam looking after her and he'd been an absolute peach over the last day or so. She wondered why she'd never really noticed him before. He was very attractive and, strangely, growing more so by the minute.

Perhaps it was due to her rule never to get involved with anyone from the office. But, seeing as she never met anyone other than people from the office, never getting involved with anyone extended pretty much to the rest of the known universe. She was tired of being alone and she had intended to discuss this with Emily last night, but all her friend wanted to do was dwell on her own situation. Which was perfectly understandable. The least she could do was provide a sympathetic ear, and copious booze, as she felt really guilty that she hadn't been able to do anything to stop the story going into her own newspaper. Overruled by all the typical male chauvinist pigs who worked here. Except for Adam.

Cara smiled at him gratefully as he returned with her coffee, ignoring the pain it produced in her cheeks.

'Just grit your teeth and swallow it,' Adam advised. 'It'll do you good.'

'Thanks.' Cara did as she was told, shuddering as the coffee hit home. The coffee wasn't good. Frankly, it was diabolical, but this definitely wasn't a rosehip tea moment. She put the cup down on her desk in the middle of her relationship corner and wondered if it might help form a bond between her and Adam. 'Have you seen the story yet?'

Adam nodded, wincing slightly. 'It's not too bad,' he said, folding his arms across his chest as if he thought it was very bad indeed. He perched on the corner of her desk, next to the coffee cup which could, Cara thought fleetingly, be seen as an omen. 'This Declan comes across as an arrogant bastard, and your pal Emily as a bit of a harmless bimbo.'

Cara massaged her temples. 'She'll just love that.'

'There's not much we can do about it, Cara.'

She liked the way he said her name; it was gruff and very manly. It would sound good uttered in the abandoned throes of passion. Cara blushed.

'It's not your fault,' Adam said, mistaking her sudden reddening for embarrassment for her friend. 'She's the one who whipped her kit off for her boyfriend.'

'Haven't you ever done anything stupid like that?' Cara asked.

Adam looked disappointed. 'No,' he said.

Cara smiled. 'Me neither.'

'What sheltered lives we've led,' Adam laughed.

'Yes.' Oh flip, I want you to invite me out to lunch, she thought. Cara didn't want to care about copy and column inches and deadlines today, she wanted to be reckless and frivolous in a ridiculously low-key way. All she wanted was a butty and a bit of flirting – was that too much to hope for? Perhaps if she concentrated really hard she could send vibes across to Adam's subconscious to get him to ask her to the canteen. The sesame-seed tahini sandwiches that she'd brought in for lunch could be consumed later.

'I warned Emily that we'd need a photograph of her,' Cara said, trying to drag her focus back to work. 'She wasn't too keen.'

'I'm not surprised.'

'I advised her to look very businesslike. A suit or something. More clothes than last time.'

'Are you sure you don't want a pose in the Santa outfit?'

'Don't, Adam. I think she'd deck anyone who suggested it.' Cara paused. 'She was due to go into work today, but she's got a monster hangover. I don't suppose you'd fancy going round and taking the photo yourself, would you?'

'Well . . .'

'She'll be in all day.'

'I'm quite busy.'

'Please.' Cara tried her most winning smile. 'At least that way I know she'd get a sympathetic showing.'

Adam caved in. 'I could pop round there at lunchtime.'

'Oh,' Cara said flatly.

'I was . . .I was going to ask you to come to the pub.' Adam's pale cheeks flushed. 'Just for a sandwich. Or something. So that we could talk a bit more about this. Or that. Or other things. But, well . . . another time maybe?'

'No, no, no,' Cara said. 'I think it would be useful to discuss this further. In more detail. And stuff – other stuff.'

Adam fidgeted with her paper clips. 'Me too.'

'Is there someone else you could send?' Cara said. 'Anyone?'

'Well . . .'

'I mean, they're all good photographers, aren't they?'

'Well . . .'

'It doesn't have to be you, does it?'

'No,' Adam said. 'I guess not. Nick could probably go.'

'Yes, Nick,' Cara said in a voice that indicated deep consideration. 'Nick's good. Nick can be sensitive.'

'Fine.' Adam stood up. 'Nick it is.' He squeezed his hands together, cracking his fingers. 'Shall we go over the road to the Jig about twelve?'

'Yes,' Cara said. 'Twelve it is, then.'

'OK.' With an uncomfortable smile, Adam eased himself away from her desk and sauntered back to his computer.

'So who said Feng Shui was a load of old bunkum?' Cara said quietly to herself as she eyed the coffee cup in her relationship corner. Wrapping her arms contentedly round herself, she grinned happily, rejoicing in the knowledge that she had once again managed to harness the mysterious energies of the universe.

She might have been less convinced of her supernatural powers if she had heard Adam mutter under his breath as soon as he had his back to her: 'Bloody Josh!'

Chapter Eighteen

I'm supposed to be at work today, but I've got a monster hangover. Hardly surprising, if I think about it rationally. But rationale disappeared at about three o'clock this morning, along with the litre and a bit of wine we drank after we ran out of Smirnoff Ice.

I have discovered, to my cost, that getting drunk is not the answer to anything, even though it feels very nice at the time. When you wake up the morning after the night before, you will still have the same problems and one extra one. Mine is where to find painkillers and Resolve in a house that is stuffed full of all things natural.

It's lunchtime already and I've still got a 1970s Michael Jackson Afro hair-style, a budgie's birdcage where my mouth used to be, skin the colour of wet cement and I'm wearing a towelling bath robe that has seen better days – probably around the time when Jacko was sporting his Afro. But in my current state of mind, plucked, pale blue, threadbare towelling feels good. It's also several sizes too small for me, but me and this dressing gown have been through some traumatic times together and it has, unfailingly, brought me comfort in my hour of need. It's having its work cut out at the moment, mind.

I'm huddled into the sofa, staring at the phone. There are four hundred messages on the answerphone, all of them from Cara asking me to contact her, except one which was from our Headmaster, Mr Shankley, asking me to call him, and one from Declan, begging me to get in touch with him. Fat chance. I've not returned any of them yet, because I haven't the strength to make brain-to-mouth connection. All Cara has is decaff, mung bean coffee substitute which smells nothing like coffee – but this could be due to all five of my senses having been totally obliterated. Whatever the reason, mung bean jallop just isn't up to the job.

The door bell rings, shattering the inside of my cranium and, rather reluctantly, I pad out to answer it, trying not to make too much noise in the padding department. I open the door and a man is standing there in a black leather jacket and a matching Nike baseball cap. I pull my dressing gown a bit tighter around me.

'Emily Miller?' he says.

I nod.

He pulls a camera out of his jacket and, before you can say, 'as quick as a flash', he rattles off a bevy of photographs of a very bemused me with my mouth drooping foolishly agog.

'Who the hell are you?' I finally manage to stammer. But by then he has jumped back into his decrepit Vauxhall Vectra and is speeding off down the road in the manner of ace rally driver, Colin McRae.

'Oh bollocks,' I say with a heavy sigh. The world – and my bit of it in particular – is not turning out to be a very nice place.

Chapter Nineteen

Adam took in the unchanged décor of the Jig. It didn't seem like five minutes since they'd last been sitting here. Cara looked vaguely ill at ease and Adam didn't think she'd seen the inside of a pub quite so much in years. She was probably much more at home in a yoga class. He felt quite touched that she wanted to make the effort when the Jig clearly wasn't her kind of place, and he was glad that he'd asked her.

'This is nice,' Cara said over the clanking of the fruit machine and the dulcet tones of Eminen on the juke box.

'Yeah,' Adam replied.

A white, jaded sandwich sat on a plate in front of Cara. Adam gestured at it. 'Sorry about the sandwich.'

'It's fine,' Cara insisted. 'I like cucumber.'

'Me too,' Adam said. He just wouldn't want to eat an entire sandwich of it manhandled together by the bar staff at the Jig. Their bacon rolls were infinitely more lovingly prepared; he just didn't think Cara would be tempted. 'Do you fancy some crisps?'

My word, did he know how to show a girl a good time!

'No thanks.' Cara shook her head, then regretted it.

Just as well, Adam thought. They'd probably only have raw steak flavour here. His colleague sank her teeth into the white bread and then abandoned it on her plate again.

'I've been trying to phone Emily all morning,' Cara said with a little huff of concern. 'I hope Nick has managed to catch her in.'

'I think he'd have let us know by now, if she wasn't.'

'Yes,' Cara said. 'I hope it went well.'

'What could possibly go wrong?'

Cara shrugged. 'You're right. I'm worrying unnecessarily.'

'It's understandable,' Adam said. 'She's your friend. None of this can be easy for her.'

Cara sipped at her orange juice. 'I'm trying to get my Vitamin C levels back up.'

So that was the cure for a hard night on the pop! Her cheeks were wan, and now that she'd finally taken her sunglasses off, he could see that her eyes were sunk back like pee-holes in the snow. Adam smiled to himself. That Emily was definitely a bad influence on Cara. Or maybe she was a good one.

'How did your date go?' Cara asked, picking up her sandwich warily.

'Date?'

'Sorry, perhaps I'm being too nosy.'

'Oh, it wasn't a date as such,' Adam said. What was the point in trying to appear like some sort of stud, like Chris, when he wasn't? He might as well come clean. Particularly as Josh's nagging was the main reason he was trying to brush up on his social skills with the opposite sex. 'I was actually taking Josh out,' he admitted. 'My son.'

'Oh,' Cara said.

'I don't really do dating,' Adam said.

'Me neither,' Cara confessed. 'I think I'm too intense. I scare men away.'

'No,' Adam said. 'Never.' She was probably right. She scared the life out of him. But then so did the majority of women.

'What about you?'

'Me?' He scratched his head. 'I've had a few near-misses, but most women tend to object to threesomes. Particularly if one of them happens to be a twelve year old.'

'I like children,' Cara said.

'A lot of women do,' Adam agreed. 'But not if they're other people's.' He leaned back in his chair. 'To be honest, by the time I've fitted work and Josh into my life, I don't have much time for anything else.'

God, this was excruciating! He was veering between sounding desperate one minute and standoffish the next. When had he lost the art of doing this sort of thing? He looked at Cara, who was smiling keenly. It wasn't fair to use her as practice. Did he fancy her? She was very sweet, certainly. But was that enough?

There was a distinct hiatus in the conversation. Adam studied his bacon roll guiltily. Every time he saw Cara he was eating unhealthily and carnivorously. She'd think he lived on bacon sandwiches. Actually, it wasn't that far from the truth. What should they talk about now? Having exhausted the banality of his private life, should he move the subject back on to work matters? How was he ever going to get back into real dating if he found a sociable lunchtime drink more painful than plucking his nose hairs?

Cara smiled across at him and he forced himself to grin back. Help me out here, he thought. Someone! Anyone!

The door burst open and six girls from the Classified Ads

department crashed in. They were always a wild and raucous bunch. Adam decided that it came from days of sitting on the telephone with headsets on taking copy for adverts for prams and sideboards and unwanted, unused golf clubs. When they were finally unplugged from their phones at the end of the day, they all went completely mad.

'Adam!' they all shouted, and headed towards him and Cara. 'You don't mind if we join you, do you?'

One of the girls, whose name Adam could never remember, came and kissed him on the lips. 'Haven't seen you for ages,' she said, before plonking herself down next to him.

Adam looked at Cara, who appeared to be slightly aghast, and shrugged. 'No,' he said.

Amid much shuffling of stools, lighting up of cigarettes and ordering of drinks, they formed an untidy little group surrounding Adam and Cara.

'Adam,' one of the girls said, taking a drag on her cigarette, 'what do you prefer – stockings or tights?'

Adam looked bemused. 'I've never worn either.'

The girls shrieked with laughter.

Perhaps they should have gone somewhere quieter, somewhere further away from work, somewhere that was anywhere but the Jiggery-Pokery. The girls roared again. He glanced across at Cara who was looking downcast and more than a little disappointed. Whereas Adam wasn't sure that he didn't feel more than a little relieved.

Chapter Twenty

The photographic studio looked very salubrious. Well, it was in a nice, neat street with a nice, neat door and precious little evidence from the outside to show that it was, indeed, a photographic studio. Normally these places have a massive window with portraits of grinning brides and winsome children, but not this one. This one was a white stuccoed building in a well-to-do residential area and had, by the look of it, been expensively and recently restored to its Georgian glory. Through a wrought-iron arch there was a short gravel path which curved up to the front door.

Declan checked the address just in case it wasn't actually discreet and he was just in the wrong place. He wasn't. This was it – the answer to his prayers. As he nervously approached the door, he saw the small gold plaque which announced very succinctly, *Sebastian Atherton – Photographer.*

This was the guy who took the pictures for the retired lap-dancing friend of Alan the computer nerd. After much persuasion – in heaven only knows what form – she had coughed up the goods to Alan. So to speak. God, wasn't life getting complicated. Declan was starting to hanker after a time when it had been just him and Emily and relative domestic harmony. He would be glad when there could be an end to all this subterfuge and he could prove to Emily that he would forever be a caring, sharing boyfriend from now on.

Straightening his tie, Declan rang the bell and then fidgeted on the doorstep of the sleek black-glossed door surrounded by curls of variegated ivy as he waited. Clearly there was money to be made in photography, he thought, taking in the surroundings again.

Declan had come to commission some photographs. Sexy, saucy ones to replace Emily's sexy, saucy ones. Alan was designing a new website – www.cheekybits.com – which he hoped, very sincerely, would get them out of this terrible mire. The bank was phoning every day, along with the backers and everyone else they owed money to. The only person who was never at the end of the line was Emily.

Declan wanted the site to be fun, feisty and, as the title implied, a little bit cheeky. He didn't want to slither down the seedy side of the porn pole; just dipping his toe into the suburban outreaches would do just fine. He hoped it would be enough to appease Emily.

The story of her appearance on the net was starting to leak out in local places, which he could never allow to happen. Only yesterday evening, a jumped-up local hack had been snooping around for info and Declan had very firmly informed him where to go and which mode of transport to take to get there. These boys would stop at nothing for a story. But then he was a fine one to talk about ethics.

The door swung open soundlessly and a tall blond man stood inside. 'Hello, there,' he said in an accent that screamed Eton-educated.

'Declan O'Donnell. I've an appointment.'

'Ah.' The man reached out his hand. 'Sebastian Atherton. Pleased to meet you. Do come in.' And he stood aside, while Declan shuffled past him.

Sebastian Atherton's office was replete with maple furniture, fresh white paint and gothic windows that faced a long, narrow and sumptuously lush garden. It was minimalist, classy, clean and sharp. The epitome of modern taste. Declan tried not to stare. Sebastian followed his gaze. 'Comes in useful for outdoor shots,' he said, nodding towards the garden.

'Grand,' Declan said and suddenly felt like a country hick. Being the youngest of seven children had certainly left its scars. Despite his desire to leave his impoverished, downmarket upbringing behind him, there were occasions when it pushed itself enthusiastically to the fore. No matter how he tried, style was always hard work to him. For all his designer suits and his designer watch and his designer anything else he could lay his hands on, he always felt like an impostor. Whereas Sebastian Atherton had obviously been born with *effortlessly stylish* stamped on his bottom. He didn't look like a man who pored through the pages of *GQ* to find out what the 'in' thing was and what were the right names to drop in the right places. Sebastian Atherton looked like a man to whom it all came naturally – and who didn't give a flying fuck one way or the other. Perhaps that was the key.

Sebastian had seated himself at his maple desk, while Declan stood like a naughty schoolboy. 'I understand you're looking to start up an erotic website.'

Declan felt himself flush at the word 'erotic'. This guy must think I'm a real perv, he thought with a heavy heart. Declan nodded. 'There's big money in it,' he said through dry lips.

'Oh, I'm sure,' Sebastian said with an air of complete indifference

74

to the lure of making 'big money'.

'I wanted something tasteful,' Declan said.

'Tasteful is my middle name,' Sebastian assured him.

Of that, Declan had no doubt. This was not a man who would trouble himself with snaps of a willing, buxom wench wiggling her bum in a conservatory in Watford. Declan peeped at the studio beyond. Despite being predominantly black, it also managed to exude sophistication.

'Tasteful, however,' Sebastian drawled, 'does come with a rather higher price tag than tat.'

'That's not a problem,' Declan said, attempting to sound as if it wasn't. 'I'm trying to get away from the old bloke in a stained mac image of pornography. I think there's a huge market for something more artistic.' Declan was warming to his theme. 'More fresh. More fun.'

'I'm sure you're right, old boy,' Sebastian Atherton agreed. 'The market potential is huge. But then some men will look at anything.' When he crossed his legs and made a steeple of his fingers, Declan thought he looked like an aristocrat out of a Jane Austen film. 'Some sad saps actually take snaps of their girlfriends and slap them on the net!' Sebastian laughed.

Declan joined him.

'The things people do to make a few bob.' Sebastian shook his head in amusement. 'Ah well – it takes all sorts.'

Declan could feel his smile sticking to his teeth. 'It certainly does,' he said as lightly as he could manage.

Sebastian leaned over and whipped a small and unspeakably tasteful brochure from a series of stainless steel shelves. 'Here's a list of my charges,' he said as he handed it to Declan.

As he scanned it, the Irishman felt a large gulp travel the length of his throat until it hit the raft of acid rapidly forming in his stomach. There was no doubt that he had to have Sebastian Atherton as his photographer for the new site, and there was no doubt that it was going to cost him. Atherton might be indifferent to big money, but he didn't seem to mind charging it. Declan wondered if there were any Peters left to rob to pay the Pauls. This was getting into selling-the-clothes-he-stood-up-in territory. Which might well force him to go down the road Emily suggested and get his own kit off. Declan swallowed the gulp. 'Do you ever photograph men?' There was an uneasy croak to the question.

Sebastian Atherton barely raised one eyebrow. 'If I'm asked to,' he said.

'I was just wondering,' Declan said.

'Would you like to see my portfolio?' Sebastian pushed a beautiful leather-bound volume towards him. 'Girls,' he added with a twinkle in his eye.

'Thanks.' Declan groped for the nearest chair and crossed his legs. He wanted to be sitting down for this. There was no way he wanted to get a hard-on with someone like Sebastian Atherton watching him. That really would be the final humiliation.

Chapter Twenty-One

By the time Cara comes home I am distraught. With a big D. 'I've been trying to phone you all afternoon,' I wail at her before she's even had a chance to take her coat off. Then I notice that her face looks very pasty. 'What?' I say. 'What's wrong now?' She's carrying a copy of tonight's *Hampstead Observer* and there is a look of terror in her eyes.

I snatch the paper from her and there I am on the front page in my tatty, terry robe looking like some sort of drug-crazed, sink-estate harlot. 'Oh good grief,' I say and flop onto the nearest stair. 'That was your photographer who came round this afternoon?' I look at Cara for an answer and her cheeks are on fire.

'Yes,' she says. 'Yes, it was.'

'Why didn't you warn me?'

'I phoned you here about a million times!' There is a catch in her voice. And to be fair to her, I do remember a lot of calls racking up on the answerphone. 'I tried to let you know that he was coming.'

'He was a gorilla,' I shout. 'He practically jumped out from behind a bush. He was delighted to catch me looking like the wreck of the *Hesperus*.'

'I know, I know,' Cara pleaded. 'We asked him to be sensitive, but he totally ignored us.'

'I'll say he did.'

'It's all my fault.' She wrings her hands. 'Adam was going to come.'

'Adam,' I say. 'Who the hell's Adam?'

'He's the only nice photographer we've got.' Cara is trying to shrink into herself. 'And, well, he . . . he sort of asked me out for lunch . . .'

My arms are folded and my foot is tapping out the same rhythm as my heart, which is a steady pound. 'And you said yes?'

'Well . . . yes.'

'And left me to the mercy of a photographic primate?'

'I didn't know it would turn out like this.' She casts a reluctant

77

glance at my Pauline Fowler image.

'But you might have guessed,' I say.

'I didn't think,' Cara admits wearily and I notice that her face is pale and tired. I cave in. It is truly exhausting being permanently angry and Cara might be an air-headed idiot at times, but it's all done with the best intentions.

'Here, give me your coat.' I feel mean. After all, she is providing a roof over my homeless little head at the moment. And she is a very good friend. Most of the time. 'Let me get you a drink.'

'Not vodka,' Cara says, looking alarmed.

'I was thinking of a nice cranberry and ginger tea.' Although I'm not sure that the word 'nice' is entirely appropriate for that particular combination.

Cara trails after me into the kitchen.

'So,' I say as I bash around doing tea-making type things with the kettle and mugs, 'was this lunch with *Adam* worth selling your best friend down the river?'

Cara has plonked herself down at the table and is nibbling dried apricots. She nibbles one in an expressively thoughtful way. 'Emily,' she says finally, 'I think I might just be in love.'

'In love?' I sit down opposite her and present her with a cup of blood-coloured water that is supposed to contain health-giving properties. When I finally got dressed I nipped down to the local Sainsbury's and stocked up on emergency supplies of good old Tetley's super-strength, caffeine-laden, hairy-arsed tea, and as I take a sip of this welcome restorative brew now, I sigh with relief as it hits the spot. Why does tea always work when all else fails? Declan made magic tea – it could put you to sleep when you couldn't and wake you up when you couldn't do that either. It was the only vaguely domestic thing he was any good at. 'Now that's a news story.'

'I know.' Cara does not, it has to be said, look happy about this state of affairs.

'It's a bit sudden, isn't it?' My Tetley's is realigning my equilibrium considerably quicker than four hours of power meditation would, I can tell you. 'I've never even heard you mention him.'

'I've worked with him for yonks,' Cara says. 'But you know how it is, you're so busy looking for something you never see it right in front of you. He sits on the next desk to me. Right by my relationship corner.'

I sometimes forget that Cara believes the universe is responsible for everything. 'Do you think he feels the same?'

'I don't know,' she answers with a depressed little tut. 'He asked me out to lunch and all that, but it was only at the local pub. And he doesn't seem over-keen.'

'Give him a chance.'

'I want a boyfriend, Emily.' Cara pouts determinedly. 'Now.'

'How can you say that when you've just seen the tawdry results of what boyfriends can achieve when they set their minds to it?'

Cara looks as if she's about to cry. 'I don't want to be alone any more.'

I move round next to her and give her a hug. 'You won't be alone,' I say soothingly, 'because I'm never going to venture out of this front door ever again.'

This threat fails to make an impression on her. Cara is preoccupied with the new love of her life. 'What can I do to make him fall in love with me?'

'I'm sure you can think of something,' I say lightly. 'Perhaps you could make an effigy of him and sleep with it up your nightie and shower it with kisses every morning.'

Cara giggles reluctantly. 'It might work.'

'There must be some sort of incantation you can chant, or potion you could rustle up or spell you can concoct to blat him with? You're a mistress of the mysterious.' And downright wacky.

Cara's ears prick up like a Jack Russell's. 'I am,' she says firmly and a serious wriggle of a frown crosses her brow. 'I think that might just be a very good idea, Emily Miller.'

'If it is, it'll be the first one I've had in a long time.'

Cara slugs down her tea and I'm sure that I see her suppress a shudder. 'I'm going to go and get my charm books and give this some thought,' she announces and heads purposefully towards the door.

I gaze once more at the photograph of an unkempt *moi* gracing the front of the *Hampstead Observer* and shout after my friend as she takes the stairs two at a time, 'While you're at it, find one that will make my Headmaster go blind so he doesn't see this wretched picture!'

Chapter Twenty-Two

Declan sat at his desk and viewed Emily's bottom in the Saucy Santa outfit. Jaysus, she was a fine-looking woman. Why on earth had he been stupid enough to let her go? Joni Mitchell had been right all along – you don't know what you've got till it's gone.

His hand hovered over the keyboard. With only one second's hesitation and one press of a delete key, Emily's scantily clad photo was eradicated from cyberspace. Gone. As if it had never been there. Almost as easily as he'd managed to wipe out the five years of their relationship in one fell swoop.

Perhaps now that he'd done as she'd asked and consigned the offending photograph to the recycle bin of the festive season, he could set about the very onerous task of winning her back. It was a shame, Declan thought, because it had been a very nice, if revealing, picture.

He eyed the portfolio of beaming, bare-breasted lovelies that he'd acquired from Sebastian Atherton at an inflated fee and tried to select one to replace her. He doubted it would be as easy in real life. His eyes fell on a pert brunette. She would do. He pulled the photograph out of the file and studied it. That sounded a lot more callous than he felt. He was actually getting terrible pangs about exploiting women's bodies in this way even though they probably got paid handsomely for it. Strangely, he hadn't felt a similar stirring of guilt about doing the same thing to Emily. Yes, he had, but he'd just ignored it in the pursuit of brash commerce and the reducing of his debts.

Sebastian Atherton had been fully brief – or debriefed – as to Declan's requirements, and was going to produce a series of suitable images for the new erotic website. If he kept convincing himself it was all being done in the best possible taste then he could allow himself to feel less like a porn king. Declan took the photograph of 'Kimberly, Surrey' over to Alan who was making good progress on www.cheekybits.com. 'Here you go, mate. Emily's replacement.'

Alan pursed his lips in approval. 'Nice.'

'Better than a Santa with *HO-HO-HO* on her bum?' Declan asked.

Alan nodded. 'Better in that she's not likely to come after your bollocks for publishing it.'

'True,' Declan agreed.

Alan leaned back on his chair and contemplated Kimberly. 'Are you making headway with the finances?'

'Not so's you'd notice,' Declan said.

'This will help,' he said, jiggling the photograph. 'Keep at it,'

'Yeah,' Declan said. 'I will.' He patted Alan's shoulder. 'I'm turning it in for the night. See you tomorrow.'

Declan headed out through the frosted-glass doors of the building. By rights he should be looking round for some sort of seedy lock-up in Streatham, but he wanted to hang on to his prestigious suite of offices until his luck well and truly ran out. He still hoped to give the impression of a successful young entrepreneur – even though he was flat on his arse.

Declan flicked the remote control key fob at the BMW. This would have to go. It wasn't top of the range and it had a few miles on the clock, but it was definitely on the list of 'expendable items'. He inhaled the aroma of the pleasingly expensive leather interior as he swung his legs inside. He'd never imagined himself as a Ford Ka man. Ever since he developed an interest in all things material, somewhere around puberty, he knew he was born to drive BMWs. But it would have to be replaced by something more sensible, much more affordable and infinitely more boring.

This is what Emily's failure to temporarily lend him her bum had reduced him to – Ford Ka Man. Declan listened to the purr of the engine as he fired the Beamer and sighed longingly as he turned it out of the car park.

He really didn't want to do what he was about to do. It seemed to be happening a lot these days, and there was no one else to blame but himself. In the boot were two large suitcases of clothes. One of his and one of Emily's. The rest of their stuff was in U-STORE, an extortionately priced airless tin box in Swiss Cottage. There were times when he seriously questioned his choice of career. If he'd embraced photography or general storage, he'd have been bobbing about on a floating gin-palace in Cannes by now. Instead he'd had to give the keys of the house back to the building society this morning. He and Emily were now officially repossessed. They would both have a black mark against their credit ratings in the future and they still owed, among other things, mortgage arrears for the best part of nine months. The money for that had also been side-lined to prop up his ailing dot.coms. If Emily still had some top left to blow, she'd have blown it.

He swung out of the offices and inched his way into Camden High Street, joining the stream of traffic clogging the road, all eager to escape the centre of London. All eager to escape the office so that they could get home early and watch more television before they had to turn round and do the same journey the next day. The shops selling cheap leather and avant garde, metal-studded clothing were shutting up for the night. Tourists were more scarce at this time of the year. Though the mounting piles of rubbish at the side of the road, the peeling fly posters and the choke of car fumes made Declan wonder why people wanted to come here at all.

Having endured the worst of the rush-hour traffic, thirty minutes later, he pulled into one of the wide sweeping streets which bordered Hampstead Heath. Negotiating gilt-tipped gates, he stopped in the carriage driveway of a darkened house. He turned off the engine and stared at the front door. This was Adrian and Amanda's house and a very fine residence it was, too. Adrian had made his money in computers when computers were the thing to make money in and he'd invested it wisely in property and shares that hadn't plummeted and had generally been a very lucky bastard. And Declan hated him almost as much as he admired him.

Adrian and Amanda were currently in the Amazon, canoeing up rivers and chasing pretty birdies in an effort to escape the rat race. Their words, not Declan's. This was going to be followed by a jaunt to the Galapagos and a few weeks sunbathing in Cancun. They were going to be away for three months and this was where Declan was going to live while they were gone. It was just a shame he hadn't told them.

Declan got out of the car and went round to the boot where he removed the suitcases and the crowbar he'd brought for the job in hand. Adrian and Amanda's house had a very sophisticated alarm system. It kept a seven-day log of all entries and exits to the house; you could, if the fancy took you, isolate particular zones, set pet alleys, contact the local police and fire stations directly. It could probably even rustle up a decent omelette if required. And Adrian and Amanda had been foolish enough to write down the code for it last year when they had escaped to the peace and quiet of the Seychelles and had called upon Emily to water their hanging baskets and plants on her way home from work. The number had stayed pinned to their cork noticeboard in the kitchen ever since. Among other things, Emily was desperately well organised. Declan looked at the piece of paper and committed the number to memory. He only

82

hoped to God that it was so bloody sophisticated that Adrian hadn't managed to work out how to change the code number for it in the intervening period.

Declan tiptoed up to the front door and squeezed himself inside the ornate brick arch that formed a nice secluded porch. Checking that he wasn't being watched, which was highly unlikely in the middle of London where no one gave a toss about their neighbours, he eased the crow bar into a hairline crack in the door near the lock. Declan leaned heavily against it and the door groaned in protest. He leaned some more. The door gave way and, as he was catapulted inside, the alarm started to clang. Loudly. The alarm box must be by the door. They always were. It was. Declan leapt on it and punched in the code. The clanging stopped dead. You could have heard the proverbial pin drop. Declan breathed a huge sigh of relief and smiled to himself.

This was a particularly nice house. A little grand, but tasteful. And 'tasteful' was becoming Declan's new watchword. It would suit his purposes just fine. He walked back to the front door and collected his suitcases, whistling contentedly as he did so. He was sure Emily had told him that Adrian and Amanda had a hot tub in the conservatory. Perhaps his luck was starting to change.

Chapter Twenty-Three

It takes me longer to drive to work from Cara's house and, if I was feeling particularly masochistic, I could go straight past my old house. Instead, I take a longer route and the queuing-in-traffic option. In Hampstead High Street, I crane my neck to look at property prices in the plethora of estate agents' windows. The price tags round here are truly frightening and I wonder, for the millionth time, how much we'll get for our home. Whatever it is, it won't be enough.

I jam my poor little Peugeot into gear and it strains up the hill towards school. I can't face going into work, nor can I face ringing up and telling them that I'm ill again. It's easier to just go in, I guess.

The school I work at is fabulous. And comes at a fabulous price to all those parents who register the spermatozoa who will one day people its classrooms. It's a very posh school and our pupils are mainly drafted in from the ranks of minor and major celebrities who grace this area. Probably because they're the only ones remotely able to afford the fees. Calling the daily attendance register is fun too, as they've all got fanciful names like Moonbeam and Sky Pixie. And that's just the boys. You'll not find anything as boring as a David or a Paul in this place. But, other than that, I doubt anything much has changed since I was at school. Nothing much ever does. Except that all the parents are divorced these days, meaning that you have to send two end of term reports to two different addresses. Not that the kids seem to suffer too much. Teenagers of any generation or social strata are still too self-obsessed to worry over-much about their parents' marital wranglings, even if they do feature in the pages of *Hello*! Magazine. The only detrimental thing I see is that most fathers at the annual Parents' Evening, rock star or not, look like spare parts and never have a clue what their sons or daughters are up to. Most only come as a token effort as, even in these enlightened days, it tends to be their name on the fee cheque at the start of each term. Not that the kids appreciate the effort, thought and expense that has gone into their education – even if it is to make up for familial shortcomings elsewhere. They are just as unruly as the lot I used to teach at the inner London comprehensive before this. Except this lot are unruly, rich and confident with it, which is a rather deadly combination.

I teach English to teenagers. Doesn't that make you envious? We are currently studying *Hamlet*, *Lord of the Flies* and the poems of Keats – and they're finding it all less than enthralling. Even though Mr Keats used to live just down the road. In my day we also studied *Hamlet*, *Lord of the Flies* and the poems of Keats and, despite going on to do an English degree, I also found it less than enthralling. But I do rather like the fact that I can now tell people that I live just down the road from Keats. Then again, if your dad is on *Top of the Pops* every week or *Never Mind the Buzzcocks* it must be doubly difficult to be impressed by dead poets.

I was rather more enthralled by Christopher Ashton than Keats in my day, I seem to remember. He didn't write anything but, for a fifteen year old, had a great collection of Depêche Mode records. At my school the choice of progression involved studying Maths, French or English at University, polytechnic for those with aspirations of brains, and a job in a bank for those who were planning to be pregnant at the age of twenty-one. I was crap at Maths and any European language except my own and so opted for English. Now I love it all. I wish I had the time now that I had then to sit and spend the afternoon at leisure with Shakespeare. That's why I adore my job so much. Even if it doesn't entertain the children, it keeps me happy. And I have found that the size of the term fees doesn't necessarily relate to the amount of enjoyment per pupil to be educated. It is still a purely arbitrary process.

The school is housed in an old Edwardian manor, shrouded in ivy and steeped in history. I love the majestic feeling I get every morning as I swing through the barricade of wrought-iron gates and crunch up the gravel drive, which probably carries too many weeds these days. Unfortunately, I don't feel it this morning, since, because of the traffic, I'm late. The manor house now bears the air of faded elegance. The finely proportioned rooms have been chopped up to form small, high-ceilinged classrooms, a distinctly 1970s science block has been tacked thoughtlessly on one side, and the vast expanse of worn tarmac playground isn't so much used for play as for lounging against its moss-encrusted walls looking cool.

I have my own parking space, suitably labelled and, sad as it may seem, that little recognition normally gives me a thrill. Today, it fails to work its magic.

As I walk up the entrance steps I can hear the strains of

'Jerusalem' coming from the hall and realise that because of the traffic, I've missed the opportunity for a quick cuppa in the staffroom and will have to go straight into Assembly. That's no bad thing. Although I'll spend the first part of the morning tea-less, it also means that I shall avoid being quizzed about my unauthorised absence over the last few days. I don't have many friends in the staffroom, but I do have a lot of very nosy colleagues. I'll have to make up an excuse that doesn't involve the Internet and my life crashing round my ears.

I tiptoe towards the hall, my kitten heels clacking on the slate floor. I'll just sneak in the back and no one will be any the wiser. Creaking the door open carefully, I sidle in. All the other teachers' heads swivel to look at me and I'm sure I hear someone gasp. I look down at my suit, making sure I'd remembered to wear one.

Now all the children turn to look at me and there is a definite hiatus in 'Jerusalem' – just after 'And did the countenance divine . . .' and before 'Shine forth upon our clouded hills'. It is a silent hiccup. The children turn back, facing towards the front of the hall where they should be, but there is a lot of nudging and giggling going on as they struggle through the bit about satanic mills and chariots of fire before the last strains descend into total disarray.

On the stage the Headmaster is looking very dark and brooding. More in a Hannibal Lecter way, mind, than in Mr Darcy mode, it has to be said. I hope Cara has more success with her spell to make the lovely Adam fall in love with her, because it is clear from the reaction of everyone in this room that they are all avid readers of the *Hampstead Observer*.

Chapter Twenty-Four

Chris and Adam were sitting in a battered red pool car outside Declan O'Donnell's offices in Camden. Waiting. For what, neither of them was sure, but they were doing it anyway.

They were parked on a double yellow line and hoping not to get a ticket from a jobsworth traffic warden. Adam huffed. 'What a bloody waste of time,' he complained. 'I hate doing this.'

To relieve the boredom, he was playing with his camera, a whizzy new digital Nikon D1 that he'd bought with his last flush of camera allowance from work. He'd also treated himself to a wide range of lenses for purely professional purposes and now he was zooming in and out on the front door of Mr O'Donnell's offices for no particular reason other than he could.

'The big boys on the nationals do it all the time,' Chris said as he stuffed chips into his mouth. Despite it being shortly after ten-thirty in the morning, he'd inveigled Adam into stopping at McDonald's to grab emergency supplies on the way. Consequently, the car stank of greasy chips and burger. Shreds of wilted iceberg lettuce were scattered in the footwell.

'That doesn't make it right,' Adam pointed out.

'Come on,' Chris said enthusiastically. 'This is the biggest story we've had in ages. It's normally some bollocks about the Heritage Society or a poncy literary club or something. This is meaty.' Chris did a 'meaty' look which wasn't remotely attractive.

'It's tawdry,' Adam said.

'Look, mate,' Chris snapped with a sigh. 'Have you ever thought of becoming a homoeopath or some bollocks, because I don't think you're cut out for the hard-edge world of international news.'

'What?' Adam said. 'Sitting outside some sad bastard's office trying to catch him with his trousers round his ankles?'

Chris sat up straight. 'Do you think we will?' He grabbed Adam's camera with his greasy fingers and tried, unsuccessfully, to focus it.

'Get off,' Adam said, snatching it back. 'Oh man, you've got ketchup all over it!' Adam polished his camera on his T-shirt, huffing and puffing in dismay until it was clean again.

Chris stuffed the remains of the burger into his mouth and threw the empty box over his shoulder. It didn't look as if he was the first person to do so. 'A little bird told me,' he said as he licked his fingers free of unsightly stains, 'that the lovely sensitive photo-journalist Adam Jackson took our lord and master Dippy Chick Cara out for lunch yesterday.'

'We went to the Jiggery-Pokery,' Adam confirmed briskly. 'There was nothing in it. I bought her a sandwich.'

'Not bacon?'

'Cucumber, if you must know,' Adam said. 'The Jig doesn't specialise in an extensive range of vegan food.'

Chris looked impressed. 'I thought the Jig was a green-free zone? I'm surprised they had any cucumber.'

'Me too,' Adam admitted. But failed to add that he'd phoned up beforehand just to make sure they'd got at least one green thing in stock.

'So what was this in honour of?'

'Nothing.' Adam tutted. How could he tell someone like Chris that he'd been press-ganged by a wily twelve year old into sampling the delights of female company once more. Chris would never understand; Adam wasn't entirely sure that *he* did. 'She's down at the moment. This Emily, bottom-baring babe, is her best mate. Cara's in a very compromising position.'

'So was her mate!' Chris gave a belly laugh.

Adam smiled reluctantly. 'Have some sympathy for her. I know you. You're determined to make matters worse.'

'I was going to come to work in a Santa's hat this morning.'

'Don't,' Adam warned. 'Not if you want to keep your job.'

'It's just a bit of fun!'

'It's people's lives, Chris. Take some responsibility for that.'

'I don't make people get themselves into a mess, mate.' Chris wagged his finger belligerently. 'I just report the facts.'

'Make sure you do. *Just* the facts.'

'You have very little joy in your life, Adam,' Chris said. 'Has anyone ever told you that?'

'Yes,' Adam sighed. Himself. Frequently.

'So, are you taking her out again?'

'No,' Adam said. 'It was just a cheering-up sandwich.'

'Does she know that?'

'Of course. Cara may be a bit weird, but she's not stupid.'

'Women get very stupid when they're in love.'

'Yeah? And so do men when they've been sitting in a car for too long doing nothing.'

88

They had been here for hours. Adam checked his watch. Well, about an hour, but it felt much longer. Much, much, *much* longer. 'I am seeing my life flash by me, Chris, while I am sitting here waiting for something deeply uninteresting to happen.' Adam slammed back against the worn velour seat. 'I must have some sort of special talent I can work on.'

'Snarf, snarf,' Chris snarfed.

'You know what I mean,' Adam pressed on. 'We all have them.'

'Adam, mate. Every time I'm with you, you want to talk about the meaning of life. It's piss-pot boring and makes me want to drink heavily.'

'Oh come on, Chris. You can't be as vacuous as you make out.'

'I am,' Chris insisted.

'You can't be. That would be just too pathetic for words. You must have hidden depths. A special talent.'

Chris looked up thoughtfully. 'I do, actually.'

'Go on then,' Adam said. 'What?'

'No, mate. You go first. You started it. What's your hidden talent?'

Adam stared out of the windscreen, lips pursed, and thought. Hard. For quite a long time. 'I don't know,' he said eventually, and his voice sounded sad and ever so slightly depressed. 'That's what I'm hoping to discover.'

'Oh, very bloody insightful,' Chris snorted. 'At least I know what mine is.'

Adam looked at him expectantly.

Chris puffed out his chest. 'I can burp "The Archbishop of Canterbury".'

Adam's mouth dropped open. 'That's it? That's all it is? You can burp "The Archbishop of Canterbury"?'

Chris looked offended. 'It takes a lot of preparation,' he said, wounded. 'And about five pints of particularly gassy beer.'

'And that's really the sum total of your abilities?'

'I didn't say that,' Chris snapped. 'I hope one day to expand my repertoire to include *all* Church Leaders of the World. Although I think "Pope John Paul the Second" will be a bit of a bastard.'

'I've heard it all now,' Adam said and closed his eyes. The whole of his life was futile. A bit like putting a resealable lid on Pringles. What on earth was the point? And the most galling thing was that, as well as not knowing what his own special talents were, unlike Chris, he didn't even have a decent party trick to perform.

'Eh, up,' Chris said excitedly. 'There's Toff!'

And sure enough, their good friend Sebastian Atherton was strolling confidently up to the offices of hot news property, Declan

O'Donnell, clutching a heavy-looking briefcase.

'What's Toff doing here?' Chris said out loud.

Adam was wondering the same thing.

'We'll have that bugger when he comes out.' Chris turned to Adam. 'Now that's what I call bloody exciting.'

And even Adam had to admit there was a certain *frisson* about it.

Chapter Twenty-Five

'I would like to see you in my office, Ms Miller,' the Headmaster says as he walks past me. 'At break.'

His tone is very threatening. And no 'please', from a man who is such a stickler for politeness. This is not looking good, is it? Somehow I don't think he wants to discuss my next pay rise.

I am going to have to do a serious amount of grovelling to get myself out of this one. I could start with the fact that I have an exemplary employment record up to now. No pupils have ever skied off a mountain whilst in my care. I have no anorexics. I have never beaten a pupil with the attendance book, although I have felt severely moved to it on several occasions. I constantly provide the school with pleasingly high marks that go some way towards justifying their unpleasantly high fees.

We are also so short of teachers in this country that they are starting to import them from China – or somewhere. There is a list of unfilled vacancies on the noticeboard in the staffroom as long as an orang-utan's arms. I just hope the Headmaster remembers that.

I have only an hour or so to think about this, so I go straight up to my classroom and avoid doing so. English with Form 5S, Year 10. The pupils from hell. Form 5S are mainly boys and are, mainly, a pain in the neck.

I should have taken more care over what I'm wearing today. The skirt seems rather short on this suit to be entirely sensible and my shoes should be less clippy-cloppy. My fitted jacket's a bit on the shapely side too. Even if I put on things that start out without shape, I poke shape into them eventually. Being an English teacher with a 36 double-D cleavage has always been a disadvantage. The boys are at that age when their hormones are all on the rampage anyway, and being faced with a figure of authority with a chest like Martha Melons or Kirsten Bigcups can't be easy. From my point of view, it's OK being an object of desire to a brood of spotty teenagers when you're in a stable adult relationship, but right now it's just downright depressing. I don't know how Britney Spears copes. I suppose being a mega-millionaire might help.

We still have fairly small class sizes here – around fifteen pupils – which is, I guess, what the parents pay for. Who wants their kid educated in a seething mass of forty-odd others, all with sweaty trainers? Particularly when you can afford for them not to be. When I go into the classroom, there is much scrabbling of youthful feet and I see several copies of last night's *Hampstead Observer* disappearing into school bags, which is something I should have expected – but hadn't. It would normally take a miracle to get these little darlings anywhere near a newspaper – unless, of course, it featured their teacher in a sex scandal on the front page.

'Good morning.' I take up my place at the front of the class and am faced by a group of inanely smirking individuals. One or two of them might be drooling. And there is an awful lot of extraneous nudging going on. It is hard to gain respect from one's pupils when they've all seen you looking like a two-bit whore in your dressing gown. I wonder how many of them rushed up to their bedrooms and logged onto the net to see me in my full glory. I hope their parents have had the sense to program their Internet access with parental restrictions, but as the majority of parents are totally computer illiterate, I doubt it.

I look up and they are all still grinning toothily at me. This promises to be a very long morning. Followed, I expect, by an equally long afternoon. Getting them interested in *Hamlet* is going to be a real challenge when all they want to do now is get an eyeful of my boobs.

At this precise moment, I could quite cheerfully murder Declan. Followed by this lot. I turn and make an attempt to start the lesson, before hysteria seizes 5S. 'OK, show's over,' I say. 'Let's get started, shall we?'

The white board is obscured by a pull-down cover and as I release it, I see, written large in red marker pen the words *HO-HO-HO*.

Chapter Twenty-Six

Toff came out of Declan O'Donnell's office building a mind-numbingly boring hour later, by which time Adam had long lost interest in the delights of his camera. In a frenzy, Chris wound down the window. 'Toff!' he shouted urgently. 'Hey – Toff! Over here!'

Looking slightly bemused, Sebastian Atherton ambled over to the car and leaned on the roof. He poked his head inside. 'Morning, chums.'

'Toff,' Adam said in acknowledgement.

'What are you two likely lads doing here?'

'Surveillance,' Chris whispered, looking round in the manner of a dodgy criminal.

'Surveillance?' Toff sounded surprised. As well he might.

Adam shrugged.

'Get in. Quick!' Chris spat impatiently. 'We need to know what's going on.'

Toff, not in the same hurry, glanced at his watch. 'I've got half an hour or so.' He ambled a bit more to the back door of the car and took his time as he eased himself in.

'Drive! Drive!' Chris barked.

It was Adam's turn to look bemused. 'Where to?'

Chris took his turn with bemused. 'How should I know?'

Toff leaned forward. 'I know, let's go to the pub. There's one just round the corner. I could kill a gin.'

Two pints and one gin later, they were all comfortably ensconced in the Princes Arms public house which was one step from being the least tastefully decorated pub in London, including the Jig, but was packed with arty types from the nearby Camden Market so the clientèle had a more cosmopolitan air than the dossers it otherwise might have attracted. It was getting near to lunchtime and if Chris had to forgo his midday tipple he started getting obnoxious. Even more obnoxious.

'So. What's this all about?' Toff said, sipping his gin and tonic.

'We were hoping you'd tell us,' Chris replied, trying to inject an air of mystery. 'Why are you mixing it with the likes of that scumbag Declan O'Donnell?'

Toff gave Chris a withering look. 'Darling,' he said with a tut, 'don't be such a drama queen.'

Chris relented. 'What's the score then?' he said in his best, most macho voice.

Toff shrugged. 'I'm supplying the guy with some photos. He's starting a website.'

'What? Porny ones?'

'Erotic, old boy,' Toff sighed. 'Very nice. In the best possible taste.'

'But still girlies in their undergarments at the end of the day?'

'Yes,' Toff admitted.

Chris harrumphed decisively.

Adam put a copy of last night's *Hampstead Observer* on the table. 'He's the guy who put his girlfriend on the net.' Adam pointed at Emily in her dressing gown. 'Chris's future intended.'

'I'm not interested any more,' Chris said, turning his nose up. 'Who wants a bird whose bum's been seen by half of the world?'

'She's Cara's best mate,' Adam continued.

'You don't think Cara'd fix me up with a date with this Emily?' Chris interjected.

'Of course,' Adam said. 'Why not?'

Chris rubbed his hands together in glee. Sarcasm never was his strong point. Nor was playing hard to get.

'She doesn't look up to much,' Toff said, leaning towards the newspaper.

'Nick took the photo,' Adam informed him. 'I'm not sure how he managed to get her looking quite so scuzzy. She's actually a bit of a stunner.'

'You're suddenly very keen,' Chris complained.

'An impartial assessment,' Adam replied.

Toff took the paper and examined it more closely. 'Emily Miller?'

Chris pulled a print-out of Emily in her Saucy Santa's outfit from his jacket pocket.

His friends stopped and stared at him. 'What?' Chris asked. 'This is purely for research purposes.'

Adam and Toff looked at him incredulously.

'You don't think I'm carrying this round because I'm a sad bastard who's in love with her or anything, do you?' Chris tutted.

Toff took the photograph.

'Don't smudge it,' Chris snapped.

'She certainly looks more festive,' Toff said after studying Emily's

94

picture. 'And considerably more attractive. I wouldn't mind taking some snaps of her myself.' He handed the photo back to Chris. 'The Santa suit would have to go though.'

'My sentiments exactly,' Chris said, kissing the print-out before refolding it lovingly and putting it back into the safety of his pocket.

'Do you think this guy's into anything else, Toff?' Adam wanted to know. 'Is there a story here?'

Toff shrugged. 'Seems a perfectly nice chap. A bit pushy, perhaps. Maybe a bit strapped for cash. Seems overly desperate for this website to work.'

'Will it?' Adam said.

Toff nodded. 'Probably. Like it or not, the majority of money on the web is made from pornography.'

Chris leaned forward conspiratorially. 'Did you see any evidence of drugs?' he asked, narrowing his eyes. 'Money laundering? Vice?'

'This isn't *The Bill*, old bean.' Toff frowned. 'This is Hampstead we're talking about.'

'There are some dark and dangerous things going on behind these designer curtains,' Chris said darkly and dangerously, and got up and disappeared towards the men's loos.

'I think there are some dark and dangerous things going on in our dear friend's brain,' Toff remarked.

Adam sighed.

'How do you put up with him?'

'He's my only friend,' Adam said. 'And that is a truly pathetic admission.'

'Don't forget me, old fruit.'

'And you,' Adam said.

'You're still looking rather ticked off, Adam. Even this exciting little charade failing to stimulate your juices?'

'Totally.'

'My offer's still open.' Toff leaned back, hands behind his head. 'Come and work with me. I've got more than enough to do. Loads of dosh and it's a doddle.'

'No offence, mate, but I don't think it's my bag either.'

'Like everything in life, Adam, you never know until you try. Come over one night. Sit in on a session.'

Chris wandered back towards them.

'You can even bring Chris, if you must.'

'Where?' Chris said as he sat down again.

'To my studio.' Toff gathered his belongings. 'I want Adam to see what I get up to.'

'We can come and watch?' Chris's eyes were out on stalks.

95

'I can't come with him,' Adam said. 'He'd embarrass me.'

'He'd embarrass himself more,' Toff said.

'I won't.' Chris crossed his heart. 'I promise. We could go tonight.'

'No,' Adam said flatly.

Chris pulled out his diary. 'Tomorrow,' he enquired. 'Next week? How about Tuesday?'

'*No!*' Adam repeated.

'Put away your little black book, old fellow,' Toff suggested. 'Adam needs to do this in his own time.'

'Thanks, Toff,' Adam said as he pushed back his chair, knowing that he wouldn't hear the last of it from Chris until he did.

Chapter Twenty-Seven

'This is not the sort of behaviour we expect from our staff, Emily.'
The Headmaster is pacing up and down. His room is sumptuous
and stuffed with antiques and hand-woven carpets from a bygone
era. Normally I love the feel of tradition in here, but today it's
suffocating me and I'm in desperate need of some fresh air before
I pass out.

'I've been fending off calls from irate parents all morning.' He has
been going on like this for some time. 'They think we're running
some sort of . . . bordello here.'

I am becoming numbed to his rantings, but not because I don't
think he's absolutely right. If I were him, I'd be ranting and raving
too, and pacing up and down if one of my staff had been such a
stupid arsehole, but that doesn't make it any the easier to listen to.
And the indignity of it all is that it wasn't really my fault. My only
fault was in trusting the man I loved and having a healthy sexual
appetite and a silly outfit to prove it. I cannot believe that this one
mistake is going to cost me my job, my career. This is all I have
worked for since university. I'm a bloody good teacher and, as I've
said, there aren't a lot of us about.

He stops and stares at me. 'You are supposed to set an example to
your pupils.'

I take it that he means a good one.

'Do you understand the gravity of this?'

I fold my hands on my lap and look chastised. 'Yes, Frank.'

Frank is an old-fashioned Headmaster, not one of these new-
fangled headteacher jobbies. I had previously viewed this as a
positive thing in an age of declining standards. He wears a tweed
jacket and Hush Puppies and walks with his hands clasped behind
his back. The man drives a Volvo. At five miles an hour below the
speed limit. We don't often call him Frank, or even, Mr Shankley; he
likes to be and is usually known as 'Headmaster'. I am trying to
appeal to his human side. And appear to be failing.

'The parents are furious,' he continues. 'They cannot afford this

97

sort of publicity. Several very well-known celebrities send their children here. They trust us.'

Perhaps they will appreciate the fact that one of the teachers at the school understands the double-edged sword that accompanies fame.

'They're calling for your resignation.'

Perhaps not. This is probably the wrong moment to point out that several of the very well-known celebrity parents have been in the newspapers for doing far worse things.

'We have rules.'

Frank loves rules. The sillier the better. He'd probably be in favour of caning children if corporal punishment was still legal.

'I think this is very unfair,' I say. 'I have been betrayed already, Frank. I want you to support me on this.'

'I don't know if I can, Emily.'

I am astonished that I'm being seen as a corrupting influence on teenage boys. Don't any of these parents watch *EastEnders*? All the kids do, and look at the stuff that goes on there. How corrupting is that? But then I conclude that I don't know how many of my pupils' parents would be *EastEnders* watchers. Some of them are *in EastEnders*. The others are all too busy arranging world tours and Christmas specials and leave soap-watching to their au pairs and offspring.

'This puts me in an untenable situation,' the Headmaster says pompously.

How do you think *I* feel, Frank? I shout silently. I have lost my lover and my home – and now my job is going down the pan. But I say nothing.

'I think it's best if we suspend you.' He sits on the edge of his desk and folds his arms. 'On full pay.'

That goes some way to providing a bit of relief.

'For the time being,' he adds.

And the modicum of relief ebbs away. Still, suspended is better than sacked. I hope they consider this slip in the manner it was executed, but I suspect the Headmaster isn't the sort of person who could understand the bringing of some festive cheer into your love life. I'm beginning to question the wisdom of it myself.

'Let's hope this whole blasted thing dies down,' he says next, as if it's *his* bum that's been on the Internet.

'I'm sure given a few days everyone will have forgotten about it,' I offer.

'I wish I had your confidence, Emily.' The Headmaster retreats behind the barricade of his sturdy mahogany desk and spreads his fingers on it. 'Go home,' he says. 'Lie low.' I hope that wasn't supposed to be a joke. Frank carries on regardless. 'I'll get a supply teacher in to cover your classes for the next week.'

'Thanks, Frank.'

'The Board of Governors have asked for an emergency meeting about this and I am duty bound to agree.' Frank loves being duty bound. 'You're not out of the woods yet.' He sounds as if he's about to add 'my girl'. He has only one mode of telling-off voice and he uses it for both pupils and teachers alike. He probably tells his wife off like this. 'Penelope, you've burned the dinner again and it really, really isn't good enough.' He concludes my telling-off by saying, 'I'll speak to you tomorrow.'

'Thanks, Frank,' I mutter again and prepare to take my leave.

'There's one last thing, Emily,' he says as I reach the door. I hear him clear his throat and when I look back there is a flush to his cheeks and he is fingering his bow tie. Frank coughs lightly. 'It's a very nice photograph.'

And I take it that he doesn't mean the one on the front of the *Hampstead Observer*.

Chapter Twenty-Eight

Adam and Josh were sitting on a bench on Hampstead Heath overlooking the duck pond. This was the same bench where Laura had first persuaded Adam to make love outside. When they met, Laura was very much an 'outdoors' sort of person. Whereas Adam was not. Having graduated from the back of a Fiesta to his own flat, comfy bed and fluffy duvet, the idea of making love in cramped, uncomfortable or generally exposed places had lost its appeal. Laura found the fresh air on her body exciting. Adam found the whole experience rather marred by his urge to look round furtively every five minutes to check that no one was watching them. Laura found the idea of someone watching them exciting. Adam didn't want to give half the perverts in Hampstead a free peepshow. He'd once seen Melvyn Bragg jogging round here. That was enough to put anyone off. So they had compromised. Sometimes he pretended to enjoy himself whilst lying on damp grass tinged with the aroma of dog pooh. Sometimes when they were at home in the centrally heated comfort of their first-floor flat, they'd pretended they were on a palm-fronded beach. It had rarely been satisfactory. Laura usually complained that he wasn't pretending enough or was pretending too much. Adam always had a sneaking suspicion that Laura was pretending, too. When Josh had joined their merry band, the occasions to pretend or not, either indoors or outdoors, became infrequent to the point of non-existence. He sighed to himself. It wasn't so surprising that they'd split up. There had been irreconcilable differences since the outset. The strange thing was that now Adam wouldn't be too adverse to a bit of fresh air frolicking, but Laura now looked as if she was an advocate of indoors on a Saturday night with the light off. Times change. And so do people.

It was cold and it was starting to get dark. A few stoic dog walkers were hurrying their charges homewards. He looked across at his son.

'Are you cold?' Adam put his arm round Josh.

'No.' His child's teeth were one step away from chattering.

Up on the Heath, they'd been kicking a ball around since Adam had enjoyed a rare treat and collected Josh from school. They'd both been a bit half-hearted and although Adam knew why *he* was lethargic, he didn't know why Josh was.

'I enjoyed that,' Adam said too brightly. 'I've been stuck in a car all day. It was as boring as hell.'

Josh rolled the football round with his foot, not looking at it. 'Would hell be boring, Dad?'

'I expect so.'

'I think heaven sounds worse,' Josh said, staring at the few shivering ducks on the green, scummy water. 'I don't think I'd like to sit around all day on a cloud.'

'Perhaps they'd let you take a football,' Adam suggested.

'What's Australia like?'

Adam smiled. 'Why? Are you planning to go there instead?'

'Mum is.' Josh looked up at him and Adam could see that his son's eyes had filled with tears. Adam felt his heart miss a beat.

'Australia?' he said as lightly as he could manage.

Josh picked at his puffa jacket. 'There are brochures all over the house. And forms. Mum says we'd have a better standard of living.'

'Well . . .' Adam cleared his throat. 'It's nice and sunny there.'

'On *Survival Special* it said that Australia has more poisonous spiders than anywhere else in the world.'

'Well . . .' Adam coughed again. 'I think they've got quite a few of them.'

'I hate spiders,' Josh said firmly.

'How long has Mum been talking about this?' Adam asked.

'For ages. She's always going on about it.' Josh looked at Adam again. 'But then she goes on about loads of stuff that she never does.'

'Women do that,' Adam assured him. 'It's probably just one of her phases.'

'Yeah,' Josh agreed, but he sounded deeply unconvinced.

They sat and watched the ducks some more. Street-lights were coming on all over London and people were starting to draw their curtains, patches of yellow, orange and pink giving a soft coloured glow to the encroaching night.

'You won't let Mum take me to Australia, will you?'

'No,' Adam said quietly. 'I won't.'

'You could get custard of me.'

'Custody,' Adam corrected.

'You could though, couldn't you?'

'I don't know,' Adam said. Josh's face fell. 'I need to talk to your mum about it.'

It had never been a possibility, him having custody of his son, because of his work. Doing shifts, the hours were too erratic to be able to provide Josh with the stability he needed. But then, if he was halfway round the world, where would the stability be in that? Josh would forget about him. Bloody boring Barry the building society manager would become his only father figure. What was Laura thinking of? Whatever happened, he would fight tooth and nail against his ex-wife taking their son overseas.

'Don't worry, Josh.' Adam pulled his son into the crook of his arm and ruffled his hair. Not that it needed much ruffling. In the untidy hair department his son was very much a chip off the old block. 'I'll sort something out.'

Perhaps it was time for him to consider Toff's offer. Topless models probably didn't work erratic hours, and he could fit them all in during the day when Josh was at school. He looked down at his son. God, he could squeeze the life out of him, he loved him so much. Josh was the only thing that kept him sane. If working for Toff meant the difference between losing his son and compromising his principles, then it would have to be done.

'Do you want to go to Luigi's?'

Josh shook his head. 'I'm not that hungry.'

'Well, I'm starving,' Adam lied. 'What about if we get Mrs Luigi to make you some special ice cream?'

Josh smiled reluctantly. 'OK.'

'Good.' Adam pulled his son up by his small, cold hand. 'What are we hanging around for?' He picked up the football and squeezed it into Josh's rucksack, hoping that it wouldn't deposit too much mud on his school books.

They set off down the path towards the High Street and the warmth of Luigi's restaurant. And Adam hoped to God that he'd be able to force some food down so that Josh wouldn't see he was dying inside.

Chapter Twenty-Nine

I am lying on Cara's sofa surrounded by an army of alternative remedies. There's incense burning which smells like old socks, a relaxation CD playing featuring the squeaks and pips of dolphins which is not *relaxing* it is bloody *irritating*, particularly if you're not a dolphin, and Cara is doing reflexology on my feet which is also annoying me intensely. I can't stand having my feet touched, but she insisted it was good for me.

'Relax,' Cara says, yanking my foot.

'I can't,' I huff. 'I'm wound up.'

'You have to let go of your anger,' Cara says.

I punch the cushion behind my head. 'Oh – and how do you suggest I do that?'

'By relaxing,' we both say together and start to laugh.

'How did things go today with the lovely Adam?'

Cara wrinkles her nose. 'He was out all day.' She twiddles my toes a bit more and I try to grit my teeth and enjoy it. 'Doorstepping.'

'What's that when it's at home?'

Cara looks a bit sheepish. 'He was sitting outside Declan's offices, actually.'

'Why?'

'To see if anything happened,' Cara says.

I can feel my brow dig into ploughed furrows. 'Like what?'

She shrugs tensely. 'Anything.'

My attempts at relaxation disappear and I push myself up. 'Can't you let this story drop now, Cara?'

'Emily, if it was up to me I would,' she says. 'It's out of my hands.'

'I can't believe you do this for a living.' I want to scream in frustration and can't make it come. 'You're principled. You're green, for heaven's sake. This . . .' I find the paper stuffed down the back of the sofa and wave it, 'this is obscene.'

'Emily . . .' Cara stops twiddling my toes.

'Can't you see what this is doing to me? It's costing me

103

everything, Cara. I've been suspended. I'm literally hanging around waiting to see if a bunch of strait-laced do-gooders think I'm fit to teach any more. I need this all to go away. Quickly. What chance do I stand if you lot keep plastering me on the front page?'

'I will do all I can to help, Emily. I promise you.'

I fall back against the cushions. My life is out of control – and for a control freak, that's a pretty unnerving experience. The telephone rings and Cara pats my feet consolingly before she moves to answer it.

'Hello.' She pulls a face at me. 'How are you?'

'*Who is it*?' I mouth.

'Yes. She's here.' Cara covers the mouthpiece and holds out the phone. 'It's Declan.'

'Tell him to fuck off.'

Cara frowns at me. 'I don't think she wants to talk to you just at the moment, Declan,' she says sweetly. 'Emily's still very upset.'

I think that warrants the title of Understatement of the Year.

'He says he wants to know how you're feeling.'

'Like shit,' I snarl.

'I think she's been better, Declan,' Cara says into the phone. 'Her chi is disorientated.'

At least I still have chi. Even if Cara thinks it's up the spout. 'Tell him he's now lost me my job as well as my home.'

'Er,' Cara lowers her voice as if she's trying to keep it a secret from me. 'She's lost her job.' She looks back at me. 'He says he's sorry.'

'It's a little bit too late for that,' I snap in honour of favoured clichés in times of stress. If I had long hair I'd toss it about like Miss Piggy.

'He says he feels it's all his fault.'

'Of course it's all his fault!' Declan has not only kissed the Blarney Stone, he must have pushed his tongue down its throat.

'He says he'll ring you in a few days when you've had a chance to calm down.'

'Tell him to leave it a few years!'

'Maybe I'll get her to call you, Declan,' Cara says. 'That might be better.' She pulls on her dreadlocks as she always does in times of crisis and turns nervously towards me. 'He says he still loves you.'

'Give me that here!' I'm off the sofa like Linford Christie out of the starting blocks and wrest the phone from my friend's hands. '*Love*?' I shout. 'You don't know what love means, Declan O'Donnell. You have ruined my life.' And, for once, I don't think I'm being melodramatic. 'I hate you. I'll always hate you.'

104

And before Declan can say one lying, slimy word in his defence, I slam the phone down. 'I really do hate him,' I say to Cara.

'I'd say you made that pretty clear.' She looks sadly at me. 'Remember, Emily, there's a very thin line between love and hate.'

'Yes,' I say, 'and I've crossed it.' Hurling myself back onto the sofa I try to make my breathing return to normal. I feel like bursting into tears, but I won't give into this. Instead I clench my palms like the Royals do to prevent themselves from crying.

'Tweak my toes a bit more,' I say in a shaking voice to Cara. I might not like having my feet massaged, but at least the discomfort takes my mind off other things.

'I've had enough of the dolphins,' Cara says and immediately switches the CD to a recording of whale song. Which I have to say is not a lot better.

She comes and sits at my feet again. 'You know, Emily,' she says, 'there is a manhole cover directly outside the front door.'

I assume she'll tell me why this is relevant.

'I think it's making our energy stagnate. If I paint it gold, I'm sure it will attract good things to our door.'

'Yeah, right,' I say and close my eyes. I do wish everything in life was as easily solved as Cara believes.

Chapter Thirty

It takes me ages to make my eyelids open. Whatever Cara did to my feet last night, it certainly helped me to have a good night's kip. I slept like a baby. Actually, I've never understood that saying. Don't babies wake up and scream the place down every two hours?

I lie here waiting for the ceiling to come into focus. This could be the day that my fortune starts to change. Cara read my tarot cards last night and they came up with all sorts of good things for my life ahead. Well, at least the Hanged Man and the card with the skeleton on it didn't turn up, thank goodness. But then she did have to do three readings on the trot, to get me a halfway decent one. The first two were crap. It's a good job I don't believe any of it.

There's a faint murmuring of voices and I think it's that which woke me up. It sounds like it's coming from outside the house, but I'll just have a little stretch and a yawn, and curl up again before I investigate what it is. Could be roadworks or yet another renovation project about to start.

The hum of noise is getting gradually louder and finally curiosity forces me out of my bed. I pad over to the window, pull the curtains back and it's one of those gorgeous crisp winter days with a sky of the purest baby blue broken only by a few fabulously fluffy cotton-wool clouds and the dark slender fingers of the trees reaching up towards them. I stretch and give thanks for the morning and all that is good. Perhaps Cara was right, after all. Life could be an awful lot worse.

No, it couldn't. My eyes snap open sharply as I focus on the hubbub outside our house. This is a disaster. A total, utter disaster. I think Cara should have painted her manhole gold some considerable time ago, because what it has attracted to our door is not good. Not good at all.

'Cara!' I shout. 'Cara!' I can hear the panic in my voice. My psychic friend certainly didn't manage to foretell *this* little lot.

It would seem that the world's press has taken up residence outside Cara's cottage. There are men and women huddled into

106

their coats on this cold and frosty morning, dozens of them. They bear pads, pens, tape recorders, video cameras, sound booms. You name it, they've got it. There are even three mobile television units parked along the street, which is extremely reckless because this place has more parking attendants per square inch than anywhere else in the world. They are all flirting with yellow boot territory. The journalists and camera crews are chatting amiably amongst themselves and someone is passing round tea. This is unbelievable. Equally unbelievable is the fact that my knees are holding up. They've started to wobble at a truly scary rate.

'Cara!'

Just then, I spot my friend struggling down the road. She has her head lowered and is battling through the throng of people. She's clutching a batch of newspapers to her chest and when she gets to the front door of her house – her own house – she is nearly engulfed by the mob. I hear her grapple with the keys and I dash to the top of the stairs.

The front door flies open and she is catapulted inside and then leans on it to stop anyone following her. She sags back against the door. 'Oh my giddy aunt,' she says breathlessly. Which for Cara is pretty strong stuff. And then she looks up at me. 'Oh, Emily,' she cries.

I run down the stairs. 'What? What?'

'This is terrible,' she says.

I've sort of gathered that. I grab the pile of newspapers from her and lower myself in a state of near catatonic shock to sit on the bottom step of the stairs. I can't believe what I'm seeing.

I'm front-page news on the *Sun*, *Daily Sport* and the *Mirror*, reunited with my Saucy Santa image. Oh my God, what do I look like? I scan through the stories on fast-forward. They make Declan sound like some major sleaze-ball setting up in competition with the *Playboy* empire and they make me sound like some sex-crazed slapper. I have only made page three of the *Daily Mail* and I would be thankful for small mercies, but they have printed the dressing-gown shot too, under the heading 'Squalid Sex-Games for Tarty Teacher to the Stars'.

'Oh bollocks,' I say.

Cara is wide-eyed with horror. 'What are you going to do?'

'Ooo,' I say sarcastically. 'I'm not sure. I could just slit my wrists now. Or I could take ever-increasing doses of arsenic and prolong my death.'

'Be serious,' she says.

'What makes you think I'm not?'

107

Cara comes and sits down next to me. 'This can't be as bad as it seems.'

'Why?'

'I don't know.'

'Anyway,' I say, 'how come you nipped out to get all these?' I flick through the newspapers again, feeling increasingly desperate.

'I heard the story on the radio when I got up,' Cara admits, 'and thought I'd better find out how bad the damage was.'

Pretty bad, I should say.

'Why didn't you wake me up?'

'I thought they might have gone by the time I got back.'

'Oh, fat chance of that,' I snort. 'You're in the profession yourself. You know that they'll be here until they get their story.'

'At least you don't have to try to get into work,' she says in an effort to comfort me. I suppose in the scheme of things, being merely suspended from my job could be viewed as a positive step.

'You wait,' I say. 'It will only be a matter of time before the phone rings and I've got the sack.'

The phone rings. Cara and I stare at it.

'You get it,' I say.

Cara dashes over to the phone and snatches it up. 'Hello,' she says. Her hand goes to her throat and she coughs gently. 'It's the Headmaster.'

I stand up and smooth my tatty terry dressing gown down with as much dignity as I can muster and before the Headmaster can speak, I say, 'I know. I'm sacked.'

Chapter Thirty-One

Adam sat by the window in the Café Blanco, waiting for Laura to turn up and stirring his coffee more than it needed. He never paid for his coffee in here. It was one of the very few perks of being a photographer on a local newspaper. The café was situated in a quiet side alley just off the High Street, nestled between a very arty art gallery which never seemed to have any customers and a property lettings agent who seemed to have more than his fair share.

Café Blanco was a traditional establishment in this age of faddism, and its primary attraction, apart from the secluded location, was the fact that it produced a fabulous all-day breakfast for under a fiver. Definitely a disappearing art on this High Street. The inside was a cramped affair of French-style beech chairs and the obligatory wooden flooring. Outside it had stainless steel tables and a smattering of patio heaters arranged on the worn cobbles which meant that the British could demonstrate their on-going battle with their weather by sitting outside shivering in all elements, all year round.

This is where Adam came on his quiet news days and just kicked around, reading the nationals, getting hyper on coffee until his mobile rang and Cara or someone from the office contacted him to tell him that something suitably newsworthy had happened.

Once upon a time when he was keen, he used to chase after the emergency services just for the hell of it and the hope of a decent story at the end. You could pick up the route of a fire engine from the trail of water it left in its wake as it turned corners. Wasn't that an incredibly sad fact to know? Adam couldn't remember the last time a speeding ambulance had raised his pulse. Probably around the same time as a woman had. Now that his ambulance-chasing days were over, he justified this inert downtime as vital mingling with the community. From the gossip he gleaned from the two middle-aged female owners and the young waitresses, he probably produced more headline stories than the news reporters who were now mostly office-bound.

How he longed for those heady days of inactivity now. Since the breaking of the Emily story, the local rag was in danger of becoming a very serious newspaper. Everyone was chasing round like blue-bottomed flies making sure every angle was covered. He still wasn't sure, however, that this justified the number of poster-size pictures of Emily that seemed to be appearing on the newsroom wall.

He stirred his cappuccino and tried to prepare himself for the forthcoming conversation. He'd spent the whole night lying staring at the ceiling, trying to imagine what life would be like with Josh living on the other side of the world. He'd looked at the prices of flights to Australia on the Internet and that was truly depressing.

Red-eyed and wracked with anxiety, he'd phoned Laura at eight o'clock and had asked to see her. She did not sound happy, but then Laura never did these days. Adam scratched at his chin and wished he'd had time to shave. The smell of frying bacon drifted through the café, but for once he had no appetite. His stomach was a gurgling mass of tension. He hadn't been able to eat at Luigi's last night after Josh's bombshell. Josh, on the other hand, had stuffed his face. The terror of becoming an Antipodean had been assuaged by a plateful of pasta followed rapidly by home-made *gelato di cioccolato*.

The door chime heralded Laura's arrival. She was tight-lipped and bitter-looking. The woman who used to spend hours in front of the bathroom mirror meticulously painting her face before she would venture out of the door wore no make-up and her hair was scraped back from her face as usual. Sometimes when he saw her, it was like looking at someone he'd never seen before. It was very hard to remember that he'd once been married to this harassed stranger.

She sat down opposite him and started unbuckling her jacket in the same movement. 'I don't have time for this, Adam,' she said. 'It had better be important.'

'Do you want a coffee?'

'No.'

'Go on, have a coffee,' he urged. 'It'll make you feel better.'

Laura's head snapped up. 'There's nothing wrong with me.'

'You know what I mean.'

She shook her head impatiently. 'Oh, all right,' she said. 'I'll have a double espresso.'

Jeanette the waitress pricked up her ears and motioned to Adam that she'd got the order.

Laura pulled a packet of cigarettes from her pocket and went through the ritual of lighting up.

'I didn't know you smoked,' Adam remarked. 'You never used to like it.'

Laura puffed the first plume of smoke out of her nose. 'I spend a 'lot of my life doing things that I didn't used to like.'

'It was a comment, Laura,' Adam said. 'Not a criticism.' He could never understand why his ex-wife wanted to make a battle out of everything. Surely they should be able to talk civilly to each other after all this time. It must be exhausting holding a grudge for so long.

Jeanette delivered the espresso, gave Adam a sympathetic glance and disappeared quickly.

'So what was it you wanted?' Laura said.

It was always so difficult to talk to Laura. He just wanted to have a reasonable conversation about Josh's future and their plans. The fact that he was his father should still involve him in major life changes and he knew she'd view it as confrontational. 'I talked to Josh last night,' Adam said. 'He told me that you're planning to move to Australia.'

Laura met his eyes levelly. 'And?'

'And . . . it would be nice if you'd have talked to me about it.'

'This has nothing to do with you, Adam.'

'How can you say that?' Adam lowered his voice. 'I'm his father. Josh is worried that he won't see me.'

'Because you're such great company?'

'Josh and I are very close and whatever happens, Laura, I'm the only father he'll ever have.'

Laura gathered her cigarettes and lighter from the table and pushed them into her pocket. 'And is that all you wanted to say?'

'No.' Adam sighed. 'I don't want you to take him away.'

'And what about what I want, Adam?'

'We promised each other that we'd bring him up together.'

'We promised each other a lot of things, Adam, and all of them have been broken.'

For a moment, Adam had a picture of them laughing and smiling together on their wedding day and felt a pang of regret that they were now reduced to talking together in impersonal cafés about their son's future.

'I'm sorry, Laura.' He reached out and touched her hand and was surprised that she didn't pull it away. 'I never meant things to end up like this. And I think you and Barry are doing a great job bringing Josh up.' Laura pulled her hand away. 'That's not my worry. I'm frightened that I'll lose him, Laura. And he's the only thing I've got.'

Laura looked at her watch. 'I've got to go.'

'Not yet,' Adam pleaded. 'I just want to know how far you've got. Has Barry got another job out there? Where are you planning to go? Have your visas come through? Or are you still both thinking about it?'

111

Laura stood up. 'This isn't about Barry. If I go to Australia, it's just me and Josh.'

Adam was stunned.

'That's why I'm not ready to talk about it.' Laura's voice softened. 'This is a big decision for me.'

'I had no idea,' he said. 'I don't know what to say.'

Laura allowed herself a rueful half-smile. 'You never did.'

'No,' Adam said.

Laura stubbed out her cigarette, picked up her coat and walked briskly out into the cold, leaving the door bell clanging behind her.

Adam looked at Jeanette the waitress.

'Another cappuccino?' she said.

He nodded. 'How do you think that went?'

Jeanette pushed herself away from the counter and shrugged. 'It could have been worse.'

'Yes,' Adam said. And wondered if that was true.

Chapter Thirty-Two

Cara is preparing to go out into the mêlée again. The phone has rung so much we have taken it off the hook and I've put it in a bucket with a towel on top so that we can't hear the disconnected tone.

'Don't move,' my friend says as she belts her coat against the elements. She actually looks as if she's armouring up to go into battle and she may well be. Cara is going to get the cavalry in the form of Adam. 'He'll know what to do,' she says for the hundredth time. 'Adam will sort this out.'

And I do hope that she's right. I'm not sure that I have as much faith in this Adam bloke as she does.

'Wish me luck,' Cara says as she heads towards the door. My friend's face never has the healthiest of blooms, because she doesn't believe in sunbathing, but now she's looking white with terror.

'Good luck,' I say and she hesitates only slightly before she whips the door open and plunges headlong into the heaving mass of bodies.

They all know her name, probably supplied by the kind neighbours, and shout after her as she legs it to her untrustworthy 2CV parked further along the road in a resident's parking bay beyond the clutches of the double yellow lines.

I don't really know what to do with myself now, so I go upstairs and get showered and dressed, making sure that all the curtains are closed between my bedroom and the bathroom in case any particularly intrepid photographer should decide to point a long-range lens in my direction. I feel totally neurotic about my privacy and wonder how Madonna and Michael Jackson cope with their lives.

I feel better now I'm washed and scrubbed. I've had some tea, but can't manage any breakfast, so I sit and switch on the daytime television. This is a luxury I can't say I've enjoyed previous to my infamy. I watch *Kilroy*, *Garden Invaders* and *Supermarket Sweep* all punctuated by shouts from the journalists outside of, 'Emily! Emily! Emily!' through the letterbox. Then I turn over to *Richard and Judy* and find them discussing my bottom. Their researchers are probably among the people trying to ring my bucket. Richard and Judy are holding up all the day's newspapers in turn. I want to switch it off, but am drawn by a masochistic and morbid curiosity to view my own life in this way. Will this never end?

I'm very pleased to say that Richard and, in particular Judy, are very sympathetic to my plight. This could be because Judy was once splashed all over the dailies having accidentally popped out of her blouse at a prestigious awards ceremony. These are sad times when Judy Finnegan's exposed baps in a lacy black bra makes front-page news. But there it is.

They are going to have a phone-in later on about me and I wonder whether I might ring in just for the hell of it. No one has yet mentioned that I have lost my job over this or that I am up to my eyeballs in debt due to my scheming bastard boyfriend. They are more concerned with the fact that it is possible to do all sorts of wicked things on the Internet now and I have to agree. They might be even more concerned if they knew the fallout. Another thought occurs to me. My mother might well watch *Richard and Judy*. I've told my parents nothing of this. How are they going to cope with seeing their daughter's rather festive bottom paraded all over ITV? They won't have seen it in the newspaper, because they buy *The Times* and I'm pretty damn sure I haven't made the front page of that. If I have, then the world is truly off its rocker.

I think my next job is to ring them and confess all. I wander over to the phone and rescue it from its ignominy in the bucket and put it back in its cradle.

It makes me jump by ringing immediately. The answerphone clicks in and records a message from the *Daily Mail* asking me to ring their *Femail* Editor. The call is quickly followed by ones from the *Sun* and the *Mirror* in exactly the same vein. And, as I suspected, from someone called Annabelle who is a researcher for *Richard and Judy*, practically begging me to contact her. Look what a media expert I am already!

I'm just about to consign the phone to the bucket again when it rings again and a rather cultured voice starts to speak. 'Hello, Emily. You must be terribly tired of the phone by now. But if you're there, I would like to help you. My name's Jonathan Gold and I'm a publicity agent.' I don't know much about publicity agents. We don't generally have much to do with them in the hectic, celebrity world of teaching, but he's the only one I've ever heard of. He sounds very calm and in control. 'Together we can handle this pressure and turn it to your benefit. When you're feeling up to it, give me a call.'

And I don't know what makes me do it, but as he reels off his telephone number, I scrabble for a pen and write it down on the back of my hand.

Chapter Thirty-Three

'Where's Adam?' Cara said, her voice rising in panic as she noted his empty desk.

'Behind you.' Obnoxious Chris pointed across the office and sure enough Adam was sauntering towards her. Chris turned back to his group of henchmen and sniggered. Cara could have cried with relief. She didn't think she'd ever been quite so pleased to see anyone.

Coming into the office was a nightmare. There were pin-ups of Emily plastered everywhere just to spite her, she was sure. Everyone seemed to be staring at her and pointing behind her back as she walked past. It was as if she'd been branded by association with Emily. They were probably imagining Cara running round in a French Maid's outfit or dressed up in head-to-toe PVC like Michelle Pfeiffer as Cat Woman. Poor Emily, she could only imagine how her friend must be feeling.

As Adam came closer she could see he was frowning and he didn't look as if he'd been to bed. But then he normally looked like that.

Cara rushed over to him. 'Adam,' she blurted out. 'You've got to help me.'

He lifted his eyes and looked wearily at her. 'What's wrong?'

'It's Emily.' Cara followed him to his desk and perched on the corner. Adam sat down. She lowered her voice, making sure that Chris and any of his cronies were out of earshot. 'Oh flip, Adam, she's in such a mess! *We're* in such a mess.'

The extent of her distress didn't seem to be registering in Adam's expression and he continued to stare at her blankly. Cara grabbed the bundle of daily papers from the news desk. 'Look at this.' She waved the *Sun* under his nose. 'It's the same in all of them.' She spread the other papers out before him. Emily featured large in all of them. 'We are under siege, Adam. There are reporters knee deep camped outside my house. Emily can't move. She's been sacked from her job.' Cara stopped blathering and looked at Adam. 'We don't know what to do.'

116

Adam looked terribly, terribly tired. 'I'm not sure that I do,' he said.

Cara sagged. 'I thought you might have some ideas?'

Adam shook his head and raked his untidy mass of black hair back from his forehead. 'I don't think so.'

'You said she could come and stay with you,' Cara reminded him. 'It might be a good idea. Then they wouldn't know where she was. She could at least get some peace to think about things.'

Adam inhaled slowly and rubbed his hand over his stubble as he thought about it. 'She can't come to me, Cara.'

'But you said—'

'I know.' Adam stopped her. 'Things have changed since then. I've got . . . I've got some problems myself,' he said.

Cara sneaked a look over at Chris who was carefully monitoring their conversation. She desperately wanted to touch Adam, to reassure him, but it was dangerous territory with so many people watching. He did look particularly careworn today. 'Anything you want to talk about?'

Adam also checked to see if Chris was ear-wigging. He moved closer to her. Cara went very warm. He was giving off very strong chi. Very manly chi. Very yang chi. Cara licked her lips.

'It's Josh,' he said, completely unaware of the effect his chi was having on her.

Until yesterday lunchtime, Cara had almost forgotten Adam had a son. He spoke very rarely about Josh, but she could tell they had a deep bond. It felt good that he had started to open up and talk to her about him. That was a positive sign, wasn't it?

'I'm going to fight for custody of him,' he continued. 'I just don't think it would be a good idea if I had Emily staying at my flat. If my ex-wife found out, it is exactly the sort of thing she could use against me.'

Cara sighed.

'You do understand?' Adam said.

'It would only be for a few days,' Cara pleaded. 'Until she can get herself sorted out.'

'I would love to help,' Adam said. 'Really, I would. You know that. But I can't risk it, Cara. I just can't risk it.'

Cara folded her arms. 'I don't know what else to do.'

'Something will come up,' Adam said. 'Besides, this story might run for a few more days and then it will be old news and Emily can start rebuilding her life.' He looked at the picture of her friend on the front of the newspaper. 'I feel as if I know her,' he laughed.

'You'll have to come and meet her,' Cara said. 'When all this is over.'

'I'd like to.' Adam surreptitiously flicked his thumb towards Chris. 'It would make someone very jealous.'

Cara snorted. 'Emily is way out of Chris's league. She's lovely, Adam. You'd really like her. And she certainly doesn't deserve all this.'

'Well, I suppose she found out about her boyfriend's true colours before it was too late.'

'I think losing your home and your job could possibly be classified as being "too late".'

'Yeah,' Adam said. 'I take your point.'

'Declan's lovely too,' Cara insisted. 'He's such a charmer. Fantastic-looking. But Emily was too soft with him. Declan needs someone strong to keep him in check. It's a shame,' Cara tutted. 'He realises he's made a mistake and he's desperate to get back with Emily.'

'If he's so desperate to get her back, he's the one who should be helping her,' Adam advised.

'Emily won't let him near her,' Cara said. 'She won't even talk to him.'

A little twinkle returned to Adam's tired, red-rimmed eyes. 'But that doesn't mean you can't.'

Cara let her mouth curl up into a slight smirk. 'No, it doesn't, does it?' She jumped down from Adam's desk. 'I think I might just pay Declan O'Donnell a visit,' she said.

'What a fine idea, Ms Forbes,' Adam said with a smile.

'I have a very good adviser,' Cara replied with a grin. 'You know, Adam, if there's anything I can do to help, you only have to ask. I mean it.'

'Thanks. But I need to sort this out myself.'

'Do you have any healing crystals in your flat?'

'Er . . .no.'

'They can be very helpful.'

'Er . . .right,' Adam said. 'I'll try to remember.'

Cara checked Chris again and he was still watching them intently. 'I want to give you a big hug,' she said softly to Adam.

Adam followed her gaze. 'I don't think this is the right time, do you?'

'Maybe not,' Cara said. But the time will come, she added to herself.

Chapter Thirty-Four

I have just discovered that *HO-HO-HO* means the same thing in about eighteen different languages.

Cara and I are sitting watching some sort of twenty-four-hour digital news channel. It is terrifying. Truly terrifying. They are showing clips from news programmes all around the globe and I'm staggered to see that my bottom is doing a world tour all by itself. There is a lovely blonde presenter behind a desk in the UK studio, recounting my story in suitably sombre tones and, I have to say, that again I'm coming out of this reasonably well – betrayed, if slightly bimbo-ish girlfriend and bastard boyfriend, etc. However, that doesn't stop them from flashing my naughty bits all over the place.

I finally managed to speak to my parents today, who are denying all knowledge of me and are thinking of emigrating to New Zealand on the strength of this. I did consider going with them. They too have had a minor press posse camped on their doorstep. My mother has come over all peculiar and is convinced she'll be excommunicated from the Bridge Club. I don't think that's a bad thing; if she's at home every now and again it might force her to have a conversation with my father for the first time in twenty years. Anyway, it won't matter if they're going to live in New Zealand, will it? I didn't, however, voice that opinion. Instead, I apologised for being the worst daughter in Christendom and for bringing shame on their household and slurring their good name. I also apologised for a lot of things I'm not responsible for too. I'm not going to ring them again for ages. If they want to know how I am, they'll have to start buying the *Daily Mail*.

I pop up in Italy, my cheery picture lurking behind a tiny, immaculately groomed presenter and the majestic Coliseum. Why? Why on earth are they bothered about this? They have housewives stripping off on their telly all the time. One more isn't going to make the slightest bit of difference. They don't have a game show on that doesn't feature some woman's bare chest. I know this from a particularly rainy holiday Declan and I spent at Lake Garda. It was

119

impossible to tell where the rain stopped and the lake started. We spent seven days cramped in the television lounge surrounded by damp Germans. Believe me, there was *nothing* else to do. I've never been back to Italy since.

'This is dreadful,' Cara says, helpfully echoing my own sentiments. 'Really dreadful.'

I think I'm well aware of that by now. I am trying to dull my pain through the *vin-ordinaire* route. Cara has lit some aromatherapy candles and is dropping Rescue Remedy down her throat like it's going out of fashion.

'You should take some of this, Emily,' she says, waving the bottle at me.

'I'm trying to give it up,' I say, waving my own bottle on the way to filling my glass again.

My bottom pops up next to a small Japanese presenter. 'This is unbearable.'

I close my eyes and when I open them again I'm in New York. Boy, do I get around. And that's the general theme of the presenters – how easy it is to humiliate your girlfriend on a truly awesome scale without really trying. Such is the power of the worldwide web.

Declan always used to complain that his Internet service was too slow. I think slow is a relative concept these days. This is something that can enable you to send instantaneous email messages, very cheaply, to anywhere in the world. Tap a few keys, click a couple of buttons and – bang – they're gone. Timbuktu, tropical rainforests, Totleigh Barton – there is nowhere out of its reach.

These days there are varying degrees of slowness. It all depends on your perspective. In the days of the stage-coach we used to think that one week was quick to deliver a letter. Actually, in these days of gross inefficiency in the post office, we still think that's quick. I've had Christmas cards posted in Hampstead that have winged their way to my door three streets away via Timbuktu, tropical rainforests and Totleigh Barton.

Personally, I can't believe how quickly I'm being whizzed round the world. To me, this feels as if it is spreading like wildfire. And I thought it was only good news that was supposed to travel fast.

'You need to do something about your image, Emily,' Cara says, pointing at me pouting on the screen. 'They're portraying you as a brainless harlot.'

Thank you, my friend.

She turns away from the television where I'm now Down Under. I don't think my parents will manage to escape my notoriety even in the sleepy backwaters of New Zealand, which is only a hop, skip and a jump away from Australia. My mother will be dogged by her dodgy daughter in bridge clubs across the globe.

'I think it's your chest that does it,' Cara continues in a considered manner. 'No one is going to take you seriously while you have boobs the size of nuclear warheads.' This is a dangerous conversation to be having with someone who has had rather a lot to drink. 'Have you ever thought of having them surgically reduced?'

'No,' I say. But I do wonder whether it's possible to get your friends surgically reduced.

'They make you look like a pin-up, Emily.'

'That's obviously why Declan chose to parade them on the Internet.'

Cara points at the television where I'm now in France, juxtaposed against the lovely, slender Eiffel Tower. 'Over ten million people have seen them already,' she says.

'What a comforting thought,' I answer. 'Thanks for that.'

'I was only telling you.'

'Well,' I huff. 'Tell me something I don't know.'

'You can't get away from it, Emily. Big breasts make women look stupid. You become mere sex objects.'

I quite like being a sex object, but that's not something I'm going to share with Cara. And I didn't particularly want to share it with the rest of the Western world either.

'Your stance on this wouldn't be down to the fact that you're a 32AA in a Wonderbra?' I suggest. Cara is the only thirty-two-year-old woman I know who doesn't confine her sock-wearing to her feet.

'Flat chests are making a comeback,' my friend informs me through pursed lips.

'Yeah? And so are Showaddywaddy.'

'Big chest and blonde hair, Emily. Recipe for disaster,' she says sagely. 'You'll be recognised wherever you go.'

The news moves off my bottom and onto slightly more weighty subjects – earthquakes in Pakistan, world famine, the destruction of the ozone layer, the relentless spread of terrorism. That sort of thing.

But Cara is right for once: I do need to do something about my image. Certainly in the short-term. If I want to shop in Sainsburys with a degree of anonymity I need to get a disguise. I don't want to be recognised on every checkout across the land while I'm out buying my Pot Noodles.

'Have you got any hair dye?' I ask, putting my wine to one side. I'm in a decisive mood.

Cara flicks the television off. 'Probably.'

'Come and dye my hair for me,' I say.

'Can't.' Cara twiddles her dreadlocks. 'I'm going out.'

'Where?'

'I'm meeting a friend for a drink.'

I grin. 'Not the lovely Adam?'

'No, unfortunately.' Cara sighs. 'The lovely Adam is playing hard to get.'

'You need to up your chanting a bit,' I say.

'I think so,' she nods earnestly.

Sometimes I could strangle my best friend.

'Can I come with you?' I'm getting very bored with being a recluse. I don't know how Howard Hughes coped.

'How can you, Emily?' she says. 'I'm going to have to run the gauntlet of the world's press.'

It's very easy to forget that you have twenty-seven journalists sitting on your front lawn when you really try.

'I feel so trapped,' I whine.

'Remember, Emily, staying in is the new going out,' Cara says.

Which is a very hip thing for her to say even though it's bollocks. Still, I suppose it makes a change from her talking about tofu.

'I won't be long,' she promises and I suddenly realise that she is looking a bit spangly for a night sitting in watching telly.

'OK,' I say and it's very hard not to let my lip tremble. I feel so very alone. One minute I think I'm coping quite well with all this and the next it hits me like a tsunami wave, threatening to leave me drowned, battered and beached.

'You'll be all right,' Cara says.

'Yes.' I nod too vigorously. 'I'll be fine.' And as she leaves, bracing herself for the renewed interest of the waiting press, I put my wine bottle to one side and decide that I'm not going to drink any more. Because – and I know I'm mad – what I actually want to do more than anything in the world at this moment is to ring Declan.

Chapter Thirty-Five

Declan was already sitting waiting in the wine bar when Cara arrived. They had decided to meet up in the West End, which smacked a bit of subterfuge, but Cara wasn't sure whether she would be followed by one of the journalists. And anyway, it was subterfuge. After all, she was meeting Emily's boyfriend, ex-boyfriend, behind her back and she felt very underhand. She comforted herself with the thought that it was for Emily's own good.

Cara dodged backwards and forwards on the crowded evening Tube, doubling back on herself just to make sure she wasn't being followed. Which was probably a bit over the top, but then real life was sort of suspended at the moment. She and Declan had arranged to meet in The Place and it was already crowded. It was always crowded. The Place was one of those wine bars where everyone wanted to go and then when it was too packed and popular because it was 'the place' to go, no one wanted to go there any more because it was too busy. And now it was chock-full of people who wished they'd been here when it was 'the place' to go. Cara shook her hair and pushed her way through the squash of bodies towards Declan.

He was looking very debonair in a Ralph Lauren shirt and chinos. It was nice to be seen with someone handsome and smart, Cara decided. She'd never had a trendy boyfriend. The last three partners she had endured had been out of the Eco-Warrior mould and there were only so many places that you could go with someone whose dress sense was modelled on Swampy. Consequently, she had never been here when it was 'the place' to go. And, to her surprise, she wished that she had – although being trendy seemed to involve not much more than lots of chrome fittings, wooden flooring and doubling the drinks prices. She wondered if the wooden floors all came from sustainable forests. Perhaps she was at that age where it was no longer suitable to be going out with unwashed men and hanging out in brown-painted folk clubs in the back streets of Kilburn. While it was nice to date someone who cared deeply about the planet, it would also be nice if they cared deeply about her, too. It was high time to address her own requirements in a man. It might be a little late to be considered a trendsetter, but Cara was definitely feeling upwardly mobile. And Adam certainly seemed to be a step in the right direction.

As Cara headed towards the table, she noticed that Declan was trying very hard to look languid. He was draped aesthetically across a black velvet armchair, but he was tapping his foot impatiently and drummed his bottle of beer on the table. Declan could also do with a good dose of Rescue Remedy, Cara thought. The boy was a complete bag of nerves.

Declan stood up as he saw her approach. 'Thank God you're here,' he said.

'Declan.' Cara kissed both of his cheeks and she shook her coat off as they sat down again.

'I took the liberty,' he said and indicated a bottle of chilled white wine and two glasses. 'It's always so crowded in here.'

Cara was about to launch into her monologue about it no longer being 'the place' to go, but thought better of it. Declan looked in no mood to indulge in small talk.

'I am out of my head with worry,' he said as he downed the remains of his beer and poured out two rather large glasses of wine. And she had to admit that his normally hollow cheeks had taken on a downright gaunt look.

'*You* are?' Cara said. 'Have you got an army of reporters following your every move? Are they camped outside your house?'

Declan shook his head.

She didn't tell him she knew that two had been stationed outside his office all day. 'Look – Emily is bearing the brunt of this.'

'I know. I know,' Declan said. 'I was so relieved when you called. I knew you'd understand what I'm going through.'

'I'm doing it for Emily,' Cara told him firmly. 'She's in a right royal mess due to you. And I've come to you, Declan, because I didn't know what else to do.'

'I want you to help me,' Declan said. 'How can I put it right, if she won't even talk to me.' He closed his eyes like a man in pain. 'I need to see her, Cara. Sweet Jesus, I need to see her. I need her back.'

'I think the best chance you have of getting her back is to try to sort out this tawdry business.'

'I am,' he insisted. 'I am. So help me.'

'You know that she's lost her job?' Cara said, savouring the sharp taste of the cold white wine.

He nodded. 'After you told me, I rushed out and bought all the papers to read about it,' he said without irony.

'She hasn't got any money.'

'I'm a bit strapped myself,' Declan admitted.

He looked it, Cara thought. The very picture of poverty, sitting here with his smouldering movie-star looks, kitted out from top-to-toe in designer labels. She could see why Emily was so mad with him. She could also see why Emily was so mad *about* him. Or *had been* so mad about him.

'I think you're very lucky she hasn't taken a contract out on you.' Cara smiled in spite of herself. It was very difficult to stay cross with Declan. He must have had charm delivered by the lorryload at regular intervals.

'I feel like I'm going insane.'

'You must have been insane to do what you did.' Cara looked at him in exasperation. 'Whatever possessed you?'

'Desperation,' he said candidly. 'I was in debt and drowning.'

'And you thought you'd drag Emily down with you?'

'I didn't mean for it to get out of control like this.' Declan wrung his hands. 'I took that damned photo off the Internet the minute Emily told me to.'

Cara gave him a sideways glance.

'I swear to you, Cara. It was no more than a couple of days.' Declan cleared his throat. 'A week at the most. And that was due to technical difficulties.'

'Yes,' Cara said. 'The technical difficulty of you remembering you had a conscience.'

'You are looking at a man who has lost everything dear to him.' Declan spread his hands wide.

Cara tutted.

'Talk to her. Get her to see me.'

'She needs money, Declan. She needs concrete evidence that you're going to make this good, not some of that old Irish flannel.'

'I have started a new business, Cara. And it's doing really well. I'm sure this will save us.'

'What sort of business?'

Declan hesitated. 'An art site.'

'Art?'

'Well, sort of arty.'

'Women taking their clothes off in arty ways?'

'Er . . .yes.'

'Declan!' Cara was outraged. 'Have you learned nothing?'

'I've learned that there's a lot of money to be made from men who want to look at buck-naked women.'

'You are insufferable!'

125

Declan smiled and Cara started to laugh.

'Stay and have dinner with me,' he said earnestly. 'I've had enough of eating alone.'

Cara looked round. The place was full of couples, huddling tightly together, laughing, joking, loving. Suddenly, she didn't want to go back to Emily and her whining or fidget round her big double bed on her own.

'Do they do vegetarian food?'

'Not here.' Declan picked up her coat. 'But I know a little place that does.'

'I should get back.'

'Perhaps Emily could do with some space,' he said.

Cara wavered.

'I'm thinking of becoming a vegetarian.'

'You liar, Declan O'Donnell!' she said. 'And if I didn't know you better, I'd think that was the most awful chat-up line I've ever heard.'

'I love vegetables,' he insisted. 'Mange-tout are a particular favourite.'

'Mange-tout, indeed,' Cara huffed. 'I'm going to order you a great big plate of them.'

'It's a deal.' Declan grinned and held out her coat.

Chapter Thirty-Six

'Oh golly gosh!' Cara plods into the kitchen, huddled in the floaty kaftan thing she uses as her dressing gown and stares at me with her mouth ajar. As well she might. Last night I went upstairs a natural blonde and this morning, came down a bottle brunette – which I realise is flying in the face of the normal run of things.

'Do you like it?' I say, giving a twirl.

'It's different.' She steadies herself on the table and sits down.

I can't even believe that Cara had a bottle of dark-brown hair dye in her cupboard. She's never been brunette in her life. Pink, purple and once a very alarming shade of orange, but never anything as drab or ordinary as brunette. I am now officially a deep shade of Chestnut Burst. I think I have a look of Winona Ryder. As a further element to my disguise, I have left my contact lenses soaking in their solution and have opted for my reading glasses.

'You look like a librarian,' Cara says gingerly.

'And you look like someone very fragile,' I point out. 'I heard you come crashing and banging in at some ungodly hour.'

Cara hangs her head. The psychedelic theme of decoration carries on through to her kitchen. Every ceramic tile is a different colour and she's painted the chairs and tables in strident shades of purple, turquoise, hot pink and crimson. And she looks like she might be regretting it.

'Did your quick drink with a friend turn into a session?'

'Yes,' Cara croaks. 'I'm going to give up alcohol. I think I'm allergic to it.'

'You only get allergic to it after the third bottle, and that's commonly known as a hangover.'

'You're a very bad influence on me, Emily Miller.' Cara starts to shake her head and then realises it's a bad idea. 'I never used to drink until you moved in here.'

'Oh yes, you did,' I protest.

'My body used to be a temple,' she says. 'Now it feels like a disused brewery.'

127

'Here, drink this,' I say and hand her a cup of tea so strong that you could stand your spoon up in it. And to think that they say tea is no longer a popular drink in Britain. Are they mad? It's the cure for all ills and is particularly efficacious in the area of excess alcohol.

'Thanks,' she says and drinks it without complaining. 'It's a good job I'm on the late shift today.' And it is, because it's nearly lunchtime already.

My body has soon grown accustomed to its lack of gainful employment and, I have to say, I'm not really missing work at all. I expect I'll feel differently when pay day rolls round and I don't get one. I've considered taking Declan to court over all this. I probably could sue him, but what would it achieve? Dragging myself through more pain and humiliation and for what? He is as penniless as I am. I take a leisurely sip at my tea and say: 'Do you think I should sue Declan?'

'That's a bit hasty,' Cara says, looking very alarmed.

'Why?' I say. 'He's a bastard and he deserves it.'

'He might be trying to sort this out.' Cara has her reasonable head on. 'Why don't you phone him and see what he says?'

'No.'

'Think about it, Emily,' my friend advises. 'Declan may be suffering as much as you are.'

'And how do you work that out?' I think the alcohol is fuddling Cara's brain.

'He has lost the woman he loves,' she points out in a slightly Mills and Boon voice.

'No,' I reply tightly. 'When you *lose* something, or someone, you do it by mistake. Declan purposely set out on a course of action that he knew would destroy our relationship.'

'You're being very hard on him, Emily.'

'I'd like to see you be so forgiving if he'd done the same thing to you,' I say.

'Ah, but that's where we differ, Emily,' Cara says, smiling at me over her Tetleys. 'I wouldn't have been seen dead in a Saucy Santa outfit in the first place.'

And I can think of nothing to say but '*Grrrr . . .*'

Cara is giving me a lift to Hampstead Tube station on her way to work. It would be a lot quicker for me to walk rather than endure the traffic, but I'm terrified that I might get set upon by a pack of rabid news hounds.

We are hovering by the front door and I am curtain-twitching to see how many journalists and photographers are still loitering in

128

Cara's bushes. There are a fair few, although they have a much more lethargic air about them and are sitting around on the pavement smoking copious ciggies rather than standing huddled together in a tense, tightly coiled bunch clutching notepads or cameras.

'Ready?' Cara asks.

'Ready,' I say.

'Where exactly are you going?' Cara queries, hand poised on the door knob.

'I'm going to see an adviser,' I say vaguely. 'To discuss my future.'

'Oh,' she says. 'That sounds like a good idea.'

It might sound like one, but I think she would be less enthusiastic if she knew I'd made an appointment to see publicity guru, Jonathan Gold. I'm not sure I should be doing this myself. Jonathan Gold has a bit of a reputation himself and it's not always a good one.

Mr Gold is known for representing women who have affairs with footballers, pop stars and MPs and then decide to kiss-and-tell – for a suitable sum of money. He also deals with disgraced prime-time television entertainers, shoplifting chat-show hosts and the mistresses of people in power who should really know better than get caught with their pants down. Still, what harm can it do? All I'm going to do is find out what he advises for someone in my situation – degraded, destitute and desperate.

It starts to drizzle and the members of the waiting press pull their collars up round their ears; when the rain gets a little heavier they drift off towards their battered Mondeos and Vauxhall Vectras.

'This is a good time to go,' Cara says. 'They might not give chase.'

I pull on a beanie hat and study myself in the mirror. It isn't only Chris Evans who looks awful in a beanie hat. I don't look like myself at all and, in a strange way, I don't feel like myself. There is still an element of me that refuses to believe all this is happening.

I look at Cara and steel myself. 'OK,' I say and we dash out into the rain.

We rush down Cara's path, my friend shielding me and we nearly get to the gate when they spot us and start to run back towards the cottage.

'Come on!' Cara shouts and we belt off down the road in the direction of her 2CV which is about a million miles away, as she can't get any nearer to the house because of all the journalists' cars parked in the way. Despite the fact that they all smoke like troopers, they still seem to be able to run with all the speed and agility of youthful greyhounds and are snapping at our heels as we reach Cara's car.

'Get in!' she screeches and we yank the doors open and fall inside, locking them behind us.

The journalists bang on the roof and on the windows and cameras flash at me as I try to hide my face. We are both breathing heavily, puffing out air like beleaguered steam trains and, as some sort of compensation, the glass starts to mist up, thwarting the photographers.

Cara starts the engine and we lurch away. As we turn into the traffic, I risk lowering my hands. Half a dozen puffing journalists are pounding down the road after us, but even in Cara's 2CV we are leaving them behind.

'That was fun,' I say.

Cara is white and visibly shaken. 'Will this never end?' she spits.

'Still feel that Declan is a caring and deeply misunderstood individual?' I ask.

She doesn't reply, but stares ahead at the cars in front, willing them not to slow down and to keep moving. The journalists are still giving chase and the shouts of 'Emily! Emily! Emily!' follow us all the way down the road.

Chapter Thirty-Seven

I take the beanie hat off outside the offices of Jonathan Gold with a trembling hand. The great publicity guru's offices are slap bang in the middle of Oxford Street, although I doubt Mr Gold himself shops here. He looks like a Jermyn Street hand-tailored shirt man from the little I've seen of him on the television. It's stopped raining and I rake my hands through my hair in an effort to coax it back into some sort of style as I push through the heavy revolving doors that take me into a cavernous marble reception area. Two bored-looking security guards man the only desk.

'I'm looking for Jonathan Gold's office,' I say, trying not to sound as nervous as I feel.

One of the guards eyes me suspiciously, clearly trying to decide if I'm the type to have a one-night stand with a famous footballer. 'Fifth floor,' he says flatly and I scuttle off to the lift, shooting inside just as the door is closing.

I'm alone in the lift and grow steadily more anxious as it whisks me silently up to the fifth floor. Normally, I hate the tinny, twinkly music they play in lifts, but hey, you certainly miss it when it's not there. I can hear the blood rushing through my ears. What I wouldn't give now for a bit of Gary Barlow.

To pass the time, I study the list of other companies who reside here. There's a successful independent film company that even I've heard of, a prestigious publishers, a firm of management agents and a well-known modelling agency, as well as Mr Gold. The lift stops and pings as the door opens and I step nervously out into carpet three inches deep. I walk along the corridor, conscious that I'm leaving little wet puddles of accumulated raindrops on their Axminster whenever I move.

A beautiful black and impossibly slender receptionist smiles coolly at me. She really looks as if she'd be more at home one floor down in the modelling agency. Naomi Campbell would be in deep, deep trouble if they signed this girl up. 'Can I help you?' she says.

'Yes,' I want to reply. 'You are making me feel like a fat, ugly elephant and I wish you'd stop it.' But I don't, I mumble that I'm here to see Jonathan Gold and she too looks at me to see if she can assess the nature of my misdemeanour.

The reception area is plush. I never really knew what that word meant before, but this is it. Plush. A mixture of posh and lush. Jonathan Gold's reception area is about as plush as it comes. Cream lamps with gold bases adorn copper side tables, giving the room a soft glow. Chestnut-brown leather chairs that shine like polished conkers invite you to linger too long in their arms. I sink into one of them and wonder who else's bottom has warmed it before me. Which scandal makers? Which fillers of the tabloids?

'Emily?' A handsome man in his early forties strides across the frothy cappuccino carpet and his highly polished brogues are the same colour as his armchairs. Jonathan Gold is much more beguiling than his television persona portrays. He takes my hand. 'I didn't recognise you,' he says.

And I wonder if he's making the obvious joke, until I realise that he has only seen me as a blonde. As well as without my clothes.

'Disguise,' I say, probably unnecessarily. He is the type of man who is used to clients who need to dodge the press. 'I've two dozen journalists on my doorstep.'

'Good,' he says and I realise that we are, indeed, seeing this from entirely different perspectives. 'Come on. Come on,' he waves me ahead of him. 'Come through.'

I enter his inner sanctum and this is double plush. Walls lined with leather-bound books, a yew desk, more leather and probably one of the best views in London. But I'm not invited to look out of the window, instead I'm motioned to a chair near the imposing desk and we take up our places on the respective sides of it. I wish I'd dressed more smartly. I just threw on some jeans and borrowed one of Cara's jackets in the vain hope of fooling some of Fleet Street's best. Oh, naïve and unaccustomed celebrity, thou art a bit of a twit! I look more like Billie Piper than I think is good for someone who wants to present themselves as a respectable pillar of the community. But at least I don't look like Chris Evans any more.

Jonathan Gold is the epitome of dandyism. I was right about the hand-tailored shirts and I think his suits are the same. On his wrist is a watch worth enough to settle all my debts and have enough left for a fish and chip supper and a bottle of cheap Chardonnay. My mother always used to say that you could tell rich men by the type of watch and the shoes that they wear. I think Jonathan Gold would fit her criteria.

There are pictures of celebrities, mainly in compromising positions, all over his walls. Headlines scream of salacious scandal and threatened careers. And I wonder if he keeps them here to remind them of how valuable he is to them.

'Now, Emily,' Jonathan says, making a steeple of his hands. He stares seriously at me over the top of them. 'You've been having it a bit tough lately.'

And I'm amazed that tears spring straight to my eyes. I nod wordlessly.

'I can help you,' he says, passing me a tissue.

I think I like the sound of this.

'It depends how far you're prepared to go.'

I like the sound of this less.

'Let's get the nasty end of it out of the way,' Jonathan continues. 'Normally,' he says, 'I charge a retainer of around ten thousand pounds a month.'

It's a good job he hasn't offered me a cup of tea, otherwise I probably would have spat it all over his shag pile.

'Or I can work on a commission basis – which I do for interesting cases.'

I'm glad he seems to view me as an 'interesting' case. In fact, I feel ridiculously grateful that he's interested in me at all. Is that pathetic? Don't tell me. I don't think I want to go there. Suddenly I feel as if I have totally lost my judgement on this subject. I'm acting as if I'm at a job interview rather than a desperate woman who's trying to do something to rescue her rear end from global ridicule.

'It's up to you,' he says. 'We can get you on *Trisha, Esther, Vanessa, Gloria, Kilroy, Richard and Judy*. They're all keen.'

I'd never thought about appearing on television. Not in the flesh. I'll rephrase that. Not in person.

'In America you're looking at *Oprah, Ricki* and *Montel*.'

America? Yikes!

'If you're looking at newspapers, we can get you in the tabloids – the *Sun, Mirror, Sport, News of the World*. They'll pay the most, but they'll want more inches of bare body in return for column inches.' Jonathan smiles at me.

I realise that I haven't yet spoken. He's probably thinking that I'll make a wild and untameable chat-show guest. I must rescue this and show him that I'm more than a bare bum and a pair of boobs. I need to demonstrate how witty and sparkling I am. 'Er . . .yes,' I stammer.

Well. It's a start.

'Then there are the men's magazines. *Loaded. Front. FHM. Maxim. GQ.* They'd be interested. *Playboy* would probably offer you a fortune,' he says. 'Would you consider nude spreads?'

What exactly would I have to spread? I want to ask.

'Er . . .' Nothing else will come out.

'You're a very attractive woman, Emily. The hair suits you,' he says, pointing a long, slender finger at it. 'Makes you look demure.'

That's a laugh. The whole world knows that I have moments when I'm distinctly not demure.

'I like it. The two faces of Emily Miller. Schoolteacher and good-time girl.'

Oh God. What am I doing?

'We may need to change it if you agree to a photo-shoot. But let's talk about that later.' He doesn't even pause for me to consider it. Do I want to look like a victim or a whore is what he actually means. 'We can turn this round,' Jonathan assures me. 'Turn it to your advantage. You can come out of this a very wealthy woman. You need never go back to teaching.'

I open my mouth and close it again. It seems rather pointless to mention that I actually quite liked teaching. Love it, in fact. There is a world shortage of teachers. But not, I feel, a world shortage of women who will get their tits out for some hard cash.

'How does half a million sound to you, Emily?'

'Er . . .' I say again. But I sound much more confident this time.

Half a million? Pounds, I take it. The devastation of my life turned into a lottery win? Is it possible?

'It's a very achievable figure.' Jonathan nods at me as if I've spoken my thoughts out loud. 'As I've said, it's up to you.'

At this point, he gets up and walks round his desk. God, he's so persuasive. A halo of confidence shines round him. He'd have had no trouble getting me into a Saucy Santa outfit, on the Internet or anywhere else for that matter.

He pulls a card out of a silver container on his desktop and hands it to me. 'Here,' he says. 'I want you to give this guy a ring.'

I look at the card. It says *Sebastian Atherton, Photographer* in classy black type.

'Get him to do some shots of you. Nothing seedy. Tasteful stuff. He can send the bill to me. Do it quickly before the press lose interest in you.' Jonathan shrugs. 'Next week they'll snap a Member of Parliament with someone else's wife and you'll be old news. If you want a decent retirement fund, we need to move quickly.'

'Yes,' I say. I know. It's a bit late to be finding my voice now.

'A friend of mine is opening a wine bar on Saturday night. Be there,' he instructs with a soft smile and hands me another card which turns out to be an invitation. *Temptation*, it says. Quite. 'I'll see you around nine.'

Jonathan moves forward. 'So?' He touches my elbow as he shakes my hand and his sparkling eyes fix on mine. 'Do we have a deal?'

I feel a hot rush leap up my throat. 'Yes,' I say. And as I leave his office, feeling slightly dazed, I realise that I've absolutely no idea what I've just agreed to.

Chapter Thirty-Eight

Adam sat on Toff's desk, leafing through page after page of scantily clad women. It was a grey winter evening and icy fingers of rain tip-tapped sharply at the window. Toff's office was bathed in a mellow, warm light and the temperature inside was sweltering. Adam was boiling alive in his sweater, but then apart from Toff, most of the people who passed through here in the course of a day didn't have the benefit of warm jumpers.

'And you call this work?' Adam said, looking down on his friend who sat swigging one of the cold beers that he'd pulled from the fridge for both of them.

'Absolutely, sweetheart,' Sebastian Atherton said. 'Many's the day I've had to take to my bed with camera clicker's finger.'

'Alone?'

'Sometimes it helps to have company.' His friend smiled. 'It takes one's mind off it.'

Adam put down Toff's portfolio. 'I've got to do something,' he said. 'How can I pursue Laura for custody of Josh if I'm working shifts? Speaking of which . . .' He checked his watch as he was due at the *Hampstead Observer* this evening. He wasn't even sure why the paper needed overnight staffing – it was known as the graveyard shift and, normally, it was indeed quieter than one.

'It would suit me down to the ground, old boy,' Toff said. 'I could toddle off on all these exotic assignments abroad . . .'

'Risking a tropical strain of camera clicker's finger . . .'

Toff nodded enthusiastically. 'And I'd know that I could leave this place in safe hands while I was away.'

Adam folded his arms and blew out an exasperated sigh.

'What rent do you pay on that poky flat of yours?' Toff asked.

'Too much,' Adam said.

Adam had moved back to Hampstead as soon as he could to be nearer to Josh. He rented a tiny attic flat in Parliament Hill that had been advertised with a stunning view over Hampstead Heath. And it did, indeed, have *a* view of Hampstead Heath. It was just that you had to stand on the toilet seat and peer out of a window the size of a cornflakes box to enjoy it.

There was just enough room in the main bedroom to walk round the bed. The spare room held a single futon and served as a wardrobe, office-cum-camera store and general dumping ground for things that he didn't know what else to do with. When his son had first started to stay at Adam's flat when he was four, Josh had cried because he missed Laura so much. Adam had taken him home at midnight still in his pyjamas, distressed and bawling the place down. Even though it was now eight years later, it was something his ex-wife had never forgotten. Although, thankfully, Josh had, he was still only allowed to stay overnight on rare occasions – usually when it suited Laura's plans. When Josh was smaller he had been able to roll out the futon for him. Since then, Adam's store of clutter had grown in direct proportion to his son's gangly limbs and it was no longer a viable option. Now, when Josh stayed, he took Adam's bed and Adam was relegated to a 1950s sofa bed which had more foothills nestling in the mattress than the Himalayas.

Yet, despite its cramped and compromised conditions, the rent for the flat still took up most of his salary. After his maintenance payments had been scooped off the top, he was invariably broke. Perhaps this was why his social life didn't consist of eating out in bijou little restaurants every night. On the plus side, the flat was within walking distance of both Patel's Off Licence and Curry Paradise.

'There's a flat upstairs,' Toff said. 'It's huge. Take that.' He nodded towards the garden. The thick lush trees were being tugged back and forth by the wind. Adam knew how they felt. 'Josh would love that,' Toff continued. 'You could play football together.'

Adam ground his teeth together. 'It's tempting.'

'I'll charge you the same rent.'

'I couldn't do that,' Adam said. 'What about you?'

'Darling,' Toff tutted, 'Daddy has places all over Town. I've never got round to moving in here. Anyway, it's not good for me to live above the shop.'

'Would it be good for Josh though?' Adam said. 'Supposing he bumped into some of your "clients"?'

'He's a twelve-year-old boy, for heaven's sake,' Sebastian said. 'The biggest problem you'd have would be keeping his friends away. Think of the street cred.'

'Think of what his mother would say,' Adam gloomed.

'It strikes me, old bean, that you think far too much of what his mother would say. It's time to break free from the lovely Laura and start doing what suits *you*.'

'I can't,' Adam said. 'We are locked permanently together by the fruit of our loins. You've no idea what it's like with your carefree single life.'

'No,' Toff admitted, 'I don't. But I am trying to help.'

Adam grinned. 'Do you know, Toff, I've been looking for someone like you all my life. If you weren't a bloke, I think I'd be seriously in love with you.'

'Now you're starting to sound like Chris,' Toff said.

Adam jumped down from his perch on Sebastian's desk. 'Kill me,' he said.

'Come out with me,' Toff said. 'Tomorrow night.'

'I was only joking, Toff. You're not really my type,' Adam laughed.

'When did you last have some fun?'

'Last Tuesday.'

'You did not,' Toff said. 'Don't you ever go out and let your hair down?'

'No,' Adam said.

'Well, you're coming out with me.'

'I'm on night shift all week.'

'On Saturday?' Toff asked. 'You're not working then?'

'No,' Adam conceded.

'It's fixed then.'

There seemed little point in arguing. Adam shrugged on his coat, mentally preparing himself to dive out into the cold and rain from the warmth and cosiness of Toff's cocoon. Looking round him again, Adam decided that he and Josh could do a lot worse than take up Toff's kind and wholly uneconomical offer.

'Cheers, Toff,' Adam said, hugging his mate. 'I warn you though. I never do sex on a first date.'

Toff grinned. 'You might change your mind when you see who your date is, old fruit.'

Chapter Thirty-Nine

Cara was feeling terrible. Waves of nauseous guilt washed over her whenever she pictured Emily bounding out of her car in the pouring rain and rushing down into the depths of the Underground. Emily had turned and smiled at her as if she, Cara, was the best friend anyone could ever have. Little did Emily know that she had spent yesterday evening with her boyfriend, ex-boyfriend, and had enjoyed every minute of it.

Cara chewed the end of her pen, careless of the fact that she might well end up with a mouthful of blue ink, gazing aimlessly at Emily's poster on the wall. The office was empty, a graveyard of computer headstones stretching out across the paper-strewn wasteland of the newsroom. Whatever had happened to the concept of the paper-free office? Computers seemed to generate more paperwork than ever, if that was possible. It didn't matter whether it was day or night here. The office was soulless, windowless and airless. Flickering banks of fluorescent lights shone down relentlessly directly over the desks, giving even the hardiest members of staff headaches by the end of their stint. At night-time, the effect was softened by a few well-positioned desk lamps. The money tree in the wealth corner of Cara's desk wilted in the battle between the chilly onslaught of air-conditioning and the dry, baking central heating. This place was probably a hotbed of germs, Cara thought, and vowed to increase her uptake of Echinacea.

Declan was a mystery. Cara rubbed her fingers over her throat. Last night had been great. She hadn't enjoyed herself so much since . . . since before she could remember. This was a very bad sign. They had laughed too long and too loud over Declan's continued declaration of vegetarianism – particularly when he was eating a medium-rare steak at the time. She'd always liked Declan. He was Emily's boyfriend. And he was very hard not to like. OK, so he was a complete rogue, but he had a bit of life to him, a spark of character missing from so many browbeaten men these days. Perhaps it was the crushing pressure of work and climbing the corporate ladder that squeezed the fun out of people. Declan had teased her relentlessly about her beliefs, calling them superstitious nonsense, but she hadn't minded. She had laughed with him. Declan could do that to you.

And he had talked about Emily a lot too. They both had, she consoled herself. They both wanted what was best for Emily. It was just that she had thought a lot more about Declan today than she had her best friend.

Adam sat down in front of her. 'Penny for them,' he said with a smile.

'Oh, Adam.' Cara snapped back to the present. She leaned forward on her desk. 'I was thinking about Emily.'

'How's she doing?' He slipped off his coat, shaking raindrops from his mass of dark hair, and settled himself in front of his computer before turning to face Cara instead of his screen.

'Better, I think,' Cara said. 'She's dyed her hair. A sort of disguise. It looks great. She went out for the first time today.'

'Good,' Adam said. 'That's good.'

It was fair to say that Adam seemed to care more about Emily – someone he had never met – than her own boyfriend, ex-boyfriend, did. Adam was such a nice guy.

'Sorry I'm a bit late,' he said.

Cara glanced at the deserted offices. 'I don't think this place will fall apart without us.'

'No,' Adam said, following her gaze. 'I was just trying to sort out a few bits myself.' He looked uncomfortable.

'Anything I can help with?' Cara asked.

Adam shook his head. His hair was curling damply round his face. Cara swallowed.

'No.' Adam pulled at his earlobe. 'Well . . . Laura's trying to take Josh to Australia,' he said in a rush. 'And I'm trying to stop her.' His cheeks flushed.

'Oh.'

'I think I might have found a solution.'

'Can you share it?'

'No,' Adam said. 'Not yet.' He fidgeted around with some copy on his desk. 'I'll keep you posted though.'

Cara smiled softly at him and Adam turned back to his desk, scratching at his stubble. It had clearly taken an effort for him to confide so much in her and Cara felt a warm glow spread through her tummy, which was an awful lot nicer than the way she had been feeling. She was going to have to up her campaign of letting the universe direct love into her life. At the moment it was doing nothing but confuse her.

140

Chapter Forty

'He said *what*?' Cara is outraged.

'Keep your voice down,' I hiss. The press were late arriving this morning and so we sneaked out to the Café Blanco for breakfast. The Café Blanco is the nearest Hampstead will ever get to a greasy spoon. And, to my shame, I was sort of peeved that there wasn't the usual battalion of photographers waiting to greet my arrival at Cara's front door. It makes me feel shallow, and hypocritical, but I guess that's the lure of celebrity. Don't want to live with it, don't want to live without it.

'You can't possibly be thinking of getting your kit off for a men's magazine!' At least Cara has lowered her voice.

'Half a million quid,' I point out. 'That's what he said. Wouldn't you consider it?'

Cara stops to consider it. 'No,' she says righteously. 'I have principles.'

And tits that aren't big enough for you to be asked in the first place, I think maliciously.

'I have principles too,' I say. 'And I also have priorities. Right now, my main one is to get myself out of debt.'

Cara looks unconvinced. She is so disgruntled that she hasn't even touched her chocolate croissant.

'You're forgetting,' I point out, 'that the world and his wife have already seen my bum, and I haven't received a penny for it. The only one who's made any money out of it is darling Declan.'

Cara goes red. Which I take as an admission that there is some truth in there.

'I have to consider this, Cara.' I rip my own croissant in half. 'Much as I'd rather not.' I stuff the buttery pastry in my mouth with a defiant gesture. What I really wanted to eat was sausages, but bowed to my friend's sensibilities in the eating animals department. Now I wish I hadn't bothered.

'And he's going to organise all this for you?' Cara says. 'This Jonathan Gold.' I see the thundercloud scud across her face.

141

I nod. 'That's where I was yesterday.'

'You're mad,' she says.

'Desperate,' I correct. 'I have a few weeks to capitalise on my notoriety and try to stop my debts spiralling out of control.'

There is very little Cara can say to disagree.

I avoid looking at my friend. 'He asked me to go to the launch of a wine bar with him.'

'In what capacity?'

I feel myself cringe as I admit this. 'I'm not really sure.'

'Oh great!' Cara's eyes shoot upwards. 'You may have dyed your hair brown, Emily, but you are still very much a blonde inside.'

At the moment, I haven't the strength to deny it. Cara picks up her croissant and puts it down again. 'So is it a date with him or what?'

'I don't know.'

'And are you going to go?'

I lay awake for most of last night trying to work that one out. 'I think I'll have to,' I say. 'To show that I'm willing.'

'To do what?' Cara snorts.

'To do whatever it takes to get me out of this mess!' I can't eat this croissant. I'm going to throw up. I'm glad I didn't have sausages. 'My reputation is in tatters. I've no home and no job. Now I could go and work in a shop for five pounds an hour or I could think . . .' Cara opens her mouth; I hold my finger up and she decides against speaking. 'Or I could *think* about what Jonathan Gold is proposing to do and become a wealthy woman. What would you do in my situation?'

'I would think very, very carefully, Emily.' Cara takes my hand. 'This may be a quick fix to your problem and, no doubt, it would bring you much-needed money. But don't forget, my friend, in going down this route there will be a price to pay. And you may not realise how much until it's far too late.'

Chapter Forty-One

Adam was sitting in the back of a black cab feeling very uncomfortable. There were probably fish out of water who were more relaxed than he was. Adam tried to smooth down the more maniacal of his curls with his hand, but he could see from his reflection in the cab window that they were just springing spitefully back into their chosen place the minute he let go. He turned and smiled at his date for the night.

She was called Jemima and he could quite safely say that he'd never dated a Jemima before. Jemima smiled back. She was poured into a tight Lycra creation that she said was a Herve Leger, whatever that was. Adam thought he was supposed to be impressed and smiled at her and nodded thoughtfully as if he was. He had never been out with anyone before, Jemima or not, who had worn so little clothing. The Herve Leger seemed to press her chest upwards and outwards at a gravity-defying level and, at the other end, it barely skimmed her bottom. It gave the impression that she was encased in a very small, tight elastic stocking.

Toff was sitting opposite him and Toff's date, Fenella, was similarly attired. It was a good job they weren't going to the Jiggery-Pokery. Walter the barman would have passed out. Shame, though, that Chris wasn't here to witness it – although he, too, would have needed smelling salts and a bucket to drool into. Adam smiled to himself. He was going to try to relax and enjoy it. Jemima was definitely going to turn heads and he felt thrilled, in a vaguely embarrassed fashion.

There was no way, he knew, that Jemima would have gone out with him if Toff hadn't set it all up. Jemima would have looked more at home on the arm of a leather-tanned, seventy-year-old multi-millionaire with white shoes, a large yacht and a bad cough. Fenella and Jemima were both models who worked regularly with Toff, and Adam was beginning to appreciate more and more the obvious attractions of his friend's rather glamorous job. And he was sure that if he hadn't felt quite so tense, he'd be having a great time.

143

They were going to the opening of a new wine bar. One of Toff's friends who owned a model agency had branched out into ritzy hostelries too and had invited Toff along to the launch. Toff had decided that Adam needed to live a little and he was probably right. Being able to recite the entire programme content of the *Radio Times* was not necessarily a sign of a man living a wild social whirl.

Adam tugged at his shirt collar. He'd forgotten what proper grown-up going out was like. His suit felt like it belonged to someone else, it was so long since he'd worn it. Adam wasn't sure when he'd lost his zest for dating. When he and Laura had split he'd embarked on a campaign of short-lived flings – all with perfectly acceptable women. Perhaps it was when Josh had started to play a more active part in the proceedings that women-hopping had lost its lustre. There were only so many 'aunties' that you could introduce to a messy, boisterous five year old.

The women, in turn, had either treated Josh as if he were some sort of temporary inconvenience to be dealt with or they'd cooed and gooed over him in gushing terms, indicating that they too were keen to start a family. It was soul-destroying really. The worst type of man to try to interest in starting a family is one who already knows what it's like. Having done it once, Adam was in no way keen to rush in and repeat the experience. And, despite the theories about men wanting to spread their genes to every woman they met, he didn't want London to be littered with a band of Adam lookalikes borne by a dozen different mothers. Unfortunately, most of the women that he met these days were over thirty and had neon lights flashing over their heads saying: *Desperate for a baby! Desperate for a baby!*

He smiled over at Jemima again and she, in turn, smiled back. It was one of those sickly smile exchanges that says 'I really haven't a clue what to say to you.' How old was she? he wondered. Twenty-five? Maybe less. Certainly not the type who would want to rush into handing over the ruination of her figure to Mother Nature.

He would have to start talking to her soon, Adam thought. But what about? It was ages since he'd done the small-talk thing and he'd never been very good at it then. That's why he enjoyed talking to Cara. She was the sort of person who seemed to understand every-thing, even though most of the time she was on a completely different planet than the rest of them. At least it gave you a refreshing new perspective on life.

'We're here,' Toff said as they pulled up outside a swish-looking wine bar.

A crowd of young, trendy people thronged outside as two burly dinner-suited security guards checked their invitations. His friend jumped out and settled the cab fare whilst the two girls tried to feed themselves out of the door without showing their underwear to the world.

'OK?' Toff asked.

Adam nodded. He couldn't have been more nervous if he'd tried.

Toff slapped him on the back. 'Stick with me, old fruit. You'll be fine.'

'Come on, Sebastian,' Fenella said. 'Chop, chop. There's ice-cold champagne waiting to be drunk.'

'OK,' Toff said and strode off to join her. And as Adam and Jemima fell into step behind them, he wondered whether he'd ever be able to call Toff by his real name without laughing.

Chapter Forty-Two

We pull up outside *Temptation* in Cara's battered old 2CV. The engine clatters to an ungainly halt. I am clutching my clutch bag and now know why they're called that. A row of heads from the waiting queue turns to stare at us and I'm trying to convince myself that it's because Cara's car is like O'Rafferty's motor car – forty different shades of green – and covered in a rash of politically correct stickers, anything from SAVE THE WHALE! to HOW GREEN IS YOUR WASHING POWDER? It's a very embarrassing car to be seen alive in.

'You are going to be all right?' Cara says nervously, nibbling her nail.

'Fine,' I answer nervously, nibbling mine in return.

I've borrowed Cara's beaded bag and raided her wardrobe to find something that wasn't tie-dyed in the 1970s or hand-embroidered by ethnic gypsies. I also needed something that would accommodate the difference in the size of our respective chests and settled on a floaty chiffon number in hot pink that Cara had picked up second-hand from the Portobello Road Market. If I buy things in the Portobello Road Market they look second-hand, but this is fabulous and not at all the sort of outfit that I'd normally wear. It's wraparound and wispy and strappy, and I think it probably looks more wraparound on Cara than on me. But if I am going to launch myself into the world for my fifteen minutes of fame as an exploited sex symbol then I must get used to showing a bit of flesh.

I check my newly dyed Chestnut Burst hair in the vanity mirror for the thousandth time. 'Do I look OK?' I say to Cara.

'You look a lot more tarty in that dress than I do,' she says candidly and I detect a distinct note of pique.

'Thanks.'

'You look tarty, but great,' she concedes. 'They'll probably think you're a soap starlet or the latest pop singer or something.'

'That's the general idea.' I spent hours carefully applying layer-upon-layer of make-up too, rather than my usual five minutes of scribble before I rush out of the door. My nails are filed and painted

– all twenty of them. I am exfoliated and depilated to within an inch of my life.

'Are you sure you don't want me to come in with you?'

Cara is wearing flared, frayed denims and a faded FCUK T-shirt that was probably once black. Her dreadlocks are tied in a bunch on top of her head with something that looks like string.

'No,' I say with an emphatic shake of my head. 'I have to do this alone.'

'Ring me when you want collecting,' my friend says.

'You don't have to collect me. I can get a cab.'

'Call me,' Cara insists. 'I don't want you to do anything stupid.'

'Isn't it rather too late for that?' I point out.

'Take this,' Cara says and she thrusts a small, clear stone into my hand.

'What is it?'

'A quartz crystal,' she says.

Ah! Why didn't I know that? I examine it closely. 'What am I supposed to do with it?'

'It will help to protect you.'

'From what?'

'Anything the universe can throw at you,' Cara tells me solemnly.

'Oh, good.' One little stone? You've got to be joking. I tuck it into Cara's beaded bag. It's the thought that counts. At least someone is worrying about me – other than myself, of course. I squeeze Cara's hand. 'I feel better already.'

Cara looks at the queue. 'Go on,' she instructs. 'There aren't many people waiting now. You won't have to hang around.'

'Thanks.' I lean over and kiss her on the cheek. 'You're a pal.'

'Have a good time,' she says. Cara looks worried to death. You'd think I was going to have an operation, not a few convivial drinks at a new hip-hop happening wine bar.

'I'll try to.'

'Not too good,' Cara adds with a sigh. 'I don't want to see you on the front page of the *Sunday Sport* tomorrow snogging a Second-Division footballer.'

And I wonder, if I'm caught in a compromising position with a publicity supremo, would he be able to keep it off the front page?

Chapter Forty-Three

The wine bar was packed. Very. Adam and Jemima were squashed up against one of the bars and Adam was finding it very difficult not to stare down the top of her Herve Leger creation. Her breasts were forming milky-white flawless domes that brimmed over the edge of her black dress like the head on the top of a well-poured Guinness.

There was a sprinkling of people who Adam thought he recognised, but then he was utterly useless on names. They were pretty television-type guys and girls who were probably out of *Casualty*, *The Bill* and *London's Burning* – that sort of stuff. Josh would have known them all. They squeezed past Adam and Jemima, making a beeline for the free bar just as they'd done.

The place was decorated in an eclectic pseudo-French style – Louis XVI meets *Eurotrash*. The chairs were ornate, gilt-backed with crushed Burgundy velvet seats and the walls were deep turquoise, studded with ruby-coloured jewel lights and curving gilt mirrors. It was hard to see the rest of the decoration as there were so many people obscuring it, but it was clear that the white ash floor was getting stickier by the minute.

A matchbox-size dance floor was situated at one end and a dozen or so beautiful babes strutted their funky stuff to the pounding beat. Boy George had been drafted in as DJ for the night and the music was great, but loud enough to make conversation impossible. Adam leaned closer to Jemima, enveloping himself in the cloud of her sweet perfume.

'Do you enjoy being a model?' he shouted in her ear.

She smiled. 'What?'

'A model?' Adam yelled. 'Like it?'

'Yes,' Jemima shouted back.

Adam nodded appreciatively. 'Have you been doing it long?'

'What?'

'Long?' Adam realised his vocal cords weren't going to last out for the night at this level. 'Long?' he shouted again. 'Doing it?'

'Yes,' Jemima yelled.

Adam stifled a sigh and swigged his freebie champagne. Why was it that fizz always tasted better when you weren't providing it yourself? Toff looked across at him from where he was sandwiched between the bar and Fenella. He gave Adam a surreptitious thumbs-up and Adam nodded, feeling that he ought to try harder at communicating with his date. After all, Toff had gone to a lot of trouble to set this up and drag him out of his shell. Although, sad as this may sound, he was acutely aware that he was missing *Stars in Their Eyes Kids Special*.

Adam cleared his throat. 'Do you travel a lot?' he shouted.

'What?'

'Travel?'

'Yes.' Jemima was clearly determined to save *her* vocal cords.

'Where to?'

'Yes.'

Perhaps they should have gone to a restaurant first and got all this inane chit-chat out of the way first. This was a terrible situation. He didn't know Jemima and, consequently, wanted to make the effort to, but it all felt rather like trying to push water uphill. She patently did not have the same desire to enquire about any aspects of his life. Maybe Jemima had been to too many of these things to consider putting more effort in than it warranted. But then they couldn't just stand here and grin inanely at each other all night. There was only one thing for it.

'Do you want to dance?' Adam shouted.

'What?'

'Dance? Do you want to?'

'What?'

'Dance!' Louder this time.

'What?'

'DANCE!'

'Yes,' Jemima said.

Things were looking up. He was a bit of an old twinkle-toes on the dance floor even though he said it himself. Well, he usually said it himself because no one else did.

Jemima gave him her empty glass. 'Champagne!'

Adam took the glass and stared at it. Jemima was scanning the room to see if there was anyone more interesting to shout at.

'You really haven't a clue what I'm talking about, have you?' Adam said quietly.

Jemima turned to him and smiled. 'No,' she said.

Chapter Forty-Four

My nerve nearly gives out as I have my invitation checked and walk through the doors to *Temptation*. I turn and give Cara a sickly-looking wave and realise that I could quite happily jump into her car and scoot straight back home.

I've always cringed at those young starlets who display more naked ambition than they do talent or modesty when they appear in the newspapers, snapped at the National Television Awards, dressed only in their underwear and something little bigger than a crisp packet that's supposed to be a dress. And here I am doing the same thing. I have a vain attempt at making the pink chiffon cross further over my breasts and fail. I blame Liz Hurley for starting it all in 'that' non-existent dress and I'm beginning to wish I'd worn something a bit less revealing. But this is hardly the behaviour of Hampstead's latest 'It' girl and so I gird my loins and do all that sort of British stuff that gets us through these situations and I push into the heaving mass of bodies, wondering how on earth I'm going to find Jonathan Gold in the midst of this lot. I had planned to be fashionably late, but old habits die hard and I'm massively early as I always am for everything.

Weaving my way through the chattering glitterati, I give up saying my litany of 'excuse me', 'excuse me', 'excuse me', 'excuse me' and just end up shoving inelegantly until I reach the complimentary bar. I'm glad that everything's free. I'm not sure my bank account would stand the bashing if I had to pay to go to a celebrity party. Cara is being wonderful about putting my rent on the slate at the moment, but I can't continue accepting her charity for ever. Why should she fork out for the mistakes I've made? I can see, at this point, how useful a sugar daddy would be to a wannabe 'It' girl.

I take my glass of champagne from the waiter with a tinkling laugh, which I hope disguises the fact that I'm the only person in the room who knows absolutely no one here. It fails miserably. He looks at me as if to say, 'You don't fit, do you, sweetie?' and I give him a cool, disdainful look, but really what I most want to do is push

Cara's quartz crystal up his nose or cry. My friend should have given me a bigger bit of stone – one the size of a house brick, at least – because this one is doing absolutely nothing towards providing protection. Against anything.

I move away from the waiter, only to find I'm surrounded by an ecstatic bunch of air-kissers, who are all clearly bosom buddies, or soon will be, and every one of their *mwoa, mwoa, mwoas* makes me feel lonelier and lonelier.

I'm used to doing coupley things. For most of my life I've been one half of someone else and I'm beginning to think this independence lark is overrated. Doing things on your own is not a lot of fun. Walking hand-in-hand in the park, watching sunsets, paying bills – all infinitely better when shared. Declan and I would have been giggling intimately over something ridiculous by now and I'd be hanging onto his arm for grim death and just that silly little act would have given me all the confidence I'm now lacking. This is the sort of do that Declan would adore – being seen in the right place with the right people, wearing the right clothing. In the midst of all these half-dressed people, I realise that I am nothing without a publicist to promote me. I am a little inconsequential splash of paint on a big, blowsy Jackson Pollack canvas. It's an interesting lesson. 'Interesting' in a self-esteem crushing way. I squeeze back towards the front of the bar and try to look for Jonathan without staring too overtly at everyone.

This looks like a wonderful and trendy place, but I'm far too stressed to be enjoying it. If I grip my champagne glass any harder, the stem will shatter. A waiter stops by my side and foists some canapés on me that I don't really want. They're little circles of raw fish on pumpernickel bread with a blob of pesto poised on the top. I'm not doing them justice, really they look very nice. And fiddly. Reluctantly, I choose one because I haven't a clue how I'm going to manage juggling my fizz and food. I smile politely, which comes out as a case of rictus, and he moves away.

Elbowing through another happy crowd lingering at the foot of the stairs, I'm jogged by a short man in a suede jacket and nearly end up wearing my food down the front of Cara's dress.

'Sorry,' he says, but he barely pays me any attention and doesn't look sorry at all and I feel like pushing my fish and pesto in his face.

I climb up a few steps, hoping that it will give me a better overview and I can keep an eye on the door to see the late arrival of my date/business contact/manager/guru/saviour – I have no idea what to call him.

I lean on the banister, eat my fishy bit without tasting it and survey the scene. All the women are showing acres of flesh and rather than feeling underdressed, I feel a bit overdone. Their paucity of clothing serves to make the world their gynaecologist. They are all candidates for indecent Internet exposure and I wonder why it had to happen to me rather than any of them. I only pranced around my bedroom in suggestive outfits, not your local hostelry. I hitch my insubstantial pink chiffon round my chest. How times change. You never know what goes on in people's lives behind closed doors. We all have secrets, don't we? And most people seem to manage to keep it that way. Declan certainly gave me no indication that he was going to turn into a complete git overnight.

I let my eyes rove over the couples at the bar and as I do, I'm brought to an abrupt halt by the sight of the most gorgeous man I've seen in years. I'm so astounded that I start to cough and splutter my mouthful of champagne. He's tall and very dark, with mad ruffled hair and fabulous soulful eyes. He looks bored to death by the woman he's with, even though she could give Kate Winslet a run for her money, and his eyes are roaming round the room too. Suddenly he looks up and catches me staring at him. And I have a thunderbolt moment.

I've never had one before, but now it's happened, I know exactly what it is. My arms are all buzzy and numb and my heart has decided to have a palpitation. I think it's playing a Ricky Martin tune. I know instinctively that I should be with this man. My nipples are tweaking towards him all of their own accord and I can safely say that my nipples have never taken on a life of their own before. Hormones are crazy things, aren't they? Some days I can't control mine at all. They are clearly operating on the random chaos theory at the moment and have decided that this man, despite the fact he is with someone else, is the man I should breed with. Nor have they paid any attention to my declarations of being a man-free zone. I specifically lodged in my brain that I was allowed to do dating, but that I was not to have these sort of emotions for a long, long time. My body pays about as much attention to me as my pupils in Year 10.

This man looks like trouble with a capital T. An all-action totty magnet if ever I saw one. There's mischief written in every line on his face and I've done mischief and it hurts. This time I wanted nice with a capital N. A Goldilocks boyfriend – someone who's not too hot, not too cold, but just right. I want someone who likes children and is kind to dogs and who doesn't laugh at the joke about women wearing white when they get married so that they match their kitchen appliances. I suspect that this man, for all his heart-melting deliciousness, will have LOVE THEM, LEAVE THEM tattooed on his rather attractive biceps. I have developed an instinct for these things, over the years. Believe me, this is one dude to avoid.

I can feel myself flush and as our eyes meet, he twitches his lips in an amused smile. Be still my beating heart! This is ludicrous. My legs seem determined to collapse under me. They've gone all jellyfied and I'm glad that at this moment I'm not required to perform any walking skills. Cara's little crystal is still doing bugger all to protect me. Particularly from myself, it seems. I think it's about time that it kicked in. I really want to smile back, but I'm terrified his girlfriend will turn round at that precise moment and I'll end up on the front page of the *Hampstead Observer* having a bar-room brawl with a jealous harpy. That would be all I'd need. But I'd like to bet you a pound to an organic pumpkin seed that they've got one of their low-life photographers lurking in here somewhere.

Chapter Forty-Five

Cara was fed up. She was watching the clock go round and worrying about Emily. Worrying was very bad for releasing free radicals in the body, so she would get old and wrinkly before her time and it would all be Emily's fault.

Staring at her pot of camomile tea, Cara tried to ignore the native North-American Indian chant droning away on the CD player. What exactly was she doing at the tender age of thirty-two, sitting at home alone on a Saturday night listening to Navajo pining the demise of Buffalo and fretting that her friend was enjoying herself too much?

Cara scooped up another spoonful of water from the small white china bowl in front of her. The water was infused with rose oil, a rose quartz crystal and rosemary. She wore a pink ribbon tied round her hair and three pink candles burned in white saucers in a neat line in front of her. Cara eyed the water suspiciously and sprinkled it over her hair. She sighed deeply. 'Lover, lover, come to me. I have spoken, so it will be.'

This was supposed to be a spell to attract a reluctant lover. Someone who should be in love with you but didn't yet realise it. Cara didn't feel it was working, but then to be fair she hadn't really given it much chance. She'd only been doing it for half an hour, which wasn't long enough for it to travel round the deep recesses of space and find its target. Also, she kept getting interrupted by thoughts of Emily and what she might be up to.

This spell was also supposed to help her feel more loved, and she didn't. Not by a long chalk. With all the magically enhanced water she'd dripped on her hair, she was feeling like nothing more spiritual than a drowned rat. It was all very well trusting in the universe, but sometimes the universe required you to do very silly things. She knew that everyone else thought she was potty and sometimes, just sometimes, she suspected they might be right.

Cara looked at her mobile phone. Adam's number was lurking in there and she wondered what he might be doing on a Saturday night. Probably out enjoying a nice quiet candle-lit dinner for two with some air-headed bimbo somewhere. She was certain that he wouldn't be sitting in alone drinking herbal tea and throwing rose water on his curly locks. Cara's fingers hovered over her phone. Would it be wrong to ring him just to find out? After all, she was only being sociable. There was nothing in it. Biting her lip, she carefully pressed the numbers into her keypad. The phone rang and, in a rush of panic, Cara hung up. No, she wouldn't ring him. It smacked of desperation. If he wanted her he was going to have to make the first move. Cara flung herself back on the sofa. The North-American Indians reached a wailing crescendo. She could always ring Declan. Hopefully, he was so flat broke that he'd be in on a Saturday night. Perhaps she might offer to take round a bottle of wine.

An hour later she stood outside Declan's new front door clutching a bottle of Chardonnay like a security blanket, disheartened to see her little 2CV looking particularly shabby parked in the rather majestic drive.

This was the posh end of Hampstead. Multi-millionaires row. The habitat of film stars, Arab sheiks and ex-Spice Girls. Seven figures round here wouldn't even buy you a lock-up garage. These were the houses with grilles on the windows, security lights that would give Blackpool Illuminations a run for their money and twiddly wrought-iron railings that made up in quantity what they lacked in taste. Declan grinned as he stood aside and let her in. Cara had to admit that its over-the-top style suited him.

'This is a bit posh,' she said, taking in the opulence of Adrian and Amanda's hall. The ceiling bore a replica of *God's Creation of Adam* from the Sistine Chapel and several very sparkly chandeliers. Cara shook her head. 'You even do poverty in style.'

'Friends are letting me stay here while they're away on holiday,' Declan explained, taking the wine and her coat.

Cara followed him through to the kitchen, trying to remember which of Declan's and Emily's friends were so well heeled. 'That's kind of them.'

'Yeah,' Declan said. 'I've got to try to remember to water their plants in return.'

'It seems a very small price to pay.'

'Yes,' Declan said as he busied himself with the wine.

'It's lovely,' Cara said, examining the Smallbone white, hand-painted kitchen and the Conran furniture. Bourgeois, but nice. Everything that her parents would hate and for which Cara feared she had a secret hankering. She slid onto one of the stools by the breakfast bar and stroked the marble top lovingly. 'It's a bit close to

155

home though,' she remarked. 'Aren't you worried about bumping into Emily in the High Street?'

'I'm half hoping that I might,' Declan admitted.

'Yeah?' Cara looked concerned. 'Well, I hope that she's not carrying a large French stick at the time.'

Declan looked like a lost little boy. 'Is she still mad at me?'

'Of course she's still mad at you!' Cara said. 'She will be until you give her back some of the money you've filched from her.'

'I'm trying,' Declan assured her. 'Jaysus knows, I'm trying. It won't be long, I promise.'

'How's business doing?' she asked.

'Better,' Declan said with a feeble shrug. 'There have been some new developments and I'm starting to claw my way back.'

'Good. Emily will be pleased.'

Declan stopped and looked at her. 'Where is she tonight?' he asked, struggling in an effort to sound as casual as he could manage.

'Out,' Cara supplied. 'She's gone to the opening of a wine bar.' She thought it wise to leave out any mention of her date, or whatever it was, with Jonathan Gold.

'I'm glad she's getting out and about,' Declan said, but he didn't look as if he was.

'Mmm,' Cara agreed, as Declan handed her a glass of wine.

'Why didn't you go with her?'

'She's on an independence kick,' Cara said. 'I think she wanted to feel the fear and do it anyway.'

'Oh.' Declan looked very down-hearted. 'I thought we both could have gone down there.'

'Invitation only.'

'Oh.' Declan's heart seemed to sink a little bit further. 'So she's managing all right without me?'

Cara pressed her lips together. 'Yes,' she said, then reached out and patted his hand. It didn't seem pertinent to mention that Emily was managing all right *in spite* of Declan.

'I've got a hot tub,' he said brightly in an effort to change the subject.

Cara could tell he was trying to sound cheerful, but the twinkle had gone out of his eyes and she wondered how responsible Emily had been for putting it there.

'Wonderful,' she said. 'I've never been in a hot tub.'

The twinkle sparkled into life again. He nodded towards the conservatory. 'Want to try it out?'

Cara shook her head. 'I've nothing to wear.'

'That's the general idea.'

156

Declan strolled through to the hot tub and motioned for Cara to follow him. She slid off her stool and, taking her wine with her, walked after him.

The conservatory was a huge hexagonal shape and the tendrils of luscious tropical flowering plants twined their way up towards the glass roof. The hot tub sat directly in the middle, echoing the geometric lines. Declan pulled away the wooden cover and a waft of warm steam rose into the air. The heavy, colourful flowers of the plants seemed to lick their lips in delight. He flicked on a switch and the room was bathed in a subdued golden glow that flowed from brushed steel uplighters.

'Wow,' Cara said.

'Candles too.' Declan picked up a conveniently placed box of matches and worked his way along the row of candles, taking his time to light them and watch as the flames flickered tentatively and then caught.

The inky blackness of the night pressed in against the windows and Cara wrapped her arms round herself as she shivered in this warm, safe cocoon.

'Sure that you won't change your mind?' Declan raised an eyebrow, his words part invitation, part challenge.

'If you'd said, I would have brought a swimsuit.'

'Have a root through Amanda's cupboards,' Declan offered. 'You're bound to find something there.'

'Won't she have taken them on holiday?'

'Oh. I guess so.' Declan blew out his final match. Dozens of church candles gave the room an ethereal mood. He flicked another switch and the water in the hot tub sprang into life, swirling and bubbling, frothily alluring like a witches' cauldron. The soothing mist filled the air and breathed against the cold windows giving them a natural frosting.

Cara chewed her nail. This was proving very hard to resist. She could always go in just wearing her underwear. Cara gave her finger the benefit of her teeth again. On the other hand she was wearing extraordinarily boring undies. There was nothing remotely exciting about her plain white sports bra and big white sports knickers, bought specifically to allow extended stretching in her yoga classes, and she was definitely not in a hurry to share them with Declan. This was a man who was used to seeing women in scanty Santa outfits, and she'd seen enough of Emily's glamorous smalls in the linen basket to realise that she was not a big- boring-knicker person. If Emily ever changed religion and ventured near a yoga class, she'd still do it wearing a dental floss thong. It was impossible to try to

157

compete with that. Cara didn't know why she'd slipped into the realms of comfort underwear. There was nothing in the Green Manifesto to say that wearing frilly undies would seriously endanger the world supplies of lace. Perhaps it was because no one ever looked at them these days.

'I don't know how you can resist,' Declan said, as if reading her mind. 'I thought being an earth mother and all that, you'd be keen to get in there *au naturel.*'

'Well' Cara said, frowning. 'I would if you weren't here.'

'We're old friends,' Declan said.

'I know.' Cara looked longingly at the hot tub. It would probably soothe aches she didn't even know she had.

Declan put his hands on her shoulders. They were warm and strong and a vision of them caressing a naked body flashed across Cara's brain. But whose body was it? Emily's or hers?

Cara's frown deepened.

'You know you want to,' Declan whispered, like a naughty devil sitting on her shoulder. 'What if I bring you a warm towel and leave you to get undressed? Would that work?'

Cara nodded and stood transfixed by the beckoning water until Declan reappeared, as promised, with a warm towel.

'Back in a minute,' he said and melted away into the kitchen.

Cara put the towel on a cane chair by the side of the conservatory and, checking that she was alone, slipped off her T-shirt and jeans. The boring bra and knickers, were, she decided as she peeled them off, going straight into the wastepaper bin. Next week she would take herself off to Agent Provocateur, batter her credit card into submission, and buy herself some *seriously* hot lingerie. And if she did herself an intimate injury during her yoga class, then so be it.

Wrapping the towel round her, she tiptoed across the cool, tiled floor towards the hot tub and abandoning the towel, lowered herself into the steamy, bubbling water.

She let out an involuntary sigh of relief as the water washed over her, massaging every tight knot of tension from her body. This was nirvana, heaven, bliss. Cara let her shoulders sink beneath the bubbles. Letting her head rest back, her heavy eyes closed without much persuasion. All this business with Emily was taking its toll on her too. And, no doubt, Declan was also feeling the strain.

On cue, Declan came back and she opened her eyes.

'Thought you'd fallen asleep,' he said.

Cara resisted the urge to blink or to close her eyes again and check that she wasn't still asleep and dreaming. Declan was naked and not the slightest bit shy about it. His long, lean body was taut and well toned. And clearly, in between becoming a dot.com bankrupt and prancing around in festive mood with Emily, he found plenty of time to do sit-ups. Cara felt a cartoon-sized gulp travel down her throat and hoped Declan hadn't noticed it.

He sank into the water opposite her and sighed gratefully. 'That feels good, doesn't it?' he said, relaxing back.

'Mmm,' Cara mumbled, not quite sure where to position her gaze.

'I told you it would.' He winked at her across the steam.

Personally, Cara felt the water temperature had shot up several more degrees than was entirely comfortable. She was feeling all hot and bothered and her cheeks were burning as brightly as the dozens of candles. Declan smiled as he inched his way through the bubbles towards her.

'I'm glad you came over,' he said. 'Bathing alone just isn't as much fun.'

'No,' Cara agreed hesitantly. Not that she had indulged in multiple bathing before.

'Here.' He reached over and pulled her glass of wine towards her. 'Be careful with it,' he said, and their fingers touched as he made sure that she had a firm grip. The glass seemed to be the only thing that she *did* have a firm grip on, Cara thought.

Declan was inches away from her and she didn't think she'd ever been so close to him before. His skin was as smooth as polished wood. His dark eyes were as rich and warm as mahogany. The water teased his hair, making it curl damply round his shoulders. Declan's mouth curled into a lazy smile.

'Cara . . .' he said softly.

There was a noise. A click. A rattling of keys. And then the front door opened. The smile on Declan's lips died and he pressed them together.

At the door to the conservatory a white-haired elderly woman in a navy blazer, a pleated skirt and very sensible brogues stood looking faintly bemused and slightly alarmed. In her hand she clutched a small green plastic watering can.

'Who are you?' Declan asked.

'I'm Amanda's mother,' the woman answered. 'I'm here to water her plants. Who the *hell* are *you*?'

'I'm Declan,' Declan said and stood up out of the water, extending his hand, and everything else, in friendship. And he did, Cara noted, look particularly pleased to see her. 'Declan O'Donnell.'

Amanda's mother didn't take his outstretched fingers. Her eyes widened and the hand that wasn't preoccupied with her watering can, went instead to her heart. Declan's hand remained unshook. Cara

159

lowered herself in the water in an attempt to hide her embarrassment and, more particularly, not to be eye-level with Declan's old lad.

'And I bet you any money,' he continued with a canny laugh, 'that they forgot to tell you I was staying here.'

Chapter Forty-Six

I've only just realised that the old queen in the big hat behind the mixing desk is, in fact, Boy George. And do you know what, that makes me feel completely mortified and totally unhip. Particularly as I've always professed to be a fan of Culture Club. If he'd been up there singing 'Karma Chameleon' then I might have recognised him a bit earlier.

Most of the people here seem to be happy gyrating to the thumping beat of the music, which has all the subtlety of being hit very hard with a ten-pound sledgehammer over and over again, but it's giving me a humdinger of a headache. There's something very self-conscious about standing and swaying on your own. It makes you look one step away from a strait-jacket and I'm already considering that I might be a candidate for one after agreeing to come here by myself.

I've been wandering round in *Temptation* for nearly an hour – woefully unaccompanied. It's way beyond Jonathan Gold's scheduled time of arrival and there's no sign of him anywhere. If this is his idea of being fashionably late then he's clearly a trendsetter. I'm beginning to wish I'd thought of putting his telephone number into my mobile directory – but I didn't, of course. All this wonderful technology and you can never quite dial out human fallibility.

I've had a few more drinks, which may or may not be a good idea. Why is it that when you're standing on your own clutching even the most delicate of glasses, it seems to take on the size of a large household bucket? I'm painfully aware of every casual sip I take and when you've no one to talk to, it's amazing the rate at which you can glug through booze.

This is not how I'd imagined it all – which seems to be happening more and more frequently in my life. By now, I thought I'd be drifting round on my PR guru's arm, being dazzling and enigmatic. I could actually hear the whispers of, 'Who's that girl?' following me. I was going to be all smiley and charming to Hampstead's answer to the paparazzi and by next week I was going to have been offered my own chat show at the very least. What bollocks!

The people here seem very friendly though, which is unusual in a London wine bar. Usually everyone ignores you. Perhaps this is down to it being a private party, but loads of people have smiled widely at me as I've squeezed past them and, after resisting the urge to check that they weren't grinning at someone behind me, I've actually begun to relax and smile back. The Hunk has also smiled at me several times over his glass of champagne, although he's still ensconced with his posh-looking girlfriend.

I feel like a real idiot hanging round here on my own and I don't know how much longer to do it for. I could ring Cara and get her to come early for me, but there's something very defeatist about abandoning my debut foray into the big, wide world. How can I make glib statements about wanting to regain my independence, if I fall at the first hurdle?

I decide to gird my loins again and pop off to the loo. That's always a good move to while away ten minutes of spare time. Making my way towards my previous eyrie at the top of the stairs, I pass The Hunk and I can feel his eyes following me. What on earth his girlfriend must be thinking about this, goodness only knows.

Needless to say, there's a queue for the ladies. When isn't there? It snakes back from the door, down the stairs and I join the end of it, thankful for the first time in my life that I'll have to wait. That's another five minutes ticked off my ordeal-by-celebrity party. I wonder what some women do in the loo. I think they take the time to fill in their tax returns or knock off a quick novel or contemplate the theory of Big Bang.

I lean against the wall and take up a stance for the duration. The queue is full of ABBA women – All Boobs, Brain Absent. And for the first time I realise that I might well be viewed like that by the casual observer. I think I'd like a badge that says: *Actually, I'm a schoolteacher*. And then it hits me that, actually, I'm not one any more.

This evening is giving me far too much time to contemplate how my life has changed over the last few weeks. This is not the giddy whirl of excitement I expected. As I glance down the stairs, The Hunk is coming up towards me. He appears to be looking for someone, and my heart has a little adrenaline rush as I wonder if it might be me.

I grit my teeth. Suppose he thinks I look like the sort of woman who would consider chatting up a man who's already with someone else? As he comes level with me in the queue, he looks up and seems genuinely surprised to see me standing there. And then he looks

162

flustered and his pale cheeks take on a bashful glow. I love men who can do bashful, don't you? They are a dying breed. He takes a quick glance up and down the queue and all the other women ignore him. I would like to take some playing-hard-to-get lessons from them.

The Hunk presses his lips together and then smiles uncertainly. 'Hi,' he says.

My mouth has gone dry, despite the zillion glasses of champagne I've swigged. 'Hi,' I respond as sexily as possible given that I've only had a few moments' notice. The other girls in the queue look at me as if I'm letting the Sisterhood down.

His smile widens. 'Did you know that you've got a big blob of pesto sauce on your nose?'

I immediately take the opportunity to go into a catatonic trance. 'No,' I say through frozen lips. And when I regain control of my limbs I push past him and the rest of the indignant queue and barge my way into the toilets, unheeding of the angry shouts of 'Oi!' and 'Do you mind?' that follow my progress.

Elbowing some more women out of the way who are taking time to carefully reapply layer-upon-layer of crimson lipstick to their immaculately painted faces, I fight my way to the mirror.

'Oh, fuck,' I say out loud when I see my reflection. Which is not really fitting language for a teacher, but believe me it's the only word suitable in the circumstances.

I do, indeed, have a very large portion of pesto sauce balanced with sculptural accuracy on the bridge of my nose. I must have acquired it when the guy nudged me when I was holding my canapé. Which means that I've been parading around looking like this for the majority of the evening. Next to me, women are nudging each other and giggling, and I realise that's what people have been doing all night. They weren't being unseasonally friendly. They've been laughing at me. Even The Hunk.

Snatching a tissue from the box by the sink, I wipe the smear from my nose. Believe me, I could weep. Just lie down on the floor of the loo and weep. Tears hover dangerously on the brink of my eyelashes and I think that if I hadn't engendered such anger in the queue already, I'd just bolt into one of the cubicles, lock myself in there and never come out ever again.

Instead, I turn on my heel and rush out again, pushing past a sea of smirking faces. And as I break out of the door, I see The Hunk waiting. There's a vaguely stricken expression on his face. He's leaning against the wall and looks as if he's hanging around waiting for me. And, although I can see some merit in the fact that he actually bothered to tell me that I looked like a prize prat, I'm not

163

feeling magnanimous enough to acknowledge it. I just want to be out of here. Out of here fast!

I run down the stairs, spilling drinks as I make my exit. I burst out onto the street and it's freezing cold and I regret the absence of a coat. In my haste to be a hot sex kitten I've forgotten that creature comforts in the form of a woolly over-garment might have been a good idea.

Shivering, I reach into Cara's beaded bag and fish out my mobile. It's turned off and when I switch it on, my message service rings and there is a voicemail from Jonathan Gold.

'Hi.' Jonathan's recorded voice crackles over the airwaves. 'Emily, I'm going to be late. Wait for me. I'll be there about eleven. Sebastian Atherton will be there and I want you to meet him. Ask Paul behind the bar to point him out to you. Sorry about this.'

The line goes dead. I look back at *Temptation*. Nothing on God's earth is going to persuade me to go back in there again. Not the chance of a date with Jonathan Gold. Not the chance of meeting a society photographer. Not the chance of a chat with The Hunk. Nothing. Not even the offer of a night of sensational sex with Brad Pitt would clinch it.

I punch Cara's number into the phone. The Vodaphone I have called is switched off. Damn! Knowing Cara, she's decided to retire to her bedroom for the night to meditate.

Then my luck changes. Perhaps the crystal quartz has decided that it has a job to do, after all. A cab whizzes down the road and even stops as I jump off the kerb to hail it.

'Where to, love?' the cabbie says as I hurl myself inside.

I give him the address and settle back down in the seat. As we pull away from the wine bar, I look back and The Hunk comes crashing out of the doors. He scans up and down the street and then his shoulders sink as he sees my cab disappearing.

I turn to face the front and force myself to study the back of the cab driver's head. He has a very large bald spot with a dark brown mole slap bang in the middle of it.

The cab driver looks in his rearview mirror. 'Had a good night, love?'

'Yes, thank you,' I say. And then I mentally go through every single swear word I can think of.

Chapter Forty-Seven

Adam and Josh were cycling along the Thames Cycle Path which skirts the southern fringes of the Greenwich Peninsula. They were working their way down from the crush of tourists circling round the *Cutty Sark*, pushing past the developing acres of ritzy new real estate thrusting into the skyline and towards the deserted outreach of the Thames Flood Barrier.

It was a bright, sunny but bitterly cold day and loading the bikes onto the rack on the back of the Vectra to take them out of the confines of Hampstead had been a chore of mammoth proportions. Adam couldn't help wondering how warm it would be in Australia at this time of the year.

Sundays were always spent with Josh. Unless, of course, Laura decreed otherwise. Thankfully, she seldom did these days. His ex-wife had gone through several irritating phases of trying to cock-up all of his access days by cancelling them for a variety of feeble reasons. Laura did phases well. This one, it appeared, had passed. Now, Adam thought, she seemed to be glad of the break from Josh.

Not that Josh was difficult to entertain, he just had more pent-up energy than your average Power Station. In full flow, he could make a man at the prime of his life feel like a puffed-out pensioner within ten minutes. That was why Adam tried to make sure that he and his son did challenging, character-building stuff. Boys' stuff. Stuff, basically, that Josh didn't seem to do any more. Barry the building society manager was a good substitute father in a lot of ways. Josh liked him. Well . . . that was about it, really. But Barry's idea of a wild time seemed to be sitting at home watching *The Simpsons* with Josh. Still, it could have been a lot worse.

It scared him sometimes that Josh seemed to know more about life as lived through *EastEnders*, *Brookside* and *Coronation Street* than he did about life in the outside world. Thus, despite having a huge headache, a small croaky voice and an aching void where his heart should have been, Adam was braving the elements to bring the sights

165

of London to his son. Dragging up some enthusiasm from the depths of his jollity reserve, Adam flexed his fingers to try to force some blood back into them. If only he could be as irrepressibly bright and bouncy as his son. These days it seemed to take a lot more to get Adam's red corpuscles knocking about excitedly.

Escaping Hampstead was one of the things that perked him up considerably. Even the twee expanse of the Heath could feel constricting at times, and once you'd kicked a ball about for a bit and maybe flown a kite on the top of Parliament Hill, there was little else to keep a burgeoning teenager amused. Adam loved to head for the river, battling his way through the traffic of the Elephant and Castle, The Old Kent Road and Deptford, through the tatters of South London, to hit the open stretch of the Thames where it started the long wind out of London on its way to the English Channel. In contrast to the claustrophobia of over-population, it felt wide open and positively coastal here. It was the closest you could get to being at the seaside and still be within the city.

Once they were out of the narrow back lanes of Greenwich, the air was as fresh as it possibly could be in an area that was still very much a working dockland, despite years of decline. There was a tang of yeast and chemicals in the air rather than ozone, but emotionally it had the same effect. Adam threw caution to the wind and filled his lungs. Cormorants perched expectantly on the dilapidated, weed-infested piers, before diving lazily for fish in water the colour of Brown Windsor soup. Shelducks and teal bobbed on the choppy, wind-whipped waters alongside the scattering of tiny, coloured yachts anchored just beyond the reach of the green-black mud flats and the receding sliver of shingle shore.

Josh had his head down against the chilly wind and an expression of supreme concentration on his face. Adam smiled to himself; just looking at his son could warm him through inside. 'You all right?'

Josh took his eyes off the pavement and grinned. 'Yeah.' His legs were pedalling round determinedly. 'You look a bit wasted though.'

'I am,' Adam said, feeling the cold air whistle through his teeth. 'Heavy night.'

'Yeah?' Josh brightened. 'Where did you go?'

'A new wine bar in the High Street.'

'Was it good?'

Adam nodded. 'So-so.'

Sometimes, when the weather was warmer they stopped and enjoyed a soft drink outside the Cutty Sark pub – one of the many inns in London that claimed to be the oldest – and watched the day-trippers take in the sights from the water. Today they pushed on, the path narrowing as they moved past beached wooden river barges and the rusting hulls of long-defunct passenger ferries and pleasure boats. They whizzed past Josh's favourite part, the gaudy, artistic graffiti scrawled on the corrugated-iron fences protecting the backs of the chemical companies and refineries of this tattered industrial stretch. The towering glass structures of Canary Wharf loomed high over the river, windows glittering in the sun. Brash new business facing off against the old, fading ways.

Josh got his breath back. 'Did you go with anyone?'

'Yeah. Toff.'

'No one else?'

'Josh,' Adam said, 'they don't ask you as many questions as this on *The Weakest Link*.'

'They do.'

'Do not.'

'You never tell me anything,' Josh complained.

'I do.'

'Do not,' Josh said. 'I tell you everything.'

'That's different.' Gulls cried out, wheeling above them in the air currents. Adam could feel the full force of the persistent wind easing the collar of his shirt apart and blowing down his neck. It was the first thing that had blown down his neck in a long, long time, he thought regretfully. 'You're a kid. Kids are supposed to do that.'

Josh looked unconvinced.

'It's true,' Adam said. 'You're not supposed to give me advice about my love life.'

'Why not?'

'You're supposed to come to me for advice. When you're older.' Adam avoided looking at him. 'Much, much older.'

'Oh.' His son's legs worked at his pedals as he considered this revelation. When he spoke, he sounded puzzled. 'Don't you want to know about my girlfriends then?'

'Yes,' Adam said. 'Of course I do.' He grinned at Josh. 'How is Britney Spears?'

'Imogen,' Josh supplied. 'She's all right.'

'Good.'

'I'd like to marry her when I'm a grown-up.'

It was nice to think that just because his parents had made a complete hash of living in the traditional bounds of a marriage that it hadn't deterred Josh from seeing it as his ideal. Or perhaps he was hoping that he might make a better job of it. 'Does she feel the same way?'

167

'No,' Josh said. 'She doesn't want to settle down and have children until she's at least twenty-two.'

'Oh,' Adam said.

'She wants to have a flat in Kensington with Leanne Connolly and break through the glass ceiling,' his son said earnestly.

'Oh. And what does that involve?' Adam asked.

'I don't know,' Josh said. 'I thought it best not to ask.'

Adam nodded. 'Probably a good idea.'

'So did you have a date last night?' the boy asked, thinking that as he'd unburdened his soul on the subject of women it was his dad's turn to do the same. 'Or was it really just Toff?'

Clearly Josh was unwilling to take the strong hint that this was a taboo subject. Adam sighed, but the wind whisked it away. 'I had a date.'

Josh grinned broadly at him. 'I knew,' he said, trying all of his bike gears in rotation for no apparent reason. 'I could tell.'

'Well, that's very perceptive of you,' Adam said, smiling back. If Josh hadn't been hanging onto his handlebars for grim death, he probably would have rubbed his hands together with glee.

Adam mused for a few moments as they wheeled round the new path bordering the beautiful saucer-shaped white elephant of the Millennium Dome. Whatever you thought of the Civil Servant-created contents of the ill-conceived structure, Adam decided, the outside was a wonderful transformation of what was once nothing more than the derelict wasteland of a former gasworks. Now the magnificent and controversial structure lay abandoned, the too-few visitors replaced by skips, diggers, deserted car parks and ripped-up tarmac – its future still in jeopardy. It was a crime to see it standing neglected and decaying, returning slowly but surely to its previous state, Adam thought. Such a bloody waste.

'Was she nice?' Josh asked.

He glanced across at his son. 'No,' he said sadly. 'She wasn't very nice.'

'Oh Dad!' Josh was totally exasperated. 'You never like anyone!'

'I do,' Adam protested.

'You do not.'

'I do. I happened to meet someone I liked very much last night.' Adam pushed harder on his pedals. 'She just didn't happen to be the woman I was on a date with.'

'Ooo,' Josh said, eyes widening.

'You can stop that now,' Adam said.

Adam gazed out at the murky water. A floating glass restaurant pottered out towards the barrier, filled with people concentrating

168

more on the delights of their roast beef than the history of a river that had once frozen over enough for men to play football on it. A river that Londoners had swum in long before the fish decided it was too unclean. It was said that drinking a teaspoon of the polluted Ganges or the Nile would be enough to kill a man – Adam wasn't sure that he'd want to take his chances with the Thames either.

The silver shell-like arches of the Thames Barrier stretching across the river came into view – a graceful string of hi-tech gates that provided the only protection against London succumbing to the powerful spite of the sea. It was a wonderful sight on the horizon and it spurred Adam's pedalling onwards – that and the thought of hot, sweet tea in the warmth of the visitor centre.

But his son wasn't letting him off the hook that easily. 'Did you talk to her?'

'Who?'

Josh scowled. 'Oh, Dad!'

'Yes,' Adam said. 'Yes, I did talk to her.'

'What did you say?'

Adam cleared his throat. 'Not much.'

Actually, Josh, Adam thought, I told her she'd got pesto sauce on her nose and, because of me, she fled from the wine bar in tears. Despite his attempts to clear his head of his inadequacies, his son was only too keen to keep reminding him, it seemed. Adam could have joyfully got off his bike and battered his head into the gravel pavement.

There was a certain irony to the fact that he'd happened to see the only woman who'd ever made his heart skip several beats on the only time he'd been on a date in living memory. How perverse was life? He'd felt this amazing connection to the woman-in-the-wine-bar, as he'd affectionately come to regard her, and he was sure she'd felt the same. It was as if he'd known her before. She was a stranger and yet familiar. So familiar. His mouth had gone dry when he looked at her. Unlike his palms, which had gone sweaty. There was too much eye-contact, too much surreptitious smiling, for it not to be mutual. And he'd blown it. Blown it, big time. He'd spent the rest of the evening staring in a subdued manner into his flat champagne – so much so that even Jemima had noticed it.

'Did you get her phone number?'

'Not exactly,' Adam said.

'Oh Dad!' His son looked at him in disgust. 'You are hopeless!'

And for once in his life Adam really didn't feel that he could disagree.

169

Chapter Forty-Eight

I am no longer on the front of all the newspapers. Jeffrey Archer is. Again. I'm not going to go into the details. And I suspect my fickle band of attendant journalists have rushed off to Cambridge to harangue the millionaire storyteller and his lovely fragrant wife, Mary, instead.

On the one hand I'm delighted that the Archers have lured my pursuers away from leafy Hampstead and my door in particular. On the other hand, I feel very sorry for them. I now know what it feels like to be hounded by the press. I think I'll dash out and buy a few of his paperbacks to show solidarity.

It makes me think seriously about my non-meeting with Jonathan Gold and whether I want to follow up his offer. Do I really want to court this sort of attention? Is being a high-profile media person really desirable? Isn't the fact that I'm now becoming old news a good thing? It's nice to be sitting sprawled in front of a log fire on a Sunday afternoon, simply reading the newspapers for recreational purposes rather than scouring them with bated breath for any more scandal featuring yours truly. I did wonder whether they'd start dredging up my old boyfriends to ask them if I was any good in bed, or perhaps a few primary-school chums to ask them if I'd shown any signs of overt libidinous development at the age of ten. That would have put the tin hat on everything. But, thankfully, they haven't.

Cara is curled up on the sofa with yesterday's *Guardian*. She's very quiet. She looks up at me. 'You're quiet,' she says.

'Mmm,' I respond, watching the flames flicker their way up the chimney. It's nice to be cosied up with Cara like this. It reminds me of being at university when it was just me and her against the world and we had no problems controlling our men and no mortgages. She has been a good friend for a long time. Outside, it's a freezing cold day and the wind is urging the remnants of long-dead autumn leaves to skitter across the garden. The sky has turned grey and grumpy. I know how it feels. I want it to be summer again. With the return of the sun perhaps I can find the way forward and move towards a new start. For now, I feel stuck in the house and stuck in my life. Cara looks over my shoulder. I'm reading an article entitled *Sexual Positions of the Stars*. There is a diagram of a Brad Pitt stick-drawing doing something very athletic.

Cara frowns. 'How do they know he makes love like that?'

'How do you know he doesn't?'

'True,' Cara agrees.

I can only say that if he does, Jennifer Aniston is one lucky woman. No wonder she always wears a smile.

I fold the *Mail on Sunday* and lean on the edge of the sofa.

'Still brooding about last night?' Cara asks.

I nod, but say nothing. How can I tell her that in the course of one night, I met the man of my dreams and humiliated myself, deeply, in front of him?

'The lovely Mr Gold will probably ring again tomorrow.'

'Yes,' I say without enthusiasm.

'He will,' she assures me.

'Yeah.' My focus settles again on the blustering breeze.

'Emily,' Cara says, putting down her own newspaper. 'Is there anything else wrong?'

'No.' I shake my head.

'Are you sure?'

'Yes.'

'You've got the attention span of a goldfish,' she points out. 'Perhaps less. They can at least concentrate for three seconds at a time.' She swings her legs off the sofa and inches next to me. 'Every time I've looked up you've been staring out of the window.'

I bite my lip. Nothing much gets past psychic Cara. And she's right, my mind is elsewhere today. You know when you hear a really terrible record on the way to work and you can't get it out of your mind at all, and then you spend the whole day singing it to yourself over and over again – 'Achy Breaky Heart' or something equally dire? And just when you think you've finally got it out of your mind, you find yourself humming it again and you realise that nothing short of beating yourself over the head with a tin tray is going to stop it. That's what I'm going through now. I have 'Achy Breaky Heart' Syndrome. Mr Hunk's face keeps flashing in front of me. Different scenarios, always the same face, over and over again. One minute I'm looking out at the garden and the next I'm watching us walking together on Hampstead Heath, enjoying dinner at La Gavroche, lying curled up together in bed. Whoa, whoa! This is bad, isn't it?

I decide to confess. 'I met the man of my dreams last night,' I say.

Cara sits bolt upright. As well she might.

'I humiliated myself deeply in front of him,' I admit, hanging my head in shame.

'Not again, Emily! You're such an idiot!'

I can safely say that Cara is unlikely to be receiving a *Forever Friends* birthday card this year. She hurls herself back on the sofa. 'I thought you were going to have a period of voluntary celibacy? You specifically bought an "I will not chase boys" T-shirt to remind yourself.'

'It doesn't work for me, Cara.'

'How can you tell after a few weeks? You have to give it time. You never stick to anything, Emily.'

'I'll have you know I was once celibate for sixteen years.'

'You were not!'

'I was.' I grin at Cara. 'It was a hell of a sixteenth birthday party!'

Cara tuts. My sense of humour is missing its mark. 'Have you learned nothing from this terrible, traumatic experience with Declan?'

'I didn't take my underwear off,' I insist crisply. 'I went for the pesto-sauce-on-the-nose type of humiliation instead.'

A glimmer of a smile twitches Cara's lips.

'Don't laugh,' I warn her. 'He laughed at me.'

'That's the real reason why you came home early?'

I nod.

'Oh, Emily,' Cara says in her most sympathetic voice. 'If he laughed at you then he really isn't a nice person, is he?'

'No,' I agree, perilously close to a sniff. 'He looked like a lot of trouble,' I say, trying to make myself feel better as much as anything. 'A love 'em and leave 'em type.'

'There you are then,' she says. 'Nothing lost.'

'I wish I could agree,' I say miserably. 'When I looked at him, Cara, I felt like I'd been plugged into the National Grid.' I stare out of the window again, as if that will help. 'No one has ever done that to me before.'

'Not even Declan?' I see that Cara is flushed. I'm sure she keeps having visions of me in my Santa's outfit frolicking with Declan, although she'd never admit to it.

'No.'

'But you said this man looked like trouble.' Cara likes to delve. Deeply.

'Bad boys are more fun, aren't they?'

'I don't know,' my friend says with a discontented little huff. 'I've always dated nerds.'

In spite of my dark mood I smile. 'That's what comes from having a penchant for lentil eaters.'

172

Cara pulls the lacy hem of her skirt distractedly. 'I would have thought after Declan that you'd want someone nice. Someone to settle down with.'

I shrug. 'Part of Declan's fatal charm is that he's a bad boy. You never know quite where you are with him. Don't you think that's what makes him attractive?'

Cara's faint flush rushes blood-red to the tips of her ears. It's probably difficult for her to hear me constantly slagging off Declan. They did used to be quite fond of each other in a chalk and cheese type of way. Declan always used to take the piss out of Cara and Cara never used to tire of setting herself up for it.

'Declan has a lot of good qualities,' my friend says.

'And an awful lot of bad ones.'

'He still loves you,' Cara states.

'Not that it will do him much good,' I say. 'I'll never take him back, Cara.'

'How would you feel if you learned he'd met someone else?'

'I'd wish her very good luck,' I say with a snorty laugh. 'She'll need it.'

'I wish you could meet Adam,' Cara sighs. 'Adam's nice. It would prove to you that reliable men do exist.'

'You stick with Adam then,' I advise. 'Nice is good. Nice is very good.'

'He just doesn't seem very keen on me.' Cara looks a little sad.

'How will he be able to resist you with the power of the entire universe at your disposal?'

'There's no need to take the piss,' Cara says huffily and returns to the depths of the *Guardian*.

I return to staring out of the window and daydreaming about the romance of the century that might have been. I feel bad that Cara was already tucked up in bed by the time I came home. It must be awful for her to be so besotted by this Adam and for him to be completely oblivious to it. He doesn't sound nice to me. He sounds like a right dork.

Chapter Forty-Nine

Josh looked totally wrecked as they walked up the path back to Laura's house. Half an hour in the steamy café at the Thames Barrier and a glass of warm Coke had finally seen him off and they'd cycled slowly back to where the Vectra was parked. Adam, as always, was relieved to see that it still had all its wheels intact.

His son had fallen asleep in the car and was now stifling yawns and trying desperately to stay awake or go back to sleep. Adam wasn't sure which one was winning. He squeezed his son's shoulders and Josh's eyelids flickered briefly in recognition. Even after all this time it didn't get any easier delivering him back to the care of his mother. But this was infinitely easier than the thought that, very soon, he might not even have the chance to do that. Josh had nattered Adam's ears off all day long, but neither of them had mentioned Australia. Although the word hung palpably between them.

Josh rang the bell and Laura opened the door with the speed of someone who had been lurking behind the curtains watching for them to return. She nodded at Adam and leaned on the door frame, arms folded over her cardigan. His ex-wife looked so forlorn that Adam had a bizarre urge to reach out and hug her.

'OK?' he asked gently.

Laura nodded, the tight line of her lips softening slightly.

'Back in one piece,' he said and ruffled Josh's hair. It was a fairly rare occurrence. He usually took Josh back muddy, bruised and/or battered by some of their more boisterous exploits. Laura thought Adam was irresponsible. Adam thought Laura wrapped Josh in cottonwool.

Josh turned and flung his arms round Adam. 'Thanks for a great day, Dad.'

His son was so easy to make happy, just the thought of it could make Adam's heart want to break. There wasn't a day went by when he didn't worry about them letting him down by being unable to provide a stable family unit for him. Laura seemed to be less troubled by the fact. If she wanted him to have a settled upbringing, would she even be considering whisking him to the other side of the world? Adam had again looked up air fares to Australia on the Internet. It was his current obsession. And every time he did, it pained him to find out that he wouldn't be able to get there for less than eight hundred quid. How often was he going to be able to visit Josh at that price? A photographer's pay was pants.

'I'll see you on Wednesday,' Adam said.

His son pushed past Laura and struggled out of his coat, hanging it on the end of the banister where it promptly fell onto the floor.

'Be good,' Adam said after him. 'Don't give your mum any trouble.'

His son was gone. Disappeared into the depths of their suburban living room, no doubt to plant himself in front of the television for the rest of the evening. Adam shrugged.

'He never does,' Laura said.

'He's a good boy.'

'I can't say he takes after his father then,' Laura said, but her eyes were teasing him.

'No,' Adam agreed. Leaning on the door frame opposite her, he pulled a dead head off something brown and crispy poking out of a hanging basket that might once, many moons ago, have been a flower. He lowered his voice. 'Any more thoughts about Australia?'

Laura's face settled into weary lines. 'I've thought about nothing else.'

'And . . .?'

'And I don't know yet, Adam.' Laura bit her lip and looked perilously close to tears.

'Is there anything I can do?'

'To help me to leave?' Laura asked. 'Or to make me stay?'

'I'm frightened, Laura,' Adam admitted. He could feel hot tears threatening the back of his eyes. 'I'm worried that I'll miss Josh too much.'

Laura raised an eyebrow. 'It didn't stop you from leaving us.'

'I know,' he said. 'Maybe I'd do things differently now.'

'Maybe I would too,' Laura said.

Adam scratched at his stubble. 'Would it help if you and I . . . you know . . .'

Laura didn't dive in to help him out.

Adam scratched some more. 'Would it help if you and I gave it another go?'

Laura smiled sadly. 'Do you love me, Adam?'

'Well . . .' he said, 'not exactly. But I don't want to see you unhappy.' He shredded some more of Laura's horticultural corpses. 'I

175

want what's best for Josh. If that means you and I have to . . . have to come to some arrangement then I'm happy to do that.'

'You've always been an old romantic,' Laura said.

Adam sighed. 'I'm trying to help.'

'Oh, Adam.' Laura let out a long unhappy breath. 'How did I manage to get it all so wrong?'

'It wasn't just you,' Adam said. 'We were too young. Too . . . too different.'

'I'm still making a mess of things,' she said. 'At least you've got your life sorted.'

Adam smiled. 'Appearances can be very deceptive.'

'Laura!' Barry the building society manager shouted from the kitchen. 'Come here a sec!'

She rolled her eyes to the bleak winter skies.

'I'd better go,' Adam said.

Laura nodded.

Adam leaned more heavily on the door frame. 'I just want us all to be happy again.'

'*Laura!*' Barry's voice boomed out.

'I think that might be hoping for rather too much,' Laura said as she slipped back inside her house and closed the door.

Chapter Fifty

'We can't just sit here doing nothing,' Cara announces. Even though that's exactly what we've been doing all day.

The rain is now sheeting down outside and we're both hugging mugs of hot chocolate with marshmallows melted in it. It may not be very green or calorifically correct, but they are vegetarian marshmallows and it's very comforting so I don't give a jot. We're both watching the four hundredth re-run of *Singin' in the Rain* on the television, and I think this soppily romantic fare is maybe what has prompted Cara's mobilisation.

'I'm quite enjoying it,' I say and snuggle deeper into my joggers and fleecy sweatshirt – perfect vegging-out clothes. Donald O'Connor has just done that thing where he runs up the wall and flips over. I love that bit. I always wanted to be able to do it, but never had the nerve to try.

'This is not how we will change our lives,' Cara insists and, grabbing the remote control, snaps off the telly.

Now I will never know whether Gene Kelly finally ends up with Debbie Reynolds. But I suspect that he will. He's always managed it, the last three hundred and ninety-nine times I've watched it. Films are like that, aren't they? They give you false hope of finding a perfect relationship and a sense that you're never having quite as much fun as people in the movies.

Cara stands up and looks all businesslike. She paces across her smelly yak rug which she brought back from trekking in Nepal. If you ask me, she should have left it there. In this sort of mood my friend is unstoppable and, if I know what's good for me, I should just give in without protest. 'We need candles,' she says decisively.

I groan.

'Shut up,' Cara instructs. 'This is for your benefit too.'

I can feel some sort of cranky ritual coming on and I think I've had enough humiliation for one weekend, thank you very much.

'You have met the man of your dreams – admittedly shortly after announcing that you'd never fall in love again – and have let him slip through your fingers because of a simple misunderstanding about the wearing of pesto sauce.' Cara does overbearing very well. She continues without pause for breath: 'I have met the man of *my* dreams and he's currently being too dim to realise that I'm the woman of *his* dreams. We have to sort this out.'

'Can't we do it in a way that doesn't involve candles?' Cara sometimes has a very slender connection to real life and when it is at its worst it usually involves a lot of candles.

Hands on hips, she says: 'Suggestions?'

I admit by a sullen silence that I have none.

'Let's get started then,' she says with a superior smile.

Cara and I are sitting opposite each other. We are surrounded by a circle of red Waitrose dinner candles all flickering wildly in their saucers. Cara's candle expenditure budget is truly phenomenal. There is probably some gnarled and rickety factory somewhere producing wax purely for Cara's personal consumption. If she ever decides to come back down to this planet, there will be a lot of candlemakers heading towards the DHSS and signing on the following week. I am struggling between trying not to sulk and trying not to laugh. It could go either way at the moment.

'We are going to practise the ancient art of Wicca,' Cara tells me.

'Nice,' I say.

'You're not going to get silly, are you, Emily?' she says with a warning note in her voice.

'No,' I say solemnly and burst out laughing.

'Just get your sniggering over with now,' my friend advises as she places our mobile phones in the centre of the room in between us.

'He doesn't know my number,' I point out. Or my name. Both of which I think are fairly relevant.

'The universe will bring him to you.' Cara has an answer for everything.

'What's the bag of flour for?' There is a two-kilo bag of Homepride Self-Raising flour on the floor between us too.

'We're going to sprinkle it over each other.'

'You are *not* sprinkling flour over me!' I object.

'Emily.' Cara sighs tightly. 'Do you want to find this man or not?'

'Yes,' I say meekly. Flour it is then.

Cara settles herself and assumes a mystical-type expression.

'I'm not hoovering it up,' I say snippily and receive a glare as my reward.

Cara picks up her well-thumbed book of magic spells and flicks through the pages until she stops at a particular hex and smiles contentedly.

'Are you sure we should be doing this?' I don't believe in this load of old bunkum, but I wouldn't want Cara to conjure up something nasty with several heads and a spiteful nature in our living room.

'Get the flour,' Cara orders me.

Dutifully, I push the packet bearing Fred the Flour Grader towards my magical, mysterious, mystical, mad friend.

'Why flour?' I ask.

'Because it means you're accepting that you're at one with nature,' Cara says, but she doesn't sound too certain.

I think it probably means that you're accepting that you're half-baked.

'Does it have to be self-raising?'

'No,' Cara says darkly. 'It's all I had in the cupboard.'

It's unusual because I can't see the word 'organic' on it anywhere. 'Do you think because it's self-raising it will give the men of our dreams spontaneous erections?'

'That would be nice, wouldn't it?'

Cara picks up her magic wand and gives it a few tentative swishes through the air and then sharply taps the top of our mobile phones three times.

I fall on my back giggling. 'You look like Sooty,' I say, gasping for breath.

Cara treats me with the contempt I deserve, so I try to calm down and pay attention.

'Now you have to say the magic words,' Cara informs me.

'Izzy, whizzy, let's get busy!' I offer and throw myself on the floor in a fit of laughter again. Calling on the universe is the best therapy I've had in ages.

'You're not taking this seriously, Emily,' she warns.

Oh, she's noticed. I sit upright again and copy Cara's mystical pose. They say that imitation is the sincerest form of flattery. In this case I'm not so sure.

'Pick up the phone,' Cara says.

I pretend to be making a phone call.

'What was this man's name?'

'I don't know,' I admit reluctantly.

'Oh, very helpful!'

'I christened him The Hunk.'

Cara looks at me with disdain. 'Visualise him then,' she says. The tone of her voice adds, 'If you think you can manage that . . .' 'I'm going to visualise Adam too. Then I dust you with flour and you repeat these words.'

I press my lips together so that I don't spoil it all by cracking up again. Cara really has the best of intentions. I close my eyes and put on my serious face.

'Call me,' she says earnestly. 'Don't be afraid. Call me . . .'

I risk opening one eye. 'That's an old Carpenters' hit!' I say.

Cara throws a handful of flour in my face. 'It is not. Just say it.'

I cough the flour out of my mouth and blink it off my eyelashes. 'It's a Carpenters' song,' I insist. Cara looks murderous. 'If it isn't, they definitely did a cover version.'

I get another gobful of flour and a glare for my pains. 'And this is the ancient art of Wicca?' I splutter. 'A mystical ritual passed down through generations? Singing old Carpenters' hits while staring at my mobile phone?'

Cara's jaw tightens. 'You have no idea what the universe can do for you, do you?'

'I have some idea what Vodaphone can do though and I don't think it's transmitting love spells through the ether.' I fold my arms in a very unmagical posture. 'If I'm reliant on bad 1970s pop tunes to find the man of my dreams then I might as well give up now.'

'I have a lot more faith than you,' Cara informs me loftily. She is a lot more barking mad than me, I think.

Cara raps her phone three more times and then snatches it up and puts it to her ear. She closes her eyes dreamily. 'Call me,' she intones and does her Karen Carpenter impression again. I sing the song in my head, mouthing the words to Cara's rapt face. I enter into the spirit of the throwing-flour-in-the-face part quite enthusiastically. Cara splutters delicately.

She opens her eyes and a shower of graded grains flutters down from her fringe like powder snow. Cara sneezes.

'That's it, is it?' I ask.

'Yes,' Cara says. 'All we have to do now is wait.'

Chapter Fifty-One

England were playing Germany. Always a grudge match. And only on Sky TV. England were sure to get a pasting. The last time they had beaten Germany, Adam was still in nappies. The thought did nothing to cheer him.

He had arranged to watch their big match demise on the large-screen television in the pub with Chris and Toff and, accordingly, had trudged painfully down to the Jiggery-Pokery that evening, still aching from this afternoon's bike-ride with Josh. He didn't think he was a natural father – he hated other people's children, who were, without exception, snot-nosed brats. He did, however, adore his own offspring, so he couldn't be that bad. And if it meant that he constantly felt his age in the pursuance of entertainment of said offspring, then that couldn't be helped either.

On his arrival, Adam got the beers in. And the cashew nuts. Chris was already ensconced on a bar stool. And so was Toff. Not that Toff had the slightest interest in football. He just indulged them as a male-bonding ritual and usually spent the entire match asking inane questions about football formations and trying to remember which teams were playing and what colour each of them wore. Toff would have made a great girl.

Chris was eyeing up two of the more dubious members of that species who were propping up the end of the bar, delicately swigging Archers from bottles, co-ordinated elegantly with alternate drags of their cigarettes. Chris licked his lips seductively in their direction and the girls giggled back. Adam and Toff exchanged a glance.

'How long till kick-off?' Chris asked.

'Half an hour,' Adam advised.

'Go and get some good seats,' Chris said. 'I'm in here.'

They always had to get there early to get good seats. Otherwise you could spend the entire match looking at the back of someone's head. This was clearly not a neighbourhood replete with satellite dishes or the type of people who'd be interested in pay-per-view footy matches. Toff couldn't care less whether they had good seats or not.

'Time for some totty teasing,' Chris said and headed towards the two rather tarty women.

Adam and Toff watched his progress.

'Hey,' Chris said as he approached the girls. 'After the football do you want to come back to my place for pizza and sex?'

One of the girls regarded him through her cigarette smoke. 'We don't like pizza.'

'Even better.' Chris rubbed his hands together. 'Can I get you ladies a drink or do you just want the money?'

The girls laughed raucously.

Adam and Toff exchanged another glance. 'Tell me he isn't real,' Adam said.

'It's his testosterone, old fruit,' Toff said. 'It's on overdrive because he's going to see David Beckham.'

'Hey, Toff,' Adam said, impressed. 'You remembered a footballer's name!'

'Only because I did a photo shoot with him and Victoria last week.'

'Oh,' Adam said, impressed.

'Charming couple,' Toff informed him and they left Chris to his lascivious chat-up lines and went in search of good seats.

When they found them, Toff sipped his Campari and grapefruit with confidence while Adam looked self-consciously around him. A lot of tattooed people inhabited the Jig and they could easily take offence at a pale pink drink in a bloke's hand.

'What formation do you think they'll play today?' Toff asked. 'A four-four-seven?'

'Toff,' Adam said patiently, 'there are only ten players on the field. And a goalie. It's a four-four-two. You know nothing about this.'

'I'm interested though,' Toff said. 'Really, I am.'

'I am *not* going through the offside rule with you again,' Adam said firmly. 'It's a very painful process and you never remember it. Just admire their hairstyles or something. Enjoy your drink and the fact that you're with friends.'

Toff cleared his throat. 'Who are we playing?'

'Germany,' Adam said. 'It's an important match.'

'And which ones are we?'

Adam sighed. 'We're the ones in the white shirts and blue shorts.'

'Nice,' Toff said. 'It's a very smart outfit.'

'Strip,' Adam corrected.

'Who's the one in the orange top with the nice shiny hair and the rather dated Mexican moustache?'

'That's David Seaman. He's the goalkeeper,' Adam explained. 'He's the man who tries to stop the ball going into the back of the net.'

'Really, darling,' Toff was affronted. 'I'm not an idiot.'

'You're not a footballer either,' Adam said with a smile.

Toff was about to open his mouth again.

'Can we change the subject, Toff?' Adam pleaded. 'To something you're a bit more *au fait* with?'

'I know a lot about cricket,' Toff offered.

Adam raised his eyebrows. 'Well, I don't.'

'Let's talk about women then,' Toff said.

'I think Chris is the expert there,' Adam mused, flicking a glance over to his friend who was making Michael Jackson-style pelvic thrusts towards his two giggling companions, accompanied by enthusiastic monkey noises. 'I can only hope he's telling them a joke,' Adam said, 'and not going through his mating ritual.'

'Me too,' Toff agreed. 'It's a very unpleasant sight.'

They both returned their attention to their drinks and the jostling that was going on to force another row of chairs in front of the designated front row.

'Talking of mating rituals, how did you enjoy yourself last night?' Toff asked.

'Great, mate,' Adam said. 'Thanks for setting it up. I mean it. Really.'

'Did all go swimmingly with lovely Jemima?'

Adam grimaced. 'I don't think she was my type. Or, more pertinently, I don't think I was hers.' Adam was pretty sure that his bank account was much lower down the evolutionary scale than she'd grown accustomed to.

'You're not going to see her again?'

Adam shook his head.

'Don't fall at the first fence, old bean,' Toff tutted. 'The girl of your dreams is out there waiting. We just have to find her.'

'Actually . . .' Adam examined the head on his pint, 'you could help me there, Toff.'

Toff was patently surprised.

Adam avoided looking at him. 'I saw someone last night at the wine bar.' He plaited his fingers together. 'She was lovely.' He shrugged. 'Really lovely. I tried to talk to her but made a complete bollocks of it.'

'And?' Toff said with a frown.

'And I've no idea who she is,' Adam admitted. 'She raced out, jumped into a cab and sailed off into the wide blue yonder before I could stop her.'

'Oh, how romantic,' Toff mused.

'Well, not really.' Adam took a mouthful of his pint. 'It would have been a lot more romantic if I'd got her phone number.'

'Oh, of course, dear boy.'

'That's where you can help,' Adam said. 'You knew a lot of people there last night. Maybe one of them could tell you who she was.'

'It's certainly worth a try,' Toff said. 'I'll give Paul behind the bar a ring first thing tomorrow. What was she like?'

'Gorgeous,' Adam said. 'Utterly gorgeous. In a sweet and vulnerable sort of way.'

'Could you be a bit more specific? Short, tall? Fat, thin? Dark, blonde?'

'Tallish,' Adam said. 'Well, not too tall, not too short. And thinish. But not too thin. Full-figured.' Adam held his hands out in front of him. And then put them out a bit further. Toff looked impressed. 'And she was dark, but not very dark. Sort of dark blondey, chestnuty. And her hair was short, but not too short. Sort of short, long.'

Toff pressed his lips together and concentrated.

'Do you know who she is?' Adam knew he sounded too hopeful.

'Yes,' Toff said. 'She's a short, tall, fat, thin, dark blonde with hair of indeterminate length.'

'Yes.' Adam nodded eagerly.

'What was she wearing?' Toff asked.

'A pink thing,' Adam supplied. 'Sort of reddy-pink. Purplish. What colour's cerise?'

'Pink,' Toff said.

'Pink.' Adam nodded contentedly. 'It was pink. Pinky-purple.'

'Reddy-pink?' Toff prompted.

'Yeah,' Adam agreed with a sigh. 'She looked great.'

'I'm sure we'll have absolutely no trouble tracking her down,' Toff assured him. 'Leave it to Uncle Sebastian, old boy.'

'Yeah,' Adam said. He punched his friend's arm in appreciation. 'You're a real mate, Toff.'

Toff shrugged. 'Are you going to come up to the studio this week?'

Adam nodded. 'I'm working tomorrow, but probably on Tuesday night.' He glanced at his watch. Ten minutes before kick-off. 'Which reminds me – I'd better phone Cara. She called last night while we were out, but didn't leave a message. It was probably something to do with work.'

184

Chris returned and took the seat next to Adam. He waved a beer mat in front of Adam's nose that had two phone numbers scribbled on the corner. He pointed at the women he had just left. 'Those clothes are going to look wonderful in a pile on my bedroom floor,' he said with a smile.

Adam really hoped that Toff would be able to trace the woman-in-the-wine-bar, otherwise he could be forced into going out on pulling missions with Chris – and he didn't think that his constitution was strong enough for that. What's more, he preferred his women with more brain cells than they had legs, which was a requirement that didn't seem to trouble his friend.

'Are you extraordinarily jealous, Adam?' Chris asked.

'Yes, Chris,' Adam said flatly and punched Cara's number into his mobile. The only thing that would cheer him up now would be Germany losing 5-1. Fat chance! It was going to be a long and miserable night.

Chapter Fifty-Two

Cara has just gone upstairs to wash the flour out of her dreadlocks. Which in my book means they are technically not dreadlocks, but just very tight ringlets. She has decided to do this because, apart from being enveloped in a cloud of white powder every time she moved, she felt that her 'I'm not being called' energy was interfering with the 'I want to be called' psychic cry we had put out into deep space. Something like that anyway.

Despite mercilessly taking the mickey out of my dear friend Cara, I actually enjoyed communing with nature or whoever it was we communed with. It was a great laugh – which I suspect is not the desired result, but it has certainly lifted my spirits. I feel all floaty and light and it's a long time since I felt anything but very pissed off.

The mobile phones are still sitting on the floor in our circle of spent magical Waitrose dinner candles and, I'm sure you'll not be surprised by this, they have not rung once.

Cara's mobile phone rings. 'Oh fucking hell,' I say, all my eloquence having disappeared in shock along with my floatiness.

It continues to ring on the floor and I'm terrified. What if some sort of psychic poltergeist comes out of Cara's phone, enters my brain through my ear and turns me into a jelly? What? It happens. 'Ohshitshitshitshitshit . . .'

I chew my fingers a bit while its tinny mechanical tone continues to trill. 'Cara!' I shout tentatively, but I think she's gone into the shower and it makes such a noise that Aliens could, indeed, land in the living room and she'd never notice. What am I saying?

This is ridiculous. I'm looking at an innocent mobile phone as if it's about to exude Technicolor horror worms. I've spooked myself with Cara's hocus pocus. I grab Cara's phone and say: 'Hello.'

I sound scared to death.

'Hi,' a very lovely and unpoltergeist-type voice says.

'Hi,' I say back.

'Is that Cara's phone?' he says brightly.

186

'Yes,' I answer. 'This is Emily.' I think I can risk giving that much information to the universe.

'Oh hi,' he says again. 'This is Adam. Adam Jackson. I work with Cara.'

'Oh hi,' I say and we're sort of back at square one.

'We've never met.'

'No.' I can confirm that much. Boy, this man is sharp.

'So you're Emily,' Adam says.

'Yes.'

'Even though we've never met, I feel like we know each other,' he continues. 'Cara's told me all about you.'

'Oh good grief,' I say. 'None of it's true. Except the good bits.'

Adam laughs and, far from sounding like a right dork, he has a very cute laugh. 'Well, there were quite a few of those.'

'Really?' That doesn't sound like my friend at all.

'You know, Emily,' he says, 'she's tried very hard to fight your corner.'

'I know,' I say. 'Cara's a good friend.'

There's an uncomfortable little pause and we've clearly exhausted our chit-chat quota.

'I hope things work out for you,' Adam says.

'Thanks. I'm sure they will.'

'Is Cara there?' he asks.

'Oh.' Crumbs, I'd nearly forgotten why he'd phoned. There's a lot of background noise and it sounds like Adam's in a pub. This is a good sign if he's calling Cara from a pub at the weekend – and then some sort of delayed thunderbolt hits me. Cara has actually done it! Her spell has worked! She has made contact with the universe! And Adam! The man himself is phoning her and she's missing it because she got covered in flour in the process.

'She's in the shower,' I stammer. 'I'll get her.'

'Don't disturb her,' Adam says. 'I'm just about to watch the football.'

'England, Germany,' I say. Old habits die hard.

'Yes,' he says. 'Do you follow football?'

'No,' I admit. 'Not really. It was just useful if I ever wanted a conversation with my ex-boyfriend.'

'Declan,' he says.

'Yes. Declan.' And I suddenly realise that Adam does indeed know everything about me.

'Tell Cara I'll catch up with her tomorrow at work.'

'She'll be sorry that she's missed you.' That, Ms Emily Miller, is the understatement of the year.

'It's been nice talking to you,' Adam says.

'It's been nice talking to you too, Adam,' I reply.

'Maybe we can meet up sometime?' he adds.

'Yes,' I agree. 'That'd be great.'

'Bye,' Adam says.

'Bye,' I echo.

I hang up and all the hairs on the back of my neck are erect. When I tell Cara about this, her dreadlocks are going to straighten of their own volition. I think The Carpenters have a lot to answer for.

Chapter Fifty-Three

Declan stood and surveyed his new, improved and pared-down operation.

Alan, perched on his desk, licked his cigarette paper and went through the measured ritual of preparing a roll-up. 'So? How's it hanging?'

'OK,' Declan replied thoughtfully.

There were several more empty desks now than there had been. Two secretaries had gone, three accounts clerks and four Webmasters. So had the pile of brown cardboard boxes containing unrequired gadgets of varying natures.

'We've managed to get rid of these.' He picked up a silver plastic Waterproof Shower Companion CD Player. A snip at £170 and something no home should be without.

It was a deal that Derek Trotter would have been proud of, but Declan had finally managed to offload them – at knockdown prices, of course. Still, they'd gone and he'd got the money for them – that was the important thing. His head wasn't exactly above water, but his eyes were some way above the main swell of waves and at least now he could see a way forward.

'Cheekybits.com is doing great,' Alan advised him. 'Five million hits this week. No worries there.'

Alan was right. The Cheekybits.com site was proving very popular thanks to a reliable supply of exceedingly cheeky and sexy photographs supplied by Sebastian Atherton, who had turned out to be something of a life-saver. The porn equivalent to the Samaritans. As long as men continued to want to ogle a wide selection of women's breasts then that should bring them in a steady stream of advertising revenue. He had even had requests to bring back the Saucy Santa. If only he could.

He'd also launched another site on the advice of the invaluable Alan – mylifeispants.com. It was a lifestyle site, manned by a perverse, sadistic 'agony aunt' who modelled herself on Anne Robinson. Every day she 'counselled' the droves of depressed

189

people who emailed into the service threatening to throw themselves off bridges, buildings, in front of buses, over cliffs, to do just that. And, judging from the constant flow of traffic through the site, there were a lot of people whose lives did, indeed, seem to be pants. A huge number of them returned to the site time and time again, thus proving, thankfully, that not many of them took her advice; they were just life's whingers.

Declan rubbed his hands across his eyes. His own life could currently be classed as pants too. He'd still not heard from Emily and he'd given up leaving messages for her on Cara's answerphone. There was something intrinsically sad about begging into a machine. Emily never had her mobile turned on these days either, presumably to stop herself from being hounded by the press and her ex-boyfriend. The furore seemed to be dying down and, perhaps, when the status quo was resumed, she would find it in her heart to forgive him.

Cara had been marvellous. A real brick. Unlike himself, who had been a real prick. He didn't know what he would have done without her. It was a shame that Amanda's mother had turned up when she did; it had given Cara the heebie-jeebies. As soon as the old lady had disappeared again – appeased by Declan's sincere-sounding promises to look after the potted plants – Cara had scuttled out of the Jacuzzi like a frightened rabbit and was back in her towel before he could say boo. Spending the evening, however brief, with Cara had been nice. She was very relaxing company in a slightly alternative way.

He felt that he ought to ring her, but he had so much to do. The first thing being trying to find alternative accommodation, otherwise he'd end up sleeping on his new, improved office floor. It would be a serious consideration if he'd had the forethought to have an executive shower installed. Adrian and Amanda would soon be returning home refreshed and revitalised from their sojourn to the other side of the world, and the last thing they would want to discover was someone sleeping in their bed. They would find out soon enough.

'So,' Alan said, breaking Declan's reverie, 'do you think you're on the way back?'

It was one of the many lovely things about Alan; his conversation was as languorous as his cigarette rolling. You could leave an hour's gap between sentences and Alan would never hassle you. Another lovely thing was that he'd been digging harder than anyone to help Declan get out of the shit. When he had something decent to offer him a directorship of, he would make it his first priority. 'Yeah,' Declan nodded, feeling a blessed trickle of relief starting to ease steadily through his veins. 'You've been a great mate.'

Somewhere behind his hair Alan raised his eyebrows. 'That's what friends are for.'

Declan felt his throat tighten, making any reply impossible. *That's what friends are for*. It was something that he was only just beginning to appreciate.

Chapter Fifty-Four

Cara was amazed that she hadn't pulled all of her hair out by now. Adam was late. Only three minutes late, admittedly. But that was one hundred and eighty seconds and she was aching to see him. He had phoned her. He had actually phoned her!

Unable to contain herself any longer she'd gone into the office early. They were working the evening shift together and, after tearing down all the posters of Emily once again, she'd been rearranging the relationship corner of her desk into a more auspicious alignment since 9.30 p.m. Cara smiled to herself. Adam. One whole night. No interruptions. It made her feel so happy she could have broken into a spontaneous chant.

Adam, three minutes and thirty seconds late, came wandering across the office. He, by contrast, didn't look quite so thrilled at the prospect of working the night-shift. Nothing ever happened – they all knew that. Generally, it was a complete waste of time. But the office had always been run like this and, just because it was totally unnecessary, the management saw no reason to change it. Cara normally spent the night reading self-help tomes and the guys she worked with normally spent the night surfing the net to see who could find the most dubious sites.

'Hey,' Adam said, throwing his coat over the back of his chair.

'Hi,' Cara replied. She was beginning to feel ridiculously shy in his presence and it was irritating her. It was also irritating her that Adam was completely oblivious to this change in her demeanour towards him.

He sat down and stretched at his desk. 'I called you yesterday,' he said.

Cara grinned stupidly. 'Emily told me.'

'She sounds nice,' Adam said. 'We chatted away like old friends.'

A dark cloud crossed behind Cara's eyes. Emily hadn't told her that bit.

'We'll all have to go out for a drink sometime.'

'Mmm,' Cara said crisply. 'I'm not sure that Emily would be very good company at the moment. She's just fallen totally and utterly in love with some hunk and talks about nothing else.'

'That's nice,' Adam said. 'She deserves something good to happen for once.'

'Yes,' Cara said. 'She's very happy.' It wouldn't be helpful for Adam to know that she was as miserable and sour as last week's milk because she hadn't even managed to get her dreamboat's name, let alone his phone number.

'What did you want me for?' Adam asked.

Cara looked puzzled. 'You rang me.'

'I was returning your call. You'd tried to ring me on Saturday night, but I was out. Your number was logged on 1471.'

'Oh,' Cara said. Oh, fiddlesticks!

'Was it about work?' Adam said.

'Yes,' Cara said. 'Work. It was about work.'

'That's what I thought.'

'Yes. Work,' Cara said again just to be sure. 'It was about work.'

Adam nodded.

'So,' she trilled brightly, 'where did you get to on Saturday? Did you have a hot date?'

'As a matter of fact I did,' Adam said, sounding almost as surprised as Cara looked. He searched in his pockets for some change. 'Do you fancy some coffee?'

'Yes,' Cara said, glad that she had actually retained the power of speech. 'Strong. Black.'

Adam got up and sauntered over to the coffee machine. As she watched him walk away from her Cara sagged into her seat. This was beyond terrible. The object of her affections was pursuing another woman despite being under the force of the universe to head in Cara's direction. What had gone wrong? She had been so convinced that the spell would work. This was getting to the point where she might have to consider investing in a psychic counsellor.

The phone rang. Cara picked it up. '*Hampstead Observer*. News desk.' Her face blanched as she listened to the message. 'Right,' she said, scribbling notes on the pad in front of her. 'Thanks for that.'

Adam appeared with coffee as she hung up. 'We've no time for that,' she said, snatching up her bag. 'Get your coat.'

'What's happened?' Adam asked while he did as instructed. He slung his coat over his shoulder and checked for his car keys.

'It's not good,' she said with a distressed shake of her head. 'Not good at all.'

'Tell me on the way,' Adam replied.

And, grim-faced, they both headed out of the office.

Chapter Fifty-Five

I've got the house all to myself. An entire evening where I can relax without having to chant, meditate or entreat the universe to do something or another whilst pretending to mean it. Great. And what am I doing with it? Watching *Watercolour Challenge*.

A group of four disparate and faintly bemused artists are trying to paint Mont Orqueil Castle whilst sitting in the full force of the ninety-mile-an-hour breeze on the flat expanse of Gorey Sands in Jersey. And what a performance they're making of it, struggling gamely in the face of adversity. As well as the gale, it's pissing down with rain and they're all huddled on the beach under umbrellas doing their best to hang onto their canvases. Hannah Gordon is valiantly trying to inject some sort of tension into the fact that they only have four windswept hours left in which to fill up their paper with an original masterpiece. Four hours! I could redecorate Cara's lounge in that time, let alone knock out a watercolour. Dear me! Hardly the cutting edge of television, is it? Even worse, it's a repeat. I can't believe anyone would want to watch it all over again. I thought Channel 4 was supposed to be all sex and swearing after 9.00 p.m. Perhaps Hannah Gordon will get her kit off in a minute. But no. I am *actually* watching paint dry. My life cannot get any more exciting than this.

I am still pining for The Hunk from the wine bar and Cara has lost patience with me – a process that doesn't take very long. I should be using this free evening to contemplate my life, make strategy plans for my future survival and generally get my act together. It's just that my brain has entered this frozen state of suspended animation, and no matter what I do to try to persuade it to think, it just won't play ball. I think I'm in shock.

I hear a car pull up outside and, gratefully, I turn off the enthusiastic artists and go and peep out of the curtain. Call me paranoid, but I still have an abject fear of the hordes of journalists descending again when they get bored with Jeffrey Archer. It is Declan's BMW and I can't even begin to tell you how I feel when the

194

headlights fade and the car door swings silently open and I see Declan himself standing there. I'm so stunned that I go and open the front door, without giving a thought to the fact that I don't want anything to do with him any more.

Declan comes up the path and his whole demeanour says tired and weary, but his eyes brighten when he finally looks up and sees me waiting.

'What are you doing here?' I say.

'I came to see you,' Declan answers, his shoulders slumped.

'You'd better come in,' I say because I can't summon up the necessary energy to tell him to get lost and I stand aside while he goes in. The realisation that I'm spending my life watching paint dry has obviously weakened my resolve.

He follows me into the lounge and sits down. Declan looks quieter and sadder than I have ever seen him. He leans forward in the chair, twisting his hands together.

'Where's Cara?' he says.

'Out,' I answer. 'Working.'

'Oh.' Declan wrings his hands some more and does a good impression of looking tortured. 'How are things?' he asks.

'Terrible,' I say.

'Good.' He twists his hands some more. 'Good.'

I haven't even the strength to give voice to my inner sigh. 'Do you want tea?' I offer.

'Haven't you got anything stronger?'

'You're driving,' I say. 'A BMW.' I'm sure he thinks more of that car than he does of me. He certainly never treats it as badly.

'It's all I have left, Emily,' he says. 'A useless status symbol. An emblem of an empire that no longer exists.'

'Sell it and give me half,' I suggest. 'That emblem would pay my rent.'

I disappear into the kitchen to make tea before I'm tempted to punch Declan. One of us is not living in the real world, and it's definitely not me. I'd never realised before how well suited Declan would be to Cara – both of them are on entirely different planets to the rest of us.

Declan plods after me to the kitchen, transferring his bottom from the armchair to the stool at the end of the worktop.

'I haven't come to tell you that things are bad,' he says encouragingly. 'Quite the opposite. I think the business has turned the corner.' Declan perks up considerably when he starts talking on his favourite, and the much safer, subject of work. 'We've got some great new sites. You should look at them.'

'Funnily enough, I try to stay clear of the Internet,' I say. 'Both as an invaluable tool and appearing on it.'

'I can understand that,' he says, slightly chastened.

'Declan,' I say, wishing Tetley's produced arsenic tea bags, 'is there any point in this visit other than to piss me off totally?'

My heart-breakingly handsome boyfriend crosses the kitchen and comes to stand behind me. He reaches out his hand, but then thinks better about touching me. It could be the way I fold my arms across my chest. I think he's actually quite lucky that I haven't taken up a lethal karate stance.

'I miss you, Emily,' he says. He moves closer so that I feel his breath on my neck. 'I want to hear you moan like you used to.'

'That can be arranged,' I say, inching away from his warm breath. 'I hate the way you used to leave your socks lying on the bedroom floor. And you always used to leave the loo seat up and—'

Declan looks at me sadly. 'I meant moan with pleasure.'

'I know exactly what you meant.' I abandon any attempts to make tea. 'Those days are gone.'

'They don't have to be,' he says. This is the closest I have seen Declan come to begging. 'I'll prove to you that I am worthy of your love again.' Now I think he has really lost it. A grovel too far. 'I'm going to pay off all our debts.'

I decide not to point out that they're only *our* debts because he tricked me.

'The company will be even bigger and better,' he states triumphantly.

'But with money in the bank account,' I remind him.

'Yes.'

'And somehow you're going to get me my job back,' I say.

Declan retreats to the other side of the work surface. 'You should take them to court for unfair dismissal, Emily.'

'I should take you to court for fraud,' I say.

Declan has the grace to pale slightly.

My sigh finally escapes. 'But I'm not going to do that either.'

Declan tries one of his winning smiles. 'Can't we just put this behind us as one big mistake?' he says.

'It wasn't my mistake, Declan.'

'We could start all over again,' he urges. 'Maybe we should have done more things together as a couple.'

I hesitate to suggest that maybe we should have done less.

Declan must have read the expression on my face, for he says, 'I mean shopping and stuff.'

'Ah yes. The couple who shop together stay together,' I say. 'I'm sure that regular excursions to Harrods is the answer to all our problems.'

Realising that he's on a losing streak, Declan changes tack. 'Say that you don't love me, Emily,' he instructs and puts on his little boy lost face.

He is beautiful. His chocolate-brown eyes fill with tears and his perfect teeth bite his full, sensuous lips nervously.

He is beautiful. But there is nothing beneath it, not for me. I've seen the hardness of his heart and I can never forget it. 'I don't love you,' I say.

Declan looks shocked as if a sharp pain has stabbed his body. His eyes are hurt. 'You mean it, don't you?'

'Yes,' I say with a melancholy sigh. 'I do.' As I look at him my anger dissipates and I feel nothing but sadness for the loss of our relationship and the cruel gash it has cut through my basic trust of others.

Declan edges away from me. 'I'll go then.'

I have no fight left in me at all. 'I think that's for the best.'

Declan walks out of the kitchen and towards the front door. I follow uncertainly. He opens the door and turns as if to leave. 'I still love you,' he says.

I say nothing as he walks out of the door and back towards his car. This probably isn't a good time to mention that I might just be in love with someone else.

Chapter Fifty-Six

Adam was driving the company Vectra. Cara sat in the passenger seat huddled into her coat for warmth in the absence of a working heater. The windscreen wipers were losing their battle as they tried valiantly to swash the rain away. What had started out as a cold, bleak winter's night had turned rapidly into a cold, bleak, rain-lashed and deeply unpleasant winter's night. Adam was hunched forward, tense, his knuckles white on the steering wheel.

'Nearly there,' he said, and flashed a quick glance at her.

Cara nodded.

Fatalities, the report had said. A coy term for dead people. Mangled dead people. Innocent people killed in a car crash. People who had loved ones waiting for them – perhaps anxious now, watching the clock. People who wouldn't be going home. No matter how long she had been a journalist, dealing with the aftermath of a road traffic accident was never easy. It was all part of the job, but Cara always had the feeling that it was none of their business to be there. Was it so important to report a story that they had to intrude, lurk on the fringes of other people's suffering? Couldn't it all wait until the pain had died down?

Adam's lips were set in a tight line and Cara wondered what he was thinking. She wanted him to hold her hand, to comfort her. But he was silent, grim and grey-faced in the half-light of the car.

Blue police lights flashed brightly in the raindrops on the windscreen and told her that they had arrived at the scene. The police had set up a road block and Adam pulled up on the periphery of it. A lone policeman was directing traffic and was lucky, in a bizarre way, that it was such an awful night as it meant there was little traffic on the road. He was hunkered down in his waterproof coat, struggling to retain an authoritative presence in the face of the elements and he waved a few rubber-necking drivers on with an irritated expression.

There were two tangled wrecks of metal in the middle of the road. One looked like it might be a Renault. Goodness only knows what the other had been. The front was completely ripped away, leaving its innards spewing out into the road like a scene from a sci-fi horror movie. Thick, black oil trickled away like seeping blood.

Even though Adam had stopped, he kept his grip on the steering wheel for a moment as if bracing himself against the horror to come. There were three police cars, a big red fire engine, as jolly as any children's toy, and an ambulance which had its back doors open, providing a slash of warm light to the miserable night. Their Day-Glo yellow and blue checked decals looked too cheerful in the middle of the gore.

The rain pounded down, obliterating their view. Ice was a fairly rare phenomenon in London, but if the temperature continued to plummet, the roads would be like skating rinks by tomorrow morning.

'Ready?' Adam said, knowing full well that neither of them were.

'Yes,' Cara said wearily and pulled her voluminous bag from the back seat.

Adam scuttled round to the rear of the car, grabbed his camera gear from the boot and joined her in the rain. 'What a filthy night,' he said, reverting to the British necessity to comment on the weather no matter how inane it might be or how adverse the circumstances.

'Come on,' Cara said, gritting her teeth. 'Let's get this over with.'

They flashed their Press Cards as they walked past the policeman on traffic duty, who nodded curtly in response. Most policemen viewed journalists and photographers as necessary evils – neither side appreciating that they were both only brought together at times like this because they had a job to do. The firemen were usually more pragmatic about their role. Perhaps they were kept sane because they occasionally still had nice jobs to do like rescue kittens from trees for dear old ladies.

Adam pulled up his collar but, despite the rain, neither of them rushed. They both surveyed the scene with mounting dread.

'I'll see you back here in ten minutes,' Adam said briskly. And, starting to undo his camera bag, he disappeared into the depths of the crash scene.

Cara stopped next to a policeman who looked like he needed a cigarette.

'Alcohol,' he responded flatly when she asked him what had happened. 'Same as it always is. They were on their way home from that new wine bar. Why is it they never learn that drinking and driving don't mix?' He wore the weary expression of someone who had seen this far too often and just wanted to be at home, in bed, next to his wife and out of the rain and away from the crushed cars.

He gave her the facts. Only one fatality. Anthony Scarborough, nineteen years old, from Stanmore. Driver of the Renault Clio. Died on impact. Multiple injuries. Three passengers. He reeled off their names from a list. Sustained minor injuries. Other car, a Peugeot 406. One passenger. Male, forty-three. David Smith. On his way to Accident and Emergency at the Royal Free Hospital. Suspected fractured ribs. Lucky escape.

Cara jotted it all down. 'Thanks,' she said, and moved away. The policeman nodded and returned to his impassive stare.

One fatality. They were lucky, judging by the amount of wreckage. The firemen were packing up now, ready to leave and head back to the warmth of their station, their job done for the night. They'd had to cut one of the youngsters out of the car. Nothing too bad, though.

She followed the light towards the ambulance, her stomach tensing as she approached, the sound of sobbing growing louder. As she craned her neck round the open door, she saw three teenagers, a fresh-faced, ashen boy wearing a torn Nike T-shirt, and two girls, both wearing sparkly outfits, high heels and very little else. There would be no more partying for them tonight. The girls' faces were streaked with blood, mascara and lipstick smears, bright mocking colours against the chalk-white of their skins like some sort of sick carnival masks. Cara felt the bile rise in her throat. One of the girls sat silently, holding her blood-stained dress together, as the young man squeezed her hand distractedly. The other girl, looking younger and more scared, was responsible for the steady sobbing and was having her head bandaged by a portly paramedic, who was softly cooing platitudes at her. A red, sticky mark had already oozed out to mar the whiteness of the dressing, just as the memory of this night would mar the purity of whatever they did in the future. They would always remember that they, at least, had a future. One fatality, but three youngsters with their innocence dead inside them.

Cara eased herself into the back of the ambulance. 'All right?' she said.

'Flesh wounds,' the paramedic said. 'These are the lucky ones.' The sobbing intensified. His face softened in sympathy. 'Their friend wasn't so fortunate.'

She wanted to say something to the stricken-looking children who had grown up in the space of the last hour. But what words could she use? She didn't know them at all. She was simply here to do her job. And her job was to report the facts of the crash, not the fact that so many lives would be blighted by something as simple as one drink too many and a bend being taken too fast.

She took their names and addresses, scant details to titillate the masses and their version of this tragic night out. Cara was as brief

200

and professional as she needed to be, but she wanted to hug them all to her before she left. Muttering some pointless pleasantry about everything being all right, she escaped from the disinfectant smell of the stark ambulance and plunged back into the night.

Clutching her notebook to her in an attempt to protect it from the rain, Cara picked her way through the bits of metal and glass strewn across the road – hubcaps twisted and torn, fragments of red brake-light casings, a lone door handle. And then, sadder than anything, a shoe. Anthony Scarborough's shoe. Trendy, expensive, and lying on its side, shredded on the road. There was blood on it. Not oil blood, but real blood. Red, spent lifeblood. Steam escaped gently into the night as the cars breathed their last gasp.

This is where he had died. Anthony Scarborough, aged nineteen, of Stanmore. Crushed, in the middle of the road, presumably from driving too fast under the influence of alcohol. Multiple injuries. It was a cruel and silly way to die. Cara's stomach was churning. How many of us optimistically planned for the future, she thought, yet could never really know whether we would make it home safely to our bed each night? Life was a very fragile commodity; it could be snuffed out by a moment of unthinking madness.

Adam was on the other side of the car, snapping away, taking photographs as if on auto-pilot. He too looked tired and drawn. Cara went to move towards him. She had finished here and all she wanted to do was get out, get back to the office and do what she had to do to fulfil her duty.

Skirting round the dismembered wheels and their tattered tyres, treading on the muddy grass verge to avoid the worst of the debris, her feet were soon wet through and freezing cold. Cara looked down at them, thinking how unsuitable her shoes were for a night like this, and as she did so, she noticed the stains on them. Not dirt or rain or oil, but blood. Dark patches that had soaked into the leather and had crept over the edges, bleeding into the flesh tones of her tights. She gasped for breath. How had it happened? In her need to get nearer to the wreck, she must have walked in a pool of blood. Was it Anthony Scarborough's blood defying the elements, that had clung to her? The thought made Cara's legs buckle beneath her and, curling up in the gutter, lashed by the unrelenting rain, she was violently sick.

Adam was swiftly at her side, kneeling in the rain. 'What happened?' he shouted.

Cara sobbed as she wiped her mouth on the sleeve of her coat.

'Oh shit,' Adam said and fished through his pockets until he found a tissue. He tried to straighten it out before he gave it to her, but abandoned the idea and dabbed at her ineffectually with it instead.

201

Cara cried louder. For the loss of Anthony Scarborough. For the loss of herself. For Emily. For Declan. And for Adam.

'Let's get you back to the car,' Adam said, a note of panic in his voice.

He wrapped his arms round her, gathering her up from the gutter and she felt herself go limp in his embrace.

'Fucking hell,' she heard Adam mutter as he hoisted her up and carried her like an ungainly sack of King Edwards potatoes in a wobbling gait back to the waiting Vectra. After that everything went blissfully black.

Chapter Fifty-Seven

I feel really shaken up by Declan's visit, and indulge myself in two cups of Tetley's finest, swiftly followed by several glasses of Jacob's Creek's finest. But I'm still feeling rattled, if a little more blurred.

What is this love thing? I'd like to know. Declan says he still loves me, but what does that mean in his book? In all the years we'd been together, I'd hardly ever met his parents. Shouldn't that have told me something? He was never very big on family occasions. I went to most of mine on my own as my dearly beloved could always find some work he needed to do. I'd assumed Declan was ashamed of his mother and father or something in his background, but perhaps he was ashamed of me. I don't know.

We never went to garden centres together either. How weird is that? Whenever we needed shrubs I had to go and buy them on my own. Don't couples normally share the pain and expense of horti-culture? The closest we ever got to commitment, apart from our joint astronomical debt, was the fact that after six months he presented me with a neatly word-processed list of his family's birthdays and I had, ever since, become responsible for their cards and presents. But isn't that always the way? Show me a man who sends his own birthday cards and I'll show you Callista Flockhart trying to struggle into size fourteen jeans. It's not going to happen, is it?

I've tried phoning Cara, but her office phone goes straight to voicemail and her mobile's switched off. She's probably having a high old time in the staff canteen with Adam. That girl could not wait to get to work to see him! I tell you, she was like a teenager off to an S Club Seven concert – knicker-wetting levels of excitement, scattered hormones and a face-full of war paint. Never in the history of journalism has anyone chosen their clothes so carefully for a night-shift. And, I have to say, after my rather brief conversation with him the other night, he did sound a little bit yummy.

Cara is convinced that all her spells are finally doing their business, and I can only hope she's right. Cara is a dear, dear friend, but a total pain in the arse once she gets a bee in her bonnet. If this

Adam doesn't give in gracefully, then the full might of all sorts of things will be brought down on his head. Cara will be up the garden gathering eye of newt and toe of frog before you can say 'RSPCA'. This is a woman who is against all cruelty to animals, unless, of course, it involves them being put in a magic potion. She's already rented *The Witches of Eastwick* on video. Twice. I'll end up living in the middle of a coven if I'm not very careful.

I wanted to do girly bonding with her and whinge about Declan and The Unknown Hunk, but after fourteen attempts, she's still not there. That's friends for you.

Taking the second bottle of Jacob's Creek upstairs with me, I decide on an early night. Tomorrow, I really ought to think about bracing myself to make an appointment with Sebastian Atherton, photographer to the nearly-clothed. It is a very sobering thought. Well, not quite.

As I climb onto my bed, the soft fluffy duvet welcomes me, embracing me like a long lost lover. I take a lingering glug from the bottle of wine and let it dangle over the side until it finds the floor, then I roll over and curl my knees up and hug them. I'm just going to have forty winks before I do the getting undressed thing and take off my make-up. My pillow gently cradles my head, sucking me down into deep, deep sleep. Getting undressed can wait.

Chapter Fifty-Eight

'Cara!' Adam said, gently shaking her shoulder. 'Come on – wake up.' He'd driven straight to Cara's place, which seemed like a good idea at the time as he hadn't a clue what else to do with her. She'd gone spark out the minute he'd picked her up, and had shown no signs of coming to all the way back here. Maybe he should have taken her to one of the paramedics, but they seemed to have their hands full with rather more pertinent matters than passing-out journalists.

It had been a particularly gory crash scene and Adam had, unfortunately, been forced to cover rather more than he cared to remember in his long career as a photographer. Even he'd felt faint, so no wonder Cara had flaked out.

'Cara,' he said again. 'Time to wake up.'

Her eyelids flickered briefly as if she was in REM sleep and then her eyes opened fully. 'What?' she said, dazed.

'We're here,' Adam said softly. 'We're back at your house.'

The journey had taken ages. As always after covering a fatal crash, Adam drove like he was on his driving test for the next week or so – push-pull steering, mirror-signal-manoeuvre, sticking resolutely to one mile below the speed limit. Eventually, the demands of his career would require him to fly round the place like a mad thing and all his carefulness and consideration to other road-users would be forgotten and he'd be back brewing with road rage like the rest of them.

Cara looked out of the window to confirm that they were, indeed, outside her front door. Then she sank back against the seat.

'Are you feeling OK?'

'No,' she said and put her hand to her head.

'You fainted,' Adam explained. Cara looked as if she was starting to remember. 'Do you think you can walk to your front door?'

Cara nodded weakly. Great. He certainly wasn't in a rush to carry her again. Cara might look like she'd blow over in a stiff wind, but Adam decided she must have very solid bones. 'Wait there,' he instructed and scooted out to rush round to Cara's side to help her out.

She wiggled to the edge of her seat and let Adam ease her out. Cara looked pasty and her hair was plastered flat to her head.

'Got your key?' he asked.

Looking at him with eyes that were dead and dazed, Cara fished it out of her coat pocket and handed it over. Half propping her on his shoulder, Adam staggered down the path, wishing that the rain wasn't still trying to swat them off their intended course.

The hall light was on, which helped Adam in his efforts to connect key with lock whilst precariously balancing Cara on one arm. He guided her inside, and headed in the general direction of where he thought the kitchen might be. Fortunately he was right. He sat Cara down on one of the kitchen chairs and flicked on the light. Adam winced. His friend was not a pretty sight. Mascara streaked her face and there was a horrible mélange of stains merged on the front of her coat – dirty rain, mud, vomit, blood.

Adam knelt before her. 'Feeling better now?'

'Yes.' Cara's voice was as weak and wobbly as she was, but at least she was speaking again.

'Tea?'

Cara burst into tears, sobbing nosily.

'Something stronger,' Adam said.

'Brandy.' Cara pointed to the appropriate cupboard and he duly headed towards it. He pulled out the bottle of brandy and rinsed out two mugs that stood on the draining board. He splashed a generous measure into one and a smaller one for himself – after all, he had to drive back to the office.

He gave Cara the mug and gently folded her fingers round it. 'Here,' he said. 'Drink it. It'll do you good.'

Cara took it, coughing as she sipped it. Adam tasted his. The hot, peppery liquid warmed his mouth. No wonder Cara was in such a state; the images of twisted metal and shattered lives still burned against his eyelids. When you were on a job like that, you just got on with it. It was only afterwards, when you were away from it and your brain started to digest the full horror of it, that the trauma began to sink in. He'd been through it enough times to recognise the symptoms. Cara shuddered and huddled her coat round her.

'I think you ought to get out of those wet things,' he said, noticing that she had bloodstains on the tops of her shoes. 'Is Emily in?'

Cara nodded. 'She's probably in bed.'

'Do you want me to wake her?'

Cara nodded again. 'Please.'

'I'll be back in a minute,' he said tenderly and went off in search of Emily.

Chapter Fifty-Nine

Adam stopped tiptoeing up the stairs when he realised that his prime mission was to wake Emily, and he stomped up the last few steps just for the hell of it. The first door he tried turned out to be the bathroom, so, in an effort to be useful, he switched the shower on in the hope that the initial jets of freezing cold water would eventually start to run warm.

The upstairs of Cara's house continued the eclectic theme of the downstairs – challenging colours in a vaguely 1970s scheme that had 'Cara' stamped all over it. The next door he tried was her room. He could tell that by the incense burners, the crystal mobiles that dangled from the ceiling and the horoscope posters on the walls. The room had a naïve, girlish feel to it and his heart went out to his friend in her suffering. Cara was so wacky that you couldn't help but like her. She was so sweet too. He would love to be able to cushion her from the harsh realities of the world. What she needed was some woolly-jumpered, sandal-wearing vegetarian chap to take care of her. Why she insisted on sticking at this soul-destroying job, heaven only knew. But then he felt much the same about himself. Except for the woolly-jumpered, sandal-wearing, vegetarian chap. He closed the door and moved down the landing.

There was a deep steady stream of snoring coming from the next room, which he assumed must, in turn, be coming from Emily. Adam paused, his fingers curled ready to knock on the door. He hadn't had her down as a snorer. This was weird. Adam had the feeling that he was going to walk in through the door to find her sitting around in her Saucy Santa's outfit. It was the only picture of Emily he had. And a very pleasant one it was, too.

Adam knocked gently on Emily's door. The sound of snoring remained unbroken. 'Emily,' he called softly. Then louder: 'Emily. It's Cara's friend – Adam.'

He put his ear to the door. Emily slumbered on unhindered. The sound of Cara crying again drifted up the stairs.

'Oh shit,' Adam muttered and reluctantly eased open Emily's door.

There was no sign of the Saucy Santa's outfit in Emily's bedroom, only a huge, shapeless lump in the bed with a duvet pulled over its head. A tiny white pair of feet with red-painted toenails peeped out of the bottom. The snoring intensified. Adam moved gingerly across the room. 'Emily,' he said and shook the sleeping mound. 'Wake up. It's me – Adam.'

Emily, if it was possible, snored more loudly. It could have been Jude Law dressed only in his boxers and she wouldn't have cared less. Adam looked down and saw a bottle knocked over on its side; a puddle of red wine had seeped out onto the carpet. He righted the bottle and sat down heavily on the edge of her bed. 'Oh, Emily,' he said. 'What am I going to do now?'

At which Emily stretched her legs, kicked him firmly in the bottom with one of her painted toes and grunted indelicately in her sleep.

Chapter Sixty

What Adam did do was go back downstairs where he found Cara sobbing more forcefully as she drained the contents of the brandy bottle into her mug.

'Emily's asleep,' he said. 'I tried to wake her up, but she's out for the count.' He turned another empty wine bottle upside down in front of Cara. Not even one solitary drop fell out.

'Oh,' she said pathetically.

'I turned your shower on,' Adam told her. 'Do you want to go upstairs and get cleaned up?'

'Yes.' Cara hugged her arms round herself. 'That would be nice.'

Adam finished his own brandy. 'I'll be off then.'

'Don't go, Adam,' Cara said.

'Er . . .'

She looked a pitiful sight. 'I need to talk to someone about this.'

Adam glanced at the clock. 'I should get back to the office.'

'Stay a bit longer. I'll take the rap if Martin kicks up a fuss tomorrow.'

It wasn't Martin the Editor who was worrying him. This had a distinct flavour of intimacy; it was creeping round the edge of 'getting very cosy' and Adam had long-since forgotten how to do cosy.

'I have no one else, you see,' Cara admitted and the tears welled up in her eyes again.

Adam abandoned his mug and rushed to her side. Wrapping his arms round her, he held her to his chest until the wracking sobs stopped again. 'Haven't you got any potions and lotions you could rub on?' he suggested helpfully. Whenever anyone injured themselves at work, Cara always managed to conjure up something to fix it out of her desk drawer.

'I've got some Bach Flower Rescue Remedy in the bathroom,' she said. Adam thought it might be a good idea for him to have some too.

'Come upstairs.' Cara stood on legs that were still wobbly.

Make that a double, Adam decided.

Cara stumbled slightly as she let go of the death-grip she had on the kitchen table.

'Here,' Adam said, offering her the support of his arm. 'Let me help you.' And he walked her up the stairs, step by painful step, as if she'd been crippled by the emotional scenes.

They finally reached the bathroom door and Adam helped her inside. There was a fog of encouragingly warm steam seeping out of the shower cubicle. Cara peeled off her coat and let it drop to the floor.

'Where's the wotsit stuff?' Adam said.

'Rescue Remedy.' Cara kicked off her shoes and whimpered a bit more. 'Bathroom cabinet.'

Adam picked through the copious bottles squashed onto the shelves until he found the tiny brown bottle of Rescue Remedy.

'Here,' he said.

'Three drops,' Cara advised. 'Under the tongue.'

Adam filled up the pipette, Cara opened her mouth and he squirted the entire contents straight in. It felt like feeding a helpless baby bird. Adam squirted some into his own mouth for good measure. It tasted bitter and, more importantly, as if it wouldn't do very much.

Listlessly, Cara started to drag her jumper over her head. It was time for Adam to leave.

'Look,' he said. 'I'll wait outside while you shower. Shout if you need me.'

Cara's lip puckered again. 'Thanks, Adam.'

Adam slipped out of the bathroom door, closing it gently behind him. The snores still emanated from Emily's room. That girl could clearly sleep for England. The sound of a heavy sigh and Cara getting into the shower came from behind him.

Adam settled himself down on the carpet, took off his jacket and leaned his back against the bathroom door. When he was in the shower he had a list of favourite songs to sing. They bore no relation to his usual musical taste, but were all good soul-cleansing, armpit-scrubbing, head-banging, joy-inducing numbers – Bon Jovi, 'Living on a Prayer', anything by Meatloaf, and the full-length version of 'Bohemian Rhapsody' by Queen was always a good standby for a particularly long sloosh after a stressful day. All of which he performed loudly, trying to get at least every other note on key. It was the only type of therapy he indulged in. Shower-gel containers were the perfect shape to be pressed into service as microphones. By the time he'd Scaramouched, Scaramouched and done the Fandango a few times most of the cricks and knots had disappeared from his neck and shoulders and he was ready to face the world again. He wondered why no one had thought to make shower sponges in the shape of air guitars. What a winner! Adam closed his eyes and drifted. Poor Cara. She'd had a plateful. He didn't think there'd be any singing coming forth from the shower tonight.

Chapter Sixty-One

'Better?' Adam said when Cara finally emerged from the shower and opened the bathroom door.

'Yes.' She tried a weak smile as she edged past him and stepped daintily over his feet. 'Come through.'

With an anxious wiggle in his stomach, Adam pushed himself up from the floor and followed her through to the bedroom.

'Sit,' she said, indicating a sofa piled high with cushions glittering with silver thread, mirrored-bits and tassels. Adam sat.

There were sumptuous drapey bits everywhere. Swags of silk, velvet throws, plush rugs. Half a dozen different gauzy fabrics made up the curtains. It looked as if a Sheikh's tent had collided with a New Age shop – and it made his own MFI-furnished place look very sparse by comparison. If he did ever manage to get Josh to live with him on a permanent basis, they'd have to do something about the décor. Perhaps Cara might help. Though only if he could tone her down to somewhere approaching magnolia.

Cara was wearing, he couldn't help but notice, a Demis Roussos-style kaftan in a shade of pink that made your eyeballs vibrate. It swamped her, making her look like a vulnerable little girl. All the smudges of make-up had been scrubbed from her skin and some colour had come back to her pale cheeks. He didn't think he'd ever seen one of his colleagues in their dressing gowns before and it was a strange feeling. A strange, *nice* feeling.

'It's a traditional Berber fertility gown,' Cara informed him as she caught him studying her. She spread out the skirt of the kaftan so that he could admire the embroidery.

'Oh,' he said. 'It's pretty.' He might have known that she wouldn't wear a dressing gown from Top Shop.

'Mummy and Daddy brought it back from one of their many trips to Morocco.'

'Oh,' Adam said. 'What do your parents do?'

'Good,' Cara answered. 'They do good. All over the world. The more horrid the place, the better.'

212

'That must be difficult to live up to,' Adam said.

'Terribly,' she agreed flatly.

Cara padded across the room in her bare feet. They looked better without her bloodstained shoes, dainty and white. She lit some sort of incense stick and the heady scent of melting chocolate drifted into the room. It was relaxing and sensual and made Adam realise how tense he was himself. There was a great temptation to kick off his own shoes and stretch out on the welcoming bed of cushions.

'Vanilla,' Cara said as if she'd read his thoughts. 'It'll help us to relax.'

Adam sat up straighter and checked his watch. 'I really should get back.'

Cara came and sat down next to him. 'Adam,' she said, 'do you think I'm cut out for this sort of work?'

'Well, er . . .' Adam said, 'no.'

'You could have pretended to think about it,' Cara said with a glimmer of a smile.

'Sorry.' Adam cursed himself for being insensitive. 'It's just that I'm not sure that I'm cut out for it myself. I guess it makes detecting another square peg in a round hole that much easier.'

Cara inched closer to him. 'Sometimes, I think we have an awful lot in common.'

'Mmm,' he said, not sure whether he agreed or not. A mutual dissatisfaction with one's chosen profession didn't seem a lot to go on.

'I'm too sensitive to be doing this,' she said, her eyes filling with tears again. 'But I don't know what else to do.'

'Oh Cara,' he said, patting her hand.

'It's horrible when you live alone; you've got no one to talk to about important things.'

'What about Emily?' Adam suggested. 'Can't she help?'

Emily's snores permeated the convenient pause in the conversation.

Cara looked rueful. 'I think she has enough to think about at the moment.'

'I guess so,' Adam said. He felt he knew Emily inside out by now. One day it would be nice to meet her – when she hadn't been on a bender or was obscured by a mountainous duvet, and was wearing normal clothes.

'No one else at work understands me like you do, Adam,' Cara said. 'Tonight was so awful. It made me realise the pointlessness of what we do.'

Here Adam agreed totally. Who would benefit from front-page pictures of a car crash? Not the victim's loved ones, for sure. Would

213

it help them to see how their son had died? Splattered on the tarmac like roadkill.

'Chris would have been in his element, wouldn't he?' Cara said.

Adam nodded. She was right. Chris would have loved it. He wouldn't be sitting here knotted up and tearful over some nineteen year old they didn't even know. Chris was never happier than when he was ambulance chasing.

Cara had tucked her knees up into her kaftan, snuggling up on the sofa next to him. Adam knew how she felt. There was a need to share a closeness, the need to feel skin on skin, a need to give thanks that they were both alive. Not that he could articulate any of it. But that was the good thing about Cara – you didn't need to. Somehow she always understood.

God, Adam thought, she looked so delicious. Her tiny pink mouth pouted sadly. A solitary fat tear slid silently over her cheek and he resisted the urge to reach up and brush it away. Cara looked a million times better without the inch of colourful make-up she usually wore. She was a natural beauty and didn't need all that stuff to obscure it. Her mad hair curled round her face, springy tendrils clinging damply to her throat.

Adam coughed. This was so difficult. He wanted to pull her to him and hold her until she felt whole again. It would be so easy to take advantage of her in this situation. Easy to run his hands over the contours of the silky fabric of her kaftan. Easy to tease his fingers through her hair. Easy to cover her mouth with his.

Cara's hand was hot and dry on his chest, burning through his shirt. She eased herself nearer to him, her hand caressing his neck as his arms slipped round her. Their lips came together tenderly, and then more eagerly, searching, bruising.

'Take me to bed,' Cara whispered in his ear.

As Adam swung her into his arms for the second time that night and carried her to the bed, his only lucid thought was, how the hell did I manage that?

Chapter Sixty-Two

Cara was on the point of orgasm – Adam was sure of it. But then it was always difficult to tell when you didn't know someone very well. It was always difficult to tell anyway, he'd found. Women were so good at pretending. You were never quite sure whether you were hitting all the right spots or they couldn't wait to get it over with and were trying to hurry the proceedings along. This, however, definitely felt like bliss. Pure bliss. Losing yourself in the sheer delight of someone else's body. Blotting out all thoughts but sensation, pleasure, softness. Adam realised that it had been a long, long time since he'd done that.

At that moment, Cara cried out. A startled little bird's cry. He held her tighter. Her cry became more intense. Louder. Her fingers clutched at his back and he buried himself further inside her, welcoming the comfort of her warmth, the oblivion of making love. Cara's cry turned more strangled. Adam opened his eyes. A sob caught in Cara's throat. She was crying. Beneath him, she was crying. Cara's face was contorted and he wasn't sure it was with ecstasy. She was all red and screwed up. Tears spilled out from beneath her eyelashes, soaking the pillows, splashing on the duvet. Adam's orgasm trickled out of him, cold, wet and deflated. He rolled over on the pillow.

'What's wrong?' he murmured, pulling her towards him.

Cara wailed louder.

'Is it something I've done?' he asked, patting her back.

She clung to him and wept.

'Is it something I've said?'

Cara howled.

'It's emotional release,' Adam decided. 'After the crash.' He hoped he was right. 'It'll be okay.' God, he was crap at dealing with crying women. It was years since he'd had any practice. In the last few years it had been women who'd reduced *him* to floods of tears. 'Do you want a cup of tea?' It was always a good standby in times of crisis.

More tears. Apparently the answer was no.

'Do you want me to leave?'

Cara clung more fiercely to him.

Now Adam was deeply confused. And, no matter what he said or what he did, she wasn't to be placated. He was running out of options. For the next half hour she snivelled, sniffed and sobbed into his chest until finally she fell into a restless, twitching, mumbling sleep.

Adam lay on his back looking at the ceiling. Cara lay curled up, knees hugged tightly to her, back towards him. The cool winter dawn eased itself through the kasbah-style curtains, bathing the room in a flat grey light which did nothing to subdue its colour scheme. Adam didn't know quite where he wanted to be, but it wasn't waking up in an orange and purple, clothes-strewn bedroom with his work colleague.

Adam shaded his eyes with his arm, pushing back the unwelcome intrusion of light. His eyelids closed over them with all the comfort of a cheese-grater. He, in contrast to Cara, hadn't slept a wink all night. This was a bad, bad situation to be in. And one that he definitely should have avoided. He stared at the tense contours of his friend's sleeping back. She looked so white and fragile against the rich Burgundy sheets that he felt moved to reach out and touch her. He didn't. Perhaps her tears weren't about the crash. Perhaps it was because she suddenly realised who she was in bed with. She was probably wondering how the hell she was going to face him over the news desk in the morning. This was a terrible, terrible mistake. They were naked and making love before either of them, it seems, had considered the wisdom of their passion.

He silently berated himself for being totally hopeless at this sort of thing. What should he do? Would it be better to wake Cara and risk upsetting her again, or should he sneak out without disturbing her? This was ridiculous! He was a grown up – an adult who should be used to handling adult situations. Why did he always go to pot as soon as someone of the opposite sex became involved? Didn't other people grow out of this kind of emotional torture shortly after Josh's age?

The snoring coming from Emily's room had stopped. Adam wondered if she was awake. Perhaps *she'd* know what to do. He knew that he couldn't lie here any longer or he'd drive himself barmy with indecision. Adam slipped out of the bed and felt around on the floor until he located his boxers, and then grappled with them quietly so as not to wake Cara. Their clothes were scattered to the four corners of the room and Adam gradually located them all, feeling foolish as he crept around like a naturist cat burglar.

216

He pulled on his jeans and his roll-neck jumper, keeping his eye on Cara for any signs of life. Perhaps he should write her a note. But in the gloom, he couldn't focus on anything that looked like something he could scribble on. They'd have to deal with it in work later on anyway. This was stupid. Stupid of him. Adam retrieved his jacket from the sofa and shrugged that on too. He didn't dare look in the mirror; he knew without seeing his reflection that it would be a truly terrible sight. His chin probably looked like Desperate Dan's. Adam scratched his fingers through his hair, straightening the worst of its excesses. His mouth felt as if something small and furry had crawled into it and died.

He stood over Cara, not knowing whether he should risk planting a farewell kiss on her cheek in case it woke her up and set off a whole new avalanche of tears. As he didn't feel emotionally capable of dealing with it, disappearing was the best option. Casting a fond glance at Cara's frowning face, he tiptoed out of her room.

As he passed Emily's door, he paused. All was quiet. Adam tapped gently but there was no answer, so he opened the door tentatively and peeped round. The shapeless hump of duvet looked unmoved and the wine bottle was where he had left it. Emily, it seemed, was still off with the fairies.

Adam continued down the stairs, hoping that none of them creaked too loudly. At least escaping like this, it would give him a few hours to think of what to say to Cara. He inched towards the front door, turned and took one last melancholy look back up the stairs and then went outside into the chill, fresh dawn.

Chapter Sixty-Three

I'm sitting in the kitchen, making love to a cup of tea and contemplating my Declan-induced hangover when I hear the front door click shut. Strange.

I push myself upright and pad out into the lounge. No one. I carry on out into the hall when I hear a car start up and do my nosy neighbour bit and pull the curtain back and have a peep. A dark green Vectra is just pulling away outside, but I don't recognise the car and wonder with a little pang of jealousy whether Cara has had company. Perhaps she's finally got lucky with the lovely Adam.

There are times when I wish I was a morning person and this is one of them. The early greyness is giving way to a beautiful dawn. A pink swish is appearing above the houses and the clouds turn indigo as the sun deigns to put in a rare appearance. This is a wonderful time of day. So still and quiet. By the time I hit the ground running, the hell that is my usual day has already broken loose. I drop the curtain into place and go back into the kitchen and make Cara a cup of ginseng tea – although waking up to something that looks like gnat's pee cannot be very inspiring – and then plod up the stairs to deliver it.

When I stick my head round the door, Cara is cuddled up in a tight ball in her bed. There is indeed evidence of a visitor not long departed. Cara is a nightmare to share a bed with as she normally sleeps splayed out like a starfish. I have only experienced it on a few enforced occasions, and it's not something I'd hurry to repeat. Her eventual life-partner will have to get used to sleeping on a four-millimetre strip at the edge of the bed.

'Hey.' I shake her shoulder gently. 'Tea.'

Cara opens her eyes dreamily and looks rather disappointed to see me standing there. She's awake in a nano-second and shoots upright, grabbing the duvet round her.

'Where is he?' she hisses, looking at the empty space next to her.

'Who?' I say.

'Adam,' she says. '*The* Adam.'

218

'Does he drive a Vectra that looks like it's on its last legs?' I put her tea down and make myself comfortable on the bed in Adam's vacated space. It still feels warm and smells of nice man smells.

'Yes.'

'Gone,' I say.

'Gone?'

'Ten minutes ago.'

'Ten minutes ago?' Cara is turning into Little Sir Echo. 'What did he say?'

'Nothing.' I shrug.

'Nothing?' There she goes again.

'He sneaked out without me seeing him.' In fact I'm quite glad he didn't catch me in my raggy old dressing gown with mascara-panda eyes. 'I just saw his car disappearing down the street.'

'Oh wombats!' Cara snarls.

'So?' I give her a nudge. 'He's finally succumbed to the greater power of the universe?'

'I seized my moment,' Cara says, sounding like a conquering emperor. 'He melted into my arms.'

'Wonderful.' I wish I sounded less envious.

Cara sighed dreamily. 'Emily,' she says, snuggling down, 'it *was* wonderful. Fabulous.'

I lift an enquiring eyebrow.

'More than fabulous,' she says, warming to her theme. 'He is sensitive, caring, sexy, sensual.' My friend is going all squirmy. 'And has a gorgeous bottom.'

Is this really Cara I'm talking to?

'He is all I have ever wanted in a man.'

I think we can safely assume that Adam was a pretty good shag.

'The sex was sublime.' Cara smiles, serenely happy. 'It is the most spiritual experience I've ever had.'

Ah yes, that's more like it.

'I felt lifted up,' she continues.

I'm beginning to wish I'd never asked. This makes my romp in the Saucy Santa outfit seem as sordid as the tabloids have portrayed it.

Cara fixes me with one of her more scary earnest stares. 'I felt our souls merge,' she says, breathily candid.

I don't quite know how to respond to that. I've had some pretty hot-to-trot sex in my time, but I don't think I've ever had a soul-merge – and I lack the emotional strength at this moment to ask Cara for a blow-by-blow description.

My friend takes my hand and her eyes fill with tears. 'Emily, can I tell you something?'

'You haven't agreed to marry him?' I say suspiciously.

'No.' Cara is dismissive. Clearly nothing as earthly as that. 'It's personal.'

'Shoot,' I say.

'When I came to orgasm,' Cara looks bashful, 'I cried, Emily. I cried with sheer joy at the beauty of it.'

She looks like she might do so again. Cry, that is. Not the other thing. I purse my lips. 'And what did Adam think?' Did he have to be peeled off the ceiling with ecstasy too? I want to ask.

'I don't know,' Cara admits, chewing at her fingernails. She casts a glance round her bedside cabinet which is littered with essential oils, herbal potions and lotions and generally healthy detritus. 'I thought he might have left a note or something . . .' she tails off unhappily.

I feel a frown draw my eyebrows together. It's true – he high-tailed it out of here in the cold light of day without so much as a by your leave. He might have a nice, smiley voice and Cara might be in a state of sexual nirvana, but I'm beginning to think that this Adam sounds as much of a bastard as the rest of them.

Chapter Sixty-Four

Adam sat opposite Chris in the staff canteen of the *Hampstead Observer* and wished that he could feel quite as engrossed in the joys of his bacon sandwich as his friend apparently did.

It was nine o'clock in the morning and a desultory straggle of staff were queuing up for breakfast orders. Adam had drunk three cups of strong black coffee in an effort to kick-start his system, but to no avail. He still looked, and felt, like shite.

After a few moments of Neanderthal devouring, Chris looked up as he realised that Adam wasn't eating. 'What?' he said with his mouthful.

'What?' Adam replied defensively.

'What's up?'

'Nothing.' Adam picked up the greasy bread.

'Mate,' Chris said, putting his down, 'there's always something up. It wouldn't be you if there wasn't some sort of crisis in your life. This one just happens to be putting you off your bacon butty. And it's about to put me off mine.'

'It's nothing.'

'You're in here developing photographs when you should be at home in your bed and you're not eating.' Chris gave him an I-rest-my-case look. 'Come on – tell Uncle Christopher.'

Adam huffed and put his sandwich down again. Chris picked his up. 'Promise you won't tell anyone,' Adam said.

Chris frowned. 'Not even Toff?'

'Well no,' Adam conceded. 'You can tell Toff.'

'It can't be that bad then.'

Adam pressed his lips together. 'I think it is.'

'Is it about women?'

'Yes,' Adam said.

'One woman in particular?'

'Yes,' Adam said.

Chris abandoned his sandwich. 'Perhaps you'd be better off talking to Toff in the first place. You know I'm crap about giving advice about the fair sex.' He leaned forward and spoke in a low voice. 'It was me that advised you to ask out that Sophia from Accounts. Look what a can of worms *that* turned out to be.'

'True.' Adam nodded.

'Then again, mate,' Chris said, 'I haven't had a decent piece of gossip for ages. You might as well dish the dirt.'

Adam leaned forward too. 'You mustn't breathe a word of this in the office.'

'Cross my heart and hope to die.'

Adam threw his friend a warning look. 'I will ensure that you do die if this gets out. Slowly and painfully.'

'I promise. On my mother's life,' Chris swore.

'Your mother's dead,' Adam reminded him.

'It's purely a figure of speech,' Chris said.

Adam checked round to see that no one else in the canteen was listening. He dropped his voice. 'I spent the night . . .' He checked for eavesdroppers again. 'I spent the night with Cara.'

Chris was unfazed. 'You were both on the night-shift.'

'No,' Adam said patiently. 'Not on the night-shift.' He paused, and when the penny still didn't drop: 'I *spent the night* with her.'

Chris cocked his head on one side and looked thoughtful. 'Can you define "spent the night"?'

'Chris!' Adam shouted and then checked again that they weren't being watched.

'What?'

'*I.*' Adam pointed to himself. '*I. Spent. The. Night. With. Cara.*' Then he waited.

Chris appeared to be hard of hearing. 'At the crash?'

No, Adam thought, he was just hard of understanding. 'Not at the crash,' Adam stressed. '*After* the crash. I spent the night with her.'

Chris still looked blank. With an impatient sigh, Adam put two fingers from each hand next to each other on the table and rubbed them up and down.

Chris's eyes widened. 'What – you shagged Dippy Chick?'

'I was trying to put it another way.'

Chris's brow creased. 'Is there any other way?'

'What do you think?' Adam said.

'Mate!' Chris said, turning the full force of a perplexed expression on Adam.

'I know,' Adam said. 'I know.'

'Are you mad?'

'I'm beginning to wonder.'

Chris rubbed his hands over his eyes. 'What on earth possessed you?'

'I couldn't help it,' Adam told him. 'You know that we'd been to cover this terrible, terrible car crash and we were both feeling very . . .'

'Randy.'

Adam scowled at him. 'Traumatised. We needed to comfort each other.'

Chris looked doubtful.

'Okay, mate. What would you have done in that situation?'

'Shared a bag of chips?' Chris suggested.

Adam ploughed on regardless. 'She went all sort of girly and vulnerable and I was a goner.'

'Oh man!'

'Chris,' Adam said, 'I haven't made love to a woman in months.'

'Any men?'

'Be serious.'

Chris's frown deepened. 'I am.'

'The spirit was willing and so was the flesh.'

'What can I say?' Chris said, sounding suitably exasperated and shaking his head in disbelief. Adam felt mortified. His friend sat back and studied him with his arms resting on his burgeoning beer belly. 'Cara?' he said, astounded. 'Fuck.' Then he laughed loudly. 'Oh, you already did.'

'This is not funny!' Adam snarled.

He brooded silently as Chris struggled to suppress his mirth and returned to demolish the remains of his bacon sandwich. With a little chuckle, Chris wiped the grease away from his mouth and said: 'Was she any good?'

Adam looked outraged. 'How can you ask that?'

'She's my boss,' Chris said. 'I need to know these things.'

'I wish I'd never started this conversation,' Adam said.

'You must have something to unburden from your soul, otherwise you wouldn't have,' Chris pointed out with a surprising amount of insight for someone whose intuition was normally limited to predicting the outcome of premiership matches. 'It must be something pretty dreadful.'

'It is.'

'Did Mr Floppy put in an untimely appearance?'

'No, he did not.' Adam was indignant. 'As a matter of fact, I thought the whole thing was going rather well until . . .' He ran out of words.

'Until?' Chris prompted.

'Until she cried,' Adam said flatly. 'She cried. When we . . . when she . . . at the point of . . . She cried. Lots. Inconsolably lots.'

223

'Ooo,' Chris said.

'I didn't know what to do.'

'Well, you wouldn't.'

Adam raked his hair. 'Has it ever happened to you, mate?' he asked. 'Has anyone ever cried when you were making love to them?'

Chris thought for a moment. 'As a matter of fact, they have,' he said sagely.

Adam brightened. 'Really?'

'Yeah. But then her husband had just walked in.' Chris rubbed his chin. 'I don't know if that counts.'

'I'm bloody sure it doesn't!' Adam snapped.

Chris started to laugh.

'Stop taking the piss and help me out here,' Adam begged. 'I don't know what to do. She obviously thought it was a dreadful, dreadful, mistake.'

'I think she's probably right,' Chris said. 'There's a little saying about not doing doo-doo on your own doorstep. I think there should also be one about definitely not doing it on your boss's doorstep.'

'I was trying to be nice,' Adam said.

'Well, the next time you think about being nice, stick hot pins in your eyes instead. It'll hurt a lot less.'

'What do you think she'll do?' Adam ventured.

'I think she'll make an effigy of you and, if you're really lucky, she'll saw its bollocks off quickly.'

'I've got to apologise,' Adam said.

'Resign,' Chris advised. 'Then you won't have to face her.'

'I can't do that!'

'She'll come in early and look for you,' Chris warned.

Adam shook his head. 'She wouldn't do that.'

Chris glanced out of the window. 'Oh no? Her car's just pulled into the car park.'

Adam blanched, shot out of his seat and craned his neck to get a better view of the car park. 'Where? Where?'

Chris laughed again.

'Oh sod off,' Adam said and sank back into his chair, realising that he wasn't going to be able to rely on Chris to provide any useful advice in getting him out of this mess. He had got himself into it, he was just going to have to get himself out.

'It could be worse,' Chris said.

'How?' Adam couldn't wait to hear this one.

'You might have persuaded the lovely Emily to join you in a threesome and now you'd have two of them after your testicles.'

'Mmm . . .' Adam said thoughtfully. Emily. Perhaps Cara had confided in Emily exactly what she was thinking. She might be willing to help him out. Goodness only knows how, but Chris might have hit on something there. Maybe, just maybe he'd give Emily a call.

Chapter Sixty-Five

My first job today – and I have quite a few on my list – is to take Cara's pink number to the dry cleaners. It, unlike me, escaped the *Temptation* launch party unscathed by a pesto sauce experience. However, it does reek of booze and cigarettes and general unpleasantness, so I am, quite rightly, treating it to a well-deserved wash and brush up at the local Perkins dry cleaning emporium.

Buckling up my sensible winter coat against the cold, I get ready to face whatever the weather has to throw at me. One of the few advantages of the British winter dragging on and on and on, is that it provided me with the perfect excuse to go out dressed in the entire contents of my wardrobe. But no more. All the people that were previously hanging round on our pavements have gone. There's not even a token reporter left, and I'm already settled back into the routine of not having to disguise myself before I go out or fight my way through hordes of marauding journalists. A quick glance at myself in the mirror and I decide that, very soon, even the Chestnut Burst can go. Although it makes me look demure, I do not feel like a brunette.

It is actually a very fabulous winter day. The sun is shining. There are no birds tweeting, but then they're probably all sunning themselves somewhere nice and hot. And all is reasonably well with the world – if you don't count the fact that I have no job, no home, no money and no man. I'm not going to risk saying that things could be worse, because whenever I do that they invariably and immediately become worse. Today there is a spring in my step, small buds of hope blossoming in my heart and two chocolate croissants I found in the bread bin resting in my tummy.

The High Street is just waking up. At this hour the main crush of commuter traffic has passed through and has now been replaced with a crush of shopping traffic. London would be a really great place if you took away all the cars. If you're a resident in Hampstead you can buy a parking permit for less than a hundred quid a year. If you are just an unfortunate visitor it costs round about that to park for an hour. Whatever time of day you drop in here, the High Street always has a lively feel. Lively, at the weekends, means that there isn't a square inch of pavement left to walk on. It has a cosmopolitan atmosphere with posh designer dress shops, upmarket chain stores, a few glitzy little cafés, some great bakeries and restaurants far too expensive for the average pocket. Dropping the dress off at the dry cleaners, I lash out on their one-hour service, even though I have nothing to lash out with. To fill the time, I decide to take a long walk on Hampstead Heath and make the most of the crisp, clear day.

Dropping down into the back lanes, I wander through the narrow cobbled streets and the tightly packed terraced houses, picking my way back towards the open expanse of the Heath. I stroll through the snarled-up car park and past the green slime that is the winter coat of the Hampstead Ponds, and head up towards Parliament Hill.

I like being up on the Heath, as high as I can get. It's basically a huge green hill peeping its head above the canopy of trees, aloof from the rest of London. When you're up here, right at the top, it's easy to forget that you're still part of a busy, bustling city. And it's nice to think that people have been using this same spot for recreation for hundreds of years. There are always folk up here flying rainbow-coloured kits, kicking a ball, reading a book. This is also serious dog-walking territory, as the handful of ever-present Westies, Yorkies, Corgis, Alsatians and Labradors will testify. Compared to the melting pot of the High Street, this is a typically British patch of land and helps give the area its character and unique atmosphere. I reckon it's the nearest you can get to village life and still be on the Underground line. At a price. I'm good at this, aren't I? Perhaps I should consider becoming an estate agent?

This why the rich and famous still flock here to live, I guess. There are loads of celebs who live in Hampstead – and once upon a time I even used to teach some of their kiddy-winkies. I can't divulge who or where, because now I appreciate why they try to guard their privacy preciously – except when they have a new book, film or TV show to promote, of course. There are also loads of famous dead people who once inhabited Hampstead. A walk through any of the lanes will show you that the place is a veritable banquet of blue plaques marking historical moments from the lives of Constable, Dickens, D.H. Lawrence, Keats, Sigmund Freud and Florence Nightingale among others. All famous for much more cultured escapades than getting their bottoms out on the Internet. How times move on.

I trudge up through the trees which clasp their bare fingers together above the path, listening to nothing else but the crunch of my boots on the path. The view from Parliament Hill is spectacular.

London in miniature is spread before me. Canary Wharf peeps out above the tree-line against a backdrop of wild, massing dark clouds teasing the populace as they decide to rain or not to rain. The slender needle of the Telecom Tower eases effortlessly skywards whereas the mighty dome of St Paul's Cathedral struggles to find its space on the skyline as it competes with the office blocks springing up around it. I wish Sir Christopher Wren had got his way when he wanted to redesign London on symmetrical lines after the Great Fire. It would be a lot tidier than it is now. I snuggle down into my coat and enjoy the view. On a clear day you can see as far as the Crystal Palace Television Transmitter.

A jogger struggles stoically up the hill aware of nothing but the pounding of her feet. I head for my favourite bench – the one inscribed to *Cid and Maurice, The Armchair Philosophers*. I think there are a lot of those in Hampstead. Sitting down, I let the cool air rush over my teeth and fill my aching lungs. The jogger puffs past me and I realise that I am definitely not as fit as I should be. I feel knackered just watching her. A career as a personal trainer is out of the question, although I could probably do with employing one myself. I realise my mind is turning to all things concerned with employment and take that as a sign that I'm getting better, getting on with my life. Getting desperate, more like.

What does an unemployed teacher, who hasn't got the remotest chance of getting a good character reference, do? If I went for another teaching job, would my notoriety as an international Internet porn star have preceded me? Would my interviewers already be familiar with my credentials? I don't think I'm keen to find out. I have considered going for auditions for *Soap Stars* or *Pop Idol* but, aside from the fact that I can't sing and have absolutely no acting talent and/or experience, I hate queuing up.

I also considered, at some length, an insane get-rich-quick scheme similar to those favoured by my ex-boyfriend, Declan Up-to-the-eyeballs-in-debt O'Donnell. I thought about joining a Women Empowering Women pyramid. The craze seems to be sweeping the country quicker than space-hoppers did in the 1970s. Britain is officially pyramid-crazy. I suppose it's a very noble idea – if a little flawed. Loads of women who have more cash than they know what to do with buy 'hearts' in order to donate to others who are more needy, and then they get loads back themselves as a bonus. Nice, if it worked. But it's like one of those chain letters where you're supposed to send six of your friends a pair of knickers and they send six of their friends knickers, and *they* send six people they hardly know six pairs of knickers, and those people in turn send six total strangers six pairs of knickers – along with a lot of innocuous threats of disasters that will fall upon your house if you don't comply with their lingerie demands. Then one day, when your postman least expects it, you get more knickers than Marks & Spencers have in stock, as not one single person has broken the chain because they were all too fearful of the plague of locusts that was promised to them if they did. Do you see where I'm coming from?

With this particular chain reaction you're expected to stump up three thousand quid to buy into it – and that's where I hit my first problem. If I had three thousand pounds to buy into it, I wouldn't need to buy into it in the first place! And it's like most things that seem too good to be true. It is. You'd have to be mad, desperate and unemployable to consider it. And even though I'm all of those I still wouldn't touch it with a barge-pole.

But that leaves me with the vexed question of what I would touch with a barge-pole and what barge-pole would touch me. By now, I've decided that I'm going to take up Jonathan Gold's suggestion and ring the saucy photographer Sebastian Atherton. Cara will go ballistic, I know that much. She will rant on about feminist principles and exploitation and all that stuff I have gone through in my head a thousand times. It hasn't been an easy decision. In fact, my fingernails are chewed to ragged little stumps because of it. But the truth of the matter is that I am utterly, utterly strapped for cash and I am being offered a very slender window of opportunity through which I can grab a load of it and secure my future – which is currently looking decidedly wobbly. Wobblier than my bottom. Which, incidentally, I feel owes me a favour. So? Do I stay principled and impoverished or get my kit off and clear my debts? What would any sane woman do, faced with this choice?

For once, my mobile phone is blessed with a signal. I dial the number before it decides to give up the ghost, and am answered immediately. Which is sort of a shame because I haven't quite decided what to say.

I try, 'Hello.' Too timid by half. 'Is that Sebastian Atherton?'

'Yes.' He sounds scary and terribly posh.

'This is Emily Miller,' I stammer. 'Jonathan Gold asked me to phone you. I'd like to make an appointment to have some photographs taken.'

'I've been expecting your call,' he says.

'Oh.' Have you? I wasn't sure I was going to ring at all.

'Let's see when I can fit you in.'

I bite my lip as I hear Sebastian Atherton shuffling through the pages of his diary trying to find a vacant spot for me.

'I could see you tonight at nine,' he offers. 'If that isn't too short notice.'

'No,' I mumble. 'It's fine.'

'I'll look forward to it,' Sebastian Atherton says.

Will you? I don't think I will. And I hang up sharply before I can change my mind.

The sun scoots behind a big, black cloud and the hope of a warm spring is crushed in one blow; I shiver as the cold wind cuts straight through me. I'm not sure whether I'm going to cry or not, but as I look out over the rooftops of London, I wonder what on earth I've done.

Chapter Sixty-Six

'Where's Adam?' Cara said as she slung her coat and bag over her chair. 'I thought he was working today.' She gave a quick glance at her shift rota which showed that, indeed, he was.

'He's out on a job,' Chris shouted over to her. 'It's World Milk Day. He's gone to snap some school kids dressed up as cows.'

'Oh,' Cara said and flopped down at her desk. She was physically and emotionally exhausted. She still felt subdued after last night's traumatic visit to the crash scene, plus elated because she and Adam had finally got it together on both a sexual and deeply spiritual level. However, Adam's pre-dawn departure had prematurely darkened her post-coital rosy glow. Why did modern-day relationships have to be so fraught and complex? Her stomach sloshed around with a mixture of utter joy and fear. 'Did he say anything?'

Chris sat himself down on Adam's chair and whizzed it over to the front of Cara's desk. He leaned his elbows on it and smirked. 'About what?'

'Anything,' Cara snapped. She still hadn't forgiven Chris for his hard stance on featuring Emily on the front page, and she noticed that the blown-up festive poster of her was once more above his desk.

'No,' Chris said. 'But he did look really, really, *really* knackered.'

Cara's head shot up and Chris gave her a leery grin. Perhaps he suspected something, she thought. Well, if she and Adam were going to be a couple from now on, everyone in the office would just have to get used to it.

'We were out late covering a bad smash,' Cara said.

'Yeah,' Chris replied. 'He told me.' He winked at her and with a little trickle of alarm, Cara wondered exactly how much Adam had told him. Surely he hadn't confided in him? Chris's middle name was not, after all, discretion.

'Haven't you got anything better to do, Chris?' Cara growled.

'As a matter of fact, I have,' he said, standing up grandly. 'The Prime Minister is paying a visit to our humble little outpost. He's

231

coming to the launch of a new Saturday-morning film club for over-privileged children.'

It certainly helped that this part of North London had more movie stars per square inch than a Hollywood studio when they wanted to attract big gun politicians for publicity.

'All part of a developing arts drive,' Chris continued. 'And yours truly is orchestrating the coverage.'

Her colleague, *one* of *her* reporters, beamed widely. Cara looked at him open-mouthed.

'If you look at your in-tray, you'll find some copy pertaining to it,' he said smugly and started to walk away with the air of someone who has managed to get one over on someone else.

'Who said you were to cover this?' Cara asked. It was her job to allocate stories.

'Martin.' Chris flicked a cursory glance at the Editor's office. 'He was really pleased with my coverage of the Saucy Santa school-teacher exposé,' he continued with barely suppressed glee. 'I was the obvious choice.' And, he failed to mention, he'd been in Martin's office begging to be allowed to do it since first thing. 'If you have a problem with that,' Chris added slyly, 'take it up with Martin.'

'I don't have a problem,' Cara said and Chris, grinning like the cat who had got the cream, waltzed off.

Cara fumed quietly and scrabbled through the pile until she found the story about Tony Blair's impending visit to Hampstead. Yes, she did have a problem with Chris covering the story. It wasn't that his capabilities were in question, he just shouldn't have gone over her head to bag it for himself. And although she hated the fact that her friend was the subject-matter, his coverage of Emily's story had been first class. The ridiculous twist was that she probably would have allocated this latest story to him. But she wanted to do it. That was what she was paid to do. She was his boss.

Cara scanned the story. Pretty routine, but interesting nevertheless. Chris would be perfectly capable of covering it. The visit was scheduled for tomorrow. It was a shame they hadn't been given more notice about it, but in these days of tightened security, the Premier's plans were often shifted, postponed, cancelled or arranged and rearranged at five minutes' notice. They would have to do follow-up pieces to add the background colour, instead of previewing it.

She needed to talk to Adam about the photographs. She needed to talk to Adam full stop! Cara took anxious little nibbles of her fingernails and gazed at her mobile. Now wasn't the right time to ring him. Their first conversation after 'the event' needed to be in private – or, at least, not in the middle of a busy newspaper office with everyone's ears flapping like Dumbo.

Cara tried to settle to her work by re-reading the piece on Tony Blair and pretending that she was making extensive plans for his visit in her head, and by chewing the end of her pen as if she was deep in thought. But it was no good, she couldn't think of anything or anyone but Adam. In the end, Cara gave up trying to think and gazed blankly out of the window. She would give anything to know how he was feeling right now.

Chapter Sixty-Seven

Adam was feeling like a bagful of shite. He rubbed his hands over his eyes and prayed for someone to give him superhuman reserves of strength. He was at a nursery school surrounded by children dressed in black and white. Some of them sported complete cow outfits and black, bovine splotches on their cheeks. There were World Milk Day posters all round the walls of the classroom confirming the reason why he was here.

Three tiny belligerent children sat in front of him in various stages of scowl. If the superhuman strength didn't arrive soon, he was going to belt one of them over the head with his Nikon. And he knew exactly which one.

'Charlene,' the teacher coaxed gently, 'hold the carton up to your mouth.' She held up a brightly painted milk carton complete with stripey straw.

'No!'

'Just pretend you're drinking the milk,' the teacher advised, inching the carton further towards Charlene's mouth which was clamped firmly shut.

Charlene was obdurate. 'I'm not drinking it,' she said without opening her lips. 'It comes from a cow's bottom!'

The teacher appealed wordlessly to Adam for help. Adam closed his eyes and sighed. What he really needed now was sleep. Deep, dreamless sleep. Lots of it. He'd only decided to do this job instead of sending one of the juniors so that he had an excuse to get out of the office and delay his first encounter with Cara after doing the big It. 'Can't you just get another child?' he suggested, silently adding, 'Before we all die.'

'But Charlene has such a lovely smile,' the teacher pleaded.

The little girl briefly bared her teeth. Teacher's pet, Adam thought. It was very hard to imagine Charlene's lovely smile as he eyed the uneven bunches in her hair and her cow jumper and her eyebrows in a dark, stubborn line above her eyes.

'I'll take some photos with the milk on the table in front of her,' he

234

said and proceeded to snap the other children to Charlene's left who were marginally less belligerent, cutting her out of the photo completely. With a Prime Minister's visit in the offing, it was unlikely that children drinking milk would make the paper anyway.

'Thanks,' he said to the teacher as he completed the photo-shoot and high-tailed it out of the door as quickly as he could.

Adam trudged back to his car and slung his camera in the boot. He felt bad about avoiding Cara, but he hadn't quite decided how he should play this yet.

Pulling his mobile phone from his pocket, he dialled Chris's direct line at the office.

'Love Rats Anonymous,' Chris said when he answered.

'Yes, very funny,' Adam said. 'Is she there?'

'Who? Space cadet?'

'Yes. Is Cara there?'

'Why didn't you ring her number?'

'Because I don't want to talk to her.'

'Am I missing something here?' Chris asked. 'Maybe you should talk to her. She's been looking for you. All morning.'

'Has she?' Adam could hear the panic in his own voice.

'Shall I pass you over?'

'No, mate,' Adam said hurriedly. 'I've got to dash. I just wanted to know if she was in work.'

'You're going to have to face her sometime,' Chris said.

'Yeah,' Adam sighed, 'but not yet.'

'Are we still going to Toff's studio tonight?' Chris asked.

'Yeah,' Adam said. 'Let's meet up for a drink at the Jig first.' He was going to need some sort of Dutch courage. 'About eight.'

'What do you think I should wear?' Chris said.

'Get a life, Christopher,' Adam advised. 'We are going to Toff's studio for the purposes of research and to decide whether I should change career direction.'

There was a disappointed-sounding pause. 'So we're not going to see naked women?'

'They are purely arbitrary to the process,' Adam stated.

Chris brightened. 'But there is always the chance that they might fancy us?'

'Yes,' Adam admitted wearily. 'There is always an outside chance.'

He could hear Chris clapping his hands together and he wished that he could get as excited as his friend over the simple things in life. 'Great!'

'I'll see you later,' Adam said, and hung up before he could get drawn into an extended discussion about the selection of Chris's outfit.

Leaning on the steering wheel, deep in thought, Adam considered his options. There was another job-sheet tucked in his pocket for this afternoon – a man working for a computer firm was having his head shaved for charity – but he had a couple of hours to kill before then. He could follow his usual pattern and head straight to Café Blanco for a couple of convivial coffees and a ciabatta. But if Cara was safely ensconced in the offices of the *Hampstead Observer*, then that might well mean that Emily would be at home alone.

It was very weird because he felt that he already knew the infamous Emily, even though he'd never clapped eyes on her in the flesh, as it were. It was high time that they did meet. Adam wondered how she'd feel about him turning up, unannounced, on her doorstep to discuss what a bollocks he'd made of his one-night stand with her friend. He looked at his watch. He could just pop in for five minutes.

Adam started up the Vectra and, still not sure whether he was doing the right thing or whether he was going to make a bad situation very much worse, he turned and headed towards Cara's house.

Chapter Sixty-Eight

I am terrified. I'm walking back home towards Cara's house, but I can't feel my feet on the pavement at all. I might as well be treading on sponge cake. Everything is numb from the neck down. I've collected Cara's now spick and span dress from the dry cleaners, but I'm not sure how.

I have my appointment all booked up with Sebastian Atherton, but how in heaven's name I'm going to get through it is another matter. To think that women strive for years to get their photograph on page three of the *Sun* and here's me having to strip off because I feel backed into a corner. I know that I won't get any sympathy from Cara, so there's no point discussing it with her, but I need someone to understand why I'm doing this. Partly, I think, because I don't myself.

The High Street is still busy. It's getting towards lunchtime and I should think about eating, but can't. I just want to be at home, back in the safety of the house, four solid walls surrounding me when everything else in my life is formed of ever-shifting shapes.

Adam was parked outside Cara's front door. It was purple, something which he hadn't noticed as he'd carried her through it last night or as he'd tiptoe-rushed out this morning. It was probably purple because it was an auspicious colour, knowing Cara. It couldn't be anything as basic as having dreadful taste in paint.

Before he could think better of it, he swung out of the car and headed with determined step up the path. Once at the door, he knocked, loudly and bravely before his courage departed. It was nearly lunchtime. Emily would surely be out of bed by now. He leaned on the wall as he waited, a tight curl of nervousness unfurling in his stomach. It seemed so unfair; it was the first time he'd made love to anyone in a long, long time and it had got him in a right royal pickle – despite the fact that he'd rather enjoyed it at the time. Chris, on the other hand, was intent on blithely shagging his way through the entire female population of the Western world without one moment of regret, remorse or retribution. That boy was born lucky.

Adam gave another cursory knock at the door. It was clear that Emily wasn't at home. A quick sandwich and then he would make tracks for the head-shaving extravaganza. One of these days he might yet get to meet Cara's mate. He sighed and turned back down the path. He had tried, but Plan A had failed. Now he had to think very hard what Plan B might entail.

The same dark green Vectra I saw departing this morning has just pulled away from Cara's house. I'm sure of it. Well, I'm not really. I'm not sure of anything any more. I stand and watch it drive down the street, straining to catch a glimpse of the driver. Not that I would know Adam from Adam, if you see what I mean. There must be a million dark green Vectras in the world and they don't belong exclusively to journalists and photographers. It could be anyone in a Vectra. I think the fact that I'm about to launch my body into the public domain again is making me paranoid. I forgive Michael Jackson anything he does with monkeys now. I think he's fully entitled. He must live in a mad, mad world.

I let myself into the quiet, incense-scented house and hang Cara's killer dress on the coat-stand in the hall. This afternoon I'm going to get rid of my Chestnut Burst and go back to being bimbo blonde – although it says Light Honey Gold on the box of hair colour I've bought. If the cap fits, wear it, that's what I say. I need to have a trawl through my wardrobe again to see what's suitable. But what exactly do you wear for an appointment when you know you're going to be required to take all your clothes off anyway? Once again, I curse my luck for ever having clapped eyes on Declan O'Donnell. He has ruined my life. No man will ever do that to me again.

But as I climb the stairs, I ruefully acknowledge that, for the second time in a matter of weeks, I have agreed to get my clothes off for a man armed with that most dangerous of weapons – the camera.

Chapter Sixty-Nine

Adam was feeling furtive, whereas Chris, always excitable at the best of times, was at his hyperactive worst. He was gabbling at ninety to the dozen about nothing remotely interesting as he leafed through Toff's portfolio of scantily clad females, his conversation interspersed with appreciative, guttural snorts and mutterings. Beside Chris, Beavis and Butthead would have looked like a pair of smooth-talking sophisticates.

Toff was setting up his studio and Adam watched as he worked. Their friend always made everything look so easy. His movements were pared to the bone, calm, fluid and confident. Everything Toff did was laid back. He lived in a borderline world of serenity somewhere between sleep and wakefulness. He'd probably only break into a saunter to escape from a burning house. However, this unhurried manner belied a business brain that was sharp and professional, and Toff's attention to detail was that of an utter perfectionist. Adam wondered how his friend had ever coped with stuff like World Milk Day and charity head-shaving contests.

'Come through, guys,' Toff said as he waved them into his studio. 'Our model is waiting for us.'

Adam shuffled through, blocking the way of Chris, who had shot off his stool with all the charm of a rampaging bull. This was ordeal enough. Why on earth had Toff said that Chris could come? It was like setting a bulimic loose in a biscuit factory.

A pretty Oriental girl draped in a silk kimono sat with her knees tucked up on a precisely placed low velvet couch, bare legs and feet exposed. Her long, silken black hair trailed to her waist. Just looking at her nonchalant composure gave Adam butterflies.

'This is Leila,' Toff said. 'Leila, these are my good friends, Mr Adam Jackson and Lord Christopher Seymour.'

'Hi,' Leila said, smiling at them. Adam nodded back while Chris tried to keep his recently upgraded peer-of-the-realm tongue off the floor.

'Adam is a respected photographer,' Toff informed her. 'He may be coming to work with me.'

'Nice to meet you.' She smiled at Adam again.

Chris nudged him in the ribs and announced in the loudest stage whisper Adam had ever heard: 'You're in there, mate.'

Adam wanted to curl up and die. Leila smiled some more. Two steel mesh chairs had been arranged at the back of the studio and Adam and Chris sidled into them.

'Wish we'd got some popcorn,' Chris mumbled.

'Quiet in the Dress Circle, please.' Toff took up his position behind the camera. 'By the way,' he said over his shoulder, 'these are for your friend Mr O'Donnell.'

Which, very effectively, shut both Adam and Chris up.

'When you're ready,' Toff spoke soothingly to Leila.

The model lay back and draped the kimono more provocatively and then proceeded to pout and pose in a very inventive manner. Chris started to slobber. Toff fired off shot after shot, but said little save the odd encouraging 'Yes' every now and again. Adam had imagined that Toff would sort of prowl around, barking orders like David Hemmings had in the 1960s film *Blow-Up* – woefully, Adam's only experience of the giddy world of glamour photography.

Adam wondered if he was really cut out for this. He felt deeply embarrassed. Leila, however, seemed not the slightest bit concerned about baring her body. But then it was a very nice body she had to bare. Could he ever be as confident and cool as Toff?

'Tell me,' Chris leaned over and muttered in his ear, 'why are you *thinking* about doing this as a job?'

Adam looked blankly at him.

'If I were you,' Chris went on, 'I'd be biting Toff's arm off before he changes his mind.'

Adam lowered his voice. 'But—'

'Adam,' Chris interrupted, 'there aren't any buts. It's better for you. It's better for Josh.'

'But—' Adam said again.

'Tell me,' Chris said, 'what would you rather do? Stand on a windy, rainswept touch-line on a Saturday afternoon photographing Golders Green United in the vain hope that they might score a goal, or be here in a nice, warm, centrally heated studio photographing some of the most beautiful and least-clothed women in the world?'

'But—' Adam tried.

'And when you reply,' Chris interrupted again, 'please give me an answer that doesn't make you sound as if you're criminally insane.'

What *was* the decision? Adam thought frantically. If he were to have any hope of gaining custody of Josh, he had to get a job with more regular hours. OK, this was a late-night session for Toff, but that was because he couldn't keep up with the workload he had as he was in such high demand. A nice position to be in, Adam thought.

Chris was right, he should grab this chance in a million. It was a world away from the *Hampstead Observer*. Better pay, great flat, a garden for Josh to play footy in and, he glanced over at the beautiful exotic Leila, a few other perks he could mention. It wasn't going to meet his lofty ideals of making a difference to world peace, but maybe he could do that in other ways; there must be a charity somewhere that could use a few of his skills. Besides, didn't the worthy cause of his own dear son take priority over everything else?

Toff's voice brought Adam back down to earth. 'Want to take a turn behind the camera?' he asked.

Adam blinked a *South Park* blink. 'Me?' he squeaked.

'Yes,' Toff laughed. 'Come on, don't be shy. Leila won't bite you!'

'She could bite *me* any day,' Chris exclaimed under his breath.

Adam stood up and wiped his clammy hands on his T-shirt, suddenly realising that Toff had set this up just for him. All at once he felt quite emotional. What had he done to deserve such kind treatment from his friend? Toff was bending over backwards to make this easy for him. Surely it would be churlish to refuse his offer?

Adam stepped up to the camera, and Toff took his place next to Chris. Adam chewed nervously at his lip. This should be like falling off a log. It wasn't as if he was trying to fight his way to the front of a press scrum. He had all the time in the world to get some good shots. And Leila was the ultimate professional. It would be impossible to take a bad photograph of her. She smiled an encouraging, pouty smile and knelt up on the velvet couch, ruching the silky material of her gown until one pert little handful of buttock pointed his way. And as Adam positioned himself and looked through the viewfinder at Leila's beguiling pose, inexplicably, an image of the woman-in-the-wine-bar flashed through his brain.

Chapter Seventy

I can't go in. I just can't. I *cannot* go in.

It's a freezing cold night. Brass monkey weather, my father would call it, but I've no idea what that means. I expect it's rude. My father always favours the hearty, Anglo-Saxon turn of phrase. I think it runs in the family. I've certainly muttered a few myself in the last few minutes.

My trusty little Peugeot is parked several streets away, due to all the parking restrictions round here, and I've been pacing up and down now on the pavement outside Sebastian Atherton's photographic studio for the best part of half an hour. I wish I'd thought to have this agony of indecision while I was still inside my car with the heater on. I've got my coat pulled tightly round my doubtful choice of clothing. I opted for jeans and a jumper – goodness knows why. My reasoning was that if Sebastian Atherton wants me to wear anything at all, then I'm sure he'll supply it. I get a vision of scarlet crotchless knickers and a feather boa and want to race for the nearest loo. My knees are knocking like a band of mad woodpeckers.

The only thing I feel confident about is the fact that my hair is now happily restored to its rightful colour. I chickened out of adding a blonde rinse to my chestnut locks, fearing some sort of colour-mixing mayhem – I didn't want to end up lime green for my first professional photo shoot. And so, credit card in sweaty hand, I popped along to A Snip In Time. Lorraine, my hairdresser and fount of all knowledge, told me that the fair-haired gene is recessive and that very soon there'll be very few of us natural blondes around. Some people might think that's for the best. Whatever. We'll all be getting it out of a bottle one day. In the time-honoured tradition of spilling the beans to your hairdresser, I confessed my impromptu Internet appearance courtesy of Declan the Dirty-Deed-Doer. Lorraine has a boring boyfriend and wishes he had the balls – her phrase, not mine – to put her arse on the Worldwide Web. It takes all sorts.

I suppose I should have consulted my new guru, Jonathan Gold, on my change of image. But, hey, it's my hair, my life and it's probably the only thing I've still got some control over. If I want to be blonde again, I'll damn well do it! I have a comforting chew on a fingernail. Hope he doesn't go bonkers though.

I wish I'd told Cara I was coming to see Sebastian Atherton so that she could have come with me for back-up or talked me out of it – whichever. But I didn't. I sneaked out without telling her where I was going and now I'm regretting it. I could ring her on my mobile and 'fess up and get her to rush her butt down here – but I think she'd just give me the bollocking of a lifetime and I'm feeling far too delicate to cope with that.

I arrived here massively early and have spent all that time vacillating. Why did I ever think I'd have the nerve to go through with this? There's a world of difference between romping around with your boyfriend and a digital camera, and setting up a cold-blooded, pre-meditated professional photographic session. Sebastian Atherton might expect me to know what I'm doing. Everyone in Hampstead seems to smoke Gauloises cigarettes and I wish I did – I'd have puffed my way through about ninety by now!

I have agreed to take my clothes off for a guy I don't even know. How sensible is that? Not very, I think you'll agree. He could drug me and parcel me up in a crate and send me to Bangkok to be a white sex slave and no one would be any the wiser. Perhaps you think my imagination is getting the better of me, but he could. These things happen. Look what happened when I got my kit off for someone I *did* know!

I have a quick glance at my watch for only about the zillionth time. I'm due in now. Right this very minute. Shitshitshit! I think I must be having an adrenaline rush because all my veins have gone fuzzy and indistinct. I cross the road and do loitering right near Sebastian Atherton's front door. It does look very salubrious, I must say. He inhabits a grand Georgian mansion and if it was a person, not a house, it would be someone with not a hair out of place. Not quite the premises you'd expect for a white slave-trader. But it doesn't do a great deal to calm my nerves, which by now are screaming, 'Run away, run away!'

I count to ten, practise some deep breathing, abandon that and do a bit of creative visualisation, but that scares me to death, because the last thing I want to visualise is me in my birthday suit adorning the pages of the *News of the World*. Pushing it all to one side, I march up to the front door and brace myself to ring the bell. Instead of doing so, I hop about from foot to foot. It's such a tiny bell and all I have to do is give it one little push.

But I can't do it. My nerves and their 'run away' chant have won. I could be missing out on the biggest opportunity of my life or I could have just come to my senses in time. Whichever way, I turn on my heels and, obeying my deepest instincts, run away.

Chapter Seventy-One

After the photo session, Leila disappeared into a changing-room in the back of Toff's studio to get dressed while Adam, Toff and Chris filed through to the office to flick through some of the images that Adam had taken on the digital camera.

Chris flopped into Toff's caramel leather armchair, wearing a sulky expression. 'I would die for a job like this. You are such a lucky, lucky, *lucky* bastard, Toff.'

Toff smiled wryly at his friend, sat at his desk and plugged into the computer. The photographs instantly popped up on the screen. Adam sucked in his breath. They were good. Very good. But he suspected it had more to do with Leila's comfortable professionalism than his own inherent skill.

'Surprised?' Toff asked.

'Yeah,' Adam admitted.

'I'm not,' Toff said. 'I knew you had it in you.'

'Thanks, mate,' Adam said, feeling ridiculously grateful that he hadn't made a complete fool of himself.

'Leila's a law student,' Toff supplied. 'She does photo-shoots to supplement her measly grant.'

Adam didn't know whether that made him feel better or worse. Was she doing this because she wanted to or because she was forced to? Then again there were other ways for students to supplement their incomes, but you wouldn't get paid nearly as much for working in Miss Selfridge on a Saturday. Life was a constant compromise. Morality versus money. Principles caving in under pressure. Eat or be eaten.

Toff crossed to the fridge, pulled out a bottle of champagne and took some tall, slender flûtes from the shelf above it. 'So,' he said, waving the bottle. 'Have we something to celebrate?'

Adam laughed. 'Yes,' he said. 'Yes, we have.'

'Woo! Woo!' Chris whooped with joy.

Toff popped the champagne cork and expertly let the bubbles tumble into the waiting glasses. He handed one each to the two men.

'Congratulations,' he said, clinking his glass to Adam's. 'You won't regret it.'

'To Adam,' Chris said, toasting his glass.

'To Adam,' Toff echoed.

'To me,' Adam said, his throat suddenly tight and constricted. This was a new start for him – the kick he'd needed to provide a better home for Josh. He hoped and prayed that Josh would be sticking around to enjoy it with him.

They all swigged their champagne.

'Oh no!' Chris wailed. 'You know what this means?'

Adam and Toff looked at him blankly.

'If Adam's going to be a sexy, glamour photographer, I'm the only one with a totally boring job!'

Just then, Leila came through. Her make-up had been scrubbed away and the long tresses of hair tied up in a pony tail. She looked fresh-faced and very ordinary. You'd walk past her on the street and not notice her beauty. 'Am I missing a party?'

'Adam's coming to work with me,' Toff announced. 'Join us for a drink, sweetheart?'

'I can't,' Leila said. 'I have to dash. I've got an essay to finish.' She turned to Adam. 'Good luck though. Maybe we'll work together again. You're good.'

'Thanks,' Adam said, aware that he was blushing.

Leila handed him a business card. 'Call me if you're free for a drink later in the week.'

'Thanks,' Adam said again.

'I can be free too,' Chris said, stretching out his hand.

'I think I'll be busy when you're free, *Lord* Seymour,' she joked. She kissed Toff lightly on both cheeks. 'Speak to you soon.'

'Absolutely,' Toff said. 'Great session.'

Leila waved to them all and left.

'God,' Chris complained to Adam, 'I'm *really* starting to hate you.'

Toff checked his watch. 'Looks like my next client has thought better of it,' he said, looking at his diary. 'She should be here by now.'

'I must love you and leave you,' Chris said, downing his champagne. 'I've got a date with Lassie and Fido, the girls I met in the Jig the other night.'

'What? *Both* of them?' Adam said.

'I think they're *very* close friends, if you know what I mean.' Chris winked lasciviously.

'You are unbelievable, mate.' Adam shook his head.

'*I'm* not the one sleeping with my boss,' Chris pointed out.

'Oh, you didn't, Adam,' Toff said with a sigh.

'I couldn't help it,' Adam said miserably. 'It just happened. It felt very natural at the time.'

'It's only now that you're regretting it,' Toff said.

'I'm not. Not really,' Adam insisted. 'But I think she is.'

'He's avoiding her,' Chris said. 'Like the plague. He's swapped his shift so that he doesn't have to see her tonight.'

'I have not.' Adam scowled. 'I had to see Josh tonight because . . . because it was the only night he wasn't doing something else.'

'A likely excuse,' an unconvinced Chris retorted.

'Now, now, children,' Toff interrupted. 'Some of us have work to do.' He clicked the computer mouse and the photographs sprang into life once more.

'I'd go blind working here,' Chris said. 'I'm off.' He rubbed his hands in glee. 'Wish me luck. I might just need it.' He clapped Adam on the back. 'See you tomorrow, mate. I wonder what Dippy Chick will think when you hand your resignation in?'

It was something Adam hadn't considered.

'Anyway,' Chris continued, 'that's your problem.' He shrugged on his leather jacket and headed towards the door. 'See you round, Toff,' he called. 'If you ever need anyone to sit and watch you work again, you can always count on me!'

'I'll bear it in mind, old bean,' Toff said with a shake of his head.

Chris left them alone.

'I'd better be off too,' Adam said. 'And thanks, Toff. Thanks for everything.'

'You're welcome,' his friend said. 'I think we'll work well together. Today Hampstead, tomorrow the world.'

Adam laughed.

'Just one thing before you go,' Toff said, and pulled his appointments schedule towards him. 'The girl who was supposed to be here tonight was Emily Miller – Cara's friend.'

Adam pursed his lips. That was a bit of a turn-up for the books.

'I didn't dare tell Chris beforehand,' Toff said. 'I thought he'd spontaneously combust.'

Toff was probably right.

'She's arranged it through the publicist Jonathan Gold,' Toff continued. 'I'd like to bet a pound Cara doesn't know anything about it.'

Adam scratched his stubble. 'Do you think I should tell her?'

'Client confidentiality, old chap,' Toff said. 'What Emily does, is Emily's business. Looks like she's changed her mind, anyway.'

247

'What would Jonathan Gold do with the photographs?' Adam asked.

'I suspect he'd make her a very rich woman,' Toff said. 'Very rich indeed.'

Chapter Seventy-Two

When I reach Cara's house, the lights inside are burning brightly and I feel a warm, happy wave of relief wash over me. I've made it home unscathed. I pull up outside and jump out of the car.

Cara is sprawled out on the sofa in the lounge watching repeats of *The Bill* when I bowl in, which is most un-Cara-like.

'*The Bill*? Are you sick?' If there is one thing Cara hates more than women who wear fur, it's television cop dramas. 'I thought you were supposed to be in work.'

'I swapped my shift,' she says. 'To avoid Adam. I'm going in during the day tomorrow instead.'

'Why are you trying to avoid Adam?' I say, throwing myself down next to her. The relief at having a lucky escape is making me slightly giddy.

'I think he's trying to avoid me.'

'Right,' I say, struggling to find a crumb of logic in there somewhere.

'Do you think I'm doing the right thing?' she says anxiously. Clearly her levels of Rescue Remedy have fallen dangerously low.

'No,' I say with a tut. 'You should talk to him.'

'I don't know if I can,' she says.

'Good grief, Cara.' I huff with exasperation. 'You think he's Keanu Reeves and Rufus Sewell all rolled into one, don't you?'

Cara nods reluctantly.

'You've had the best sex of your life with him.' Cow! I add silently. 'And, according to you, he's kind to children and small furry animals. Isn't he worth the effort?'

'When you put it like that . . .' Cara says, brightening.

'And at least you know the object of your affections,' I point out. 'I, on the other hand, am chasing some elusive will o' the wisp man whose name I don't even know.'

'True,' Cara says, and I can tell that her attention is drifting from *The Bill*.

'I'll put the kettle on,' I say. I love tea in a crisis. It's very nearly

249

every bit as good as vodka. 'Then why don't you and I turn our attention to the universe and have one last go at bagging Adam for you?'

Mention anything utterly wacky and Cara perks up immediately.

'Don't the Native-American Indians have the love equivalent of a rain dance?' I suggest.

Cara's forehead is furrowed into a frown. A scarily serious frown. I must try to remember that she doesn't think all this stuff is a joke.

'I have one spell,' she says earnestly, 'that will blow his socks off.'

I'm not sure that's exactly what we want, but decide to say nothing.

Cara glances up at me. 'I need your help.'

Oh crumbs! What have I let myself in for? 'Go on then,' I say. If I'm really nice to her, I keep hoping she'll forget that I owe her loads of money.

'Make a cup of tea while I go and get my things,' she says. Tea? *Tea*? I think this has just turned into a vodka moment.

Chapter Seventy-Three

Everyone in Luigi's seemed quiet tonight; the atmosphere was unusually subdued. Pale-faced, Josh listlessly pushed his spaghetti round his plate. There was something wrong, Adam knew. He abandoned his own food. 'What it is?' he asked his son.

The boy looked up and pressed his lips together. 'Bad.'

'Very bad?'

Josh nodded.

'Plane tickets bad?' Adam tried.

Josh shook his head. 'Visa bad,' he said. And then looked at Adam for confirmation. 'That is bad, isn't it?'

Adam shrugged. 'What does Mum say?'

'Nothing,' Josh said. He poked at his spaghetti. 'She doesn't know I know.'

Adam raised an eyebrow in question.

'The postman brought them this morning,' Josh said, avoiding eye-contact. 'I steamed open the envelope when Mum was in the shower. She takes ages,' he added.

'Women do,' Adam said.

'There was a visa for Mum, but I couldn't tell what else,' he admitted. 'Then Barry came in and I had to hide it. I stuck it up with Pritt Stick and put it back with the other stuff.'

Josh was heartbreaking in his inventiveness.

'You shouldn't steam open your mum's post,' Adam said gently.

Josh stared at him with tear-filled eyes.

'Except in extreme circumstances,' he relented.

'I didn't know what else to do,' his son said.

Adam smiled at him and rubbed a thumb across his cheek. 'You could talk to your mum.'

'I try to, but she won't talk back,' Josh said.

Adam knew exactly how that felt.

'You talk to her,' Josh suggested.

'I've tried,' Adam admitted. 'She won't talk to me either.'

'Is this a women thing too?' Josh asked.

'No,' Adam said. 'Women usually want to talk too much.'

'Oh.'

Adam took Josh's hands and squeezed them. 'This isn't the end of the world,' he tried to reassure his son who looked more worried than a twelve year old should. 'A visa means that you *can* go to Australia. It doesn't mean that you *have* to.' Plane tickets are a worse sign, Adam said to himself. 'I'll try to talk to her again,' he promised.

Josh smiled. 'Thanks, Dad.'

'You know that I'll do all I can?'

'Yeah,' Josh said. Adam just wasn't sure that it would be enough. Once Laura set her heart on something, she was immovable in her determination.

'I've got a new job,' Adam said, changing the subject. And I hope that's going to help me to keep you here, he thought.

Josh was attacking his spaghetti again, despite the fact that it was long cold. 'Doing what?'

'Still in photography,' he said. 'Just different stuff.'

'Like what? Cars?'

'No,' Adam said, trying to sound confident. 'Models.'

Josh's fork stopped halfway to this mouth. 'Girl models?'

Adam cleared his throat. 'Yes. Mostly.'

Josh frowned. 'Models like Kate Moss and Naomi Campbell?'

'Well . . .' Adam raked his curls. 'Sometimes.'

'Or models like Jakki Lodge and Holly McGuire?'

Adam felt his eyebrows shoot up in surprise. 'Aren't they page three girls?'

Josh avoided his gaze. 'They might be.'

'How do you know the names of all these models?'

Josh went red under the collar of his Nike T-Shirt. 'Barry gets the *Sun*,' he said. 'Sometimes it falls open at page three.'

'Oh,' Adam said, biting back a smile.

Josh flushed redder. 'Look, I'm growing up,' he said sharply, 'OK?'

'Yeah,' Adam said, pushing aside the thought that his son might not be around for him to see it.

Chapter Seventy-Four

I cannot believe what I'm doing. This is Cara's idea of me helping her. It is one step beyond the magical throwing-flour-in-the-face incident.

It has started to drizzle and the grass is unpleasantly damp. I know this because I am picking my way up the garden by the light of a very feeble torch, wearing only my slippers on my feet, and have already used every expletive known to man. I am not a happy bunny.

The trees are being stirred by a growing wind and the clouds are scudding swiftly and spookily across the bright, shining face of the moon. It's a full moon. What else? But I don't think this has any bearing on Cara's spell. She says it's just a fortuitous coincidence that will make her magic more potent. I say it's a stroke of good luck because otherwise I wouldn't be able to see a bloody thing.

I am looking for spiders. Big, hairy-arsed ones. Some people think that witches don't use spiders in their spells – well, they bloody well do. At least my witch-like little friend who is sitting in the warmth of her lounge, scanning ancient books of magical text, says they do.

I bloody hate spiders. I never used to. I was all right until Declan got *Arachnophobia* out on video because he said Blockbusters didn't have any copies of *Four Weddings and a Funeral* as I'd requested. Strangely, the next day when I took *Arachnophobia* back, they had four copies, all sitting expectantly on the shelves, Hugh Grant smiling out winsomely.

OhGodohGod. I hold up the leaves of a laurel bush and check for spiders. I've got two already in my jam jar. But guess what? I need six. And you know the thing about spiders and jam jars? They become Houdini personified. The minute I screw off the lid to pop one in, another one shoots straight out. I've probably manhandled seventy-eight spiders in the last half an hour and I've still ended up with naffing two in the jar. The star of *Arachnophobia* is sitting winking at me from his web. Ugh.

Cara opens the French doors. 'What are you doing out here?' she shouts above the wind.

I wonder if the patio is big enough to bury her under.

'I'm ready now,' she says impatiently. 'All I need is the spiders.'

All she needs is a pick-axe through her head.

'You could come out and help me,' I suggest tartly. 'I don't actually like spiders!'

'I'm not asking you to eat one, Emily,' she responds.

There aren't names bad enough to call my friend.

'I'm going in,' Cara informs me. 'It's cold.'

As if I don't know this. 'My knickers have probably frozen to my bottom,' I snarl.

'At least you're wearing them.'

Grrr!

'I'll practise my wand technique until you've done your bit,' she says magnanimously.

How much practice does waving a little black stick about take?

'I can feel bad vibes coming from you,' my one-time friend advises me.

'Really,' I say. I can't imagine why.

'I don't want it to have a negative effect on the spell,' she says. 'This may be my last chance to nab Adam.'

Whatever this man has done I don't think he deserves Cara as a girlfriend. 'I'll just carry on grubbing round in the mud then, shall I?' I say. 'We shouldn't let a bit of wind and rain and my utter discomfort stand in the way of your love life.'

I can hear Cara puff grumpily and just before she firmly shuts the French doors, she adds, 'This *was* your idea in the first place, Emily.'

I know. It isn't the best one I've ever had. I clench my jaw and prod a spider leg back into the jar. And to think that I could have been in a nice, warm photographic studio rolling around on the floor in the nip.

Chapter Seventy-Five

Adam walked Josh up the path and rang the door bell. His son looked up at him dolefully, two extra scoops of chocolate ice cream having failed to lift his mood. This was too much to ask him to go through, and Adam wondered how much longer they could both take this living in limbo, not knowing how many access days remained before Josh left his life for another continent.

Barry opened the door. He looked tired and drawn, but his face lit up when he saw Josh. With a tiny jolt of shock, Adam realised that he'd never noticed that before. But then he rarely saw Barry; it was Laura who usually provided the barricade at the door. 'Hi,' Barry said. 'Did you have a good time?'

Josh nodded and threw himself against Adam. He crouched down and squeezed his son to him. 'Be good,' Adam said. 'I'll see you at the weekend.'

Josh rushed inside. Barry hesitated before following him.

'I need to speak to Laura,' Adam said. He paused, not knowing how much to say.

'She's out,' Barry said. 'At a women's group meeting.'

Both men raised their eyebrows.

'Can you get her to phone me?' Adam said. 'About this Australia thing.'

'Ah,' Barry said wearily. 'Australia.'

'It's upsetting Josh.'

'It's upsetting us both,' Barry stated. 'You know that she's talking of going without me?'

'Yes,' Adam said. 'I did.'

'What do you think about it?' his ex-wife's husband asked.

Adam wasn't sure that it was his place to comment. 'You know what Laura's like,' he ventured, being as non-committal as humanly possible.

'Yes, I do,' Barry said. 'I wouldn't mind,' he complained, 'but she's not a great wife. Or even a great mother.' He hung his head. 'But then you'll know that.'

'Yeah,' Adam said. 'But then I don't think I was a great husband.' I thought so at the time, he mused. But hindsight was a truly wonderful gift.

'You're a great father though,' Barry said, a tinge of envy staining his voice.

'I don't know about that . . .' Adam began to protest.

'Josh is like a son to me,' Barry interjected. He shook his head sadly. 'I might not be able to show it like you do, but I love him as best as I know how. I can't have children of my own. I expect Laura told you that?'

'No,' Adam said, uncomfortable at this unexpectedly intimate exchange with a man to whom he'd barely spoken two sentences in the last nine years. Barry clearly didn't appreciate that Laura only ever revealed snippets of information on a need-to-know basis.

'Josh is the closest I'll ever know.' Barry gave a sad twist of his lips that in better circumstances might have suggested a smile. 'It's difficult to live up to a father who's a superhero, you know.'

Adam shrugged. 'It's easy being a superhero if you only have to do it for a handful of hours each week.' He tried a smile at the pale, drained face of Barry. 'I'm not the one who has to make him eat his broccoli.'

'Adam,' Barry said, 'if you do get custody of Josh, do you think that I could take him out sometimes?'

'Do you think Laura will let him stay with me without a fight?'

'No.' Barry wrung his hands together. 'I'm clutching at straws, mate.'

'Me too,' Adam said. His hands were going numb with the cold.

'She might not be a good wife, but I still love her. I can't help it.' And Adam guessed that love sometimes made you like that. Despite all the evidence to the contrary, some people soldiered on for years trying to make unsuitable relationships suit. Barry looked more miserable than ever. 'What do you think would make Laura happy?'

'I don't think Laura knows that herself.' Adam jammed his hands into his pockets. 'But I'm sure it isn't moving to Australia.'

'I don't want her to go.'

'If that's how you feel,' Adam said, 'then fight for her.'

'I don't know how,' Barry admitted.

'I can't help you with that one, mate.' Adam studied his feet. 'Women are a complete mystery to me. Particularly my ex-wife.'

'Whatever happens,' Barry sighed, 'let's keep in touch.'

'Yeah.'

'I'll see you round,' Barry said and closed the door.

'Yeah,' Adam said to himself and wondered why he'd always thought Barry was such a complete tosser when he was actually quite a decent bloke.

Chapter Seventy-Six

Cara has a piece of red cloth placed in the middle of the lounge carpet. The Navajos are doing their stuff on the CD player and there are so many candles that it looks like the set of *Phantom of the Opera* in here. All the spiders have legged it. The minute Cara opened the jar, they were off. I think Lester Piggott was riding one of them. The little bastards are probably lurking in the sofa and down the bathroom plugholes to exact their horrid, hairy-arsed revenge on me when I'm least expecting it.

'This is a spell to attract my perfect lover,' Cara intones gravely.

And, do you know what? I haven't even the strength to laugh. I've got soaking wet hair and a soaking wet heart and I think I've probably just performed the traditional ritual for attracting pneumonia.

Cara has a little red velvet pouch and she puts in all sorts of different coloured crystals. When she's finished, she gives it a tender kiss. I have a feeling she's done this before. There are also two glasses of red wine, which seems like a jolly good idea. I reach to take the nearer one to me, but Cara slaps my hand. 'That's not for you!' she snarls. 'It's for Adam!'

I perk up. 'Is he coming?'

'Only in spirit,' Cara says mysteriously.

I might have known. Just when I thought things were about to liven up. Then again, it's probably a good job he's not coming. The poor chap would have thought he'd arrived in the middle of *Macbeth*.

'I'm supposed to have a picture of my perfect lover,' my friend says, admitting to a rather fatal flaw in her magic. 'I'll just have to visualise him instead.'

I hope a picture of Austin Powers doesn't flash through her brain instead. Would it be cruel of me to focus on him? Ha, ha! Mind you, I'd probably end up with him then.

'And you're missing a few spiders,' I say helpfully.

From Cara's black look, I don't think this has escaped her attention. 'We do, however, have a full moon,' she says. 'That will help.'

Cara settles herself into a mystic pose, which in time-honoured tradition, I mimic. 'We should move back the sofa and do a circle dance,' she tells me.

'Oh, let's not,' I beg.

She tuts at me. I will never secure my place in the universe at this rate, her frosty glance tells me.

Cara's hair is spiralling madly round her face and she's wearing a flowing silk number in a rich, scarlet red. Her mouth is painted with a matching red slash. She looks stunningly beautiful in a slightly insane way.

'This is my altar of love,' Cara says, indicating her red cloth and putting a piece of white paper in the middle of it.

I don't like to mention it, but it is actually an old cushion cover. The white piece of paper has Adam's name scrawled over it several hundred times. And lots of kisses. This is the sort of thing I used to do in my Biology lessons when I was supposed to be paying attention.

Cara smoothes out the piece of white paper signalling that magic is about to commence.

'Where does the red wine come into it?' I say, hoping that I still might get a snifter.

'I'm going to infuse it with these herbs,' Cara says, indicating a saucer of what looks like basil, crushed cardamom seeds and a few dried-up-looking cloves. But I suppose all cloves look like that. 'Then all I've got to do is persuade Adam to drink it before the next full moon.'

'Which is when?' I say.

'I'm not sure,' Cara says. Another flaw in her supposedly omnipotent knowledge of the black arts. 'A while, I think. Two weeks on Thursday.'

A guess if ever I heard one.

Cara waves her wand about, nearly knocking over the glass of wine, and then closes her eyes. I, respectfully, close mine.

She performs a bit of deep breathing and, to show solidarity, I do likewise.

Cara draws in a huge, sucking breath and exhales it sharply before she speaks. 'When will I see you again?' she says solemnly. She utters the next line under her breath, running the words together like an incantation.

My eyes shoot open. This is the number one hit by The Three Degrees from the seventies! I remember it well. My mum rushed out and bought it and we used to play it over and over. I flip over her book. It might say *Ancient and Effective Magical Potions Passed*

Down Through the Centuries on the cover, but this isn't a book of spells, it's a book of old song lyrics! This is a Three Degrees' song. It is! Just as the other spell was a Carpenters' one.

Cara has opened her eyes. 'What?' she says with menace.

'Nothing,' I say innocently. She's paid £17.99 for this. She's been robbed.

She opens her eyes to slits, daring me to intervene. I clasp my hands together in prayer and gaze serenely towards the ceiling, which is only slightly in the way of the celestial skies above while my friend continues to mutter Three Degrees' lyrics in a mystical fashion.

Even Cara is starting to look doubtful now. I resist the urge to burst into song. This was a great record – one of the best. I wanted to be one of The Three Degrees when I was younger. And would have been if I hadn't been hampered by the fact that I wasn't black, beautiful, and I couldn't sing a note. And I was only four at the time. But, hey, we can all dream.

Cara rushes through the rest of the spell with a distinct lessening in enthusiasm. When she's finished, she feigns exhaustion.

'Right,' I say, rubbing my hands together. 'Can we get pissed now?'

'Yes,' Cara says. And she does, indeed, look like she needs a drink. 'Just don't touch this,' she says, moving Adam's special, spell-laden glass of wine with an exaggerated degree of reverence. 'I'll pour it into one of the empty bottles when we've finished.'

We're obviously in for a session. 'And then what?' I want to know.

'I'll take it into work or try to lure him here,' she says. 'Then all I've got to do is get him to drink it.'

'And then what?'

'Bingo!'

'Bingo?'

'Bingo,' she reiterates. 'He falls madly in love with me and we live happily ever after.'

'Nice,' I say. Cara deserves a bit of happiness, even though I haven't quite forgiven her for sending me out in the rain to collect spiders. I will get my own back some way, some day. And, as spell sessions go, this one wasn't too painful and didn't involve me in suffering too much abuse. I might even consider doing it again to snare The Hunk from the wine bar. Then I remember the spiders. Cara would definitely insist on them next time.

'I'll get the plonk then,' I offer.

'By the way, Emily,' Cara says as I head for the door. 'Where did you get to earlier tonight?'

'Nowhere,' I say as glibly as I can manage with my tongue stuck to the roof of my mouth.

Cara regards me coolly. 'Are you sure you're not up to something?'

'No,' I say and, as I rush out of the kitchen, I just hope that I don't look too guilty.

Chapter Seventy-Seven

Adam was languishing over his breakfast. He was reclining on his sofa in front of GMTV watching the chubby-cheeked Eamonn Holmes and the irrepressibly chirpy Fiona Philips as they dished the dirt on the daily news. Even the orange sofa was failing to give him a headache.

As he sat and munched his way through his Weetabix, Adam decided he was in a very strange mood. He was feeling very elated and positive about his new career move. So much so that he'd decided to go out and buy himself some new threads. Trendy photographer-type clothes rather than has-been news snapper-type stuff. He looked down at his fraying jeans. Soon.

By contrast, he was also feeling very flat re. The Josh/ Antipodean situation. The sooner he got himself a solicitor and applied for custody of Josh, the better things would seem. If it hadn't been the day of the Prime Minister's visit to the new cinema club in Hampstead, he would have been tempted to phone in sick and sort out a few of his pressing domestic problems. As it was, he was going to be massively late and he still had a shirt to iron.

But, before he did anything work-related, he urgently needed to talk to Cara about the photographs she wanted him to take, although the only plan they'd probably have would be to do blanket coverage and get as near to the front of the press scrum as possible. It was that sophisticated an operation. The other advantage of today marking a rare appearance in their borough by Tony Blair and entourage was that it would make him far too busy to talk to Cara about anything else.

Also, he'd need to start packing things up at home as soon as possible, as Toff had said he could move into his new flat whenever he liked. Adam couldn't wait to move. This place wasn't exactly a dump – where in Hampstead was? And it wasn't a sad bastard bachelor place, but it wasn't a million miles away either. In Toff's place, Josh could have his own bedroom and Adam wouldn't be relegated to the lumpy sofa-bed every time he had his son to stay overnight.

Fiona Philips kindly announced the time. Time to get a move on, Adam thought – just as his door bell rang. Padding to the door in his bare feet, he opened it, and the last person in the world he had expected to see was waiting there.

'Hi,' Laura said.

'Hi,' Adam replied, standing there with his empty Weetabix bowl and a bare chest. He held his bowl a bit higher, though why he should feel embarrassed, goodness only knows. Laura had seen everything he'd got and from several different angles.

'Can I come in?' she asked.

'Yes, yes,' Adam said. 'Of course.'

Laura nervously picked her way past him, taking in the peeling paint in the hall.

'I've got a new flat,' Adam said, a defensive note in his voice. 'Two bedrooms. Nice garden.'

'Good,' Laura said with a heavy exhalation of breath.

'Tea?' he offered.

'Yes,' Laura said. 'That would be nice.'

Adam tried not to look at the clock. This was important. If Laura was here at this hour in the morning, it was very important. 'I take it that this isn't a social visit?' Adam said, broaching the subject as he clanked about with the cups waiting for the kettle to boil.

Laura sat on one of his rickety kitchen chairs. God, he'd never realised that everything in this place was falling down around his ears. She picked at the paint on his table with her long slender fingers. He handed her a mug and then leaned against the sink, arms folded.

'Barry told me you wanted to talk to me,' she said.

'He's a nice guy,' Adam observed. 'You could do worse.'

'I already have done,' Laura said, giving him a pointed look.

Adam laughed. 'I guess I deserved that.'

'No,' she said. 'I was just teasing.'

Adam chewed his lip. 'Have you come to a decision?'

Laura had dark circles under her eyes and lifeless skin. 'Yes.'

'You know,' Adam said, 'this isn't just about me. Josh is finding it very hard.'

'I don't think he wants to go to Australia.' Laura looked up at Adam. 'Do you?'

'No,' Adam said quietly. 'I think he wants to stay here. Where he can be with me.'

'You love him very much, don't you?'

Adam felt his throat close up. 'Yes.'

'I do too,' Laura said and Adam could see her eyes fill with tears. 'I want what's best for him.'

263

'I'm not sure that dragging him halfway round the world is,' Adam said.

'You're right.' The tears rolled down Laura's cheeks. 'You seem to make a habit of it.'

'Laura . . .' Adam stepped forward, but she stilled him with a wave of her hand.

'I'm going to Australia,' she said, her voice brittle.

'And that's it?' Adam said, his heart sinking. 'No more discussion?'

'There's no need to discuss it, Adam,' she pointed out. 'You've said all you need to.'

'I haven't, Laura. Not by a long chalk.' His voice sounded calm, but inside he was shaking. 'I'll fight you all the way on this.'

'I don't want to fight you, Adam,' she said wearily. Laura gazed at him levelly. 'I'm going to Australia alone.'

It wouldn't even have taken a feather to knock Adam over. *'Alone?'*

Laura nodded hesitantly. 'Alone.'

Adam couldn't find his voice.

'I'm going alone. For six months. Maybe less – I don't know. I might miss my son too much.' Laura looked up bleakly. 'Josh can stay with you. If you'll have him.

If he'd have him? Adam could have broken down and wept like a baby. 'Laura . . .'

'Josh will be better off with you,' Laura said. 'This is about me being fucked-up, isn't it?' Her dark eyes appealed to him. 'How can I make anyone else happy, if I'm not happy inside myself?'

'I'm not sure that running away will help.' Adam wanted to say more, so much more. 'I did it once and I've lived with the guilt ever since.'

'You tried your best, Adam,' Laura said. 'Even I know that now.'

'Stay,' Adam pleaded. 'Stay and let's sort it all out together.'

'I've made plans,' she said. 'I need the freedom to find out who I want to be. Just for a while.'

'And what about Barry?' Adam asked.

'He's said he'll wait.' She gave a sad half-laugh. 'He is a good man.'

'Josh needs you around too,' Adam said. 'You're his mother.'

'Perhaps he'll like me better when I come back,' Laura said. 'Perhaps I'll like myself.'

'When are you going?'

'Next week,' Laura said.

'So soon?'

'There's no point hanging around now I've made the decision.'

'No,' Adam said. He was sure there must be a point, but didn't know how to voice it.

Laura pushed her tea to one side and stood up. 'I'll bring Josh round on Saturday,' she said. 'With his stuff.'

Adam put his head in his hands. Shit. This was heartbreaking. It felt worse than the day when he'd walked out on them both. Even though Laura had decided not to take Josh with her, there was an emptiness at the thought of her child, their child, being left behind while Laura breezed off to 'find herself'. Knowing Josh, he would adapt admirably to it and his heart went out to his stoic little son.

'Laura,' Adam said, 'is there any other way we can do this?'

'I don't think so,' she answered uncertainly. It seemed a very big decision to take if you weren't absolutely sure. 'I'd better go now.' She chanced a smile. 'And you'd better iron a shirt before you go to work.'

Adam gaped stupidly at his bare chest. 'How did you know . . .?'

Laura regarded the ironing board standing on permanent duty in the corner of the kitchen. 'You used to iron a shirt every morning before you went to work. And you only ever did the front.'

Adam chuckled.

'There are some things I'll never forget about you, Adam Jackson,' she said, and she came to him and ran a finger tenderly down his cheek.

They looked at each other and their faces crumpled with pain and sadness, love that had been lost, and regret, and the tears flowed. Adam wrapped his arms round the person whom he had once loved so much and held her sobbing body tightly to him. Laura was right. He still only ever ironed the front of his shirts.

Chapter Seventy-Eight

She was going to have to get Emily to move out, Cara thought as she moved her limbs in the same leaden fashion that wading through treacle might involve. Her friend was definitely a bad influence on her liver. This weekend she was going to drink only wheatgrass juice in an effort to detoxify herself. She sat down at her desk and sipped her coffee gratefully. Her caffeine level was at an all-time high too. Yes, she'd detoxify at the weekend, but today her fragile constitution was in need of chemical jump-starting.

Chris was sitting quietly at his desk, tapping away at his keyboard. Hangover territory too, Cara guessed. She nodded in his direction and the reporter smiled back weakly.

'All set for today?' Cara checked. Tony Blair was due at two o'clock, just in time for a bit of party-political mumbo jumbo to the waiting press and then a matinée showing of *Snow White and the Seven Dwarfs*.

Chris gave a slight nod. Cara looked puzzled. He wasn't gloating. He was definitely ill.

She returned to her in-tray, stacked with incoming stories. As she sorted through the first few, out of the corner of her eye she noticed that Adam had arrived. He was hideously late, but looking very bouncy. His usually pasty cheeks were positively blooming. Wherever he'd been, it wasn't out drinking with Chris last night.

'All right, mate?' Adam said to his colleague as he passed his desk.

Chris managed a feeble, 'Fine.'

'Feeling a bit delicate?' Adam enquired.

'Yeah.' Chris's voice was hoarse.

'Lassie and Fido a bit too much to handle?'

'Yeah,' Chris said miserably. 'Ha, ha.'

When Adam came over to his own desk, Cara busied herself with the day's stories, shuffling them furiously in an important manner.

Adam leaned over and gave her a heart-stopping, toe-tingling smile. Her heart, obliging, stopped momentarily and all of her toes tingled in the confines of her combat boots. 'Sorry I'm late,' he said, lowering his voice. He looked over his shoulder. Chris had his head sunk towards his desk. 'And I'm sorry too that we've not had a chance to talk since . . .' he checked on Chris again, 'since – you know.'

'That's OK,' Cara said, her heart taking up a steady thump.

Adam's eyes went all sort of dreamy. 'I've loads to tell you. But not here. Let's catch up later.'

'Yes,' Cara said. 'I'd like that.'

'Now you need to tell me what photographs you want,' he said, switching to work mode.

'Fine,' Cara said and reeled off a list of shots that she thought they ought to get.

Adam shrugged out of his jacket and Cara noticed that only the front of his shirt was ironed. He was definitely in need of a good woman, she mused, casting her eyes over the creases in the fabric.

'Anything else in?' Adam asked, nodding at the pile of news stories.

Cara flicked at them. 'Not much,' she said. 'Ooo, wait!' She cast her eyes over the piece of paper in her hand. 'This is an interesting little story. How come this is down at the bottom of the pile?'

She glanced over at Chris who slunk lower in his chair.

'What?' Adam took the paper, read it and smiled.

'I think we should cover this,' Cara said.

'Me too,' Adam looked over at Chris, grinning broadly.

Chris narrowed his eyes at him.

'Hey, Chris!' Cara shouted over. 'What do you think?'

The reporter cleared his throat.

'It's just come in,' she said. Cara took the paper back from Adam and read from it: ' "Last night a major security alert was sparked by intruders in the car park of St Winifred's Primary School, close to where the Prime Minister is due to visit today." ' Cara looked up. 'That's the little school just behind the cinema, isn't it?'

Adam nodded.

Cara returned to the news copy: ' "The area was being monitored by CCTV equipment in advance of the PM's visit. Sources say that police helicopters swarmed the area and armed officers surrounded a suspicious-looking car only to find a man and *two* women involved in activities of a sexual nature." ' Cara hooted with laughter. '*Two women!*'

Adam looked over at Chris, who fidgeted uncomfortably. 'Greedy.'

'*Lucky!*' Chris mouthed back defiantly.

267

'And careless,' Cara snorted. 'What sort of idiot would do that?'

Adam eye-balled Chris. 'I've absolutely no idea.'

Chris flushed a nice shade of beetroot.

'We've got to cover this,' Cara exclaimed, 'seeing as we're now known as the newspaper for exposing sleaze in the community. Do you want to get onto it, Chris?'

He coughed delicately. 'Not really, thanks, Cara.'

Her face fell. 'I would have thought this was right up your street.'

'No,' he said vehemently. 'It's a non-story.'

'A non-story? But it's great.' Cara was stunned. She turned to Adam, who was standing smiling inanely. 'What do you think?'

'What does it matter what Adam thinks?' Chris interjected crossly.

Adam pressed his lips together as he gazed thoughtfully across the office at his colleague. 'I think we should do an in-depth exposé,' he said sincerely. 'Find out who they are, fill the front page with it and pillory them as unfit members of society.'

Chris snarled silently at him.

'Well, I wasn't thinking of going quite so strong,' Cara said, 'but you're right, maybe we ought to really go for it.'

Cara looked expectantly at Chris, who said nothing.

'I don't understand your stance on this,' she said when he didn't respond. 'You were so keen on sleaze before.'

Adam smirked at Chris and said innocently, 'What else does the copy say, Cara?'

'Er . . . blah, blah, blah . . .' Cara said, picking up the story again. ' "Police have named Christopher Jeremy Seymour, aged thirty . . ." ' She stopped and looked up, openmouthed.

Chris's hair roots turned red.

' "Christopher *Jeremy* Seymour, aged thirty. Mr Seymour is believed to be a journalist on the *Hampstead Observer*." ' Cara looked up again. '*Jeremy?*'

'Yes. Fucking *Jeremy*,' Chris snapped. 'It was my father's name.'

Cara started to giggle. ' "Mr Seymour's companions . . . *companions*! . . . are named as Ms Karen Smith, forty-two, and Ms Rita Brown, forty-five." ' Cara was incredulous. 'Bit old for you, Chris!'

'They looked a lot younger!' Chris was getting more puce by the minute. 'Didn't they, Adam?'

Cara's head snapped round. 'You knew about this?'

Adam held his hands up. 'I know nothing!'

Cara put down the paper. 'We have to run with this, Chris. You know we do.'

'It was one little mistake,' the reporter pleaded. 'This could scar me for life.'

Adam and Cara stifled chuckles.

Chris's face took on a pained expression. 'One minute I was having a nice time . . .'

'With Karen and Rita?' Adam said. His friend glowered at him.

'And the next,' Chris continued, 'I was facing two dozen masked men with Heckler & Koch MP5 machine guns pointed at my grollies.'

Adam and Cara burst out laughing.

'It was a very traumatic experience,' Chris protested. 'This is enough to make me impotent!'

'I think that might be a blessing for womankind,' Cara retorted.

'You cannot do this to me,' Chris whined. 'I'm your mate. I work here. Please, please don't do this.'

Cara was suddenly serious. 'You didn't think of the effect on Emily's life of running her story, did you?' she said. 'That was a silly mistake too and look at the consequences she's had to suffer.'

'Awwh,' Chris moaned. 'Have some pity.' He looked at Adam for support, but none was forthcoming. 'How will I ever hold my head up in the office again? I'll be a laughing stock.'

'At least you won't lose your job. Or your home,' Cara pointed out. 'It's only your dignity you'll lose.'

'And you didn't have much of that in the first place,' Adam observed.

'Cheers, mate,' Chris said with a resigned pout.

Cara flipped open her notebook. 'I'll cover this story,' she said decisively. 'Would Mr Seymour like to grace us with a comment?'

'Bollocks,' Chris replied unhelpfully.

Chapter Seventy-Nine

I need some fresh air. My head is stuffed full of cottonwool and I'm sporting eye bags that would carry enough clothes for a fortnight's skiing holiday. I've got to move out of Cara's house and beyond the reaches of my friend's idea of tender loving care. I'm being organised to death. All this health food and the vitamins she's insisting I throw down my throat are doing me no good at all. I feel decidedly rough. I'm sure I'm allergic to ginseng.

On the other hand, when I do eventually go, I'm going to miss her loads, because despite our sparring, Cara is like a sister to me. Life is certainly never dull when she's around. I guess she could well say the same about me.

I skirt round Adam's potion – which is sitting looking faintly malevolent in the fridge door – and opt for plain old orange juice instead. In the aftermath of last night's spell session, I have decided not to leave my fate in the hands of the universe. In my opinion, the universe is far too fickle a force to leave in charge of my love life. Instead, I am going to try to track down The Hunk myself. I have decided, in the tried and tested method of television detectives, to go back to *Temptation* and quiz the bar staff in an in-depth fashion about the identity of this mystery man who has made fast and free with my emotions. Is that not a positive step forwards? Is that not more resourceful, say, than relying on some scabby arachnids and a few dodgy old pop songs to do your dirty work?

I savour my breakfast, despite feeling rather delicate in the digestive regions. It's a wonderful day and even the air is tinged with the expectancy that anything could happen. This day feels like a turning point – don't ask me why, since nothing has changed. But perhaps something has shifted inside me. For the first time in ages I feel in control of my destiny.

Breakfast done, I set off and stride out down Hampstead High Street feeling a bit fab. Even the tramps in the High Street are sipping frothy cappuccino out of tall Starbucks cups, so life can't be

270

all that bad. If I do become a down-and-out here, at least I'd get decent beverages.

Temptation looks very different in the daytime. Not very tempting at all, in fact. *Temptation* is clearly a night owl, not a lark – much like myself. The jewel colours and gilt mirrors look garish in the low, piercing winter sunlight. I creep in, aware that the bar staff are just setting up for the lunchtime trade which caters for the ciabatta crowd, and also aware that my boots are clonking on the fashionable wooden floor, which echoes loudly without a crush of bodies to deaden the sound.

There are no customers in the bar yet, just two gaunt-looking guys polishing glasses with damp tea towels listening to the melodic strains of Frank Sinatra over the sound system.

'Hi,' I say, feeling extraordinarily stupid. 'I wonder if you can help me?' They both look up and indicate that they might be persuaded to. 'I'm looking for someone.'

'Aren't we all?' the comedian of the duo states.

I laugh as if it's the best joke I've ever heard, in a pathetic attempt to win them over. 'I was at the launch party,' I say before I decide against committing my future to this listless clown. 'I wanted to find a guy that I saw here.'

The barmen raise their collective eyebrows. 'Name?'

'Emily,' I say.

'His name,' they say in unison.

'Oh.' What a twonk I am. 'I don't know.'

'What does he look like?' The taller barman pulls a notepad and a pencil out of his apron pocket.

'Er . . .' I say helpfully.

They are both poised expectantly, all thoughts of polishing glasses banished.

'He's tall. Very tall. Over six foot. Six one? Six two?'

'Six three?'

'No,' I say. 'Not six three.' Definitely not six three. 'He's dark.'

'And handsome?'

'Yes,' I say, brightening. And then realise that I'm still a twonk and that with a slight stretching of the imagination, both barmen – and ninety per cent of the male population – could quite easily fit that description.

'Anything else?'

'Er . . . No.' How do you describe a smile that makes your heart do a salsa routine?

The barman puts his pencil away. Pointedly.

'Thanks, anyway,' I say. 'You've been a great help.'

271

'Why don't you come in on a Friday and Saturday night?' the barman suggests. 'There are loads of guys here then. Some of them tall, dark and handsome. You might even find one better than the one you're looking for.'

I somehow doubt it. 'Yeah,' I say, 'I might well do that.' I somehow doubt that too.

'Do you want to leave me your name?' the barman says. 'Just in case.'

'Emily,' I say. 'I'm Emily.' And at the risk of appearing a loose harlot I give him my mobile number. 'Thanks,' I say again and walk out into the sunshine.

The barman pushes the note into his apron pocket with an appreciative curl of his lip. 'I might just ring her myself,' he says to his mate. But, of course, I'm already striding back up the High Street and don't hear that.

Adam had half an hour before he had to whizz off to the film club to snap the Prime Minister looking happy and smiling. Chris was still sulking and wouldn't come to lunch with him at the Jig, which left Adam pretty much to his own devices. He could, he supposed, have taken Cara to lunch, but he didn't quite know what to say to her yet as the right sentences were taking time to formulate in his brain.

He couldn't help smiling to himself when he thought of Chris's misfortune. His friend might be mortified, but it was very, very funny. And it could have been worse – he could have been caught enjoying carnal knowledge of two blokes rather than two women. But then it was easy for Adam to feel smug when things were going right in his life. For once. He'd got a great new job. A great new flat. And, the greatest great of all, Laura was letting Josh move in with him on a permanent basis.

While he was on a roll, he'd decided to throw caution to the wind and go in search of the elusive dream-woman-in-the-wine-bar, despite the fact that in reality she could be married, a psycho, a lesbian or a vegetarian. Or all four.

Toff had obviously forgotten his promise to help him in pursuit of his mystery woman, but after all his friend had done for him in the last few weeks, Adam had decided to let this temporary lapse go unchallenged. Toff was, after all, a bloke. And if there was dirty work to do, then Adam should be man enough to do it himself.

With a spring in his step, he swung through the doors of *Temptation*. It was quiet at lunchtime. So quiet that it hardly seemed like the same place. A few trendy guys propped up the bar. A group of giggling women sipped champagne and swung their shoes hopefully in the direction of the trendy guys propping up the bar.

Adam waited for the barman to finish serving and ordered a glass of fresh orange. The barman filled a tall glass with ice and poured in the freshly squeezed juice. He put the glass down in front of Adam with a cursory smile.

'I wonder if you can help me, mate,' Adam said before the barman started to move away.

'Shoot.' The tall, gaunt barman shrugged.

'I'm looking for a girl.'

'Me too,' the barman quipped.

'No. Someone special,' Adam said. 'I wondered if you'd know her.'

'Maybe.' Another shrug.

'I was here on the night of the launch party,' Adam pressed on. 'So was she.'

'Name?'

'Adam,' Adam said.

The barman sighed. 'Her name?'

'No idea, mate,' Adam admitted, a slight puff of his buoyant nature escaping with the noise of a deflating balloon. This might prove more difficult than he imagined.

The barman leaned on the bar. 'We might have had her in earlier.'

Adam sat up straight. 'What?'

'There was a woman in earlier,' the barman said, 'looking for a bloke of your description.'

'No?' Adam said incredulously. This was beyond good luck.

'Yeah,' the barman reiterated. 'Very pretty, mate.' He gave Adam an approving glance.

'Yeah,' Adam agreed.

'Great figure.'

'Yes,' Adam agreed.

'Nice teeth.'

'Yes. Yes.' Adam was bordering on ecstatic.

'Blonde hair.'

'Blonde?' Adam's world came crashing down. *'Blonde?'*

'Yeah,' the barman said. 'Blonde.'

'No, mate,' Adam shook his head sadly. 'This one was dark.'

'Oh,' the barman said. He looked as downhearted as Adam felt. 'Never mind. Plenty more fish in the sea.'

'Yeah.'

'Do you want her name anyway? She left it – and her phone number.' The barman concentrated hard. 'It was Imogen. Or Jenny.' He scratched his ear. 'Or it might have been Emma.'

273

'But she was blonde,' Adam said.

'Yeah,' the barman confirmed. 'Blonde.'

'She's not the right one.'

'You never know,' the barman said encouragingly. 'Fate works in mysterious ways. She's worth giving a ring.'

'Thanks, mate,' Adam said, 'but I'll give it a miss.' He drained the orange juice and pushed a handful of change across the bar. 'Cheers,' he said and jumped down off his stool.

'You could leave your number.'

'Nah,' Adam said. 'It was a long shot.'

'Better luck next time,' the barman said.

'Yeah.' And Adam walked out into the sunshine.

The other barman came behind his colleague rushing to make a Cosmopolitan cocktail for one of the giggling women whose birthday it was. 'What did he want?' he asked.

'I sometimes think we should set up a dating agency in here,' the barman said. 'We'd make a fortune.' He shook his head. 'What happened to that woman's phone number I took earlier?'

'You put it in your apron pocket.'

'Did I?' The barman rummaged in his apron, pushing past the spent cheques and receipts and spare change. 'Oh, here it is.' He tutted to himself. 'I had it all the time.' He pulled the crumpled page of his notepad out and straightened it on the bar. 'Emily,' he said. 'She was called Emily.'

But of course, Adam was already striding back up the High Street and didn't hear that.

Chapter Eighty

I'm going to have a cup of coffee and contemplate my next strategy –
seeing as my last one was so desperately pathetic. This time, my
strategy needs to be slightly more focused on *job-* rather than
man-hunting.

Café Blanco looks as dead as a doornail today, so I carry on up the
High Street and grace Starbucks with my custom instead. It's not that
busy here either, and for once there is a surfeit of brown velvet
armchairs. I can have my pick. Unless I'm beaten to it, I'm going to
sit in the window and watch the world go by. Who knows, The Hunk
could just stroll past.

As I settle down with my coffee, my mobile rings, but I don't
recognise the number from the display.

'Hi,' the voice says and I know that confident tone immediately.
'It's Jonathan Gold.'

I wince as I think that I've ignored every bit of advice he's ever
given me. 'Hi,' I say and feel slightly shamefaced. He's a busy man
and there are plenty of babes out there bonking famous footballers
who probably need him more than me.

'I'm at Sebastian Atherton's,' he says over the crackly line. 'He
tells me that you didn't turn up for your photo session.'

There's no point beating about the bush. 'I bottled out,' I admit
weedily. 'I loitered outside his studio for about half an hour and then
did a runner.'

'Emily!' Jonathan Gold chastises me.

'I know,' I grovel. 'I'm such a wimp.'

'Sebastian was very disappointed. He was looking forward to
meeting you.'

'Please apologise to him,' I say. 'I'm sorry. Really I am. I didn't
mean to waste his time. I just don't think I'm cut out for getting my
kit off.'

'Where are you now?' Jonathan asks.

'In the High Street.' I look at my cappuccino getting cold. 'Having
a coffee at Starbucks.'

'Come and meet him. Now.'

'Er . . .' I say.

'I'll come and get you.'

'I could walk there in ten minutes,' I point out. 'Probably less.'

'I know.' I hear the smile in Jonathan's voice. 'But you might not get here.'

'I . . .'

'Stay there,' he instructs. And he hangs up.

I slip my phone furtively back into my handbag and check that I'm not being watched. But, this being London, no one is taking a blind bit of notice.

Ooo. Now what have I done?

As I finish the last mouthful of my coffee and just before the first shake of my knees, Jonathan Gold pulls up outside Starbucks. I can tell it's him straight away and not just because he turns up in a sleek black Porsche Boxster. Hampstead is a place where Porches are ten a penny. To really stand out from the crowd you need to be driving a beaten-up old 2CV covered in 'right-on' slogans like Cara does – now you don't see a lot of *them* round here. No, it's not the car. It's the way Jonathan Gold drives. Direct, controlled, calm.

I do an uncontrolled, frenzied scrabble round for my coat and handbag and rush out of the door like a thing possessed. He smiles serenely as I fling myself into the passenger seat.

'I thought you might have legged it again,' he says.

'I did think about it,' I admit. And I wonder why I didn't.

'You'll like Sebastian,' he says as he glances behind him and glides out into the constant stream of traffic that is another integral part of Hampstead life. 'He'll put you at ease.'

'Good,' I say, my heart accelerating in time with Jonathan's engine. Because right now I could do with it.

Chapter Eighty-One

Prime Ministers' visits were, Adam decided, thoroughly boring affairs. He lurked behind the metal barriers of the specially segregated press pen with a couple of photographers from the *Sun*, the *Daily Mail* and a reporter from the *Telegraph* who would no doubt try to whip it up into the major event it wasn't.

The general public in Britain are, by and large, fairly ambivalent about their politicians. There has never been the same amount of enthusiasm and flag-waving that seems to accompany American politicians wherever they go. In Hampstead, there was a meagre crowd of children present who had been herded along, primarily since they were the ones who were going to benefit from the opening of the new film club. Adam wondered idly if any of them had ever been taught by Emily. There was also a straggle of bewildered-looking pensioners in tweed jackets who looked as if they might not have anything better to do and a few, fragile white-haired women who seemed to have sort of blown there on the wind like dandelion seeds.

The Premier himself looked older, wearier and more careworn since Adam had photographed him on his last visit here and that wasn't all that long ago. He wore a grey suit and a grey tie and had grey skin. And there was a more distinct smattering of grey in his hair too. Perhaps being the leader of a country meant that you started to age in bigger blocks, rather more like dog years than human ones. Adam knew how he felt. He was sure he'd acquired a Dicky Davis tuft of white near his right temple due to his rising stress levels over the last few weeks. Imagine the toll it must take if you had a cabinet and a country to control rather than a few recalcitrant work colleagues, a tricky ex-wife and a twelve-year-old son. Adam shuddered at the thought.

A few minor film stars from the local environs had popped along for the jaunt and managed to elicit a bit of spontaneous appreciation out of the crowd, as they beamed cheesily and made sure their best side was angled towards the phalanx of photographers, before being swept into the foyer by waiting flunkies.

Adam snapped away as the Prime Minister, flanked by shifty-looking bodyguards, passed by; he tried to capture on film the excitement of Tony's practised, automatic wave and fixed-on grin as he rapidly disappeared into the depths of the renovated cinema.

Adam packed his camera away and, with a twinge of regret, realised that it would probably be the last time he would be hanging around in a press posse on an occasion like this. From now on it would be a warm, centrally heated studio, bigger salary cheques and champagne all the way. Adam stopped in his tracks. And he was having a twinge of regret? Like hell! With renewed energy he headed back to the office to file the pictures.

Chris had also returned to his desk after the press briefing and was sitting, bashing away at his keyboard, sulky lip trailing the floor.

'Cheer up, mate,' Adam said as he strode past him towards his desk. 'It might never happen.'

'It has,' Chris said and flung a mock-up page that had been printed out towards him.

Adam smiled. The headline stated: 'Seymour Sets Off Security Scare.' To accompany it, there was a grainy CCTV photograph of Chris's car surrounded by armed riot police, and a close-up of his rather startled face.

'It's not bloody funny,' Chris snarled, 'so don't even think about laughing.'

'It'll all blow over in a day or two,' Adam assured him. 'No one will even remember.'

'Oh yeah?' Chris said.

Sitting down at his computer, Adam clicked his mouse. Someone had put Chris's face up as a screensaver. Adam grinned to himself. It would blow over in a day or two, sure – but until then, everyone in the office would milk it for all it was worth.

Adam looked up, aware that Cara was watching him.

'Just deserts?' she enquired.

'Perhaps we could fix him up with Emily,' Adam suggested. 'They'd have a lot more in common now.'

'Yes,' Cara giggled. 'They could swap stories.'

'How's Emily doing?' Adam asked.

Cara nodded. 'She seems fine.'

'Back with the boyfriend yet?'

'No,' Cara said. 'I don't think it's meant to be. She's fallen hook, line and sinker for someone else.'

'Lucky Emily,' Adam said with feeling.

'Yes,' Cara said with a sigh.

She was looking very cheesed off, Adam realised. 'Look,' he said, doing the customary check that Chris wasn't listening, 'why don't we go out for a bite to eat tonight. There's a lot I need to talk to you about.'

'I'd like that,' Cara said.

'I'll pick you up about eight,' Adam said and glanced at his watch, noticing for the first time the advancing hour. 'We'd better go through these photographs.' He waved the memory card at her. 'Tony Blair looking very scraggy.'

'I'll pull up a chair,' Cara said and rushed round her desk, pulling a chair tight into Adam's side. As she huddled in front of his computer screen, her arm brushed against his and Cara smiled warmly and secretly at him. She looked so happy that she seemed about to burst and ooze joy all over the *Hampstead Observer*'s vinyl flooring.

Oh shit, Adam said to himself. He'd assumed that she thought their liaison was as disastrous as he did. From the look on her face, now he wasn't so sure. How was he going to tell her that he, like Emily, had fallen hook, line and sinker for someone else?

Chapter Eighty-Two

Sebastian Atherton is a doll. A living doll. He is sweet, gentle and kind in a lovely camp and cutesy fashion. And if I wasn't in love with The Hunk from the wine bar, then I might just give Sebastian Atherton the glad eye. Jonathan Gold was right, he *is* making me feel at ease. Three glasses of champagne have also helped considerably.

Sebastian is folded into an armchair in one corner of his office, long legs swinging loosely over the side. He has 'relaxed' stamped all over him. Jonathan Gold is sitting upright and as businesslike as ever at Sebastian's desk. I'm dithering somewhere in between, the epitome of tension.

'Two hundred thousand pounds, Emily,' Jonathan Gold says – not for the first time.

It is a lottery-winning amount, isn't it? How can my head not be turned by this.

'That's what the *News of the World* have offered,' he reiterates. 'Two hundred thousand pounds. That would solve an awful lot of your problems.'

It may even solve some I haven't yet thought of, I muse. GodGod-God! Why is this so hard? I check my fingernails. 'But they want me to take all of my clothes off for that?'

'Yes,' Jonathan states flatly.

'There are ways that I can do it without you having to feel exposed,' Sebastian says over his glass.

That could be interesting. 'How?' I say, sounding suspicious.

'You need to trust me, darling,' Sebastian urges. 'I can make you look utterly, utterly fabulous. Really I can.'

Is this his way of saying that I currently look a mess? I catch my reflection in the window of his studio and think that it probably is.

'My make-up artist, Nikki, will be here any minute. She'll make you look gorgeous. Jonathan will stay in here. And it will be just you and me.'

'And the camera?'

'You'll love it. I promise.'

I glance at them both, giving them the benefit of my most distrusting stare. 'These pictures won't turn up in some seedy magazine somewhere?'

'You can have full editorial control,' Jonathan says sincerely. 'There's no point in me having unhappy clients, Emily. My reputation exists only because people like what I can do for them. I want you to be in full agreement at every stage. If, for any reason, you don't like them, we'll destroy them while you're still here.'

'Promise me?' I say.

'Promise,' Jonathan echoes.

I knock back my champagne and stand up, wiping my damp palms down my jeans. Sebastian Atherton gives me a warm, encouraging smile. 'Let's do it then,' I say, and notice that my voice and my knees have gone all peculiar.

Chapter Eighty-Three

Adam stared round at the contents of his flat. It didn't amount to much. None of the furniture was his, nor were the curtains or even the cushions. He didn't think he was a natural cushion buyer. Even in this enlightened age, that tended to be the woman's department generally. There were some things men could live without that women couldn't – cushions being a case in point.

When he'd rented this flat, the previous occupant had left a supply of mismatched bedlinen, a cupboard full of mismatched crockery and a bank of towels that looked as if they'd all been stolen from hotels. He had replaced none of them and they had all served him admirably. Did tea and toast taste any better when it was served on matching tableware? Adam thought not.

The only things he had taken with him when he left Laura had been his record collection – which was sort of a bloke thing – and his stereo and, though it had been through several incarnations since then and now sported a CD player, practically the only thing he would leave here with was his stereo, too. It gave him comfort to think that he wasn't an acquisitive person. As soon as Josh arrived, however, Adam was sure his son would try to make him see the error of his ways.

His lack of material possessions meant that packing up was a doddle. Adam had, with an amazing flash of forethought, bought a roll of bin liners and now he opened them and tipped the contents of his wardrobe inside. He would stay on here until the end of the week and then move permanently into Toff's flat. It would give him time to get Toff's place straightened out, buy some new stuff and fumigate this place before he left in the hope that the landlord wouldn't hang onto all of his deposit. It was around five hundred quid and he planned to give anything that was left to Laura to help her out in the only way he knew how.

He stacked the bin bags by the door and went to jump into the shower. There were a couple of hours before he had to pick Cara up and it would give him time to think about what he was going to say to her.

Half an hour and two full-length renditions of 'Bohemian Rhapsody' later when Adam had showered, shaved, found his least crumpled shirt and had tried to organise his hair into a less scary arrangement, he was still none the wiser. He would have to rely on his male instincts. If he sat there and said nothing, perhaps Cara would sort it out for him.

Like some yuppy tramp, he grabbed the bin bags containing his life's possessions, headed down the stairs, dumped them in the back of the Vectra and set off to start his new life at Toff's.

Chapter Eighty-Four

I am as naked as a jay-bird. And Nikki, the magical make-up artist, has made me look like some glamorous, vampy temptress even though my cheeks were bearing a nice pink, champagne after-glow. I resemble a walking advert for a make-up counter with half a pound of Estée Lauder plastered on my face. After my transformation I look, as Sebastian promised, utterly wonderful and not like me at all. My mother could walk past me and not recognise me – although, if she did, she might wonder what I was doing in Sainsbury's without my clothes on. When I was allowed near the mirror, I could only gaze in wonder at this fabulous woman who stared back at me in a faintly agog fashion. Liz Hurley, I am snapping at your heels! Ha!

'This way, Emily,' Sebastian coaxes in his soft, steady voice.

And I pout and pose like an old hand. I am loving this. I feel foxy, flirty and free. I can see Sebastian smile behind his camera. As well he might. He was right.

'Cross your arms,' he says. And I cross and re-cross, tilting my head this way and that. What an old tart I am!

Sebastian is re-creating some classic poses. I have sat astride a chair, lounged on a chaise-lounge, cavorted on a fur rug on Sebastian's warm oak floor and tipped myself backwards like Sophie Dahl in the *Obsession* adverts. I have been wild, wicked and wanton. I have bared all. And, best of all, I have shown nothing.

Thanks to Sebastian's skill, there has not even been one nipple shot. Not even a tiny one. For two hundred thousand pounds, the *News of the World* will get everything and see nothing. Ha, ha! There will be the suggestion of the rounded swell of my breast, the outline of my curving buttock, a shadow of well-formed cleavage, but bugger all else! Cara would have a blue fit.

'Feeling OK?' Sebastian asks.

'Great!' I say.

'Not tired?'

Is he kidding me? This is as easy as falling off a log compared to trying to hold the concentration of Years 10 and 11 armed only with the delights of Shakespeare's *Much Ado About Nothing*.

'No,' I say and shake my head in such a ridiculously dramatic way that Sebastian snaps away again.

Jonathan, who has stayed out of the way until now, pops his head round the door. 'How's it going?' he asks.

'Wonderfully,' I say breathily. Grief, even my voice is getting into this.

'Nearly finished,' Sebastian says. And do you know, I actually feel disappointed. I rather like prancing around without my clothes on, I've decided. It's what happens to the photographs next that rather scares me.

Sebastian click-clicks for a few minutes more and then stands away from his camera. 'I'm done,' he states.

I resist the urge to say: 'Oh!'

'Put your things back on, Emily,' Jonathan Gold says, 'and then we can have a quick look at the results.'

Ah. My confidence sinks down to somewhere round my knees, my make-up resembles a clown's mask and I suddenly feel very, very vulnerable.

'Don't worry, darling,' Sebastian says with a roguish wink. 'You'll look fabulous.'

I only wish I was as sure as he is.

Chapter Eighty-Five

Adam hauled his bin bags through the side gate marked *Private* and into Toff's secluded garden. The thought struck him that he was going to have to invest in a lawn-mower if he was intending to involve himself in grass-cutting duties. Still, it would be worth it. Adam took in the mature, weeping trees, the crush of lush shrubs, none of which he could name. This would be a beautiful green haven in the midst of the London smoke. At the word smoke, Adam had a vision of himself barbecuing sausages for him and Josh. It was a very nice vision. He might invite Barry to join them. When he'd had a bit of practice.

The flat had its own entrance, up a flight of ornate wrought-iron stairs, which meant that Adam didn't have to trail through the studio and disturb Toff every time he wanted to get in. Not that anything much disturbed Toff. It felt strange having a new key in his hand, so much more symbolic than a mere tool for opening a door. Adam tried it in the lock. The door fitted tightly, neatly, expensively. It was unlikely that anyone would be able to put their knee through it as they could through the door in his old flat.

Adam didn't think anyone had lived here for years, so goodness only knows what kind of state it would be in. It might be deeply optimistic to think that he could move straight in. Perhaps he should have thought to bring a tape measure as he'd have to buy curtains and stuff, maybe even carpets. As he edged in through the door, there was a faint whiff of furniture polish rather than the stale odour of damp he had grown used to. He resisted the urge to shout, 'Hello!'

A small hall led into one large room that stretched out in front of him in a vast expanse, and a vast *expense*, of oak flooring. It held two navy-blue sofas huddled round a wood-burning fire and a huge, square coffee table that would be great for doing jigsaws on. Adam felt his jaw slacken. This wasn't quite the poky, decaying flat he had envisaged. Did he always imagine the worst because that was what he usually got? Somewhere inside his mental processes he needed a long-overdue clearout.

The kitchen area was fitted with gleaming stainless steel units and sleek black marble tops which Adam trailed his finger over to make sure he wasn't imagining it. The fridge, when he opened it, still had the operating manual in a plastic bag sitting inside. Next to it was a six-pack of Budweiser with a gift tag attached which said: *Welcome to your new home. Sebastian.*

A large picture window, overlooking the garden, dominated the far end of the room. In front of it sat a glass-topped table and six chairs that matched the sofas. Someone had even put fruit in the waiting bowl. Adam went to take in the view. At the end of the long, slender garden, the Heath stretched out before him and this time he didn't have to stand on the toilet seat to see it. He felt like a man in the middle of a dream.

Still clutching his bin bags like a security blanket, Adam wandered through to the bedrooms. The navy theme continued into the main room, which had its own shower room complete with a fluffy new set of navy towels. Adam checked behind the door to see if there was a matching dressing gown. There wasn't, but it rather surprised him.

In Josh's room there was a raised bunk in stainless steel reached by a ladder. Underneath it a computer, ready to run, waited patiently. The ceiling was navy blue and littered with silver stars. A CD player that made Adam's look like it had come out of the Ark, sat next to a portable television and PlayStation console. Adam's emotions bumped around inside him like Dodgems. Toff had thought of everything. More than everything. In true Toff style.

Wandering back through to the living room, he looked around again, unable to take it all in. It was like something out of *Homes & Gardens* magazine. Like something out of the estate agents' windows in the High Street. Like something that was way, way beyond his normal price range. And Toff had made it all available to him and his son, complete with every creature comfort. Adam looked down at his black sacks. He had not been taking care of himself for too long, he realised. Now he would look after them both, himself and his son, properly. Josh would make this immaculate, ultra-cool palace look like a bombsite within five minutes flat. He would fill it with skateboards and Britney Spears and noise and laughter and love. As Adam let his bin bags sink to the floor, his knees buckled and he joined them in a crumpled heap. He would be forever indebted to Toff for his kindness. And as a wave of gratitude, sheer joy and relief swept over him, he cried for the second time that day. Life simply could not get any better.

Chapter Eighty-Six

I can't believe how fabulous I look. 'Wow,' I say as Sebastian clicks through the images he has taken, enlarging them on his computer screen.

'I knew you'd be pleased, darling,' he says with a satisfied smile as Jonathan Gold and I huddle round him.

'They really are great, Emily,' Jonathan agrees.

Somehow he's managed to get me looking sexy, sultry and demure all at the same time. I wish it was a look I could pull off without the aid of a camera lens.

'So what happens now?' I ask. This is the bit I'm nervous about – although appearing in the *News of the World* won't lose me my job or my house this time. I do suspect that my mother might never speak to me again though.

'Sebastian will print these out and we'll send a selection to the newspaper,' Jonathan says with the authority of a man who's done it all before. 'They'll want to send a reporter round to interview you and I think we'll do that at my office so that I can help you to control the content.' He notices that my eyebrows shoot up in question. 'I don't want it slipping out that you were a lap-dancer in a former life.'

I laugh.

'You weren't a lap-dancer in a former life, were you?' Jonathan asks somewhat nervously.

'No.'

'Just checking,' he says with a sigh of relief.

'Would it bother you?'

'No.' He gives a chuckle. 'But I would need to know!'

'Rest assured,' I say, 'that I have never been anything more interesting than a teacher.'

'Be grateful for that,' my guru says.

Sebastian clicks my photographs from the screen. 'I'll get these over to you tomorrow,' he says to Jonathan.

Jonathan nods. 'We must go,' he says. 'I've got an Entrepreneur of the Year dinner at the Grosvenor tonight.'

'Candidate?'

'No,' Jonathan says with a hearty laugh. 'But one of my clients is. He's made fifty million out of selling frogs' legs to the French.'

'There's a rather nice irony to that,' Sebastian observes.

'I'm organising the life-story splash in the papers,' Jonathan continues. 'If he wins.'

'Good luck,' Sebastian says. He comes and kisses my cheeks. 'Nice to meet you, Emily. Finally.'

'Thanks, Sebastian,' I say. 'I can't believe how much I enjoyed this.'

'You could make a career of it,' he suggests. 'You're good enough.'

And I think that's stretching the imagination a bit when I have cellulitic thighs and ankles like a sturdy Chippendale – and I mean one of the tables, not one of the male strippers.

'I'll give it some thought,' I say with a laugh.

'Come on, Emily,' Jonathan Gold says, directing me into my jacket. 'I'll drive you home.'

I follow him out into the darkness, the air cold and damp after the fuggy warmth of Sebastian's tropically heated studio.

'Where to?' he asks as he unlocks the Porsche which is miraculously parked directly outside the studio, and I give him directions to Cara's house.

As I slide into Jonathan's car, the leather seats feel cold against my back and I huddle my arms round me.

'OK?' he queries.

'Yes, thanks.' And I think I am. I feel jittery, but there's a calmness at the centre of it for the first time in ages. It may not be an ideal situation, but at least I feel I've done something towards moving my life forward. There are a lot of things I can do with two hundred thousand pounds – even after taking Jonathan's commission off, it will still be a substantial amount of money – and I begrudge him not one penny. I can pay off my debts and get on with my life. I may never be a teacher again, but I could be an awful lot of other things. Limitless possibilities stretch before me and it feels nice to have a different set of problems to confront.

Jonathan's car heater blows out hot air with industrial strength and I can feel my eyes rolling. I hope that tonight I will enjoy a deep and dreamless sleep. An unbroken night where I'm not having nightmares about busking in Oxford Street Tube station or castrating Frank the Headmaster for sacking me or arguing with the Bank Manager about my spiralling overdraft whilst dressed in a saucy Santa outfit.

289

'I'm sorry that I missed you at *Temptation* the other night,' Jonathan says as he effortlessly steers his car through the traffic.

'It doesn't matter,' I say. 'We got there in the end.'

'We could have had some fun.'

'Yes.' As it was I had a miserable time, but I won't go over that ground again.

Jonathan pulls up outside Cara's house and turns in his seat to face me.

'Perhaps we could go out to dinner sometime to make up for it?' he says, fixing me with a questioning gaze.

'Maybe,' I say with a smile, but I don't meet his eyes, and we both know that I mean probably not.

'No conditions,' he says. 'And we do have something to celebrate.'

'You're right,' I agree. It would be churlish not to. 'Thanks for getting me out of this mess.'

'Thanks for getting into it,' Jonathan says with a disarming smile. 'It's been a pleasure to help.'

'I'll wait to hear from you,' I say.

Jonathan nods and I go through an awkward moment where I don't know whether to kiss him or not and I sort of lean forward in an undecided way and we clash heads.

'Ouch,' he says and rubs his forehead.

'Sorry.'

'You'd better go,' he says. 'I don't want to turn up to Entrepreneur of the Year sporting a black eye.'

'Sorry,' I mutter again. This is a man who was once rumoured to have dated Elle McPherson. But then if I was a PR guru, I'd start rumours like that myself. I get out of the car, before I do something stupid and head-butt him again.

'I'll phone,' he says.

And I know this time that I can rely on him to do so – how often can you say that about a man? I watch the sleek love machine roar off down the street. Jonathan Gold is gorgeous in an older, smoothie sort of way, but he's out of my league and makes me behave like a gauche teenager. The Hunk in the wine bar is much more my level, and now that I'm going to be a woman of independent means, perhaps he'd be more inclined to fall at my feet. If only I could find him.

Chapter Eighty-Seven

Adam stuck his head round the studio door. Toff was shuffling papers. 'Mate,' Adam said warmly, 'how can I possibly thank you?'

He came across to Toff and hugged him gratefully. His friend patted his back paternally.

'By taking most of my workload off me, sweetheart,' he replied.

'That place has got to be worth at least half a million,' Adam pointed out. 'More. You could rent it out for a small fortune.' It was a rare slice of prime Hampstead real estate. Toff could have named his price and, instead, he was charging Adam the same as he was currently paying for his crumbling bedsit.

'Adam, darling,' Toff said, 'do I look like a man who's in need of money?'

'No,' Adam admitted.

'Then let's talk no more about it and have a beer to celebrate instead,' Toff said, reaching two beers from the fridge. 'It's nice to be able to do a friend a good turn.'

'I've just moved my stuff in, mate. I can't believe how you've done it out for us. Josh will be knocked over.'

'Good,' Toff said. 'You both deserve a little comfort and joy.'

'We'll really look after it for you,' Adam promised.

'Fine,' Toff said. 'I've organised a cleaner for you. She's called Maria and she's Armenian. Doesn't speak a work of English, but she's a devil with a duster.'

'Toff . . .' Adam began to protest.

'And someone will come and do the garden,' his friend interrupted. 'We'll put the bills through the business, so no worries there.'

'This is too much,' Adam said, beginning to feel emotional again.

'You haven't seen how hard I'll work you yet,' Toff laughed. He held his beer up and clinked it against Adam's bottle. 'To our new working arrangements,' he said. 'You might be begging for your old job back soon. All those hours of drinking coffee in Café Blanco will disappear.'

'I'll give my notice in tomorrow,' Adam said. 'Tonight I'm meeting Cara to give the glad tidings to her.'

'How will she take it?'

Adam sucked in his breath. 'Don't know. If there's one thing that you can rely on with Cara it's that she's totally unpredictable.'

Toff gestured towards the studio. 'Her friend was in here earlier.'

Adam frowned. 'Emily?'

Toff nodded.

'I thought she'd decided against it?'

'Another change of heart,' Toff said. 'She's doing a spread for the *News of the World* under Jonathan Gold's caring direction.'

Adam's eyes widened. 'I really didn't think she was the type.'

'Is there a type?' Toff countered. 'I don't think so.'

'I suppose not,' Adam said. 'She just seemed so devastated when her boyfriend posted those pictures of her on the net.'

'Perhaps that was more to do with betrayal than baring all?'

'Yeah.' He just ought to recognise, Adam thought, that he would never, ever, as long as he lived understand the workings of a woman's mind.

'I still don't know if Cara's aware of it, darling. Best not to mention it,' Toff cautioned. 'Although she'll know soon enough.'

'Yeah.' Adam snorted in agreement. 'And I wouldn't like to be in the firing line when she finds out. She did all she could to keep Emily out of the local paper, never mind the nationals.'

'We are talking large sums of money, here, darling,' Toff said. 'It can turn a girl's head. And, let's face it, she has no visible means of support at the moment.'

'True,' Adam said. 'I guess if you've got it, you might as well flaunt it.'

'She certainly has got it,' Toff said rather wistfully. 'I'd have called you down to meet her if I'd known you were upstairs. She's nice. Surprisingly shy. Great body.'

'Let's have a look at the photos,' Adam said, sliding along the desk.

Toff indicated his computer with the neck of his beer bottle. 'Logged off, old fruit,' he said, 'And I'm out of here in two minutes.'

'Romantic assignation?'

Toff nodded. 'Hermione.'

Adam didn't think he'd heard of that one before.

'We'll have a look at them next time you're over. I've got to do the prints for Jonathan tomorrow. He seems to have taken quite a shine to our Emily.'

Adam pursed his lips. 'I'd better get a wiggle on too,' he said, swigging back his beer. 'I daren't keep Cara waiting. I've got to go and pick her up.'

'You might get to see Emily at Cara's.'

'Yeah,' Adam said, 'you never know. Though, at the moment, she seems to be more elusive than the Scarlet Pimpernel. We seek her here. We seek her there. We seek the lovely Emily everywhere.'

'Not for long,' Toff said. 'On Sunday, you'll see an awful lot more of her.'

'I can't wait,' Adam said and he realised with a strange little shiver that only part of him was joking. Good grief, he was turning into Chris.

Chapter Eighty-Eight

I haven't got one foot over the doorstep before Cara pounces on me.

'Guess what?' my friend shrieks.

I put my finger to my lip, feigning deep thought. 'Brad Pitt's sitting in the lounge waiting for me.'

'Don't be stupid,' Cara says with a tut. 'It's better than that!'

'Adam's taking you out tonight.'

Cara's face falls with disappointment. 'How did you know?'

'Well, I can't think of anything else that would put a grin on your face like that.'

Flinging my coat on the end of the banister, I trail through to the lounge. I am suddenly weary right down to my bones. Cara follows and sits down, edgily, as I collapse full-length onto the sofa. 'I'm knackered,' I announce and before I think, add, 'I've had one *hell* of a day.'

'Where have you been?' Cara immediately wants to know. 'I was starting to get worried about you.'

'Oh, just out and about,' I say. Cavorting on a sheepskin rug with no togs on. I haven't quite decided how to broach the subject of my new career as a nude model with my censorious chum.

'Looking for a job?'

'In a manner of speaking,' I say, and try to stop myself grinning and fail. 'So where's Adam taking you?' I ask in an attempt to side-step any further questioning. Cara is in her element when the subject of the conversation is the lovely Adam.

'I don't know,' Cara says with a huff. 'What do you think I should wear?'

'What about the pink creation?' I suggest, nodding at the dress I borrowed to go to *Temptation* in, which is now hanging from the living-room door, all clean and fresh, in its Perkins dry-cleaning bag.

'Too tarty,' Cara says dismissively. 'Although it did look very nice on you,' she adds as an afterthought.

'Thanks,' I say, and try to look as if I don't want to punch her.

'Knowing Adam, we'll probably go somewhere quite casual,' she says with a sense of cosy possessiveness. 'I don't want to be overdressed.'

'Is he coming here to collect you?'

'Mmm,' Cara nods, her mind distractedly flicking through the contents of her wardrobe for something suitable. I know the look very well.

'My goodness, after all this time I might finally get to meet him.'

'Yes,' Cara says, looking up sharply as a frown puckers her forehead. 'This is a very auspicious day for a second date,' she announces. 'I've checked my Panchang energy forecast for today and it's a swift-supportive time.'

'What does that mean when it's at home?' I say, burying myself in the *TV Times* to sort out my night's entertainment.

'It's the perfect time for advancing elusive relationships and facing challenging issues concerning the future.'

'Ooo.' This sounds a bit of all right. 'Does that count for me too?'

'Yes,' Cara confirms.

'Perhaps The Hunk from the wine bar will turn up on my doorstep,' I say brightly. So I won't be needing the *TV Times* after all. 'I'd better go and have a shower.'

'Don't be long,' Cara warns. 'I want to get into the bathroom too.'

I put down the magazine and study my little mad friend. She is looking very worried. 'This is very important to you, isn't it?'

'Yes.' Cara goes all dreamy. 'I'm crazy about him, Emily.'

I smile.

'And don't make any clever comments about me being crazy, anyway,' Cara snaps.

'I wouldn't dream of it,' I insist. 'I really hope that this works out for you.'

'Me too,' Cara says. 'I've been floating on cloud nine since Adam asked me to meet him. It's silly, isn't it?'

'It's love,' I say.

Cara snorts. 'Even the sweet revenge of seeing Chris splashed all over the inside pages of the *Hampstead Observer* has been tempered by a general feeling of goodwill to all men.'

She tosses the newspaper at me and I abandon the *TV Times* to have a glance at the grainy image. So this is the guy who wrote the story about me. I grin as I scan the piece about his unfortunate incident. Well and truly caught with his pants down. Serve the bastard right! 'Couldn't happen to a nicer man,' I say.

'Chris is all right,' Cara says. 'For a half-wit. This might make him stop and think about what he's doing to other people.'

'I doubt it,' I say, showing my rather cynical side. Did I used to be like this? 'His type are all the same.'

'That's why I like Adam so much,' Cara says. 'He's a very nice man.' She sighs a melancholy sigh. 'I've been on my own for too long, Emily, and now it's time to do something about it.'

'Good for you,' I say as I jump up and make for the door. I need to get in the shower before Cara. Once she gets in there she'll be gone for hours. I just use the shower to wash, de-stress, that sort of thing. Cara carries out all manner of unnatural practices in there involving chanting and oils and volcanic mud. Not for Cara a quick rub round with Tesco's shower gel.

And then I remember something important. 'Cara,' I say, turning back. 'Are you still going to give Adam the spell we made?'

'Oh,' Cara says. 'I'd forgotten about that.'

'It's still lurking in the fridge,' I remind her. 'Does it go off?'

'I don't think so,' Cara says.

'You won't want to poison the poor bugger,' I point out helpfully.

Cara chews on her lower lip. 'Do you think I should give it to him? I don't want to overpower him.'

I roar with laughter. 'I thought that was the whole point!'

'Emily,' Cara says indignantly. 'You never take any of this stuff seriously. The universe is a very powerful force.'

'Sorry.' My laughter subsides to a suppressed giggle. 'I keep forgetting.'

'I wonder if we've done enough,' Cara confides. 'He has asked me out, after all. Perhaps I ought to see how things develop.'

'Cara, you had me trekking up the garden terrorising half the tarantula population of these leafy environs,' I say huffily. 'The least you could do is try the bloody stuff on him.'

'OK,' Cara nods in agreement. 'I will.'

'Not until I've seen him though,' I say. 'I don't want him to turn into a toad before I've had the chance to give him the once-over!'

'Emily,' Cara scolds, 'sometimes you can be such an air-head.'

She's a fine one to talk! 'That's why we've stayed friends for so long,' I say, smiling and blowing Cara a kiss as I head out of the door.

'You're very perky for someone who's had a knackering day,' Cara observes.

'Really?'

'Yes,' Cara says, wrinkling her nose. 'And why are you wearing so much make-up?'

'Better dash,' I say. 'Otherwise you'll still be stinky and scruffy when he gets here.'

And before I'm required to provide any further explanation, I duck swiftly out of the door.

Chapter Eighty-Nine

'He's here!' Cara shouts up the stairs. 'He's here!'

I force my eyelids open. I'm lying on my bed having a lovely reverie involving two hundred thousand pounds and The Hunk from the wine bar and it was definitely X-rated.

Earlier, when Cara and I were talking, I wanted to tell her about my good fortune, but wasn't sure how she'd take it. No, that's not true. I know exactly how she'll take it and that's why I've chickened out of telling her. She'll read me the riot act and go on and on about morals and ethics and feminism – but I bet you she'll still accept my rent cheque. Sometimes it's very difficult having a friend whose head is filled with finding a solution for world peace when mine rarely extends beyond finding a solution for unwanted flab.

'He's here!' Cara yells again. 'Aren't you dressed yet? Are you coming down?'

The answer to the first question is no. I'm still wearing my dressing gown after my shower and extreme jet-hosing of my face to get rid of the perma-layer of foundation. As I catch sight of myself in the mirror, I know that the very first thing I will do with my cheque is go out and buy a luxurious silk wrap and throw this tatty Fozzy Bear-style creation out on its ear despite my emotional attachment to it.

'I'll be down in a minute,' I shout to Cara and swiftly tiptoe over to the window to get my first, long-anticipated view of the lovely, elusive Adam. I can feel myself tingling with nerves, so I can't imagine how Cara must feel.

I turn off the light and peer into the enveloping darkness. People who say that it never truly goes dark in London haven't been down Cara's road. Adam is fussing about locking his car and I strain to get a peek of him. He looks nice. Tall, dark with mad curls. My mouth is ever so slightly dry and I wonder why.

Adam straightens up and stretches. He heads towards Cara's front door and as he does so, he looks up. I gasp. It pops out of my mouth from nowhere. This isn't Adam! It's The Hunk from the wine bar!

Gaspgaspgasp! What the hell is *he* doing here? How did he know how to find me?

I look down at myself. God, I can't see him looking like this! I check the window again and I can just see the top of his head. My knees have gone weak – and my heart. It's struggling to beat, really it is. He's every bit as gorgeous as I remembered. And he's found me! He's found me!

I jump up and down a bit and manage to stop myself shrieking with joy.

The Hunk rings the door bell.

'WhatshallIdo? WhatshallIdo? WhatshallIdo?' I mutter to myself, rushing round my bedroom like a mad dog chasing its own tail. I start stuffing my dirty clothes under the bed. What am I doing? He's not going to want to come up here the first time we meet, is he?

'Emily!' Cara shouts. 'Where are you?'

In hell, is the short answer, but I've no time to say anything before Cara wrests open the front door.

'Hi, Adam,' I hear her say.

And then my world goes all peculiar. I shrink to about two inches high, like one of the cartoons on *Ally McBeal*. I'm a tiny little person focused only on the word 'Adam' which is sort of fizzing in echoey repeats in my ears.

'Emily,' Cara shouts again. 'Adam's here!'

I'm crouched on the floor. This is a terrible mistake. Cara must have finally gone mad. How can I tell her that this isn't Adam, it's The Hunk from the wine bar that I've been telling her all about. The Hunk, who wears very small white underwear in my dreams and not a lot else. The Hunk, who has turned my insides to a slow-motion ocean. The Hunk, whose babies I want to bear. The Hunk, for whom I would lay down my life. Oh my word! And then the ground does, in fact, open up and swallow me. If this is Adam, then it's me who has made a terrible, terrible mistake. Ooo! Ooo! Ooo!

I have no idea what to do. There's no way I can go down there. I can't face Cara ever again. I'm going to have to emigrate. Preferably in the next thirty seconds. Whatever happens, I'm going to have to get out of here *now*. This minute. This second. I stand up and cross to the window, flinging it open and gaze down into the front garden. It is a very small strip of scrubby green with the insubstantial remains of long-dead summer flowers. Tentatively, I heave myself up onto the windowsill. There is nothing down there that looks like it would cushion a fall. Bollocksbollocksbollocksbigbollocks!

'Emily!' Cara shouts up the stairs again. She is losing patience with me. What a shame that patience isn't like virginity. Something that can only be lost once in a lifetime rather than with alarming regularity. 'What are you doing?'

I swing my legs out of the window. Bloody hell, it's cold outside! The ground is rushing up to meet me. I wonder if I can jump onto the porch roof from here and then shin down the drainpipe.

'If you don't come down in a minute, I'm going to come up and get you,' she calls.

It looks like I'm going to have to give it a try.

Chapter Ninety

'I've no idea what she's doing,' Cara trilled lightly at Adam who was sort of fidgeting from foot to foot. The rose aromatherapy oil she'd been burning for the last half hour clearly wasn't having the relaxing effect on Adam it was supposed to. 'She's been out job-hunting today. I think the strain might have taken it out of her.'

'Oh,' Adam said and fidgeted a bit more.

'Would you like a glass of wine while you wait?' Cara offered.

'Best not,' Adam said. 'Designated driver.'

'Oh,' Cara said. 'It's very nice. I made it myself. Specially.'

'You make your own wine?'

'Well, in a manner of speaking,' she said. 'It's really good.'

'No, thanks.' Adam waved a hand. 'I actually had a beer at Toff's before I got here. I don't usually drink at all if I'm driving.'

'Sure?'

'Positive,' Adam said and he sounded it. He glanced at the pink dress hanging on the door and Cara wished she had tidied it away. She could have sworn his face went pale. 'Is that your dress?' Adam said with a frown.

'Yes,' Cara said.

'Oh.' He looked disappointed.

'Would you like me to put it on?' she asked hopefully.

'Oh, no. No. No,' he muttered. 'It's just that well, I thought I recognised it. Never mind . . . mistake.' He lapsed into silence.

This was not going well. They were uncomfortable with each other, tense outside of the familiar world of the work environment. Perhaps Adam was thinking about the last time he was here, Cara mused. Blokes were hopeless with intimacy. Although she had to admit, she wasn't great with it herself. Put it down to lack of practice.

'Do you want to sit down?'

'We'd better go,' Adam said. 'I've booked a table.'

'Just wait a minute or two,' Cara said. 'Emily won't be long.'

Adam sat down and then looked up at her. 'We've got a lot to talk about.'

'Have we?' she said.

'Well . . .' Adam faltered. 'Yes.'

'I'll go and get her,' Cara said briskly and marched out of the room.

Adam sighed and looked very much like he needed a drink.

Cara hadn't missed a stride of her march when she clomped into Emily's bedroom. Where the hell had she got to? It was rude. Emily knew that Adam was downstairs waiting to meet her. Emily's window was open, the cold night air streaming in. Cara went over to the window and peered out. Nothing. She slammed it shut. Her friend couldn't have just disappeared.

'Emily?' Cara hissed. 'What are you playing at? Where are you?'

Nothing.

Cara stomped out of the bedroom and checked the other rooms, but there was no sign of her friend. Back in Emily's room, she looked round again. She checked under the bed, but it was simply piled high with debris. Finally, she flung open the wardrobe – and there was Emily, curled up in a ball, squashed between the shoes and the bottom of her skirts.

'Hi.' Emily waved weakly.

'Why are you hiding in the wardrobe?' Cara said.

Emily gulped. 'I've got a headache.' She rubbed her temple dramatically. 'I thought the dark might help.'

Cara nodded thoughtfully. 'I'm going to close the door now, and when I open it again and ask you the same question, I want you to have a more convincing answer prepared.'

'OK,' Emily said.

Cara closed the door, counted to three and then opened it again.

'I'm having a nervous breakdown,' Emily said. 'I'm not responsible for my own actions.'

Cara's eyes narrowed. 'This has something to do with Adam, doesn't it?'

The mechanism that produces blushes clicked into operation. Cara could see it whirring in her friend's brain. It was working up to be the mother of all blushes. Cara watched it starting from Emily's toes, spreading over her knees, disappearing beneath the hem of her disgusting dressing-gown until it surged in full flowing colour over her neck and face.

'No.'

'Are you lying to me?'

'Yes,' Emily said.

'Are you going to tell me now what it is, or are you going to force

301

me to sit through an evening of polite conversation with him until such time as I can return home and murder you?'

'Er . . .' Emily gulped.

'I'm waiting,' Cara said, tapping her foot to indicate that she wouldn't be prepared to wait much longer.

'Laryngitis,' Emily croaked, holding her throat.

'Very well,' Cara said crisply. 'If that's how you want to play it. I may be late, but I won't forget.' And with that she closed the wardrobe door very firmly and left.

Chapter Ninety-One

So, the mystery Hunk in the wine bar turns out to have been Adam, the love of Cara's life, all along. I can't believe it. How can fate be so cruel? There are millions and millions of people out there. How can my best friend and I have set our sights on the same man? Oh, this is a complete disaster.

Cara thinks Adam is a caring, sensitive, sexy man. I think he looks like a bagful of trouble, although I'd go along with the sexy bit. They've made love in the room right next door to me and I didn't even hear one twitch from the headboard. That can't be right, can it?

Given my previous history, a particularly nice bottle of red wine would help to ease my troubled heart, but in deference to my liver, I've opted instead for the Cara route and have already ingested enough Rescue Remedy to drown me from the inside out. I've sprinkled myself with some sort of smelly oil from one of the least dangerous-looking coloured bottles on her bedside table and I have before me a range of Love Tarot cards. I have no idea how these work, but I can tell you that it's not looking good.

I've shuffled them three times and cut them different ways and each time I've turned up three cards that say in big letters at the top UNREQUITED LOVE. Cara would find something positive in this, but at the moment it's eluding me. I wonder, have we got any wine in the fridge?

I toss the cards to one side. I think this is all total bollocks anyway, it's just that I'm not quite sure what else to do. I hope Cara can put a hex on me to forget all about him. They say that in the world you have just one soulmate; it's frightening to contemplate that by turning the wrong corner, missing the bus or staying just five minutes longer at work, you could have lost the chance to meet them. What are the odds against your paths crossing again? But then, what are the odds of walking into a wine bar and, despite all rationale, thinking you've met the man you're supposed to be with for ever? All my fibres, my DNA, all the whirly things that hold me together, they have decided, absolutely, that Adam is *The One*.

Perhaps I've just got a chemical imbalance.

We haven't even had a proper conversation. One brief interchange about the joys of having pesto sauce on your nose is not generally considered the bedrock of a stable relationship. I know nothing about him. What if he is hopelessly in love with Cara? What if I have to find another less fantastic boyfriend and go out with them for coupley dinners, watching as Adam puts his arm protectively around Cara's shoulders, and pretend to enjoy long, dragging weekends in the country as they walk hand-in-hand down leafy verdant lanes? I shouldn't have been so flippant about Jonathan Gold's invitation to dinner. I could be desperate by next week. I could be catapulted onto that horrible singles playground ride of dinner-snog-sex-dump, going round and round until you're sick to the heart of it all. What if I have to be a bridesmaid at their wedding? Aaargh!

I need candles. Lots of them. Cara always seems to think that helps. I feel terrible. I know that I should be pleased for my friend. She has found someone truly fabulous and she's besotted with him. If I was a good friend, I should hope that he is besotted back. But I don't. And the swirling, sucking whirlpool of emotion is making me feel nauseous. I look at the clock. I've got about two hours, I reckon, to get my act together and call on all the powers of the universe to help me pretend that Adam was just a passing fancy and to laugh and joke and be happy for my friend. And disguise the fact that my heart is very quietly breaking.

Chapter Ninety-Two

'So?' Adam said, his glance embracing the rustic décor of Luigi's. 'It's nice here, isn't it?'

'Yes.' Cara steadied herself with a deep breath that helped to keep the smile on her face. She hadn't a clue what the place looked like. It could be turquoise with pink gingham spots and have elephants swinging from the ceiling for all she cared. Her vision had gone blurred at the edges and Adam seemed to be speaking out at her from the bottom of a very long tunnel. She knew, just knew, that it was going to be one of those occasions that she'd remember for the rest of her life and yet would be able to recall no detail of it whatsoever. One part of her knew that she should be rejoicing in Adam being here, while the rest of her knew that he was gradually slipping away. And that Emily had something to do with it.

'I come here nearly every week with Josh,' Adam continued, a forced brightness to his chatter. 'He likes it here. It makes him feel grown up.'

'That's lovely,' Cara said.

'So?' Adam repeated, nibbling the end of his breadstick nervously.

'You said we had a lot to talk about.'

'Yes,' Adam said. 'So I did.' He snapped his breadstick in half and busied himself brushing crumbs from the table onto the floor.

Cara's heart squeezed tightly. 'Is it about the other night?' she said.

'Yes,' Adam said. 'It's about that. And other things.'

The word seemed to have a capital 'T'.

'It was fun, wasn't it?'

'Fun. Yes,' Adam said. 'Well, fun after the awful bit. The awful bit was pretty bad.'

Cara leaned forward. 'Do you think that it was going to the crash scene and all the emotion that made us act recklessly?'

Adam scratched his stubble. 'Recklessly. Yes,' he said. 'It was a bit reckless, wasn't it?'

'Yes,' Cara said. 'But nice.'

'Yes,' Adam echoed. 'Reckless, but nice.'

Cara forced herself to smile, while inside she could hear herself shattering like fragile glass. 'It was nice, but it doesn't mean I want to go shopping for an engagement ring.'

Adam started at the word 'engagement'. 'No,' he said. 'No, of course not.'

Mrs Luigi delivered two dishes of lasagne – one vegetarian – and a conspiratorial smile at Adam. Was she used to seeing him here with other women? It didn't seem like it.

Adam prodded the lasagne with his fork. 'I didn't know whether you . . . you know, regretted it.'

'No,' Cara said. 'I don't regret it at all.' It was the best night of my life, Adam, she wanted to say. But, of course, she didn't.

'Good.' He nodded vehemently. 'I wouldn't want you to regret it.'

I would like to repeat it, Cara thought, but again said nothing.

'I don't think we should do it again, though, do you?' Adam said.

'No.'

'It's difficult with us being work colleagues and that, isn't it?'

'Yes,' Cara said, and forced some lasagne into her mouth.

'I'd like us to be friends,' Adam continued to burble. 'Good friends.'

'I'd like that too, Adam,' Cara said and wondered how she was managing not to put her head on the table and weep.

'This isn't about you,' Adam said. 'If there weren't other complications, it would be great to have a relationship.'

'Are there any other complications besides the fact that we work together?' she asked as casually as she could.

'Well . . .' Adam looked uncertain.

'Is there someone else?' Cara pressed.

'Well . . .' Adam said again. He looked as if a dam had burst inside him. 'There is someone. Well, not really. I don't know her. Not really.'

'Oh.'

'Well, I've met her. Of course, I've met her. But only once. Just briefly. I don't even know who she is or even *where* she is. But I sort of feel . . .' Adam swallowed. 'I fee I owe it to myself to find her.'

'Lucky girl,' Cara said. Her lasagne had lodged in her throat.

'I don't know about that,' Adam said with a laugh. 'Would you want a madman pursuing you?'

'No.' Yes, Adam, she thought sadly, I'd very much like a madman pursuing me.

'I've only seen her the once,' Adam said. 'When I went to the launch of *Temptation*, remember?'

'Yes.' How could I forget? 'And she was there?'

Adam nodded. 'The dress that was hanging up in your lounge,' he said, 'she was wearing something just like that. A bit like that. Well, probably not like that at all. It's hard to remember.'

'Yes,' Cara said. The blood was draining drop by drop from her face and she was glad that she'd taken a lot of trouble with her make-up. It might help to hide it.

'But I remember how I felt,' Adam said, and Cara noticed that his beautiful eyes had gone all dreamy and distant. 'It just hit me in a blinding white light.' He glanced unseeing at Cara. 'She is *The One!* BAM!' Adam shook his head wistfully, the memory clearly playing back in his mind. 'Has that ever happened to you?'

'Oh yes,' Cara said softly. 'Just the once.'

'It feels fabulous, doesn't it?'

She made the muscles of her cheeks do a smile. 'Yes. Really fabulous.'

Adam snapped his attention back to her. 'I'm being rude,' he said. 'Going on and on.'

'That's OK,' Cara said with a shake of her curls.

'I don't usually talk like this,' Adam said. 'I don't know what's come over me.'

I think it's known as being in love, Cara said to herself. You're in love with Emily, Adam. My best friend, Emily. And you don't even know her. Cara could have fallen on her fork. All the effort she had put into harnessing the universe, cajoling, pleading and plotting with the heavens for Adam to fall in love with her – all for nothing. All Emily had done was prance around a wine bar in a slip of pink chiffon and she'd captured his heart.

'You've been a great mate, Cara,' Adam said, eyes shining.

Wasn't that the worst compliment you could ever get from a man? Cara sighed inwardly.

'You're really easy to talk to.' His eyes crinkled softly when he smiled and Cara wanted to reach up and trace the lines. 'I really appreciate it.'

'You're welcome,' Cara said and nearly choked herself.

'The other thing I wanted to tell you . . .' Adam was in full flow now. Cara could feel her eyes roll to the back of her head. She wasn't sure that she wanted to hear any more. 'I've got a new job,' he said. 'I'm leaving the *Hampstead Observer.*'

'You're *leaving*?' Cara croaked. 'When?'

'I'm giving my notice in to Martin tomorrow,' he said. 'I wanted you to know first.'

'Thanks.' Most of this information seemed to be bypassing her brain and hitting her straight in the stomach.

'It's a tough decision,' Adam said.

'Of course.' Cara had to put her fork down. It was way, way too tempting.

Adam's brow crumpled with concern. 'You're not disappointed?'

Oh God, Adam, Cara thought, I just want to pull you onto the table and snog you! I want to hurl myself at your feet and tell you how much I adore you. 'You will be sadly missed,' she said instead. 'You're a valued member of the team.' She was sure she'd read that in a management handbook somewhere.

'But that's all?'

'Yes,' Cara said. 'I'm sure if you're moving it's for a very valid reason.' Adam had been part of the fixtures and fittings at the paper for as long as she could remember. For as long as anyone could remember. How would she cope there with just Neanderthal Chris for company?

'Laura's moving to Australia – my ex-wife,' he explained. 'She's going off to find herself, or find someone else, or find that she wants what she's already got.' He shrugged. 'I don't know,' he said, 'I never understand women.'

Oh, Adam, Cara thought, that is patently clear!

'All I know,' he burbled on, 'is that she's leaving Josh with me while she does it.' He smiled a smile to break all hearts. 'I get a posh flat with this job and sociable hours.'

'That sounds fantastic.'

'Maybe you could come round to dinner one night,' Adam said enthusiastically, before adding the devastating words, 'as friends.'

'Yes,' Cara said, the void that had opened up inside her giving a hollow ring to her voice.

Adam was blissfully unaware. 'I'd like you to meet Josh,' he said. 'He's a great kid. But then all parents think that, don't they?'

'Yes,' Cara said.

'Life couldn't be better,' Adam said with a broad grin.

Cara tried to mimic it, but feared she'd end up looking like Wallace saying 'Wensleydale'.

'Well, it could be better,' he chuckled. 'I could find the woman-in-the-wine-bar. That's what I call her.'

'Oh,' Cara said. 'You don't even know her name, do you?'

'No,' Adam admitted with a rueful smile.

But I do, Adam, Cara thought. I do.

Chapter Ninety-Three

I'm sitting on the sofa, pretending to watch television, and the minute I hear Cara's key in the door, I shoot about four feet in the air. (That's about 1.2 metres, now that we're all Europeans.)

As I hear Adam's car roar away, I realise I'm ridiculously thankful that he's not coming in to spend the night again. I have vowed to face this 'situation' head-on and not run off and join a nunnery as was my first instinct. But all the same, I went and carefully re-applied my make-up and put on some particularly slimming trousers to meet my best friend's new man. Oh grief, this is all going to be terribly hard work.

I think the sound of them cavorting while I was trying to sleep would have made my head explode. Perhaps Cara is being thoughtful for once.

However, when Cara comes into the lounge, her mouth is not cracked open in a wide, gloating grin, it is down-turned and sombre. I must be in for both barrels. Clearly, I've ruined her evening.

Cara flops down on the sofa next to me. 'Stick the kettle on, Em,' she says. Which is not quite the salvo I'd expected.

'Did everything go all right?' I ask tentatively.

My friend turns to face me and her eyes are over-bright. There are high spots of colour on her pale face. 'We had a lovely meal,' she says flatly. 'Excellent lasagne.'

'Oh, Italian,' I say, nodding approval. 'Nice.'

'Yes,' Cara says.

'Lovely.' But I suspect it wasn't.

'Adam takes his son Josh there every week.'

'He has a son?'

'Yes. You get two for the price of one with Adam.'

'Ooo.' A scary thought, but not unusual these days. I could have coped with that. I am perfectly used to small, scruffy, indiscreet humans – albeit in a professional capacity. Besides, all the good blokes have got ex-wives, children and current girlfriends.

'Yes,' Cara continues. 'In the middle of it, he told me he was in love with someone else.'

'Oh. Not lovely then,' I say.

'No,' Cara agrees. 'Not lovely at all.'

'I knew he was a bastard the morning he cut and run after he'd had his wicked way with you.'

My friend looks like she's about to weep. Poor Cara! *Poor Cara*! What am I saying? *Poor me*!

'I can't believe this,' I run my hands over my face in sheer disbelief. 'You've probably worked out by now that Adam is The Hunk from the wine bar.'

'Yes,' Cara says. 'I did manage to work it out.'

'All that hocus-pocus stuff we've done,' I say. 'And all the time we've been chasing after the same man!'

Cara looks at me bleakly. 'I know.'

'And he has the audacity to be in love with someone else!'

'Yes,' Cara says. 'That's men for you.'

'Too true,' I agree. This is too dreadful to contemplate. All that time wasted. All those candles. All that flour. All those homeless spiders. All those old pop songs. I punch a cushion miserably. 'You have to laugh, don't you?'

'No,' Cara says.

'No,' I say with a heavy and expressive sigh, 'you don't.'

'So what now?' Cara says. She is anxiously picking the beads off her best beady bag.

'Well,' I say, 'we can either find out who this woman is and put a curse on her. Or we can forget about Adam the Bastard and find ourselves new men.'

'I vote for the new men option,' Cara says wearily. 'I think the universe has got it in for me.'

I agree. Although Cara is being very magnanimous in defeat, I think she'd probably have me singing the *Agadoo* spell just to spite me.

'Damn,' I say with a heartfelt tut. 'So who's this woman he's in love with?'

Cara looks away. 'I don't know.'

'I bet it's that woman he was with at *Temptation*,' I speculate. Cara swings round and stares at me. 'That was where I spotted him,' I say meekly. 'If you remember.'

'Yes. Yes,' Cara snaps. 'What woman? What was she like?'

'Gorgeous,' I say. 'Utterly gorgeous. She was trussed up like a Christmas turkey in black Lycra. A designer turkey. Mind you, he didn't exactly look like he was in love.' It's going to be a long time

310

before I forget the way his eyes followed me round the room.

'Well, he is,' Cara states.

'Bollocks,' I breathe discontentedly.

'They're getting married,' Cara adds.

'Married!'

'So that pretty much puts the tin hat on it.' She stands up.

Adam, married? I've only just found out what his name is and now I learn he's already otherwise engaged. This feels like a hammer blow to my heart. 'I don't know what to say.'

'Me neither,' Cara mutters.

'Let's not talk about him any more,' I say. 'Let's pretend he doesn't exist.' Easier said than done, I think.

'Good idea,' my friend says. She looks tired and unhappy and I'm sure that I'm partly to blame.

'Cara . . .' I sigh. 'I'm sorry about Adam, but perhaps it's for the best. I would have found it really hard to see you with him.'

'I'm glad you said that, Emily.' She concentrates on decimating her handbag. 'Because that's exactly how I feel.'

'Good,' I say, and try a watery smile. 'I wouldn't ever want anything to come between us. Particularly not a man.'

'Me neither.' Cara closes her eyes and rests her head back on the sofa. She blinks away a tear. Then she looks at me and gives a tired huff. 'Have we got any wine?' she asks.

'No,' I say, 'we drank it all.'

'Oh.' Cara looks disappointed.

'But we've got a bottle of vodka in the freezer.'

My friend casts her handbag carelessly to the corner of the room. 'Let's do it,' she says.

And I couldn't agree more.

Chapter Ninety-Four

Adam, Cara and Chris sat round a cramped table in the salon bar of the Jiggery-Pokery. It was packed and smoky.

Chris held his head in his hands. 'I can't believe you're actually leaving, mate,' he whined.

'It had to happen sometime,' Adam said over his Guinness.

'Yeah, but at the end of the week? Martin should have made you work out your notice.'

'I'm just using up all the holiday I haven't taken.'

'Sad bastard,' Chris complained. 'We could have gone to Ibiza for a week.'

'Why didn't I think of that?' Adam said.

Chris puffed and folded his arms across his chest. 'Who am I going to play cheesy anagrams with now?'

'There's more to life than cheesy anagrams, Chris.'

'Like what? Moan Sad Jack.'

'Fulfilment,' Adam said. 'Ho Hum Cissy Reporter.'

'That is *not* an anagram of Chris Seymour!'

'Christopher,' Adam said.

Chris drew a pen out of his jacket pocket and scribbled on a bar mat. 'Bollocks,' he said. 'You're right.' He threw the pen down.

'Don't you boys ever have grown-up conversations?' Cara asked.

'No,' Chris said. 'We try to avoid them at all costs.'

'It seems to me you do rather well,' she observed.

'Are you going to miss Adam?' Chris said with a smirk.

'Yes,' she replied tartly. 'You know I am.' She downed her tomato juice with a shudder. 'Does anyone want another drink?'

'I'm fine, thanks,' Adam said, indicating his half-finished, half pint. 'I've got loads of stuff to sort out this afternoon.'

'Chris?' she said.

'I'd like a double brandy,' he said. 'I've got a broken heart.'

'I'll get you a half of lager,' Cara said. 'You've got lots to do, too.' She went off to the bar.

'Lesbian,' Chris said to her retreating back.

'Leave her alone,' Adam tutted. 'You're the one who's going to have to look after her now.'

'God forbid,' Chris muttered darkly.

'Cara's all right,' Adam said defensively.

'She's barking mad and you know it.'

'She's different,' Adam insisted. 'Unusual.'

'Ah, yes,' Chris said. 'Different or not, that didn't stop you doing the dirty on her last night and dumping her.'

'Who told you that?'

'Jill from Classified caught her crying in the ladies' loo.'

Adam's voice was laced with concern. 'And she said it was my fault?'

'Two and two usually comes to about four, mate.'

'Bugger,' Adam said. 'I thought she took it really well.'

'That's women for you,' Chris said sagely. 'Strange and exotic creatures.'

'Mmm,' Adam pondered. 'And what did the two strange and exotic creatures who were caught on camera with you have to say about their surprise appearance in the local paper?'

'They were strangely pleased,' Chris mused. 'I think it's probably increased business.'

Cara returned with a mineral water for herself and put a half pint of lager down in front of Chris, who gave a disgruntled snort as he said thanks.

'What do you think of our Adam's glamorous new career then?' Chris asked.

'What glamorous new career?' Cara's eyebrows creased in alarm.

'We never really got round to talking about it last night,' Adam said sheepishly.

'I thought you were going to work for another paper?'

'Not exactly.'

'Not exactly!' Chris exclaimed. 'He's going to be the next David Bailey. Erotic photographs a speciality. Are you going to pose for him?'

Adam gave a sickly laugh.

Cara's face darkened to the colour of the pub carpet. 'You're going to be a glamour photographer?'

Adam cleared his throat. 'Yes.'

'I've heard it all now,' she snapped.

'I did it for Josh,' Adam said. 'The hours are better.'

'*Now* I've heard it all,' Cara growled. 'What happened to your principles, Adam Jackson?'

'Moan Sad Jack,' Chris interjected.

313

'Shut up, Chris,' Cara said. She turned to Adam. 'You and Emily deserve each other.' And with that she stood up and flounced to the ladies' loo.

'I bet she's gone for another cry,' Chris said, testing his drink.

'Shut up, Chris,' Adam said with a sigh. 'Why do you think she said that about Emily?'

'Who's Emily?'

'Who's Emily?'

'I can never remember girls' names, mate. Have I slept with her?'

'You wanted to,' Adam reminded him. 'She was the Saucy Santa. You wanted her to have your babies.'

'Oh, yeah,' Chris said. 'There's just too many women in the world for me, mate.'

Adam drained his drink. 'I'm going back to work before Cara comes out and has another go at me. I hope working with Toff isn't going to be as complicated.'

'Yeah,' Chris said, 'but you're not likely to sleep with him.' Chris sat upright. 'Are you?'

'No,' Adam said. 'He's not my type.'

'Am I?'

'No, Christopher,' Adam said, 'I can safely say that you're not.'

'Even if you were homosexual?'

'Even if I were homosexual and you were the last man on earth.' Adam headed towards the door.

'Why?' Chris shouted after him. 'What's wrong with me?'

Adam let the door slam behind him. Cara came out of the loo and sat back down at the table.

'Looks like it's just you and me now, babe,' Chris said to Cara, flashing her his best leery grin. 'Don't suppose you fancy a shag?'

'Drop dead,' Cara said.

Chris shrugged. 'Back to work then?'

'Yeah,' Cara said, and they downed their drinks and followed Adam out of the pub.

Chapter Ninety-Five

Cara lay reclined on her sofa with an ice-pack on her head. The incessant thump-thump-thump of a particularly thumping rave was going on inside the confines of her cranium. She had meditated, cogitated, ruminated, taken two Nurofen and still it wouldn't shift. And it was all Emily's fault. How could she have made Adam fall so madly in love with her? Friends weren't supposed to do that sort of stuff. The fact that Emily didn't know she had done it was neither here nor there.

Cara pushed the thoughts of her own betrayal to the back of her mind. Her conscience had struggled with the secret all day. Maybe she should have told Adam that she knew the whereabouts of his mystery woman. Maybe she should tell Emily that her love was, after all, requited. It was enough to give anyone a headache.

A car pulled up outside the house and for one giddy moment, Cara thought that it might be Adam. She pushed herself upright and plodded to the window, holding the ice to her throbbing temple. It was Declan, getting out of a Ford Ka.

She opened the door before he rang the bell.

'Hi,' Declan said and dodged inside shiftily. He was hiding a bunch of flowers behind his back. 'I didn't want anyone to recognise me.'

'No one round here knows you,' Cara said. 'Except me.'

'So much the better,' Declan said.

'Where's the big posh BMW?' Cara asked as he followed her into the lounge. 'What are you doing driving a Ford Ka?'

'It's symbolic,' Declan said.

'Of being poor?'

'I wanted Emily to know that I wasn't squandering money.'

'She'll be pleased about that.'

'Is she in?'

'No,' Cara said. 'Emily's gone out for the evening.'

'Oh.' Declan looked disappointed. 'Where to?'

'I've no idea,' Cara admitted. 'She'd gone by the time I got back

315

from work. She just left me a note.'

'Oh.' He pointed to her ice-pack. 'What's the matter?'

'Stress headache.' Cara ditched the ice-pack. It was making no impression anyway.

Declan whipped out the flowers from behind his back. 'These are for you,' he said.

Cara took them graciously. 'Thanks. That's kind.' Funny that the flowers were Emily's favourites, she thought wryly.

Declan was unabashed.

It was a gaudy spring bunch, the bright colours fighting each other for space, the perfume sweet and heady. She wished that Adam had bought them for her and wondered how she'd manage, knowing that she'd never spend the night with him again. Cara pushed the thought aside. 'I'll put them in water.'

'I've brought her a cheque too,' he said, still trailing after her into the kitchen and sitting on a stool. 'I expect she's getting a bit low on funds.'

'Low?' Cara exclaimed, plonking the flowers down on the draining board and pulling out a vase from under the sink. It was decorated with mosaic mirror tiles, done in the days when Cara had managed to find time for hobbies. 'Emily's been scraping the bottom of the barrel for weeks now. She's raided my piggy bank twice.'

'This will help,' Declan said. 'It's the proceeds from the sale of the Beamer.'

'I thought business was booming again?' She rooted through the drawer for the scissors and sliced through the cellophane wrapping and then carefully snipped the end off each flower. 'Why did the car have to go?'

'Money isn't everything, is it?' Declan said.

'It is when you haven't got any,' Cara pointed out.

'I know,' Declan said dismissively. 'But I've just realised that there are more important things in life. Things that money can't buy.'

'Well done,' Cara said with a nip of sarcasm, as she arranged the flowers in the vase. 'How long has it taken you to work that one out?'

'Too long,' Declan said. He gave her a doleful look.

She carried the vase to the table and set it down.

'They match the décor perfectly,' Declan noted.

'They do,' she agreed. Which was terrifying really, because the flowers were purple, yellow and orange.

Declan fondled the petal of a brazen tiger lily. 'I'm glad we're alone,' he said. 'I wanted to talk to you about the other night. At Adrian and Amanda's. In the hot tub.'

Cara slid into the seat opposite him. 'There's nothing to say. Really.'

'You were embarrassed.'

'I wasn't.' She was. It wasn't very difficult to conjure up a picture of a very fit and naked Declan in his full glory. Cara flushed.

Declan grinned an evil grin. 'You're embarrassed now.'

'I am not,' Cara insisted.

He laughed and then took her hand. 'I'm very fond of you, Cara. I always have been.'

Fond. *Fond*? What a terrible word that was. People were fond of Bambi and Thumper and Barry Manilow music. It was altogether too weak a word to apply to human passions. Being told that someone was fond of you was nearly as bad as being told you were a great mate. What was happening to her? Why did no one see her as the repressed love goddess that she was? Men she had adored for years told her that they were *fond* of her or that she was a *great mate*. All Emily had to do was breathe and strangers fell totally in love with her.

'Fond,' Cara said wistfully.

'I meant it as a compliment,' Declan said with a smile as if he'd read her thoughts. 'You've got a lot going for you.'

'Yes,' Cara agreed. And you could probably write it all on the back of a matchbox.

Declan rested his face on his hands and stared at her. 'I'm not going to get Emily back, am I?'

'I think it's unlikely,' Cara agreed.

'Do you want to give me the "you've got to move on" lecture?'

Cara hooked her finger through one of her dreadlocks and curled it round and round. 'Not really.'

Declan reached out and took her other hand. 'How's the headache?'

'Better for having my mind taken off it,' she said tiredly. Why was the process of living so exhausting?

'Let's go out,' Declan suggested. 'Have you eaten?'

'No,' Cara said.

'I'll treat you,' he offered. 'Now that I'm flush with cash.'

'I'm glad the business is picking up again,' she said sincerely. 'I know it means a lot to you.'

'It doesn't mean quite as much as it did,' Declan reminded her. 'But thanks anyway.'

'I need to get changed if we're going to go out,' Cara said. 'And slap some more war-paint on.'

'That's the spirit,' Declan congratulated her. 'I thought for a

317

minute you were going to turn me down.'

With an effort, Cara pushed herself up. She didn't really feel like going out, but she was going to plaster a smile on and try to enjoy herself. At least it would stop her from thinking about Adam and Emily.

'I won't be long,' she promised. 'Help yourself to a drink while I'm gone.'

'Thanks,' Declan said. 'You . . .'

Cara held up her hand. 'Please don't tell me that I'm a great mate, Declan,' she warned. 'I really don't think I could bear it.'

As she headed for the door, she left Declan sitting at the table with his mouth slightly agape.

Declan felt as if he was reeling slightly, but couldn't put his finger on why. Emily was gone. She was out of his life. Of that much he was sure.

It felt strange to think that he was footloose and fancy-free again. He'd spent a lot of the time when he was with Emily, looking at other women and wondering what it would be like to sleep with them. Now that was a possibility rather than a fantasy, he felt more than a little uncertain of himself.

Take Cara. No matter how much she hated the description, she *had* been a great mate. He didn't know how he would have got through this without her. OK, she was completely dappy. But dappy was fun. And there was nothing wrong with a dash of good, old harmless British eccentricity. The world didn't have enough of it these days. But just lately he'd begun to feel differently about her – ever since that night in the hot tub, if the truth was known. Who knew what might have happened if Amanda's mother hadn't turned up with all the comic timing of Attila the Hun.

Declan spun round and headed towards the fridge. He'd take Cara to the Thai place just down the hill in Belsize Park. She'd like that. Lemongrass was vegetarian, wasn't it? There was a bottle of red wine already open in the fridge door that had a plastic stopper jammed tightly into the neck. He took the bottle out and tugged at the temporary cork, which released with a satisfying pop. Declan sniffed it. Slightly strange. There was the aroma of fireworks, putty and candlewax. It might just be on the turn, but he'd get a glass and try it anyway.

He opened two or three cupboards before he remembered where Cara kept her glasses and then poured himself a drink. Declan licked his lips as he tested it. The wine tasted even more strange than it smelled. Not off exactly, but weird. It had the flavour of snuff and mouldy leaves and Jelly Babies, and there seemed to be flecks of black floating in it. Not the usual flavour for a Cabernet Sauvignon. He looked at the label. Nothing too offensive there. Should be a good drinking wine, even if it was straight out of the fridge.

Declan took the bottle of wine back to the table and, as he waited patiently for Cara, kept trying it to make absolutely sure that he really didn't like it.

Cara had decided to wear the floaty pink number she'd lent to Emily. It had been lurking in her cupboard for too long and if it could work for her friend, who knows what it might do for her. She tied her dreadlocks up into a knot on her head and then tiptoed into Emily's room and rummaged through her shoes until she found some pretty black kitten-heeled sandals and into them squeezed feet that were normally accustomed to flat boots. She hoped that Declan wasn't planning to go to Pizza Hut.

Cara glanced at her watch. Ten minutes. A quick smear of lipstick and she'd be ready. With a last approving glance in the mirror, she bounded down the stairs.

Declan looked up as Cara came in the kitchen door. 'Wow!' he said, blinking rapidly. 'You look fabulous.'

Cara smiled shyly, slightly taken aback. 'Thanks.'

'Well,' he said, 'that's a bit of an understatement really.' He glanced down at the bottle of wine and blinked again. 'You look absolutely sensational.'

'Thanks,' Cara said again.

'Your hair . . .' Declan was behaving very strangely. 'It's shining like there's a big, Hollywood spotlight behind you.'

'Is it?' Cara looked round to check.

'This is going to sound a bit strange.' Declan took a heaving breath. 'I can see diamonds sparkling from your fingertips. And there's glitter floating in the air all around you.'

Cara raised her eyebrows.

'I know,' Declan said. 'It sounds mad, doesn't it?'

'Just a bit,' Cara said.

'I can hear music, Cara.' He spoke in hushed tones. 'Soft, pure angelic chords that are plucking my heartstrings. I can feel warm, pulsating waves brushing over my skin as gentle as silk.' Declan shivered deliciously.

Cara looked down at the open wine bottle in alarm. 'Exactly how much have you had to drink?'

319

'Hardly anything,' Declan insisted. 'This stuff tastes like shite. What is it?'

He held out the glass to Cara and she took a sip. Her hand flew to her mouth. 'Oh my giddy aunt!'

'What?' Declan said. 'What is it?'

Declan had gone all soft-focus and swimmy. Tiny jewelled butter-flies fluttered round the gold threads that ran through his hair. His eyes had turned to darkest amber. Somewhere, a harp was playing. The moon shone through the kitchen windows as bright and warm as a hot summer sun. 'Oh my giddy aunt,' Cara gasped again.

'I found it in the fridge,' he explained nervously.

His voice fell on her like the cool droplets from a mountain waterfall on naked skin. Cara unpinned her hair and shook it loose. Declan gulped. She ran her hand over her parched throat, aching to taste the wine again. Without much of a fight, she gave in and had a hearty swig. Her whole body shuddered with bliss.

'Do you feel like I do?' Declan said in awe.

Cara nodded.

'It tastes like shite,' Declan reiterated, 'but it's powerful stuff. Did you get it from Oddbins?'

'It's a spell,' Cara breathed. 'A magic spell.'

'Oh Jaysus,' Declan said. 'And it makes you feel like this?'

'It makes you fall in love with the first person you see,' she said.

'So I'm in love with you?' Declan asked.

'And I'm in love with you,' she confirmed.

'Shit,' Declan puffed. 'It feels fecking great, doesn't it?'

'Yes.' Tears sprang to Cara's eyes.

Declan moved towards her. 'I thought you were lovely, anyway,' he said. 'But all this glittery stuff looks grand.'

'You have hair like spun gold.'

'I do?' Declan said, chuffed. He traced his fingers over her cheek and shivered with ecstasy. Cara's eyes closed in response.

'How long does this spell last?' he murmured, his lips searing hot against the skin of her neck.

'A hundred years,' Cara said breathlessly.

'That's a hell of a long time, Ms Forbes,' he said.

'Yes,' Cara whispered.

'We could afford to miss dinner.'

'Yes.'

Declan took her hand and led her towards the door. 'Spell or not, I'm in love with you.'

Cara laughed softly. 'And I'm in love with you.'

320

Declan pulled her to him and kissed her passionately. 'This feels beyond belief.'

Cara grabbed the bottle from the table. 'Let's not forget this.'

'It's good stuff,' Declan said as he tried to focus on the label. 'Have you got any more?'

'I don't think we'll need it,' she said as, laughing, they raced up the stairs.

Chapter Ninety-Six

I'm sitting in Jonathan Gold's office. It's late and the only light is from his desk lamp which casts soft, shapeless shadows round the sumptuous room. The coffee table is littered with dead cups.

'Well . . .' Jonathan says and spreads his hands.

The journalist from the *News of the World* has just left. Her tape recorder whirred for over an hour while she grilled me like a sardine. Now I'm feeling vaguely battered. Like cod if you want to keep up the fish analogy.

'How do you think it went?' I say anxiously.

'Fine,' he says. 'You did fine.' He comes round his desk and leans against it, crossing his long elegant legs. 'Now you have a few days' grace before notoriety shines on you again.'

'Don't remind me,' I say with an uneasy shiver.

'It'll be different this time,' Jonathan assures me. 'We'll control it.'

'And I won't lose my job and my home.'

'No,' he says. 'Quite the contrary.' He hands me an envelope from his desk. 'Inside, there's a very large cheque.'

'Thanks,' I say. I stuff the envelope in my handbag, even though I'm desperate to get a look at how much it is. 'I'm still uncertain how I feel about it,' I admit. On the one hand it was pretty easy money and on the other it cost me a lot to do it. I sigh and hope that one day I'll get my head round it.

Jonathan shrugs. 'People compromise their principles every day, Emily,' he says with the casual air of a man who has seen and heard too much to be shocked by anything. 'Some people have no principles at all. Each of us do what we have to do to get through the day.'

I hang my head. 'I am grateful.'

Jonathan smiles. 'Grateful enough to let me buy you dinner?'

I look down at my clothes. 'I'm not dressed for it,' I say.

'You look beautiful,' Jonathan insists. 'You worry too much.'

I look up and laugh. 'I get it from my mother.'

'Chinese or Italian?' he asks.

What I really want to do is curl up in my bed and sleep for a week.

322

'I don't think I'm in any fit state to make such a difficult decision.'

'Italian,' Jonathan says. 'The cutlery will take less co-ordination.'

'Great choice,' I say with a smile. Standing, I stretch and rub my hands over my eyes. I feel as if this is the end when really it is all just beginning again.

Jonathan comes and takes my hands in his. They are cool and soft. 'You've handled this brilliantly,' he says. 'You should be very proud of yourself.'

'Thanks,' I say, and realise that Jonathan doesn't know that I have yet to face my best friend, whose finest quality is that she is principled and perfect in every way. And I wonder how the hell I'm going to tell Cara that I'm getting my kit off again in one of the sauciest tabloids on the market.

Chapter Ninety-Seven

Dinner went well – but it was nothing special, and there's no way that Jonathan and I will be sailing off into the sunset on a yacht that I've bought with my filthy lucre. Perhaps it was my mood, but Jonathan Gold, however attractive he may be, just doesn't light my fire. The flames flicker a bit and then die out. It's that pesky Adam who still seems to get my motor running.

Now, here I am, key in the door, back at Cara's house and it's not yet the witching hour. Although you could say it's always the witching hour in this house.

There's giggling coming from the kitchen and my heart sinks. Perhaps Adam has decided to have one last fling before settling down in unholy matrimony, and I don't think I can bear this after my long, stressy day. Perhaps I should just sneak upstairs and let them get on with it.

Oh what the hell. I brace myself and plod through to the kitchen where I'm bemused, and more than a little shocked, to see Declan and Cara wrapped round each other. Declan has Cara's dressing-gown on and she is wearing his boxer shorts and nothing else. They are feeding bits of bacon and toast into one another's mouths as if it's caviar.

I stop in my tracks. Cara is eating bacon. I have clearly wandered into a parallel universe.

'Emily,' Declan says in a very cheerful way.

I did wonder, for a minute, whether I might be invisible. I guess I should be shocked by this little tableau before me, but I'm not. Does that mean I've become a hardened media hag, my exterior crust impenetrable? Or does it simply mean that I really *don't* love Declan any more?

'The spell works,' Cara says, licking bacon grease from her fingers with something approaching relish.

I want to sit down but daren't, because that means I'll have to linger in here. In the real world, you see, my feet are killing me. 'What spell?'

'The spell that makes someone fall in love with you.'

'Oh good,' I say. Bloody hell. Declan and Cara look dreamily into each other's eyes just like Brad and Jennifer do.

'We both drank it by mistake,' my friend explains as if it's the most natural thing in the world. And they chuckle childishly at each other.

'Oh.' None of Cara's spells have ever worked. I think they must both be hallucinating or suffering from delusions. Or both. Declan was never that stable either. Perhaps the impending threat of bankruptcy has pushed him over the edge.

'You don't mind, do you?' Cara says.

'No,' I say. And I don't really. I feel vaguely stunned and amused by it all, but that's about it. My heart has decided to tackle far more complicated situations than Declan has ever created. I think they've both had a skinful and are going to have massive hangovers in the morning and will feel very silly.

'I'm so pleased,' Cara says and lunges towards me, involving me in some sort of greasy group hug. So some things never change. 'You won't let this come between us?'

'No,' I say, and laugh even though I'm miserable. And I won't say 'I told you so' when it all ends in tears. 'I'm cool.'

'Good,' Cara slurs, 'because I love you. You are my bestest, bestest friend in the world. I love you, Emily. I really, really love you.'

'Yes. Good.' I try to untangle myself. 'I love you too.' Then: 'I'm off to bed,' I say. I want to warn them not to make a noise, but that's probably rather pointless. I can always find something to stuff up my ears with, I suppose.

'I'm sorry for everything,' Declan says. I smile at him and not just because he looks absolutely ridiculous. If I was a vengeful old cow, I'd whip out the camera right now. 'I've brought you a cheque,' he says. 'The first of many.' He is swaying slightly. 'I'll pay off everything.'

'Good,' I say. 'I'll hold you to it.'

'I'm glad we can all still be friends.' Cara is weaving unsteadily. 'We have been through so, so much together!'

'Yes,' I say, 'and there's going to be a tiny bit more.'

'Mmm . . .' Cara says, gazing at Declan.

'I'm going to be in the *News of the World* on Sunday, showing my bottom again.'

'Lovely,' Cara beams.

'Night then.' I wave to them both and rush off up to bed, before Cara realises what I've said. Mind you, there's no way she can give me a hard time after this. I rub my hands joyfully and enjoy a wicked little laugh.

Chapter Ninety-Eight

It was Saturday afternoon and Adam was nervous. He was pacing about in his new flat, trying not to make too many clonking sounds on the wood flooring. It still didn't feel quite like he belonged here. And that was probably because there was no way, even if he lived to be a million, that he'd ever be able to afford somewhere like this without Toff's benevolence. Adam felt like hugging himself. Oh, but this place was fabulous. And he was nervous because he really, really wanted Josh to think so, too.

Adam checked his watch. Laura was bringing his son over with all his stuff and it was too scary for words. He'd waited so long for this moment and now he couldn't quite believe it was here. He felt he was being given a chance to be a proper father to Josh again.

Adam had checked out the stereo in Josh's room with the latest Britney CD. It sounded dire to him, but he hoped Josh would like it. He'd bought them a new football in honour of the new garden and it stood looking vaguely pathetic and small in the corner of the cavernous room. In the kitchen there was a huge freezer, much more practical than the eight-inch ice box that Adam had struggled with for the last few years, filled with kid's type food – burgers, chips, pizzas, tons of Ben & Jerry's ice cream. The fridge held enough Coke to float a Caribbean cruise ship. Before he had time to consider, again, whether he had enough biscuits, the door bell rang.

Laura stood there looking as stretched as she ever had. Dark, distressed eyes shone out from her chalk-white face. At least she might look better if she was able to get a bit of a tan in Australia, Adam thought. She had a large suitcase and for one mad moment Adam considered asking her to move in here with them both.

Josh stood next to her looking like a latterday evacuee. His holdall, too big for his short legs, dragged on the ground. He was drowned by his jacket and jeans, a twelve-year-old slave to the ridiculous fashion of wearing everything seventeen sizes too big. Adam had never seen his son look tinier. He looked like he wanted to hold Laura's hand, but she was too weighed down by baggage to spare one.

'Hi,' Adam said in an overly manic voice. 'Come in.'

Josh and Laura clonked past him, their eyes widening in amazement as they took in the stylish minimalism of the flat. His son dropped his holdall on the floor.

'Wow, Dad!' Josh breathed. 'Do we live here?'

Adam noticed Laura flinch slightly.

'Yes,' Adam said. 'Do you like it?'

'Yeah!' Josh enthused. 'Where's my room?' And he raced off.

Adam and Laura faced each other awkwardly.

'I don't think he's going to miss me,' Laura said.

'Of course he will,' Adam assured her gently. 'It's just that everything's new and exciting here.'

'This is very flash,' Laura said, surveying the lounge.

'Toff owns it,' Adam said with a shrug. 'I haven't just won the lottery.'

'I did wonder.'

'How's it going?' Adam asked.

'Badly.' Laura studied her feet. 'Barry's devastated.'

'He can come round here any time he wants to,' Adam said.

'Thanks,' Laura said. 'I'll tell him.'

Josh rushed back in. 'I've got a stereo and everything, Mum,' he said, as if Christmas had come early. Adam wished he could remember a time when he had been so easily pleased.

'I'd better go,' Laura said. She pulled Josh to her and ruffled his hair. 'Look after your dad for me.'

Josh held onto her. 'I will.'

'I'll be back before you know it,' she said as she kissed his hair, and the tears rolled down her cheeks.

'Take care,' Adam said as she slowly disentangled herself from their son.

'I will.' She walked to the door.

'He's got his own computer. I'll set him up an Internet account,' Adam promised. 'Find yourself a cybercafé and you can contact him whenever you want.'

'I'll do that.' Laura started to cry again. Sad, silent tears. 'Why am I doing this, Adam?'

'I have no idea,' he said.

She laughed and took a tissue out of her pocket and blew her nose. 'You know, Adam, you'll need to get some new clothes if you're going to live in such luxury,' she remarked dryly, as she ran a hand tenderly over his shirt. 'You look like a scarecrow who's

327

stumbled into the middle of the Ritz.'

'He'll be OK here,' Adam said.

'I know.' And with that Laura kissed his cheek lightly and walked out of their lives.

Adam closed the door behind her and leant heavily against it. His son's miserable face looked up at him. 'You OK?' Adam checked.

Josh nodded. 'Yeah.' He scuffed the toe of his trainer against the immaculate oak floor. 'Do you think Mum will miss me?'

Adam let out a long breath and put his arm round Josh's shoulders. 'More than she realises.'

'It's great being here with you, Dad.' Josh leaned against him and a smile split his son's face. 'Can we go and play football?'

Adam grinned back even though he felt like crying. 'Yeah,' he said. 'Why not?'

Chapter Ninety-Nine

The upstairs function room of the Jiggery-Pokery had been done out with balloons. Cara had spent all afternoon exercising her lungs by blowing them up. They hung in swathes from the ceiling and floated in bunches from every table. There was an Oriental fusion buffet, provided by obliging outside caterers when Cara had realised that bacon butties were on the outer limits of the Jig's culinary capabilities. A banner which said SORRY YOU'RE LEAVING! hung limply above the large cake iced with similar sentiments.

The disco was in full flow. She hadn't really imagined that Martin the Editor would be an aficionado of 1980s' pop music, but there he was, bopping away with gay abandon to the Communards with Mad Michelle from the Classified Ads department. Then again, you never knew what people would do after a few drinks.

In the middle of the throng, Adam and Chris were dancing too, badly but enthusiastically, both looking very much the worse for wear. Adam glanced over and caught her eye and winked a very sober wink for someone whose arms and legs seemed to have no co-ordination.

Declan's arm snaked round her waist and she leaned into him, gazing up. She didn't know whether it was still the after-effects of the spell, but everything about him was gorgeous and overblown. He smelled of vanilla and pine forests and baking cakes. She looked up at him and his eyes smouldered back and he pulled her to him, kissing her tenderly. Whether it was magic or not that had brought them together, she didn't care. Cara was loving every minute of it.

The DJ slowed the music down and Adam came over to them. 'Can I take this gorgeous lady away from you for one dance?' he said breathlessly to Declan.

'You can,' Declan said and kissed Cara as she reluctantly eased herself away from him.

Adam took her hand and led her to the dance floor. Bonnie Tyler croaked out 'A Total Eclipse of the Heart'. He wound his arms round her, swaying slightly more than was necessary. Cara smiled to herself. 'I hate this song,' Adam said.

'Me too,' she laughed.

'Thanks for doing all this.' He gestured at the balloons and the cake, the crowd of partying colleagues.

'You're welcome. We had to give you a good send-off.' Cara looked bashful. 'The *Hampstead Observer* won't be the same without you.'

'No,' Adam said with a sigh. 'I'll miss it.'

'You will not!' Cara laughed.

Adam held her tighter. 'I'm sorry that things didn't ... you know ... work out between us,' he said hesitantly. 'Bad timing, et cetera.'

'Story of my life,' Cara tutted. I did love you, Adam, she said to herself.

'You look fairly well set up now,' he said, glancing back at the bar where Declan stood watching them.

'I am.'

'That is Declan the Internet rogue you're with, isn't it?'

Cara grinned. 'It is.' They stumbled round nearly in time to the music. 'It's a long story,' she said. 'One day, if you're very good, I might tell you about it.'

'Come over to the flat,' he offered. 'You'll probably hate it. It's all painted white. Come for supper. I'm going to try to learn how to cook.'

'I'd love to.' They lapsed into silence.

'I'm glad you're happy,' Adam said. 'Just make sure you don't let him near you with a digital camera.'

'Don't worry,' she giggled. 'I won't.'

Adam raised his eyebrows. 'How does Emily feel about you taking up with her old boyfriend?'

At the mention of her friend's name, her conscience pricked with guilt. 'She's fine about it. Absolutely fine.'

'I thought you might have brought her with you tonight,' Adam said. 'We've been threatening to meet each other for a long time.'

'Yes,' Cara said. 'Emily's busy tonight.' She tried not to think of her friend sitting forlornly at home alone with only Cilla Black and Matthew Kelly for company.

'Ah yes,' he said. 'Emily's in love with someone else, isn't she?'

'Yes,' Cara said and the words almost stuck in her throat. 'She is. And what about you?'

'Oh, you never know,' Adam said too brightly. 'I might find myself a woman one of these days.'

'I do hope so, Adam,' she said.

'Yeah, well. Josh keeps nagging me enough.'

'How's he liking the new flat?'

'Loves it,' Adam said. 'He's got the place looking like a nuclear disaster zone already.'

'Where is he tonight?'

'At home. Toff's babysitting. They've got a Chinese takeaway and *Terminator 2* on video.'

'Sounds like a great night.'

'Yeah,' Adam said. 'I think Toff's secretly enjoying his new role as favourite uncle and role model.'

'Are you still going to take Josh out to Luigi's every week?'

'I expect so,' Adam said. 'It's part of the Jackson family tradition. I'm taking him for lunch there tomorrow too. A sort of celebration.'

'That's nice.' Cara was choked. She squeezed Adam's arm. 'I want everything to work out for you,' she said with a crack in her voice. 'You know that.'

'Yes.' Adam looked slightly surprised. 'I know.'

Chris came blundering up to them. 'They want you to cut the cake, mate.'

Adam laughed. 'Feels like I'm getting married!'

Cara felt her smile stick to her teeth as Chris dragged Adam away from her. She had to do something to sort this situation out. There must be a suitable spell in one of her books somewhere. She looked at Adam's retreating back. Or maybe there was another way.

Chapter One Hundred

I'm going to write a book called *Depilating for Fun*. After years of tweezing, ripping and coaxing unwanted hairs from my bodily parts, I'm probably a world expert. And it really is so much fun, isn't it? I've now decided I'm going to spend every Saturday night doing it. After watching Cilla and Matthew until my eyes were square, I indulged in my second favourite pastime apart from watching telly. Shaving my legs. Ha! You can keep your trendy wine bars and your swanky Michelin-rated restaurants. Give me a Bic razor and some soap any day of the week. Staying in and shaving is the new going out and getting lashed. Aren't I the biggest party animal ever? Is this all I have to look forward to for the rest of my life? Well, at least I don't have a hangover. Unlike some.

I don't know where Declan and Cara went last night, but Cara was in a very strange, gushing mood when she got home. She did another one of those IloveyouIloveyouIloveyou Youaremybestfriendinthe-entireworld I'vehadtoomuchtodrink speeches that are becoming a regular part of her repertoire while Declan stood and swayed like a birch tree in a stiff breeze. I blame myself for encouraging Cara's consumption of the demon drink. She'll probably go on the wagon the minute I depart. I've no idea what she was rambling on about, but I lost interest after the first ten minutes and just nodded politely before I escaped off to my bed. I think this spell is the mystic equivalent of being knocked on the head with a very heavy frying pan. Their brains are both definitely doo-addled. Perhaps when Cara eventually sobers up and returns to her natural state of detoxification, she'll dump Declan.

This morning they're not a lot better. Declan is sitting at the table, thankfully reunited with his boxers, eating muesli. I think that must be a first for him. Cara's staggering round in a post-drunken state, trying to aim toast at her mouth. I sit down opposite him.

'Morning, Emily,' he says and this is too, too weird for so early on a Sunday.

332

'Morning,' I say and fight the urge to grab a cup of tea and rush out again.

Cara joins us at the table. Her hair looks like she has spent the night being shagged and her skin is all pink and scraped by stubble. I didn't hear a thing. My ears were jammed full of cottonwool and I had my shower cap on. In fact, I'm amazed that I did sleep so well last night. Apart from the fact that the two people in the world closest to me were enjoying Biblical knowledge of each other in the next room, I did start to get the late-night collywobbles about my photo-session. I know it's a bit tardy to start thinking that this may not have been a very good idea – but I am.

My friend and my ex-boyfriend exchange a furtive glance. I think I might be sick.

'We're going out to lunch today,' Cara says. 'Come with us.'

'No, thanks,' I say and try to smile. I think I'd rather have my bikini line waxed in full public view on *So Graham Norton*.

'We really want you to come,' she insists. 'Don't we, Declan?'

'We do,' Declan says, and looks like he doesn't give a toss what I do any more.

Cara scribbles the name of a restaurant down on a Post-It note and shoves it into my hand. I glance at it and think that I'd actually quite like to eat there. I've never been before, but I've heard it's good. 'Be there, Emily. Please. It's important to us. Isn't it, Declan?'

'It is,' Declan says, although it clearly isn't.

Cara looks very anxious and I think she's feeling guilty about nicking my boyfriend. That's all I can put it down to. I think it should feel more strange, seeing her with Declan, especially as they seem to be existing in a lovey-dovey glass bubble which contains only the pair of them at the moment. I shall have to make an effort to go to lunch with them, otherwise they'll think I'm sulking.

'Yes, OK,' I sigh. 'I'll come.'

Cara gets up and kisses me. Her breath smells like the back end of a brewery. 'I knew you would.'

'Grand,' Declan says, examining a raisin suspiciously before popping it into his mouth.

Cara appeased, I want to shoot out to the newsagents at the end of the High Street and buy up all the copies of the *News of the World* before anyone else can see them. I suspect though, that Hampstead isn't a *News of the World* enclave. I'd hazard an educated guess that there are more readers of the *Observer* and the *Sunday Times* here.

When Cara and Declan have finished their breakfast, they shoot upstairs holding hands. I do hope they're not going to have another sex session. But I needn't have worried. A few minutes later, they're back down again.

'Don't forget to be at the restaurant,' Cara days.

'No.' I'm not likely to, am I? How many offers am I going to get between now and noon?

'See your later,' she says and before you can say let's-have-another-snog they're out of the door and off in Declan's Ford Ka to who knows where.

There's one good thing about going to lunch with Cara. I can show her my newspaper spread in public, thus reducing my chances of getting knifed by my best friend.

I think we get more than our fair share of sunny days in Hampstead. Even though it's still technically winter, there's a milky warmth to the sky and everything looks quite perky. I have a perfect excuse for my sunglasses, and I can justify my beanie hat too, at a stretch.

I sidle into the newspaper shop, furtively grab three copies of the *News of the World*, queue up behind three *Independent on Sunday* readers, and pay up. Then I dash outside and rifle through the top copy with fingers that have all the strength of a feather cushion.

And there I am on page thirteen. Bottom-bared in my Saucy Santa outfit. My heart is pounding like an unfit jogger, but suddenly it stills. Alongside the original image, three of the photographs that I viewed on the computer in Sebastian's studio grace the page and I look great. I look great in all of them. They are sexy, but sophisticated. And though I haven't got a stitch on, I'm completely covered up. I quickly scan through the story and it is fairly and squarely reported, albeit in a sensational way. I can feel the relieved grin spread across my face.

Sticking the newspaper under my arm, I dial Jonathan Gold's number.

'Have you seen the paper?' I ask as soon as he answers.

'It's great, isn't it?' he says.

'Yes.'

'I knew it would be.' I can hear his confident smile. 'Do you want some more good news?'

'Go on.'

'Foxy Frillies have been on the phone. They want you to become the face of naughty lingerie.'

The power of speech has deserted me. The face? I think Jonathan just might mean 'the bottom'.

'I've said we'll meet them for lunch one day next week.'

'Fine,' I somehow manage.

'I'll fix something up,' he says in the cool, unruffled manner of a man who is accustomed to doing this sort of thing every day.

I, on the other hand, want to run up and down the High Street cheering and showing everyone my knickers. This could be a good qualification for my new job.

'I've just been offered a job as the arse of Foxy Frillies,' I want to shriek. 'Do you know what that means to me?' But I don't. I stand gawkily on the street corner, grinning to myself like an idiot.

'Well done, Emily,' he says. 'I'll speak to you tomorrow.'

Hanging up, I wonder whether Jonathan Gold will be the only person congratulating me on my good fortune. A rumble in my tummy makes me realise that it's time to meet Cara. I rummage in my bag and find the Post-It note she thrust into my hand. *Luigi's*, it says, the address barely legible beneath it. Suddenly I feel like I've got a huge appetite that only pasta will sate and I set off towards Luigi's with a definite spring in my step.

Chapter One Hundred and One

I recognise Adam immediately. And I feel like I've had all of my breath knocked out of me. He is sitting at a table by the window with a boy who is bound to be his son, as he is a miniature version of him, but I can't remember what Cara said his name was. They are chatting and laughing and take no notice of me.

This is actually the first time I've seen Adam in broad daylight and he looks even more fantastic than I've remembered/dreamed/ fantasised. This man could feature in the Boden catalogue, no trouble. No wonder Cara was besotted. No wonder *I'm* besotted. At least Cara can now speak in the past tense.

Luigi's restaurant is buzzing and busy – but then, where isn't on a sunny Sunday lunchtime in Hampstead? There appear to be more people than there are tables for them. A fat, grinning Italian woman comes over, bearing paper menus.

'Is there a table booked in the name of Forbes?'

'Si, si,' she says and guides me to the one vacant table, which happens to be adjacent to the love of my life. I sit down and squeeze into the corner furthest away from Adam. This is dreadful. Where the hell is Cara? It's not like her to be late. The girl is pathologically punctual. All this sex is making her sloppy.

'Drink now?' the waitress asks, her accent veering between the rolling hills of Tuscany and the back streets of the East End.

'Red wine, please.'

'Glass?'

No, just bring the bottle and a straw. 'Yes. A glass.'

She looks at me strangely. Perhaps she thinks I should take off my hat and sunglasses now that I'm indoors, but she clearly doesn't appreciate that us minor celebrities like to retain our privacy. I notice with a shiver of shock that Adam has a copy of the *News of the World* folded on the chair next to him. Oh bugger.

I suppose I could brazen this out and just go over and introduce myself and congratulate him on his forthcoming nuptials and ask him what the hell he thought he was playing at giving me the glad eye in *Temptation* when he was already betrothed . . . but not before I've had a lot more to drink.

The waitress delivers my wine and sneaking a look in Adam's direction, I catch his son's eye and the little boy smiles at me. What a sweetie he looks. GodGodGod. I am smiling at other people's children. Clearly, I'm not a well woman. I ferret about in my handbag – I really must springclean it this year – and find my phone. I hate people who inconsiderately use mobile phones in restaurants, but tough titty, this is an emergency. I dial Cara's number.

'It's me,' I hiss.

'Are you in Luigi's?' my friend says.

'Yes! Where the hell are you?' I check round to see that no one – i.e. Adam – is listening. 'Adam's here.'

'I know,' Cara says.

That takes the wind out of my sails. 'You know?'

'I wanted you to bump into him,' Cara explains.

'Why?' I lower my voice. *'Why?'*

'He isn't getting married and he's in love with you,' she says in rather too matter-of-fact a way, I believe, for such an announcement.

'Oh.' I can't think of much else to say.

'Talk to him, Emily.'

'He's got his son with him,' I point out.

'Josh,' she says. 'That's all right. Josh wants a stepmum.'

A *stepmum*! I lower my voice even further. 'So when are you getting here?'

'We're not,' Cara says. 'Declan and I are on Hampstead Heath having a picnic.'

'A picnic?'

'We thought it would be romantic.'

Nice! 'I hope you both get frostbite.'

Cara laughs weakly. 'Don't be like that.'

'You're a cow!' I slink down into my seat. 'Why did you tell me he was getting married?'

'I lied, Emily,' she admits. 'It was wrong of me.'

'How could you do this to me?' And I know the answer to that. Because Cara, too, was in love with Adam – before she got zapped by whatever she got zapped by.

'I'm desperately trying to make things right,' Cara says sincerely. 'Don't miss this opportunity, Emily. Just go over and say hello.'

My friend . . *friend*? . . .hangs up. It's all right for her to say just go over and talk to him. She doesn't know that the restaurant's packed and I feel like everyone, *everyone*, is watching me.

The Italian waitress appears again. 'Ready to eat?'

'Yes,' I say and point at the menu. I have no idea what I've ordered.

I risk a furtive glance towards Adam again and his son is still smiling at me. I'm going to kill Cara when I get home. But that still leaves me with one quandary. What the hell am I going to do now?

Chapter One Hundred and Two

'The woman on the table over there keeps looking at you,' Josh said.

'Eat your spaghetti,' Adam instructed.

'She does,' Josh insisted. 'The one with the funny hat. Look.'

'I'm not looking.'

'Go on,' Josh pleaded. 'Just a quick one.'

'No. Eat your spaghetti before it gets cold.'

'Look!'

Adam tutted. There would be no more eating done until he looked. Josh had definitely inherited his mother's stubborn streak. Adam swivelled in his seat. 'That one?' he said.

'She's nice, isn't she?' Josh observed.

Adam turned back to his pasta. 'She looks mad.'

'How can you tell?' Josh frowned. 'She's wearing sunglasses and a hat.'

'Exactly,' Adam said.

'I think she fancies you.'

'I think I'd rather go on *Blind Date* than let you fix me up.'

'Wasn't there anyone nice at your party last night?' his son continued.

'They're all people I've worked with for years,' Adam said. 'I wouldn't touch any of them with a barge-pole.'

'You're too fussy,' Josh told him.

'And you're too young to be telling me how to run my life.'

'Did you have a lot to drink?'

'Yes,' Adam admitted. 'Too much.'

'Uncle Chris threw up in the bathroom this morning,' Josh said brightly. 'I heard him.'

'Nice.' The vision reduced Adam to prodding at his pasta listlessly with his fork. It had seemed a good idea to let Chris sleep on the sofa at the time. 'Did you behave for Toff?'

'Yeah,' Josh said, returning to his own food. 'He has loads of women.'

339

'I know,' Adam said and wondered why there was a hint of envy in his voice.

'Do you think you'll have loads of women when you starting working for Toff?'

'Probably.'

Josh cheered up considerably. He gobbled down his spaghetti. 'She's looking at you again.'

'Josh,' Adam warned. 'Leave it out.'

'Just do a quick, sneaky look,' his son urged. 'Go on. Now.'

Adam turned and came to an abrupt halt halfway round. Josh was right. The madwoman in the hat was, indeed, looking straight at him.

Chapter One Hundred and Three

Oh my God. He caught me looking at him. I bury myself in the remains of my seafood pasta. That's what I ordered. It serves me right, because I'm not a great fan of seafood. Molluscs and me do not agree. I push the plate aside just as the waitress returns.

'Finished?'

'Yes. Thanks. I'll just have the bill.'

She is smiling a serene, secret smile. It's a now or never moment. I root round in my handbag for a piece of paper, thanking God that I haven't yet springcleaned it. I find an appointment card for my hairdressers and on the back of it hastily scribble my name and mobile phone number.

The waitress returns and gives me the bill. I clear my throat and decide to take her into my confidence. I hand her my note. 'When I've left the restaurant, could you possibly give this to the man at the table by the window?'

She looks up at Adam. *'Si.'* She grins at me. 'You think he look nice?'

I feel myself blush. 'Yes. I think he look very nice.'

I pay her, leaving a disproportionately large tip considering I've hardly touched my food, and busy myself collecting my newspapers. As I look up, I see that the waitress has wandered over to Adam's table and has handed him the note already. Ohshitshitshit.

I stand up and make a dash for the door. Adam stands up, knocking his wine over, the waitress has blocked the door and I'm standing there quaking like a hedgehog trapped in the path of a speeding ten-ton truck. Adam looks like he's been hit over the head by a cricket bat.

'Emily,' he says. There's a note of laughter in his voice. *'The* Emily?'

I nod, wordlessly.

Adam's full, soft lips break into a wide grin. 'Pleased to meet you,' he says. 'At long last.'

This is ridiculous but I want to cry. I want to fall in his arms and cry. Clutching my newspapers tighter, I take off my hat and my sunglasses.

'Bloody hell,' Adam says, his grin suddenly frozen. 'It's you. Woman-from-the-wine-bar.'

'Yes.'

The whole of the restaurant is basking in a stunned silence. The hush of paused cutlery pervades. Josh comes up behind Adam and slips under his arm. 'This is Josh,' Adam says softly. 'My son.'

'Pleased to meet you, Josh.' I do my best children's smile. I used to be a teacher. I have years of practice.

Josh's eyes pop out on stalks and his face takes on an expression of awe. 'Crikey, Dad,' he says in a very loud voice. Every head in Luigi's whips round to stare at us. 'It's the Saucy Santa!'

'So it is,' Adam says as he tenderly takes my hand.